THE FIRST WAVE

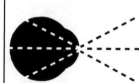
This Large Print Book carries the
Seal of Approval of N.A.V.H.

A BILLY BOYLE WORLD WAR II MYSTERY

LP
F

myst

THE FIRST WAVE

JAMES R. BENN

KENNEBEC LARGE PRINT
A part of Gale, Cengage Learning

GALE
CENGAGE Learning

Detroit • New York • San Francisco • New Haven, Conn • Waterville, Maine • London

GALE
CENGAGE Learning™

Copyright © 2007 by James R. Benn.
Kennebec Large Print, a part of Gale, Cengage Learning.

ALL RIGHTS RESERVED
Kennebec Large Print® Superior Collection.
The text of this Large Print edition is unabridged.
Other aspects of the book may vary from the original edition.
Set in 16 pt. Plantin.
Printed on permanent paper.

LIBRARY OF CONGRESS CATALOGING-IN-PUBLICATION DATA

Benn, James R.
   The first wave : a Billy Boyle World War II mystery / by James
R. Benn.
     p. cm. — (Kennebec Large Print superior collection)
     ISBN-13: 978-1-59722-928-9 (pbk. : alk. paper)
     ISBN-10: 1-59722-928-8 (pbk. : alk. paper)
     1. World War, 1939–1945—Algeria—Fiction. 2.
France—Politics and government—1940–1945—Fiction. 3.
Large type books.
PS3602.E6644F57 2009
813'.6—dc22   2008056138

Published in 2009 by arrangement with Writer's House LLC.

Printed in the United States of America
1 2 3 4 5 6 7 13 12 11 10 09

For my sons,
Ben and Jeff

I am the novelty of the time,
the wonder of nations.
I am the wily one,
who plays his wiles among Arabs and
foreigners.
But not the less a brother of need,
whom fortune vexes and wrongs.

Al Hariri of Basrah
Maqamat, (The Assemblies), c. 1100

CHAPTER ONE

Off the coast of French North Africa
8 November 1942

It was dark, and I was at sea, hunkered down in a flat-bottomed landing craft, slamming through four-foot swells and chugging noisily toward shore, leaving the relative safety of our troop transport behind. One hard mile out, me and twenty other guys, all sweating, scared, and slipping on the wet deck every time the landing craft crested another wave, rode on air for a split second, and then fell from under us. Each time it felt like hitting concrete from two stories up and each time I prayed it wouldn't happen again. No one was listening. The diesel fumes from the engine mixed with the smell of vomit and salt water and fear, giving off a new odor that wrapped itself around me, hooked into my nostrils, and wouldn't let go.

The guy next to me grabbed my arm. His

eyes were wide as they darted back and forth, searching for something that wasn't there, like a really good place to hide. His face was drained of color and I could barely hear him above the sound of the engine and the smashing waves.

"Are we almost there, Lieutenant?"

"We'll know when they start shooting at us," I said.

He looked disappointed at my answer, but I had no idea how close we were and I wasn't about to stick my head up to look. I didn't know if the Vichy French were going to put up a fight when we landed or kiss us on both cheeks. Either way, I planned to keep a low profile.

The next wave wasn't as bad as the others, and I guessed that meant we were getting nearer the shore. Our landing area was designated Beer Green, sixteen miles west of Algiers, capital of Algeria, the French colony garrisoned by the Vichy French. I thought it was funny that after being in this war almost a year, the first time we invade somebody it's the French. Not the Nazis, not Mussolini and his Fascists, but the so-called Vichy French. After the Germans steam-rollered into Paris, they took all the good parts of France for themselves and let some tame Frenchmen work out of a little town in the south, governing a sliver of France and most of her colonies. Vichy, famous for not much more than bottled water before, now stood for a divided France. Our brass hoped that the French soldiers in Algeria would see us as their American buddies come to help them liberate France from the Germans. But there was a distinct possibility that since we were secretly landing on their turf in the middle of the night, loaded for bear and backed up by a naval armada, they might think we were liberating Algeria from them. Which was sort of the truth, since they were between us and the Germans in North Africa, and sooner or later we were going to have to mix it up with Rommel and his Afrika Korps.

"Boyle! Are the motorcycles still secure?" the voice of Major Samuel Harding barked in my ear.

"Yes sir!" I was standing next to two U.S. Army Harley-Davidson motorcycles, lashed to the deck. They were for Harding and me. Not only did we have to survive the landing, we had to get these beasts up over the beach and then take them for a joy ride, smack in the middle of the invasion. The guys in the landing craft were from the 168th Combat Team, and their job was to

11

help us get the bikes and ourselves safely ashore, then wave goodbye as we took off into the night on a pre-dawn secret mission. So after landing in North Africa, with the first wave of the first invasion of the war, if I survived, I'd be celebrating my twenty-fourth birthday on a motorcycle ride from hell. Not for the first time, I wondered how a nice Irish kid from Boston like me had gotten himself into this situation.

"Okay, men, listen up!" Harding bellowed over the sounds of the engine and the surf. Bellowing was Harding's normal tone of voice. He was regular Army, in for the long haul. I was . . . well, I wasn't.

"I know you've been wondering why you're baby-sitting a couple of staff officers. We're about to hit the beach so now I can tell you." Harding paused and looked at the men. He stood straight, somehow immune to the rocking of the craft, displaying no sign of a normal sense of self-preservation. The rest of us were hunched over, to present less of a target. Harding seemed like he didn't give a damn. A couple of guys straightened up and looked around nervously. When no one got his head blown off, a few more did the same. I made believe I was checking the bikes and stayed low.

"We're landing near Cape Sidi Ferruch,"

he went on. "The French have a fortified battery at the tip of the cape, directly overlooking our landing beaches. Big 155mm artillery pieces, with new infrared thermal detectors and range finders. If the French government issues orders to resist us, we have to neutralize their artillery before they blow our ships out of the water. Lieutenant Boyle and I will make contact with friendly French officers to ensure that these guns are not used against us. Your job is to get us and the motorcycles off the beach and up to the main road. Do that and we'll do the rest. Understood?"

Pinpoints of light arced up from the beach and then exploded brightly above us, just like fireworks. Night turned to day as parachute flares floated lazily downward, light dancing on the waves and bathing us in a white, ghostly illumination. Before anyone could say a thing, there was a sound like distant thunder. Then bright flashes, reflected off the low, dark clouds. Something told me it wasn't weather.

The major reacted first. "Incoming!" Harding yelled, and then he wasn't standing so straight. We ducked as a shrieking sound split the sky and exploded to our right, sending up a column of water that drenched us on its way down. I wiped seawater off my face and looked toward the shore. Half a dozen spotlights were playing over the water, picking up landing craft as they slowly made their way to Beer Green. Flashes lit the early morning darkness from beyond the searchlights, and more shells whistled toward us. I tried to make myself small and squeezed my eyes shut, as if that might make everything go away. There were explosions all around us. Men screamed, fear making their voices unrecognizable. We rode through near misses that spewed so much seawater into the craft I wondered if we'd sink before we hit land.

Harding tapped me on the shoulder and pointed to our rear, a broad smile on his face. He was calm, really enjoying all this, like a kid at a carnival. I turned and looked back. Two destroyers were slicing across our wakes, their five-inch guns opening up on those searchlights. The noise didn't seem so bad when it was our guys dishing it out. When the first searchlight was hit and went dark, GIs, who had been screaming seconds earlier, cheered. The artillery fire from shore lessened as the destroyers kept up their barrage, and within minutes the searchlights were gone. Everyone was whooping and yelling, trying to forget the rush of fear that had gripped them moments earlier.

"Was that the big guns you were talking about, Major?" The white-faced GI who had wanted to know if we were there yet ignored me this time and went direct to Harding with his question. Smart guy.

"No, Private," Harding answered. "Those were just French 75s. Good field pieces, but popguns compared to their emplaced 155mm guns. Nothing to worry about."

"Yessir," the private said, some color returning to his face. I felt sorry for him, so I didn't point out that a 75mm shell exploding in our landing craft would indeed be something to worry about. No sense upsetting the help.

"Get ready!" Harding yelled. I untied the straps that held the motorcycles in place. As instructed, four GIs grabbed each bike, two on a side. I looked up. We were almost there. I could see the surf breaking on the beach. Other landing craft had already made it to shore. A few isolated shots were fired up and down the beach, sporadically, as if someone was target shooting. Everything seemed to slow down, and I could hear my heart pounding in my chest. My legs felt wobbly. I didn't know if I could make it out of the craft. I knew I didn't want to be here. I just wanted to be back in Boston, on the police force with my Dad and uncles, enjoying my promotion to detective. It had become effective December 1, 1941. I was in clover for a week, then the goddamn Japs had to go and bomb Pearl Harbor. Everything changed, and eleven months later, here I was in the middle of the night with a gung-ho major, playing secret agent, hoping some Frenchie didn't put a bullet in my skull before I gave the Germans and Italians their chance.

You've got no one to blame but yourself, Billy Boyle, I thought as the landing craft hit the shore with a jolting crunch. The ramp dropped and we were greeted by the sight of white churning foam on a gravel beach, and complete darkness beyond.

"We're here," I said to the talkative private.

"Gee, thanks, Lieutenant," he said as he pushed one of the Harleys into the surf. I followed him onto the shore of the African continent, an unwilling, wet, and shivering soldier in the vanguard of an invading army, longing for home and for Diana. Wondering where she was, and if she were alive or dead.

CHAPTER TWO

There were no bullets or kisses waiting for us on the Beer Green beach, both of which suited me fine. The GIs struggled in the soft sand with the big Harleys as the first faint glow of false dawn drifted up over the low rolling hills ahead of us. Dunes rose up from the beach, and for every three steps forward we took one back, as we struggled with heavy loads in the yielding white sands.

"Come on, men!" Harding yelled, "Put some muscle into it!"

He was rewarded with grunts and groans and a dirty look or two from the GIs as they pushed and nearly carried the motorcycles through the dunes. Harding was anxious and when he was worried, he yelled. I knew we didn't have much time to make contact with the French officer who was supposed to be waiting to surrender the fort and join up with us. If we didn't get there before he received direct orders from Algiers to resist the invasion, he might change his mind. That would be curtains for a lot of guys following the first wave, especially at full light. Even in the dark, those new thermal detectors could target a blacked-out troop transport and send a thousand soldiers and sailors to the bottom of the Mediterranean.

Harding got to the crest of the next dune and signaled everyone to halt. He knelt and scanned the horizon. I hustled up next to him and looked around. It was still pretty dark, but I could see that the sand dunes gave way ahead to scrub-pine woods that rose gradually from the beach.

"What is it, Major?"

"Shhh!" Harding swiveled his head, listening, then pointed to the left. I didn't hear a thing.

"Truck," he said. Then I heard it. The distant sound of an engine and of heavy tires on a gravel road. "Running with no lights."

The sound came closer, and rose as the truck passed in front of us. I could see a dark shape moving through the pines on the low ridgeline dead ahead.

"The coast road." Harding smiled. I realized that in the five months I had known him, I had never seen Harding smile this much. He looked so natural behind a desk, frowning, that I had never thought about him as a combat soldier. He gave a hand signal for the GIs to move forward, as if he'd been longing for this moment.

I put on my goggles and checked the safety on my .45 caliber Thompson submachine gun. Harding had an old .30 caliber Springfield M1903 bolt-action rifle. He said he preferred 'aimed fire' to automatic weapons. Me, I preferred to put a twenty-round clip from a Tommy gun between Mrs. Boyle's boy and anyone looking for trouble.

Harding revved his bike and glanced at me. I nodded, and played with the throttle of my Harley just to hear that rumble. It felt as if I were home, on motorcycle patrol for the Boston PD. We took off, spitting gravel and dust, toward Cape Sidi Ferruch. Harding was in the lead. I dropped back a bit and rode in the middle of the road, looking back as often as I could to see if anyone was following us. There was only the wind, dancing the dust our bikes kicked up, swirling it around in sudden clouds before it settled down again, unimpressed with our mission.

I don't know what I expected North Africa to look like. I'd imagined lots of sand, and there was plenty of that. But as we followed the road along the coast the land became greener and we passed cultivated fields. We sped through a small village: whitewashed buildings and tall trees lining the road. The houses were thick-walled, with rounded corners and smooth surfaces. Not a clapboard wood frame house in sight. I was a long way from South Boston.

A curve appeared down the road and I watched Harding slow and lean into it, his right foot out as if to hold up the weight of the bike. Then he straightened and gave it full throttle. The man could ride. I remembered a picture of my Uncle Frank sitting on his 1912 Harley, a rookie cop in Southie with his life ahead of him, a big grin plastered over his face, his gloved hands gripping the handlebars. My uncle never came home from the trenches of the First World War. I was glad my Dad and my Uncle Dan didn't know about this Harley ride. Thinking about them and how far apart we actually were made me feel lonely. I turned my head again. The road behind me was empty.

I tried to stop thinking of home. I had to notice everything around me, as if I were following a shooter up the rear stairway of a tenement with no backup. This was Indian country, after all. There were vineyards all around now, rows and rows of neatly planted grapevines, their wooden stakes looking like grave markers casting their shadows downhill as the sun rose. The ground sloped toward the sea on my right but there were rolling hills on the other side. The air was full of the ripe smell of grapes. Algeria didn't look anything like what I'd imagined. War sure is educational.

As we passed some buildings, I saw a few heads peek out of windows and doors and wondered what the locals were thinking. It might not make a whole lot of difference to them whether the French, Germans, Italians, or Americans ran the place. Whoever it was, they'd end up with the same short end of the stick. We might come as liberators, but we weren't planning to give the country back to the original owners.

Harding slowed as we came to a crossroad, and leaned hard right. I followed. We had been running without lights, but now he turned his on and rode just fast enough to control the bike. Ahead, car lights flashed on and off, twice. Harding signaled back, like in the movies.

A young French lieutenant jumped out of the car and waved his arms. "Bienvenu, mes amis Américains!" he welcomed us. He grabbed Harding's hand and pumped it like a politician on St. Paddy's Day, then planted a smack on both his cheeks. I swung my

Thompson around and casually held it pointed at the car. There might be surprises inside, or maybe I'd have to defend myself if he tried to kiss me. He jabbered some more French I didn't understand, and then Harding replied slowly enough that I could pick out a few words. I had booked enough Canucks back in my Boston cop days to know a bit of the lingo.

"Where is Colonel Baril? Did he send you?" Harding had asked.

"Oui, oui," the lieutenant answered and then added, in pretty good English, "I will take you to him. You are expected, Major Harding. My name is Georges Dupree, and I am at your service."

"Very well, Lieutenant," Harding answered. "This is my aide, Lieutenant William Boyle."

"Welcome to Algeria, Lieutenant Boyle." He made a slight, graceful bow.

"Call me Billy. Everyone does." I gave him my best Billy boy-o, happy-go-lucky smile.

Harding grimaced and shook his head. Dupree looked at Harding, then back at me. He had thick, wavy black hair slicked back, big dark eyes and a thin Ronald Colman mustache. Not my style, but it looked good on him.

"Everyone? We shall see."

He got into the car, turned it around, and set off. We followed, and within minutes were at the gate of the fort. It looked old and worn, as if it had been there since the days of the Barbary pirates. The outer ring was a mud-brick wall with large double wooden doors that swung open as the car approached. One of our General Lee tanks could've plowed right through it.

We drove into the courtyard. I could see that the place hadn't been built for defense from a land attack. Cape Sidi Ferruch jutted out about a mile from the mainland, and we were at the tip of the cape. There was enough light to see that the fort dominated the coast on both sides, and that the big 155mm artillery pieces in their emplacements could pound anything that ventured up or down the coast. There was no shortage of targets. On both sides of the cape, hundreds of landing craft, transports, destroyers, and larger warships were spread out on the water, looking like toy boats on a dark, distant pond. Crews stood at their guns. It would be a turkey shoot if someone gave the order to fire.

We sat on our bikes for a few seconds, engines idling, taking the scene in. I hadn't liked the idea of hitting the beach in the first wave but Harding had pushed his plan through and ordered me to come along. He had contacts among the French who were friendly to our side and wanted to get back into the war against the Germans. I hadn't understood why we'd had to rush ashore before the infantry cleared the area, but now I did. Harding had been right. But that didn't make me like taking risks any better and I was glad this mission was almost over.

I killed the engine and stepped off my bike, the Thompson gun still slung from my shoulder. Harding did the same and we stood there, waiting for something to happen. Dupree got out of the car and nodded to a group of soldiers standing near the entrance to the main building. Six of them trotted over and stood in front of us. Their rifles weren't pointed at us exactly, but they held them at the ready. Six other guys appeared in back of us, idly holding their rifles and watching Dupree carefully. Something told me this wasn't an honor guard.

"What's the meaning of this?" Harding demanded. "Take me to Colonel Baril, now!"

"Very good, Lieutenant Dupree. This is the right man." A voice spoke up in English from inside the entranceway. "I would recognize that loud American voice anywhere."

The French soldiers in front of us shouldered arms and stepped aside. Dupree gestured us toward the entrance, where a tall man stood in the shadows, watching us. Harding squinted, trying to see him clearly in the dim light.

"Jean, is that you?" Harding asked.

The man walked through the granite archway and down two stone steps. He was tall and lean, and wore an elegantly tailored uniform. He smiled tentatively.

"It is I, Samuel. If indeed that is who you are. The loud voice sounds the same but I do not remember the gray hairs."

Harding grinned and walked toward him. They exchanged a manly hug and a couple of those double cheek kisses that gave me the willies. We didn't do a lot of that in Southie and I was sure I'd make a fool of myself if I had to try.

"Jean, it has been almost ten years," Harding said. "I see time hasn't made you more tactful!"

"Samuel, one of your best qualities is your voice. It is well suited to the battlefield. Authoritative and distinctive. I remember it from our days in the trenches. It was, however, less well-suited to duty with your embassy in Paris. Neither of us was meant for the diplomatic service, I think. Forgive the dramatics," he said, gesturing toward the guards standing at attention, "but the times call for caution."

"Caution kept us both alive in the last war, too." Harding said to me. "Colonel Baril and I were lieutenants together during the First World War. He was attached as a liaison to my unit. He showed me the ropes when we first went into the trenches and saved a lot of our boys from getting killed right off."

"Samuel is too modest. He also saved my life, you know," Baril responded. "But let us save reminiscences for another time. We have much to discuss. Come inside."

We sat around a conference table in Colonel Baril's office next to a large window overlooking the bluff and the beaches beyond. The sea was filled with our ships and landing craft. The fort's guns were quiet. Arab servants in white coats served us thick, black coffee in little cups with handles you couldn't fit a finger through. I looked at Harding and somewhat grudgingly admitted to myself that he had really pulled off something spectacular. I was impressed with the fact that I had personally invaded North Africa and now was having coffee with these nice Frenchmen, as opposed to being blown to bits by them. I decided the survival of Billy Boyle deserved comment.

"Nice job, Major," I said to Harding, gesturing at the scene below. No need to go overboard with praise for the boss.

"Pay your compliments to Colonel Baril, Lieutenant Boyle," Harding said rather curtly. "He's the one who has put his head on the block to make sure this fort doesn't oppose our landing."

"My colonel also suggested the beach below for your landing site," Lieutenant Dupree volunteered. "It provides good access to roads and the seas are somewhat quieter here."

"So this plan has been in the works for a while?" I asked. I felt left out, like the last kid picked for a baseball team. Harding had chosen me to accompany him just two days ago, when I arrived in Gibraltar, fresh from leave in England. I was still in the dark about his mission. I sort of worked for Major Harding, who was General Eisenhower's deputy intelligence chief, except for when the general had a special job for me. Usually something involving low crimes in high places, crimes that had to be kept quiet for the sake of the war effort and Allied unity. Right now, things were pretty quiet in the military crime field, so here I was keeping the major company until Ike needed me again.

"For some time, yes, Lieutenant Boyle," Baril said. "There are many of us here who do not support the Vichy regime and wish to strike back at the Germans, instead of collaborating with them. Are you not fully aware of the situation here?"

He studied me as he asked that question, then looked at Harding with a glance that seemed to ask if I was some country bumpkin along for the ride.

"Lieutenant Boyle has been recuperating after completing a secret mission, and only joined me recently," Harding explained. I mentally thanked him for the boost, and the white lie about the secret mission. Well, it had been a secret, except that I had kept it a secret from him as well as everyone else. But I'd managed to return from Norway, where the mission had taken me, so here I was, available for duty.

Baril and Dupree exchanged glances, taking Harding at his word, even though the evidence in front of them, namely me, still gave them pause. I sipped some coffee. It was really strong, and sweet, which gave me the opportunity to try to move the conversation away from the shortcomings of yours truly.

"Wow. This joe could peel paint." Except for a roll of Harding's eyes, everyone ignored me, which is the way I liked it when I had to hang around with senior officers. They had a way of thinking up ideas that got you killed and them promoted.

"Jean, what's the situation here?" Harding said.

Baril gestured for the servants to leave. He waited several seconds after the doors closed behind them.

"General Mast, my commanding officer, is on his way here. He is with us, and will give orders to the outposts along the road to Algiers to not resist the Americans. He is attempting to stay *out* of touch with General Alphonse Juin, commander of all French forces in North Africa, until sufficient American forces are in place." Baril sat back, nodded at Dupree, and took a sip of coffee, letting the younger officer fill in the details.

"General Juin is anti-German, but he is a professional soldier, and will obey whatever direct orders he receives from the French government, even if that government kisses the boots of the *Boches*," Dupree said with disgust.

"What are your government's orders likely to be?" I asked.

"To resist any invader. Period."

"So, Colonel Baril, you and your men are risking your necks to help us?"

"No, Lieutenant," Baril answered. "We are doing it for the honor of France. Many fine young men like Lieutenant Dupree have been working to carry out this coup so we can strike back against the occupiers of our nation."

"Billy, my friend," Dupree said, "we are not risking our necks, but rather our heads. If we fail, the best we can hope for is the guillotine. If we succeed, I hope to be fighting the Germans by your side very soon."

I was impressed with these guys, so impressed that I didn't even mention that, personally, my hope was to get back to headquarters in London and my nice room at the Dorchester Hotel as soon as possible. Hell, what I really wanted was to be back home on the force in Boston, but that was too much to hope for.

"Sure, George . . ."

"Georges," he corrected, giving it that Gallic uplift I'd never master.

"Okay, Georgie. What's next, Major?"

Harding looked at Baril. "Your lieutenant goes right to the point. I must prepare to meet General Mast. When can we expect Allied forces to reach us here? If orders to resist the invasion come from Algiers first, my men may have to obey them, especially if they are delivered by an armed force."

"A detachment of British Commandos is making its way up the bluff now," said Harding, checking his watch. "They should be here within ten minutes. You can turn the fort over to them, and then follow us into Algiers."

"Algiers?" I asked. "Before the rest of the Army gets there?"

I was so happy at having made it this far that I wanted to enjoy the feeling for a while.

"Our job has barely begun, Boyle," Harding said. "We need to make contact with our agents in Algiers who are working with the friends of Lieutenant Dupree."

"There are over four hundred insurgents active at this moment. They are taking over police stations, government offices, even the official residence of General Juin," Baril explained as he strode to the door. "They need to keep orders from going out to countermand those of General Mast. If they succeed, your forces will be in Algiers before anyone can resist. You must leave quickly. Georges will drive you. He is very well informed and can put you in contact with the insurgents."

We shook hands; I felt like one of the

Three Musketeers. It was one of those moments that led to guys getting killed for the greater good.

"How'd you get mixed up in this, Georgie?" I asked as we piled into the staff car.

"My younger brother, Jerome, and several of his friends are involved. He took me into his confidence, and knowing that Colonel Baril was in favor of the Allies, it was only natural that I became his liaison. It means a great deal to us, to be able to join the fight against the Germans."

"Is your kid brother in the army too?"

"The army? Oh no, he is a student at the university. He is studying philosophy. You will meet him this morning. He is one of the leaders of the students."

Now, I always thought I had a good sense of the odds for or against me when things got tough. Back in Boston, when I was walking a beat, they were usually in my favor, unless I did something stupid, like walking alone in Chinatown after rousting a couple of tong boys. In England, I'd kept a low profile when I could. I did make a side trip to occupied Norway, but that was personal, so it didn't really count. But as we got into the car, I began to calculate. There was me, Harding, and this French kid who probably spent more time trimming his moustache than cleaning his rifle. We were way out in front of the U.S. Army, heading into an enemy capital, to help a bunch of spies and college kids — philosophy students, no less — take over a military headquarters. I did the math as best I could, and determined that our odds of survival were roughly equivalent to that of the Red Sox winning the World Series.

"Are you a baseball fan, Major?" I asked Harding.

"Sure. Ever since West Point I've been a big fan of the New York Yankees."

"Figures."

CHAPTER THREE

The staff car got waved through a couple of roadblocks without a question. Harding said he would've had those guards court-martialed if they were in his army. I thought they did a fine job.

We crested a ridge and saw the city of Algiers rising up from the harbor on a gently sloping hillside. There were a few tall hard-edged modern buildings, but mostly I saw whitewashed two- and three-story, softly rounded structures that looked like they'd grown straight out of the stony ground. The whiteness was intensified as they reflected the light of the morning sun in the sky. It was a clear day, and the Mediterranean was a deep shimmering blue, broken only by the wakes of warships that seemed to cut across the water in every direction. Up here it was quiet, the opposite of what I expected an invasion morning to sound like.

"Not much fighting going on," I commented.

"General Mast and Colonel Baril bought us some time," Harding said. "We've gotten ashore safely, but there are still organized French forces in the city and all around us. We need to get this settled, now."

"And how are we going to accomplish that, Major?" I asked.

"Well, Boyle, I've got two tricks up my sleeve. The first is a letter from General Giraud calling upon all French soldiers to rally to the side of the Allies."

"General Giraud?" asked Georgie, clearly puzzled. "What has he to do with this?"

"Giraud escaped from Vichy France recently and is with General Eisenhower at Gibraltar, organizing plans for French forces in North Africa to join the Allies."

"General Giraud is a fine officer," Georgie said with a shrug, "even a hero. But he is no longer on active duty. Why would anyone obey his orders?"

"Ike is counting on it," Harding said, evading the question.

"That may be. But for the majority of officers, any such order will have to come via the chain of command. Some of us wish for vengeance on the Germans badly enough to disregard it, but most will follow the orders they receive from a superior officer."

"But you said yourself this Giraud guy is a hero —" I said.

"There are only two things that will work," Georgie cut in. "Either General Juin or some other senior official orders resistance to cease, or your army arrives very soon in overwhelming force, leaving no choice but to surrender and join the Allies."

"So you don't place much stock in General Giraud?" I asked.

"The decision must be made by the proper French authority or on the battlefield. Those are the only honorable choices. A retired officer hand-picked by the Americans, or worse, the British, will not be obeyed."

I knew the French and the Brits didn't always get along, especially since the British Navy had shelled the Vichy French fleet at Mers el-Kebir to keep it from falling into the hands of the Germans.

"I mean no offense, of course . . ." Georgie said, looking a little embarrassed.

"None taken," said Harding, in a tone of voice that let you know he was really steamed.

"I hope your second trick is a show-stopper, sir," I said.

"You're the other trick, Boyle. I thought General Juin might be impressed when he learns that General Eisenhower sent his favorite nephew to meet him."

Georgie eyed me, then Harding. I could tell he was trying to figure out if he could trust his command of the English language.

"General Eisenhower is your uncle?"

"Well, Georgie, he is, sort of. We're connected on my mother's side. I think we're really second cousins once removed or something, but since he's older I've always called him Uncle Ike."

Georgie drove on without saying anything, through a neighborhood of European style homes and gardens.

He finally turned and looked at Harding. "So your mission, Major, is to convince General Juin to surrender due to the influence of a retired French officer and the distant relative of an American general?"

There was silence for a moment while Harding did a slow burn. "I will inform General Juin of the massive Anglo-American forces just landed upon his shores, and convince him that resistance is not only futile, but will needlessly delay the liberation of France!"

"Very well, Major. I hope for your success, perhaps even more than you do."

Harding didn't answer. He settled further down in the back seat and stared out the window. I could tell he had hoped for a more enthusiastic response. I didn't know how serious he was about using me with Juin. Uncle Ike wasn't all that famous and nephews-twice removed are a dime a dozen, so the two of us put together weren't exactly overwhelming. It seemed the odds were stacked against us.

Georgie turned a corner and we entered a small village. The signpost said LAMBIRIDI, which was the town just outside Algiers.

"General Juin's villa is just a few kilometers —" Georgie slammed on the brakes as a roadblock came into view. Two trucks were pulled across the road. Armed men with black armbands ran up to the car as it skidded to a stop.

"Who are these guys?" I asked.

"SOL," Georgie said disgustedly. "Service d'Order Legionnaire. Vichy fascist militia. They worship the SS, and do whatever dirty work Vichy asks of them."

Before Georgie could finish, the doors of the staff car were flung open and rifles pointed at our heads, accompanied by more excited French chatter than I'd ever heard. One pair of hands grabbed my Thompson while someone else took me by the collar and hauled me out of the front seat.

"Américain!" I hollered, trying to form the rest of the little French I knew into a full sentence. The next thing I knew, the flat of a rifle butt slammed into my head and plastered me against the side of the car. My legs buckled, as I tried to grab onto something to keep my head from hitting the pavement. It always bothered me that in the movies a guy got knocked clean out when someone smacked him in the head. Then he'd wake up later, rub his head a bit, and go on like nothing had happened. I knew something about getting hit in the head. It was very painful, there was usually a lot of blood, and if you were knocked out there was a good chance you weren't going to wake up again.

My head felt as if someone had rammed a ten-penny nail into my skull, and I could feel blood trickling down my ear. I was damned if I was going to pass out, although it seemed to be an attractive idea as I tried to stand up. The guy who'd batted me took a step forward. I held up my hand.

"Irish," I said, tapping my chest. "Erin Go Bragh." He didn't get it, but he didn't hit me again, either. Instead he hustled me over to the other side of the car to stand next to Harding and Georgie, both of whom had been smart enough to keep their mouths shut.

Georgie pulled out a white silk handkerchief and handed it to me. I pressed it against my head where it hurt the most and the flow of blood eased up. I looked around, counting the guns and looking for a way out. There were seven SOL thugs, all mean-looking, one of whom was smiling at the others as he showed off my Thompson. Spoils of war.

A black sedan was parked by the side of the road. The driver got out and opened the rear door on our side. He was dressed in a blue uniform, and so was his boss, who also wore a blue cape tossed back over one shoulder, and an armband similar to the ones worn by the SOL.

"Vichy police," Georges whispered to us. "The Gardes Mobiles. They run the SOL, unofficially, of course."

"Of course," I said. "Any other surprises we should know about, Georgie?" I was joking, as usual, but even I wasn't ready for the punch line. The driver went to the other side of the sedan and opened the back door. Out stepped a tall German officer, in a sun-bleached khaki uniform, complete with Iron Cross at the collar and a band around his left sleeve, in ornate German script, that read "Deutsches Afrika Korps." One of Rommel's boys.

The two of them strolled over, like a

couple of old pals. The French cop was of medium height, with a long face and a big, sloping nose at the center of it. He wasn't what you'd call ugly, but he probably would be someday. Right now, in his tailored uniform and polished boots, with his cape jauntily thrown over his shoulder, he looked like the cat that had caught the canary. Or three canaries. He smiled as he approached us, the kind of smug smile that comes from being in charge and having seven gunsels watching your back. The German was taller than him and slimmer, with a face as weather-beaten as his uniform. I could tell he wasn't a cop. Like Harding, he had professional soldier written all over him. He didn't smile, and he sure as hell looked like he didn't need seven guys to watch out for him.

"Welcome to Algiers, gentlemen," the Frenchman said in excellent, but accented English. "We have been expecting you." He walked right up to Harding, extending his hand like a precinct captain greeting a visiting dignitary. "Major Harding, I am Captain Luc Villard, at your service."

His hand hung there for a second, the smile frozen on his face as he waited for Harding to respond. My mind dully registered the fact that those first roadblocks had been too easy to get through, that he had been waiting here for us, that he knew Harding's name, and that I didn't have a clue as to what in the hell was going on. Being a trained detective, such deductions came easily to me, especially the one about not having a clue.

"Pleased to meet you, Captain Villard," Harding said, shaking his hand. He was trying to sound confident, but even Harding couldn't keep a slight tone of bewilderment out of his voice.

He gave it his best shot, though. "Obviously, you are aware of our mission," he continued. "I bring greetings from General Giraud and General Eisenhower, and offer French forces our assistance in fighting those who occupy French soil." He delivered this line with a straight face, ignoring the German standing right there. I almost believed the three of us were about to march on Paris.

Villard laughed as he turned to smirk at his German companion. "We are well aware of your pitiful mission. Also, I am aware that this is French soil, under the sovereignty of France, and *you* are the invader!"

His smile turned ugly and he smacked Harding across the face. Harding didn't even twitch, and I caught a glimpse of a raised eyebrow from the German. It was his first expression of any kind and vanished in an instant. Was it disdain for Villard, or did he think a bullet would have been better than a sissy slap?

"We have freed General Juin from the pathetic rebels who occupied his house last night," Villard said, "and we have also taken into custody the British and American agents who acted as provocateurs among them. It was not difficult to learn from them that you would arrive this morning."

"You can't expect to win —" exclaimed Georgie.

"I know who you are as well, Lieutenant Dupree," Villard cut in. "A traitor at worst, at best a dupe of the British." He motioned for one of his men, and a thick-waisted sweaty guy in a dusty black suit leaned in and pulled Georgie's revolver out of his holster. He handed it to Villard, who aimed it at Georgie's chest.

"And I have little use for either traitors or fools." He pulled the trigger before anyone could move. The sound exploded in my ears and the next thing I knew Georgie was thrown against the car, a look of shock and surprise on his face and a burnt, black hole in his chest that slowly spread scarlet as he fell.

CHAPTER FOUR

I knew Georgie was dead before he hit the ground. I knew it was a well-practiced routine, the hand gesture to the sweaty guy, the sudden, unexpected violence. I knew that it had a purpose, and that Villard enjoyed it. He smiled at us.

"The penalty for treason is death in your army too, I believe, Major Harding?"

"Yes, Captain, it is. If a legally constituted court martial finds the defendant guilty."

"In this national emergency, some legalities must be put aside," Villard said as he shook his head sadly. He casually threw Georgie's revolver down by his body, and continued as if nothing had happened.

"Search him," he ordered one of his men, who turned out Georgie's pockets and tossed his wallet onto the ground. As Villard watched them search, I looked down at the piece on the ground, then around me. The German caught my eye, and shook his head

44

no, ever so slightly. So this was part of the routine too. I looked at the sweaty guy and he had his rifle aimed right at me. Nice little game the Algiers cops had going here.

"But, where are my manners?" Villard said, after the search turned up nothing of interest. "Major Harding, allow me to introduce Herr Major Erich Remke of the German-Italian Armistice Commission. It is his job to insure that all parties adhere to the terms of the armistice that ended hostilities between France, Germany, and Italy. This includes resisting invasion by foreign armies."

Remke snapped to attention and made a slight bow in our direction. "Major Harding, you and your aide will accompany us into Algiers to the Gardes Mobiles headquarters. Captain Villard has given me permission to question you before I depart."

His English was excellent, better than mine almost. He didn't sound like a psychopath and I wondered if we'd be better off with him than with Villard.

"Like he questioned Georgie?" I asked. My gut was churning as I thought of how alive and excited Georgie was just a minute ago. I told myself to shut up if I wanted to get through this in one piece. There'd be time to even the score later, when a bunch

45

of killers didn't have the drop on me. Later, when I had Villard alone and a loaded .45 in my hand. The thought calmed me.

Villard laughed and looked at his men, translating my question as if it were a good joke. They all thought it was hilarious.

Remke locked eyes with me. "My duty here is to insure that the representatives of Vichy abide by the terms of the armistice, and to report on enemy movements to my superiors. I have no intention of shooting you, if that is your concern. As to this . . ." He glanced down at Georgie. The blood on his chest was already drawing flies. ". . . action, I have no authority to intervene in purely internal Vichy politics. Nor any wish to."

He spun around and issued orders in French. I didn't understand the words, but the tone was clear enough. Everyone jumped to, except Villard, who gave him a dirty look and got back into his vehicle. Maybe these guys weren't such pals after all. A couple of goons took our side arms, gave us a quick check for hidden weapons, and then swiped our wristwatches for good measure. They tossed us into the back seat of our car and Remke and a driver sat in the front.

As the driver headed back to Algiers,

Remke turned and gave the slightest hint of a smile. "You are new to war, you Americans. You should prepare yourselves for far worse than this. Did you really expect these Vichy French to welcome you with open arms?"

"Name, rank, and serial number is all you can expect from us," said Harding.

"You are not my prisoners of war, Major. I think it far more likely that I will end up your prisoner before the day is through."

"Well, what are we then?" I asked, eager to get back to the subject of my own future.

"You are detainees of the Gardes Mobiles, along with quite a number of very enthusiastic young Frenchmen whose ideals, unfortunately, outweigh their military prowess. Also, several American and British agents who have been apprehended with them."

"So the uprising failed?" I asked.

"Totally. There was some initial confusion, but they were all easily overcome once the sun rose and the Americans were nowhere in sight. Except for yourselves, of course." Again, that slight smile played across his face, as if this were all very amusing.

"Too bad," Harding said.

"For a number of them, like the young lieutenant back there, yes. Scores are being settled, and this is a very useful pretext."

"What do you mean?"

"You must be aware there are many factions among the Vichy. There are those who favor joining the Reich as a full ally, to fight against the British. They hate them. There are those like General Mast, Colonel Baril, and their followers who prefer to avenge France's defeat in 1940 and join the Allies. Personally, I find the most honorable men here among those two small groups."

"What about the rest?" asked Harding.

"The rest? The rest are either too frightened to act or are like Villard, and act only in their own interest. And the worst of them all is here in Algiers now."

"Who are you talking about?" demanded Harding, who was suddenly taking a bigger interest in this conversation.

"You don't know?"

Harding shook his head.

"Americans," Remke laughed. "You are in for a very long war, I'm afraid. You really need a better intelligence service if you need me to tell you that Admiral Jean Darlan, Deputy Premier of Vichy France, is in Algiers."

Harding sat there like he had been whacked with a two-by-four. Hot air from the open front windows blasted us as the driver accelerated. Remke removed his cap and mopped the sweat from his temples with a handkerchief.

"So, Major, do not feel too badly about the failure of your mission," Remke said, putting the sun-bleached cap back on, adjusting it to a jaunty, roguish angle. "General Juin would never have gone over to you with Darlan so close. With Petain's own deputy in Algiers, he would not dare to disobey orders."

"If you've got everything under control," I said, "and Darlan is in charge here, then why did you say you might be our prisoner by tonight?"

"Excellent question, Lieutenant . . . ?"

"Boyle. Billy Boyle."

"Well, Lieutenant Boyle, it is because Darlan is the biggest opportunist of them all. He will stop this plot to join the Allies precisely because he has no role in it, and if it succeeds he would become a prisoner of General Mast or of Juin himself. Darlan is also smart enough to know the Vichy divisions here cannot hold out against the Allied forces, which seem formidable. He will find a middle ground that will ensure his own safety."

"Meaning he'll cut a deal with us and come out on top?"

"Cut? Make a deal?"

I nodded yes.

"I would wager my Knight's Cross on it. He will align with the winning side, which I must admit will be yours. Here in Algeria, in any case."

"What did you mean about Villard acting in his own interests?" I asked.

"He has many connections with Vichy politicians and the local underworld. He certainly hopes to benefit no matter who wins."

"What happens next?" I asked, still not clear on where I'd be tomorrow.

"We have a little chat at headquarters, and then I leave for Tunisia."

"Back to the Afrika Korps, Major?" Harding asked.

"Perhaps you now wish to exchange a little more information than name, rank, and serial number, Major Harding?"

"Just curious," Harding answered with a grin, "as one professional soldier to another."

Remke nodded. I noticed that he didn't nod at me. I was relieved to know I still looked like a civilian in uniform.

"I was sent here on light duty to recover from a leg wound, courtesy of the British Eighth Army. I am due back at Wehrmacht headquarters in Tunisia shortly. I think we will be quite busy there in the near future."

"We'll do our best," said Harding.

"Of that I am sure," said Remke, "and you will need to."

That pretty much ended the conversation, and I realized that Remke had avoided saying what would happen to us after he left.

We drove by a three-story brick building, home of the Gardes Mobiles. There were armed police and SOL all around it. A crowd of Arabs watched from across the street, wary of the police, but curious. The car turned down a side street and entered a large walled courtyard at the rear of the building. The sun was rising in the midday sky, and it was getting hot. The car braked to a halt, stirring up a cloud of dust that settled down lazily over the hood. The driver opened Remke's door as other guards pulled us out, gripping our arms, and hustled us toward the back door.

We weren't the only ones in the courtyard. A group of about twenty young guys and a couple of girls sat in the dust. Their hands were tied behind their backs, and more than a few of them had bloody faces. Next to them another truck was being unloaded, with more of the same. Armed guards surrounded them.

"Are they being detained, too?" I asked Remke.

"Unfortunately, they are now political prisoners, and whatever happens with the Allies, the Gardes Mobiles will not release them."

"I'm sure their release will be part of any negotiation," said Harding.

"Major Harding, America has been at war for less than a year, and North Africa is your first engagement. I have been in combat since 1939, in Poland, Holland, France, Libya, and Egypt. I tell you now, those brave, helpless young men and women are already casualties, and there is nothing you or I can do about it."

I looked at the faces staring up at us. I wondered if Remke was trying to scare us, or if he just took a dim view of human nature after three years of fighting. Or, if maybe he knew what he was talking about, and I'd be joining them out in this dusty courtyard before the day was over. Or somewhere worse.

I walked by another row of prisoners, the guard holding my arm in his meaty grip. I caught a glimpse of something out of the corner of my eye, something familiar yet out of place here. I turned my head and tried to focus. Then I saw. I couldn't believe it.

At the end of the row, her long blonde hair framing a dirty face with a bloodied lip, sat Diana Seaton. Diana, who I hadn't seen for nearly two months since she'd received her orders to report to the Special Operations Executive for her next assignment.

Diana.

I looked over to Harding. He shook his head, then shouted at me, "Boyle! Name, rank, and serial number, nothing else!"

I looked at Diana, and saw that she had heard Harding. She sat up a little straighter but, except for her eyes, she didn't betray a thing. Those eyes hooked me and held on as the guard pulled me along, into police headquarters, leaving her and the others in the dusty courtyard. I wondered what kind of nightmare I had stumbled into.

My stomach felt like I'd been punched by Joe Louis. I couldn't catch my breath, and my heart was pounding so loudly I thought the guards might hear it. Beads of sweat dripped down my temples and my face felt red-hot. Diana. Here. Hands tied behind her back. Helpless. What was I supposed to do? What could I do?

The guards bundled us into a tiled entryway, with one set of stone steps descending below ground and another going up to the floor above. Remke gave us a lazy salute and went upstairs. We went down. Our guard rapped on a thick wooden door braced with rusty ironwork with a small, barred window face-high. There was a rattle of metal and the squeak of straining hinges as the door opened. A couple of rough shoves propelled Harding and me inside as the door swung shut with a thud.

A figure rose from behind a small wooden table. The narrow hallway was lit by a string of bare electric bulbs hanging from the curved ceiling. No windows, nothing but stuffy concrete dampness.

The jailer was an impressive guy, if bulk and smell counted. His blue police uniform was stained and faded to the color of a three-day-old bruise, and his mustache hung down on either side of his mouth, blending in with the stubble on the double chin erupting over his collar. One hand held a revolver, motioning us to move on down the hall. The other wiped at his mouth, clearing the remains of a meal caught in wiry facial hair. There was a newspaper spread out on his little table, and some sort of gooey cheese made little grease stains across a front-page photograph: Darlan himself.

We moved down the hall, trying to stay ahead of his odor, a combination of garlic, sweat, and rotten cheese. Another small set of stairs led to a corridor with two cells on either side, all empty. The first cell door was open and he pushed us in, jabbing the snout of his revolver in my back. The door slammed with a hard, final *clang* and he reached down and produced a large ring of keys, which had been hidden by the flab hanging over his belt. He locked the door, belched, and went back upstairs.

Just like every guy I've ever thrown in the slammer, I went up to the bars and rattled them, just in case he'd forgotten to give the key that final turn. No dice. I looked around. The cell was about six by ten, with high walls and a small barred window way above my head. No furniture, just a bucket that I didn't want to get close to. I could see some sky and hear bits and pieces of shouts from the courtyard above.

"Something's going on," said Harding.

The shouting grew louder, there was a shuffling sound and dust spilled through the cell window.

"Give me a boost, maybe I can spot Diana," I said in a rush. "Sir. Please."

"Don't call out her name, for God's sake,"

said Harding as he cupped his hands and braced his back against the wall. I put my right foot in his grip and pulled on his shoulders as he lifted me with a grunt. I got my left foot on his shoulder and pushed off, not caring how Harding felt with the tread of my combat boot digging into his collarbone. Rank be damned. I had to see Diana.

I got one hand around a bar and tried to steady myself as I put my right foot on his other shoulder. My face was plastered against the gritty concrete and as I pulled myself up I could feel my skin rubbing raw against the rough surface. I had both hands on the bars now and I could see out of the window. My legs were shaking, and Harding felt wobbly underneath me, but I clung to those iron bars.

The prisoners in the courtyard were being herded against the far wall, guards yelling and giving them a few kicks and blows with rifle butts if they didn't move fast enough. I thought they were lining them up to be shot and I almost fell as a sick feeling flooded through my body. Then I heard engines, grinding gears, and brakes, and out of the corner of my eye I could see trucks pulling into the courtyard. They were only getting them out of the way so the trucks could come in. I let out a deep breath.

There were a lot of feet and legs in front of me now, some milling around, others stationary. How could I find Diana? What was she wearing? I tried to remember . . . she had on a blue blouse, light blue, like her eyes. She liked to show off those blue eyes. I couldn't come up with what else she had on . . . slacks, a skirt? What would college kids in Algeria wear?

I didn't know what to do. What if I saw her? What the hell could I do? I was as useless as, well, a guy locked in a jail cell. I felt panicky. I wanted to jump out of my skin. I had to do something.

"Hey! Hey!" I yelled as loud as I could. I couldn't call her name, I couldn't say anything that would give away that I knew her, so I just started yelling.

"Hey! What's going on? Somebody talk to me! Hey!"

"Can you see her?" Harding asked.

"No, just a lot of legs and shoes. They either don't understand English or think I'm some nutcase down here." My hands were beginning to ache from gripping the bars.

"HEY!"

There was some commotion outside, and two sets of bare legs in skirts began backing through the crowd.

"Hey," I said, not quite as loud. I could feel my heart thumping. I didn't feel the ache in my hands anymore. Could it be? The bare legs moved closer. One pair turned, then the girl fell to her knees, awkwardly, her hands bound behind her back throwing off her balance. Now I could see: the pale blue blouse, floated above a dark blue skirt. Her chest was heaving, and I could see a bit of her long blonde hair as she bent her neck to peer inside the window at ground level.

"Hey," I said, in a whisper. "It's me."

She dropped onto her side and rolled, so her face was right up against the window. Diana. Her hair hung down over her face, and she had to shake it aside to see me. Tears streaked her dust-caked cheeks, and blood dripped from a gash on her upper lip.

"Billy," she said.

I mouthed her name, so no one else could hear. Her blue eyes flashed. We looked at each other. What was there to say?

I decided "I love you," was right.

She looked at me a long time.

"I love you too," she whispered.

I had never said that to a woman before. Or heard it. Hell of a time and place. I pulled myself closer, the muscles in my forearms quivering as they took almost all my weight. Harding was pushing up on the soles of my boots as I strained to get just a little closer. I could feel his hands shaking.

"I'll get you out of this, I promise," I said.

"Get yourself out, Billy. The SOL men are fanatics."

"I know." I didn't want to tell her how I knew. "What's going to happen to you?"

"I don't know," she said, shaking her head. "I don't know what went wrong. We must have been betrayed." There was hurt in her eyes, as if she were wondering which of her friends was the traitor.

"We'll be out soon," I said. "There's no way they can keep us here. The whole U.S. Army is on its way. I'll find you. I promise!"

"You can't mention my name, Billy. If they find out . . ."

"I know, I know. The best thing now is for you to keep quiet and pass as another kid caught up in all this."

I wished I hadn't said it like that. She was so much more. She looked away for a second. I sensed I'd hurt her.

"We almost did it, you know," she said.

"Yeah, I know. Me, I didn't even get close."

"We're quite a pair, aren't we?" She tried to smile and winced, as she shifted to get closer. I could tell she was in pain.

I looked at her face, the face I saw in my dreams every night, the face I dreamed of kissing in a place far away from here. The first time I had seen that face, lightning had cracked the sky and thunder rolled like waves over the hills. She'd been mucking out a barn at Seaton Manor when we were introduced by her sister Daphne. And despite that, and the fact that she was English through and through, committed to serving her country while I was Irish-American, and less than enamored of England and all she stood for, we had fallen for each other. Hard.

We were choking on sand and blood and smiling at each other, desperate to be closer. I wanted to cry out and make this all go away, to just go home with Diana, wherever that might be. Boston, London, it didn't make any difference. We were inches away from each other and this could be the last time we'd ever be together. Her face was bloody and dirty and beautiful and I knew she was scared. I was scared. My heart was breaking and I was terrified and I realized I had never felt this happy before, just being with her for a few seconds, here in this dusty prison courtyard, a world away from everything.

I heaved myself forward and felt my feet leave Harding's grasp.

Diana inched herself closer and pressed her face against the bars.

"Billy," she said, tears sliding sideways across her face, as she struggled to move nearer still. I didn't have breath to spare, I couldn't say another word. My boots scrabbled at the bare wall, trying to find a hold. I anchored my jaw on the concrete sill next to the bars. There was no more strength in my arms.

Our lips touched. I tasted blood, then fell away.

It was like falling in a dream, when it takes a long time but then you hit the ground and all the air comes out of you and you wake up. Except I was already awake.

Harding got me on his shoulders again but by the time I managed to hoist myself up next, all I saw was legs moving away, toward the trucks. I couldn't hold on any longer; my arms were gone, weak and shaking. I slid down to the floor and cradled my head in my hands. Sticky blood from my cheeks and jaw oozed between my fingers and I could feel gritty flecks of concrete flake away from my face as I rubbed my eyes. The worst thing was, I felt relieved Diana was gone. I didn't know if I could take seeing her again, tied up like that. I wanted to be with her, to keep her safe, not to hang onto bars while she threw herself to the ground for half a kiss before they took her away to who the hell knows where. At first, all I could think about was her, until I forced myself to recall images of home and work back in the States.

A memory came to me, a crazy one, of the time I was walking my beat in Boston and a car almost hit a lady crossing the street against traffic. I couldn't believe what I was seeing, didn't want to believe it. It was headed straight for her, then swerved, just missing her. I had felt relief, and my whole body loosened up. She stood there, scared out of her wits, and surprised she was still alive. I can still remember the look she gave me, joy and fear mixing at the sudden shock of near-death, then salvation. Then another car sped around the corner and hit her straight on, sending her flying as she bounced off the hood and rolled to the ground, arms and legs bent in different directions and no look at all on her face. I stood there, shouting "No, no, no," jumping up and down, trying to will away what I had seen, feeling guilty I hadn't been able to stop it.

I lifted my head from my hands and let it

fall back and hit the wall with a thunk. It hurt and felt good at the same time, knocking my thoughts off that track for a second. I tried to think of something positive. A little part of me was still happy at the memory of those eyes, of Diana looking at me and getting close enough for a kiss. A flicker of joy crept up but then I felt fear. I might never see her again. She might die, still wondering where I was and when I was going to come for her. I felt jittery, as if something was about to happen I wasn't ready for. And I thought once more about that lady in Boston, looking at me in the last seconds of her life, a guy who stood there flat-footed, doing nothing.

CHAPTER FIVE

Hours passed. There was nothing to do, which usually would suit me. I'm not the kind of guy who thrives on adventure. Give me a nice routine, like walking my beat back in Boston, stopping at a diner for a cup of coffee, flirting with the waitress, twirling my baton out on the sidewalk, and watching the world go by. Seeing the same folks in their shops every day. Church on Sunday. Opening day at Fenway every April. Stuff like that.

Guys like Harding, and maybe every other GI I've run into, they all want adventure. Win the war, get a medal, whip the Nazis, smash the Japs. Me, I figure it's easy to talk tough but a lot harder to stay tough when the lead starts flying. It's not that I'm unpatriotic, I just don't have enough imagination to convince myself that war is going to be like it is in the movies. I've seen too many gunshot wounds up close to believe that. That's why I appreciate a nice, predictable, routine, boring life. Sure, you could get hit by a bus, or if you're a cop you might be one of the unlucky bastards who gets shot every now and then, but the chances are slim. The risk is a lot bigger roaming around North Africa, dodging bullets.

I thought I had it made back in Boston. I sure never thought I'd end up in a jail cell, much less a stinking Algiers jail cell. I was just enjoying being called Detective and then what happens? I get pulled out of civilian life and thrown into the army, where not even Dad's political pals could keep me out of this war. Getting into another fight alongside the English hadn't played well at the Boyle household. The Holy Catholic Church, the Boston Police Department, and the Irish Republican Army are a pretty big deal at home, although not necessarily in that order. My Dad and two uncles had gone off to fight in the Great War. Alongside the English. Only two of them came back, and they were pretty bitter. So I'd been brought up to believe that the only thing worth dying for, other than family and a brother officer, of course, was a free Ireland. One night, right after Pearl Harbor, Dad and Uncle Dan laid it on the line for me. It took a few beers at the tavern before they got around to it, but I knew something was up when Uncle Dan drained his fourth draft and told me this wasn't our war because no one had attacked a Boyle, or Boston, or any part of Ireland. Uncle Dan's a cop too, a detective just like my Dad. He's also a real IRA man, unlike Dad. He didn't like the idea of another Boyle dying for the "fucking Brits," but other than that sentiment, which I couldn't really argue with, they didn't have much of a plan.

Mom did. As usual. She recalled a relative on her mother's side who had married a guy who'd gone to West Point and worked himself up to general. He worked a staff job at the War Plans Division in that new building down in Washington D.C. The Pentagon. She was sure he'd like a nice young relative with police experience to be a security officer on his staff.

She had suggested the Military Police at first, but Dad hated their guts from his days in France. He said they weren't real cops, just guys with clubs who kept an honest doughboy from his drinks and the ladies on those few occasions when he got a pass. So, no Military Police for me.

Mom called her cousin and Dad called his congressman who owed him a favor or two, and pretty soon I was going to OCS and then to Washington, D.C. to join Uncle Ike's staff. Maybe Dad had kind of oversold me. True, I was a detective on the Boston PD, but I had only been in plainclothes for a few weeks. I had worn a bluecoat and walked a beat for five years right out of high school and although Dad had me detailed to help out around crime scenes a lot, I wasn't the experienced investigator Uncle Ike thought I was. It was kind of unusual for a cop to make detective at my age. While I can usually figure things out sooner or later, I'm no scholar, and the exam they gave was real hard. A few of the sheets from the test happened to find their way into my locker one day, and I managed to pass. My Uncle Dan is on the Promotions Board, so I was in. That's the way it works. I'm not saying I'm proud of it, but it doesn't mean I'm not a good cop either. I'm not just some stranger who got the job because he was smart enough to answer more questions than the other guy. That doesn't mean a damn thing when your partner is counting on you for backup.

I had to do my best and figure things out as we went along. I hate to admit it, but I didn't want to disappoint Uncle Ike either. The guy had such a big job and such a nice smile, it seemed that it wouldn't be fair to fail and add to his burdens. He's family, after all. We were all sure he and I would sit out the war at the Pentagon. Little did we know that he had been tapped to head up the U.S. forces in Europe. And that he liked the idea of having a former cop on his staff — a family member to boot — to work as his secret special investigator. There's all kinds of crime during wartime involving top brass and politicians, and Uncle Ike doesn't like anyone getting away with anything that hurts the war effort. He also doesn't like stuff like that getting in the news. Too embarrassing for Allied unity. That's where I come in. I'm supposed to look into things for him. Quietly.

The only thing quiet about this mission was this jail cell. Everything else was loud, from the artillery fire to the gunshot that killed Georgie. Nothing I could do about that now, though. I stretched my sore back and tried to get comfortable on the hard floor.

Major Samuel Harding was not "family," not even close. West Point graduate, decorated combat veteran in the last war, professional soldier. My complete opposite and worst nightmare. He worked in the Intelligence section at U.S. Army Headquarters, and Uncle Ike had detailed me to be his aide. That was my cover story and my job between assignments from Uncle Ike. Such as now. Which is why I'm sitting in a jail cell in Algiers, in the basement of the Vichy secret police headquarters, wondering if some French homicidal maniac is going to shoot me before or after he shoots Diana.

Diana. Now that's a whole other story. Diana had had a sister, Daphne Seaton, Second Officer in the Women's Royal Naval Service, attached to the U.S. Headquarters in London when I got there last June. She's dead now, but I don't want to think about that. I met Diana just before it happened. She knocked my socks off. Diana and I saw each other pretty regularly until I was sent to Gibraltar with Harding and she was recalled to the SOE.

She had enlisted, at the start of the war, in the First Aid Nursing Yeomanry. It was a women's outfit, and they weren't actually nurses, or yeomen either. Diana had ended up as a switchboard operator for the British Expeditionary Force in Belgium in 1940. She was nearly captured, and made it out of Dunkirk only to have the destroyer she was on sunk in the Channel. It was filled with wounded. She made it, they didn't. That's when she volunteered for the SOE.

I understood that. She needed to find out

if she deserved to live after everyone around her died. I just didn't understand what possessed her to get herself in that position in the first place. I was here under protest, like any sane person, but Diana had no one to blame but herself. I got mad at her while I thought about it, which was at least a distraction from worrying about her.

I stood on the stone floor and stretched. The cell was empty, if you didn't count a sleeping Harding, me, and a rusty bucket. The walls were a flaky white limestone that crumbled easily and smelled like mold and piss. The iron bars were coated with rust, and my hands were the color of dried blood and white chalk. My head throbbed as I stood, and I remembered some of that rust color was my own dried blood.

A door clanked and I heard footsteps coming down the stairwell. Harding opened his eyes and got up instantly. He probably slept at attention. We both went to the bars and tried to peer down the hall, just like guys in the cells back home. I liked the view better from the other side.

Remke and another German officer strolled into view. They were both dressed in full-length leather coats, with goggles pushed up over their caps. If this was going to be an interrogation, it looked like it was going to be a messy one.

"Well, gentlemen," Remke said, "it appears there is not time for our little chat. Conditions are changing rapidly, and we must depart at once. While we can."

"We?" I asked. Remke smiled slightly, and glanced at his companion.

"Lieutenant Boyle is worried we might take him with us, Gerhardt," Remke said. "What do you say? Would he be better off as our prisoner or as an ally of the French?" Remke looked like he was enjoying himself. His pal didn't.

"Major, all I know is that we must leave immediately." Gerhardt looked calm, every part of him except his right hand, which held the grip of the Schmeisser submachine gun slung over his shoulder. He kept flexing it, opening and closing it over the hatch-marked grip like a nervous gunsel at a bank heist.

"My aide, gentleman," Remke said, as if we were being introduced at the officer's club. "Lieutnant Gerhardt graf von Neiderlander. Major Harding and Lieutenant Boyle."

Gerhardt snapped out a crisp salute. "Major Harding, I am pleased to meet you. Major Remke regrets he cannot discuss events further with you, since we must leave immediately." He spoke perfect English, with an accent that would have fit in at Oxford.

Harding returned the salute and looked Gerhardt up and down. He was tall and tanned, with white patches on his face where goggles had shaded his skin from the sun. A white scar ran down his right temple. His blue eyes and blond hair made him look like a high school kid, but his unusual tan, and the leather trench coat with a Schmeisser held at the ready, said he was a hardened soldier, an Afrika Korps killer.

Harding looked at me, then back to Gerhardt.

"I don't suppose you'd trade aides, Major?"

Remke laughed and said something in rapid German to Gerhardt, who cracked a smile.

"No, Major Harding. While I would like to learn more about you Americans, I cannot leave Gerhardt here. After all our difficulties working as allies with the French, I could not allow him to miss the opportunity of fighting them!"

"I'll make do with Boyle, then. Are you returning to Tunis?"

"Perhaps. Perhaps we will meet again, under circumstances that will allow me to learn more about you Americans. I am quite interested to see how you will adapt to this war. I do regret that you cannot accompany us to continue this discussion, but Captain Villard forbids it. I almost had him convinced that it would be better for him if you did not rejoin your forces, but . . ." He shrugged.

"You mean so that we wouldn't report the murder of Lieutenant Dupree?"

"That, and the fact that you were allowed to see the number of detainees in the courtyard," Remke answered.

"What do you mean?" Harding said.

"I told you old scores would be settled. Some of those people will never be seen again. Villard is very powerful here, a law unto himself."

"Why are you telling us this?" I asked. I was worried about Diana, and I needed to know if this guy was on the level.

"Most of those prisoners are ineffectual rebels who hardly know how to fire a weapon. They pose no threat to us. Perhaps you can assist in their release if you are freed soon enough. The French government here will go over to you within hours. There is no reason for Villard to shed innocent blood, but he will, and gladly."

I was trying to believe in this little speech

about the sanctity of innocent life, but it just didn't add up. Especially when I saw how nervous Gerhardt was becoming. Harding caught on faster than I did.

"You've got some of your own people out there," Harding said with certainty. "I guessed you were in Intelligence. You're leaving a spy ring behind and one or more of them was caught up in this dragnet. You figure that if we yell loud enough, Villard will let them go."

I admired Harding's smarts until I saw how right he was. Gerhardt shifted one leg slightly and all of a sudden that Schmeisser was pointed straight at us.

"I don't think so, Major . . ." I stammered, trying to think of something, anything to say. Remke put his hand on Gerhardt's arm and gave a slight, almost imperceptible shake of his head.

"I see you are already learning how things work here, Major," Remke said. "But you still have more lessons to learn if you plan to stay alive. When to keep silent, perhaps. Remember that. Come, Gerhardt."

Remke turned on his heel and was gone. Gerhardt smiled, bowed, clicked his heels, then followed his boss up the stairs.

I waited a couple of heartbeats and then turned to Harding. "Major, you almost got us killed!"

"Don't worry, Boyle. All that talk was to deliver a message, to get us to look out for those prisoners so Villard doesn't knock off a German agent among them. I knew Remke wouldn't gun us down in here. Too unprofessional. But that lieutenant of his, Gerhardt, he would've done anything Remke asked. That's my idea of an aide!"

Unsure if he was joking, and not really wanting to know, I sat on the floor and waited for Vichy French politics to run their course. I also sent up a little prayer that everything would work out in time for me to get Diana out of here. I had already broken too many promises to God to even bother making another one, so I just straight out asked if He would save her. No reason, no promises, just save her from Luc Villard, the Germans, her own feelings of guilt, and her goddamned good intentions.

CHAPTER SIX

When I woke up, I didn't have a clue where I was. My head ached and nothing felt right. I deduced from my extreme discomfort, and that fact that I was sleeping on a cold, smelly, damp stone floor, that something was wrong. Then, I remembered that floor was in the basement of the Gardes Mobiles headquarters in Algiers, I was a prisoner, and Diana was, too, if she was still alive.

I lay there thinking how nice those few seconds are after you wake up, before reality sets in. Opening one eye, I saw early morning sunlight filtering through the high, narrow, barred window above the cell. Another day in sunny North Africa. I closed that eye and wished I could fall asleep again, buying back those few precious moments of ignorant bliss. I kept my eyes shut and tried to sleep. I couldn't. I kept seeing Diana in the courtyard, blood on her face, but no fear in her blue eyes. She was brave, all right. You didn't volunteer for the SOE and go behind enemy lines if you weren't brave. And foolish, too. I tried to remember the last time we had been together in England. She must've known she was headed for North Africa. I knew I was. Neither of us had said anything. No loose lips between us. I had come to see her father, Sir Richard, concerned about how he was doing after losing Daphne, her sister. Diana showed up with three days leave, and visited me in my room each night, just as she had the first time. That first time I had only held her as she cried, and fallen in love with her. This last visit, there were no tears. We made love as if there were no tomorrow, which we both knew might be true but neither of us could admit. I smiled now as I remembered her, face shining in the moonlight, beautiful, whispering my name.

I heard a crash, and tried to rouse myself from my daydream. A loud thud followed by a rattle of automatic fire got me up fast. I rolled over with a groan and saw Harding standing by the door, trying to see down the hallway. There were shouts from outside, single shots that sounded like pistol fire, then running feet above us. More cries, some in French, more in English. The yelling grew louder and the sounds echoed down the stairway, into the cellblock, now closer to us. A single gunshot rang out, incredibly loud in the narrow stone passageway, and the French yelling suddenly stopped, replaced by the heavy sound of a body rolling down the steps and hitting the bottom with a thump. Harding and I leaned against the bars, trying to see what was happening. The smell of cordite was thick, smoke and dust drifting in the air. Through the haze a slight figure in British battle dress that looked like it was tailored just for him, which it probably had been, strolled nonchalantly. He held a Webley revolver, smoke curling out of the muzzle, in one hand and in the other, a ring of jailer's keys. The grin on his face was split by a scar that ran from the corner of one eye down to his chin, a souvenir of the explosion that had killed Daphne, ended their love affair, and broken his heart.

"Gentleman, in a few minutes the St. George Hotel will be serving breakfast. Would you care to join me?"

Lieutenant Piotr Augustus Kazimierz was the unlikeliest soldier I had ever seen. He was small, thin, pale, wore glasses, and had studied foreign languages at Oxford University before the war. Before the Germans invaded his native Poland and killed all of his family, which made him a very angry small, pale, thin guy who wore glasses. He had a heart condition that had kept him out of the army until he kicked up such a stink that the Polish Government in Exile commissioned him a lieutenant and sent him to work for General Eisenhower as a translator. That's were he'd met Daphne Seaton. And me. I was still alive, Daphne was dead, and now Kaz didn't care if he lived a minute longer.

He'd gotten involved in the Norway job with me, and did pretty well as my Junior G-man, so Uncle Ike posted him as my assistant to his secret Office of Special Investigations. He wasn't supposed to be in combat because of his medical condition, but working at HQ meant you could bend the rules a bit. That gave him the chance to get into the fight, which is what everybody else seemed to want to do over here. Between his bad ticker and the loss of everyone he loved, I understood that he didn't particularly care about planning for the future.

Kaz was supposed to be an egghead, a back room, quiet, paper-pushing staff officer. Instead, here he was leading a raid to spring us from a Vichy slammer, holding a smoking revolver in one hand and our ticket out of here in the other.

"Kaz!" was all I could manage.

"Yes, Billy, it is Baron Kazimierz to the rescue!" he said, as he tried to find the key for our cell among the dozens dangling from the chain. He winced as he struggled with the heavy ring of keys. I saw blood dripping from his sleeve. More boots thundered down the stairs as a team of Royal Commandos came into view.

"Baron, you promised to stay behind us!" shouted a very exasperated Commando officer as he signaled his men to check the other cells.

"Aha!" shouted Kaz as he found the right key and unlocked the door. "Yes, well, I saw that guard heading down here and thought he might be thinking of harming Billy and Major Harding."

"You mean that big fellow at the bottom of the stairs with a bullet in his chest?" asked Harding as he stepped out of the cell.

"The one and the same, late but not lamented, Vichy jailer. He smelled quite bad. I trust you were not mistreated, Major?" Kaz asked.

"No, we're fine. Are you hit?"

"Yes, I think I have been shot. In the arm. Quite amazing, it does not hurt at all," Kaz said, and smiled weakly.

"It will, Baron," said a Royal Commando

medic who began to strip off Kaz's sleeve, applying sulfa and a bandage. "The bullet went clean through. Nothing to worry about."

"What about the other prisoners?" Harding looked to the Commando officer.

"Place is cleared out, sir. You're the only guests. We got word that a couple of American officers were being held here, and figured it must be you, since you didn't contact headquarters this morning."

"All right. What's the situation?" Harding asked Kaz as he led us out of the basement, stepping over the body of the guard lying in a darkening pool of his own blood.

"Wait a minute," I said. "What do you mean cleared out? They were holding dozens of civilian prisoners yesterday. Aren't any of them still here?"

"No, and no one seems to know where they were taken," Kaz answered. "Perhaps they were transferred to another prison, since their jailers knew Algiers would soon be entered by the Allies."

"Kaz," I said through gritted teeth, "They've got Diana. I saw her yesterday."

Kaz looked stunned. His eyes opened wide and his mouth sort of hung open. He turned to Harding.

"Is this true, Major?"

"Yes, we both saw her in the courtyard with a group of rebels the Gardes Mobiles had rounded up."

Kaz's face went dark. I knew this wasn't easy for him. Diana made him think about Daphne, and Diana in danger would only make him think about Daphne, dead in a rigged car explosion. I still thought about Daphne all the time. She had been my first real friend in England, even though at first she'd thought I was kind of a jerk. I'd had a crush on her, but that was just loneliness. When I met her sister Diana it was like a thunderbolt. There actually had been lightning and thunder, which seemed only normal. Daphne was the older sister, dark haired, beautiful, very sophisticated and elegant whether she was in her blue uniform or in an evening gown. Diana was different. Tall, with long blonde hair, she was more at home on a horse than dressed for a night on the town. She was really good-looking, although not movie-star beautiful, like Daphne had been. She had a strength in her, something steely in her eyes, a hardness in her grip, that dared the world to deny her anything. Daphne had been at peace with her place in the world. Diana wasn't, but at least she was alive. I hoped.

"We have some of the Gardes Mobiles in

custody," Kaz said as we left the cell. "We can question them." He reloaded his revolver as he talked. I thought about the French jailer tumbling down the stairs. I thought about the cold look in Kaz's eyes, which he kept focused on his pistol.

"Kaz, had you killed anyone before?"

"Yes, Billy. Two of them, outside," he answered, knowing I had meant before today.

When I first met Kaz, he seemed like the sort of fellow who would've collected butterflies except that he couldn't stand to hurt them. A nice guy, but a bookworm. Now he had three notches on his gun — that I knew about — and was ready for more. I kind of liked the old Kaz, and was beginning to worry about the new one.

"Tell me what's going on, Lieutenant," Harding said. Kaz looked at him blankly, still trying to take in what had happened to Diana.

"With the invasion," Harding said sarcastically. "You remember, all those ships and men with rifles?"

"Yes sir," Kaz said, pulling himself together. "All the landings went well. General Giraud has arrived, but very few Vichy officers regard him as having any authority.

Admiral Darlan was here when he landed —"

"We know," snapped Harding.

"General Juin has declared an armistice in and around the city of Algiers, at the orders of Admiral Darlan," Kaz said. "It covers only this immediate area, and talks are now underway between General Mark Clark and Darlan. General Eisenhower is expected as soon as the area is secure."

"All right, let's find out what we can here and then get to headquarters," Harding said.

"Captain," Kaz called out to the Commando officer, "are your men searching the premises?"

"Standard procedure, Baron. What are you looking for?"

"Prisoner lists. Show us to the administrative section."

We trotted up the stairs to the third floor, where the main offices were located. A cooling breeze came through the open windows along the hallway, above the dusty courtyard. I searched for the spot where I had seen Diana just a day ago. Worry made my gut ache. I turned away and followed Kaz into what looked like the main office. He was already at work, going through file folders. Except for being in French, it looked pretty much like any police paperwork. Lots of forms and carbon paper. Typewriters on four desks pushed together, file cabinets around the room, a row of tall windows, and a big desk for the guy in charge at the other end of the room. A ceiling fan moved lazily above it all. The smell of sweat and stale cigarette butts was pushed around with the heat but never made it out the windows.

"Kaz," I said as I looked through piles of paperwork on the desk, "why all this 'Baron' stuff anyway? I never heard you use your title except to get reservations back in London."

"That Commando captain is actually Lord Waverly. He didn't care to have me along, so I played the fellow aristocrat. It turns out we had several friends in common at Oxford, and this warmed him up to me. A Polish baron is a rarity, and he may think of me as a mascot."

"Pretty deadly bite for a mascot," I said. Kaz ignored me and went on hunting through the files. His family was descended from one of the ancient clans in Poland, and now this Baron Kazimierz was at the end of his line. Very far from home and alone in the world.

An hour later there was a mound of paper on the floor and three sheets on a desk. Harding and Kaz leaned over them. I leaned against the wall.

"This is all we can find, Major," Kaz reported.

"My French isn't as good as yours, Lieutenant," Harding said, "but I can tell these are travel orders of some sort."

"Yes, and requisitions for food, quarters, and most importantly, petrol. For twenty-five prisoners and ten guards, no names listed." Kaz stabbed his finger at one of the sheets. "At the French Army fuel depot at Bône."

"That's not much to go on," said Harding. He turned to a map on the wall. "Bône is here, on the coast about 125 miles due east. Way beyond our advance units. If they're refueling there, it stands to reason they're headed even further out."

"Here, Major," Kaz said, favoring his bad arm as he read through one of the sheets. "This says the final destination will be confirmed when the convoy arrives in Bône."

"Confirmed by whom?" Harding asked.

"By the deputy administrative officer of XIX Corps, a Captain Henri Bessette, according to this. It says final instructions will be radioed to the commander of the supply depot, who is to turn them over when he is given the authorized password."

"What's the password?" I asked.

"It does not say here."

"Why all this secrecy about a bunch of rebels, anyway? Why didn't they keep them here, or shoot them and get it over with? It doesn't make sense," I said.

"XIX Corps covers the area from Algiers to the Tunisian border," Harding said, half to himself as he studied the map.

"But why would a staff officer at an Army Corps headquarters issue orders and supplies to a police force?" I asked.

"Remember that the Service d'Order Legionnaire militia works hand in glove with the Gardes Mobiles police force," Harding said, "and SOL draws its supplies from the army. Whatever is intended for these prisoners is connected with people in high places."

"Like General Juin?" Kaz asked.

"Maybe," Harding shrugged. "But with Darlan in town, who knows?"

"Let's get to Darlan then," I said.

Harding reached into his jacket and pulled out a pack of Luckies. He lit one and sat on the desk, staring at the wall map of the North African coast.

"Listen to me, both of you. I want to get Miss Seaton back as much as you do. I understand what she means to each of you."

He stopped and looked at us, then back at the map, blowing a stream of blue smoke toward it.

"But, we have a job to do here. That job doesn't include running off to find one missing SOE agent, no matter who she is. The best thing we can do is sort things out with the French so she can be released. If I let you go after her, you could as easily screw things up and get her killed. Let Ike and General Clark negotiate with Darlan. They should have things wrapped up in a few days."

"You mean in a couple of days we'll be pals with Villard, and he'll simply hand her over?"

"It's common to add 'sir' when addressing a senior officer, Boyle," Harding said. "Now let's get out of here and get some chow." He stood, ground out his cigarette, and walked out the door.

"Who is Villard?" Kaz asked. Neither of us had to comment on the fact that Harding had avoided my question.

"I'll tell you on the way to the hotel. You said something about breakfast?"

We set out. I can worry just as well on a full stomach.

Breakfast was powdered eggs and Spam

cooked in a field kitchen erected in the courtyard of the St. George Hotel. We sat on ammo crates in the shade beneath camouflage netting, watching swarms of GIs carrying supplies from trucks through the main entrance like they owned the place. The St. George was four stories high, surrounded by gardens and palm trees, tucked in a quiet area away from the dust and traffic, overlooking the Mediterranean. It was pretty fancy.

"I've eaten at nicer hotels," I said to Kaz, as I pushed the congealed eggs around in my mess tin. Harding gave a grunt, which passed for hysterical laughter coming from him.

"I asked if I could make a reservation," Kaz answered, "but the phone service from Gibraltar was not dependable."

"He's serious." Harding said, through a mouthful of Spam. He actually looked like he was enjoying the stuff.

"In any case, all reservations have been canceled and the guests are being moved out," Kaz said. "All except one. Admiral Darlan."

"Darlan's quartered here?" I asked.

Harding nodded. "See those French Naval ratings guarding that entrance?" Harding gestured to a far wing of the hotel with his fork, a hunk of burned Spam pointing the way. "That's where he's holed up, negotiating with General Clark. He's got XIX Corps headquarters staff in there too. Including Bessette."

I stared at Harding, wondering how he always seemed to know everything, and if he was giving me a hint about what to do next. And wondering if I could do it.

"Why are we bothering with Darlan anyway?" I asked.

Kaz said, "Darlan is the direct representative of Marshal Petain."

"But Colonel Baril, and Georgie . . ." I began.

"Darlan's arrival threw a monkey wrench into the works. It took a lot of courage to do what they did," Harding said. "But I'm afraid Colonel Baril may pay the same price Lieutenant Dupree did. Only he may be allowed a blindfold."

"So what does that mean for your mission to work with the rebels?" I asked.

"It's a military dictum that no plan survives contact with the enemy, Boyle. That mission is over. Now we collect whatever information we can on French troop dispositions until they come over to our side or Ike gives us a new assignment. It was supposed to be a quick coup. The rebels didn't pull it off, so now Darlan's in charge. He's got them in prison and we're pleading with him to come over to our side. Remke was right. Darlan's going to come out smelling like a rose," Harding said.

"What exactly does that mean for the civilian rebels in custody?" I asked, dreading the thought of Diana in Villard's hands. "A firing squad?"

"I doubt it," Harding said casually. "It's one thing for an officer to disobey orders. A bunch of kids, that's another thing. Once things get straightened out here, they'll let them go. Don't worry."

"Sure, Major." I looked over at Darlan's rooms and counted the guards. I drank my coffee. It was cold.

CHAPTER SEVEN

I only had combat boots with me, so I went out of the skylight in my stocking feet. Kaz boosted me up and I pulled myself out onto the roof. I looked down and Kaz disappeared in the darkness, his footsteps echoing faintly in the hallway. I sat on the warm tiles for a second, glad that I didn't have to shinny up a drainpipe to get here thanks to the skylights in every hallway being left open at night to let the heat of the day out. Four floors up was about even with the tops of the palm trees that encircled the hotel. I watched them sway in the slight breeze that moved the warm air around. It felt kind of nice up here, peaceful and quiet. But I wasn't here to relax.

When I told Kaz about my plan, he said it wasn't much as plans go. A guy who can't make heads or tails out of French really shouldn't expect to find a clue in a French army headquarters filled with paperwork.

The only problem was I couldn't think of anything else, so although I had to admit he was right, I was determined to go ahead anyway. Kaz offered to come along, but his arm was hurting him, and I had no idea how he'd manage to dangle from a rope four stories up, over the heads of armed guards. Some things you don't want to find out the hard way. I told him to get his arm checked and go to bed, but he wanted to wait until I set out.

I looked at my watch. Half past two. Late enough that the night owls should be asleep and too soon for the early risers. I only had to worry about insomniacs and sentries. And falling.

The roof had a slope to it, but it wasn't steep. I crouched down and moved slowly, keeping my silhouette below the top of the roofline. I passed another open skylight and listened. Nothing. I stayed low and slow, easing myself around the angle where the eastern wing of the hotel began. This was Darlan's territory. I stopped and listened. I tried to breathe deeply a few times to quiet my heart. It still sounded like a bass drum banging in my ears. I strained to blank out everything else: the palm fronds rustling in the breeze, the sound of a faraway vehicle shifting gears, the little sounds you don't really listen to until they get in your way. I only wanted to hear footsteps, coughs, murmurs, and other telltale signs of bored guards on the graveyard shift.

I had one thing going for me. These guys were rookies at security. I had watched them all afternoon, just another dumb GI strolling around, gawking at the French sailors in their blue uniforms, standing at attention with rifles sporting shiny two-foot bayonets resting on their shoulders. They formed a good perimeter all right, but this wasn't a skirmish line. They had all the entrances covered, but only in one direction. Their mistake was that they all faced outward, ready to beat back an assault at ground level. No one was stationed above the first floor, and no one was watching inside the building.

Any good second-story man will tell you no one looks up. I've seen enough of them in cuffs and heard enough of their stories to know they only got caught when they ran into something unexpected inside and couldn't beat feet fast enough. I agree, people don't generally look up. They look around. But I didn't like taking chances with Mrs. Boyle's number one son, so I started off real cautious, every step a deliberate, conscious move. Nothing sudden, nothing to flicker at the edge of a guard's vision to make him curious about what was going on up here.

I passed yet another open skylight and stuck my head inside. It was dark and quiet. I stayed there a full minute, letting my eyes get used to the darkness, listening for the sound of footsteps. Nothing. It would have been easy to get inside through the skylight, but I couldn't drop down without waking the devil, and I couldn't leave a length of rope dangling from the skylight like a cat burglar's calling card.

I had fifty feet of Uncle Sam's finest hemp rope wrapped around me, pulled tight so it wouldn't catch on anything. I uncoiled one end and tied it off around the skylight hinges. I tugged at it to make sure it was secure and wouldn't make any noise when it took my weight. Now I was starting to sweat. It was warm, but it wasn't the heat that sent a trickle down my spine. I wondered if I was off my rocker to try this, and what might happen if I screwed up. It probably wouldn't be handcuffs and a night in the slammer. I had left my newly issued .45 behind, so at least they couldn't shoot me with my own gun.

Thinking about Georgie just got me mad, and then thinking about Diana, somewhere out there with Villard, got me madder. Good. That took care of the sweats. When I got mad about somebody who did me wrong, I forgot to worry about the consequences. It wasn't my best character trait, or even one I'd recommend, but I hoped it might help keep Diana alive.

I let out some slack and slid to the edge of the roof. I knew there was a balcony right below this skylight, at the end of the east wing. I aimed myself toward the side of the balcony. I didn't want to come down smack in the middle of it, in case someone who couldn't sleep was looking out at the moonlight. At the edge of the roof, I let out a few feet of rope and eased over, lowering myself a couple of inches at a time. My arm muscles started to shake and I really wanted to slide down that rope before I fell. But I didn't. This was a dangerous spot to be in, a dark figure moving against a white wall. I had to go slowly, so slowly that even if somebody looked up for a second they wouldn't notice movement.

Finally, I was at the edge of the balcony. I swung one leg over the railing and pulled myself onto it, then squatted in the corner and let my breathing settle down. When it did, I listened, as hard as I could. I pressed my ear against the wall. It was quiet. I uncoiled the rest of the rope and tied up the slack in a loose knot. When I came out I could throw it over and climb down to the ground if I needed to, but that would only be if trouble were following me, since it would leave the rope hanging there for all to see. Otherwise I'd climb back onto the roof and pull the rope up after me. Much more desirable, since that meant Vichy guards weren't chasing me.

I peered over the balcony railing and saw a sentry below, standing at ease and looking bored. His head swiveled right as I picked up the sound of footsteps coming toward him. I froze, waiting for the other guy to show up, hopefully only a change of the guard. Instead, a French Army officer appeared out of the darkness. I couldn't make out his rank, but he seemed to be right for a captain or major, not an HQ desk jockey. His uniform was dirty and worn. He had been out in the field. Fighting us? Or rounding up rebels? I wondered which.

The sentry snapped to attention and the officer asked him something. Even if I understood French I wouldn't have picked it all up, but I did hear "Capitaine Bessette" toward the end.

"Oui, mon Capitaine," the sentry answered. At which point his captain breezed past him and went inside. I heard a door open and slam shut. Now I had trouble. A guy inside, looking for Bessette, the officer who had issued the orders for the convoy and who knew the password. Great. It meant I either had to retreat to the roof and give up, or get inside quick.

The way I figured it, if I could stay out of this guy's way, he might do me a favor and lead me to Bessette's office. I could hide out until he left. I didn't have time to think it through, so I went ahead. I pressed my face against the glass in the door leading inside from the balcony. I could see it was some sort of sitting room. No one was inside. I tried the door handle. It opened with a slight creak. I went in, made for a corner, and stood still, getting my bearings.

It was a small room, with a couple of couches facing each other and a long coffee table between them. On the wall to my right a door led to another room. I moved along the wall toward the door, listening. It was quiet, that dead of night quiet when the blood pounding through your veins sounds like a rushing river. Suddenly, a telephone rang; the shock nearly knocked me over. Looking around I saw the phone on the coffee table. I was ready to bolt out onto the balcony when it cut off in mid-ring. I heard a short, one-sided conversation in the next room, so I knew there was a bedroom extension. I ducked behind the couch when I heard footsteps, but they didn't head toward me. A door opened to the corridor, and the guy from the next room, sounding really pissed off, barked out harsh words. I went to the hallway door and cracked it open quietly, just enough so I could see through the narrow opening with my eye pressed up against it.

I saw the back of this fellow, as he yelled down a staircase at someone a few flights below. He was a short, gray-haired man wearing pale blue pajamas. I guess he didn't like being awakened in the middle of the night any more than I would. A voice answered him, and I recognized it as the captain who had entered the building. He let out a string of French that once again included "Bessette." This time he seemed angry. The gray-haired guy shouted "non" and by his tone, he meant it. He turned and I saw his face, the same face that I had seen in the papers and newsreels. Admiral Jean Darlan himself, the little Vichy collaborator who was giving us so much trouble. His face was set in a frown as he passed by the door at which I stood. I could have opened it and grabbed him by the neck, he was so close.

Maybe I should have, but I was here for my own reasons.

He went into his bedroom and I knew it was time to move on. Next door to the most powerful Frenchman in North Africa wasn't my idea of a good hiding place. Opening the door further I eased out into the empty corridor. I went down the staircase and listened for sounds to tell me which way the captain was going, as I wondered what his beef was.

He entered the hallway two flights below and I wasn't far behind. I flattened myself against the wall and peeked around the corner. The captain marched down the corridor and tried a door on the left. It opened and he looked inside. No one home. He went for the next one on his right, and I could hear him spit out the name "Bessette." No love lost there. He went in and I took my chance, sprinting down the hall to the empty room on the left. I slid into it and pulled the door almost shut behind me. It was a small office, stacked with boxes of files and rolled up maps. With the door cracked open I could see into the room across the hall. Two brass candlesticks on the corner of a desk illuminated the Army captain arguing with someone, Bessette probably, just out of my view.

French was flying fast and furious, and I could tell that Bessette was trying to calm the other guy down, but he wasn't buying. Finally, the captain slowed down. It sounded like he was delivering an ultimatum. I picked up a few words I had heard on occasion from French-Canadians sitting in Boston PD jail cells.

Contrebandier . . . that was smuggling or smuggler, I was pretty sure.

Droguer . . . drugs, I knew that one.

Américain . . . well, that was me.

Bessette got up and moved into view, calling the captain "Pierre" like they were old chums. From the conversation so far I could guess he was trying to placate Pierre. I watched him as he shook his head "no" in response to a question. He was a fireplug of a guy, squat but full of muscle. His hair was close-cropped and starting to turn to gray. His nose looked like it had been broken years ago. Maybe he had been a prizefighter once, or a stevedore. His hands were thick and beefy. He turned away from the captain and as he did one of those big hands grabbed a candlestick, and turning faster than I'd have thought he could, brought it down with a powerful swing right to the top of the captain's head. One second they were talking, and the next second Bessette was standing there, flecks of blood on his face, smiling down at the twitching body of his late-night visitor. There were some gurgles and thrashing for a few seconds, and then the only sound was my heart pounding in my chest to beat the band.

I tried to get a grip on myself and figure out what was happening. Who the hell were these people? First Villard shoots Georgie and then Bessette smashes in Pierre's skull. They were doing more damage to each other than to the Germans. My main concern right now was that no damage be done to me, so I glanced around for a quick exit. I looked out the one window, and it wasn't a bad drop, except for the sentry right below. I looked back across the hall and saw Bessette leaning out his window, giving a command and gesturing to someone. Footsteps came clattering up the stairs. I was cornered.

I wanted to shut the door quietly and hide under the desk until things settled down. It would have been the smart thing to do, but if I knew when to do the smart thing I wouldn't have been shoeless and sweating bullets across the hall from a corpse, in the middle of a B & E.

I kept my foot jammed against the door and pulled the handle toward me, keeping a quarter inch opening that gave me a view of Pierre's feet and Bessette's desk. Two enlisted men trotted down the hallway into the office. They were Army, not sailors like the others who were guarding the place. Bessette barked something at them and they rolled up Pierre in the carpet and hoisted him like two rug merchants. No surprise, no questions. As if they had done it before. They left, grunting under their load. Bessette went out after them, and as he did he looked straight at me. Instead of turning down the hall, he strode across it, and put his hand on the doorknob on his side. I released the knob on my side in the nick of time. He closed the door with a slam. Only inches had separated us and I was sure he had heard me breathe, until I realized I hadn't drawn a breath since I saw him heading for me. I waited until I heard him walk away, and then slowly exhaled. Maybe this hadn't been such a good idea.

After counting to fifty, I opened the door again and stepped into silence. Bessette's office door was still open, the one remaining candle flickering. He'd probably return after they'd removed the body from the building. I went in, stepping around a puddle of blood that had soaked through the carpet. I gave myself two minutes in there, and started counting in my head, *one-one-thousand, two-one-thousand, three-one-thousand* . . . as I checked the wall-map of the Algerian coastline. Bône was circled, but so were six or seven other places. *Eleven-one-thousand, twelve-one-thousand* . . .

I inspected the top of Bessette's desk. Green blotter, pack of cigarettes, keys, a fountain pen, and some sealed envelopes that he must have been addressing. No open letters. I glanced at the envelopes. The top one was for Madame Mireille Bessette, Marseilles, stamped and ready to go. Another was to Jules Bessette, Blackpool, England, sealed but no stamp. Was there mail service between Vichy territory and England? So Bessette kept up with his relations and had, what, a brother or cousin in England? *Twenty-eight-one-thousand, twenty-nine-one-thousand* . . .

Damn it! I was looking for a password, not evidence that Bessette was a family man. I turned to the filing cabinet, and opened the top drawer. It was too dark to see clearly, but there were so many files, each with a tiny heading in French, I knew I'd never get through them all, much less understand what was in them. I looked in each of the four drawers; more of the same. The French Army runs on paperwork, like ours. I pulled out a few files from each drawer and flipped through them. Lots of reports, charts, numbers, carbon paper. *Sixty-six-one-thousand, sixty-seven-one-thousand . . .*

I put the files back, closed the drawers, and sat at the desk. I tried the drawers on the left and found the usual junk: paper clips, rubber bands, dust. The large bottom drawer held a bottle of cognac and a revolver. What a surprise. *Eighty-four-one-thousand, eighty-five-one-thousand . . .*

I urged myself to hurry! Were those foot-steps?

I checked the middle drawer and rummaged through notepaper, an old newspaper, and a few receipts from a place called Le Bar Bleu. A blue matchbook from the same place. A street map of Algiers: I checked it for notes or marked locations, but there was nothing. *Ninety-nine-one-thousand, one-hundred-one-thousand.*

The right-hand drawers were all that remained. Blank paper in the first, nothing in the second. I pulled at the large bottom drawer. It was stuck. I pulled again. Locked! There had to be something in there. *One-hundred-twenty-one-thousand . . .*

I grabbed the keys and fumbled through them, looking for a small desk key. I found one and tried it. No go. There was another, and it worked. The drawer opened and I saw about a dozen thick file folders piled up. Why keep hundreds in the open file cabinet and lock up these? It had been so long since I saw a clue I almost didn't get it. *One-hundred-thirty-five-one-thousand . . .*

Damn! I wished I knew French! I couldn't make heads or tails out of this stuff. Then one file caught my eye. It was labeled "Ordres de déplacement." Deplacement? Did that mean travel? Travel orders? I put the file on the desk near the candle and looked through its contents. The forms looked familiar. These were all carbon copies, but they were duplicates of Villard's travel orders that we'd seen at the Gardes Mobiles headquarters. I couldn't make out the order they were filed in, so I just pawed through them. It was right at the bottom. Orders to Captain Luc Villard for the transport of twenty-five prisoners via the Bône supply depot, Captain Gauthier, commanding. Next to his name, there was one handwritten note. *Le Carrefour.* What was that, the name of a bar? Or the password? Wait a minute — I looked at the matchbook more closely. "Le Bar Bleu — Bône" was written on the back with a phone number. I stuffed the matchbook in my pocket along with the

106

orders. *One-hundred-sixty-one-thousand* . . .

Time to go! I put the files back and shut the drawer, eased around the desk, and listened in the hallway. I heard laughter, then footsteps coming up the stairwell, so I went for the other staircase at the end of the corridor. Then it hit me. I'd left the keys in the lock, but I'd found them on his desk! I turned and tried to get traction on the slippery floor. I almost fell, regained my balance, darted back into the office, grabbed the keys out of the lock and tossed them onto the desk, then ran out into the hallway, not even stopping to listen this time. I had to get out now under my own power or Bessette's office would run out of rugs. I made it to the stairs and turned the corner just as I heard the sound of boots in the hallway and Bessette's loud voice. It was close, but I beat him by a second. And I had a password, or the name of either a good restaurant or a carpet wholesaler.

Ten minutes later I was up on the roof and headed back to friendly territory. The prospect of an army cot actually sounded good to me. Kaz and I didn't have a room, but they had given us beds at the end of a hall where we could sleep and stow our gear. It felt like home, and I was glad to still be in one piece to enjoy it.

CHAPTER EIGHT

Dawn wasn't far off and I was torn between getting a couple of hours of shut-eye and waking Kaz to tell him about the murder. There was enough light at our end of the hall for me to see that Kaz was already awake, sitting on his cot, leaning against the wall.

"Billy . . ." he said, almost in a whisper. He didn't sound right.

"Kaz, you okay?" I asked as I knelt next to him. He didn't answer. He didn't have to. He was drenched in sweat and hot to the touch. His eyes were focused somewhere else.

"Billy, I waited for you." He was talking to me but looking straight through me.

"I know you did, buddy. I knew I could count on you. Now tell me, what's the matter?"

"My arm . . ." He looked down at his bandage, then his head rolled back and his eyes shut. He was breathing in quick little gulps, as if he couldn't get enough air. The bandage was loose and hanging by a few pieces of tape. I lifted it up to get a look, and brushed my hand against his skin.

"Ahhhhh!" he gasped, sucking in air between clenched teeth. His eyes were wide open now. I grabbed for my flashlight and shined the light on his wound, careful not to touch him again. Even lifting the gauze seemed to cause him pain.

It looked awful. The skin was swollen and red all around the wound, filled with bumps or blisters, a few oozing dark brown matter. Kaz had waited for me, all right. Waited instead of going to get his arm checked like I'd told him to. It had been bothering him earlier in the evening, but he wanted to see me return safely.

I knew I had to do something, but I couldn't move. I stood frozen for seconds, maybe minutes. I felt horrible. The weight of Kaz's pain crushed the breath out of me. He had been shot rescuing me, and now he looked like death itself. Forcing myself to move, I pulled on my boots and put on my web belt, my .45 in its holster. I tightened his sling as best I could, and knelt to pick him up. I was careful not to touch his bad arm. Fortunately, he had passed out. He was light as a feather. There really wasn't much to this little guy, and I was scared that whatever was wrong with his arm was going to get to his bum ticker, if it hadn't already. Kaz had suffered enough in this war, and mostly because of me. He would still be in London with Daphne if he hadn't gotten involved with my last investigation. I couldn't bring her back but I could do my best to keep him alive. And then, I'd do whatever it took to get him back to London.

I left a message for Harding and five minutes later I was in a jeep, hightailing it down the coast road, one hand on the wheel and the other on Kaz's shoulder to keep him from falling over.

"Hang on, buddy," I said, "we're almost there. Kaz, can you hear me?"

Nothing. I slammed the accelerator to the floor and skidded right at a sign for the 21st General Hospital. They were just setting up the main medical center for this area. I thought Kaz would stand a better chance here than at a field hospital or aid station, even if it wasn't fully operational yet. More doctors, more drugs, more of whatever he needed, I hoped.

I pulled up to a brick building that might have been a school or government offices before we moved in. In the courtyard stood trucks with red crosses painted on them. On either side were tents, more trucks, and piles of supplies under tarps. Even this late — or early — there were lights on and people moving around. The main door opened and a sergeant with a cigarette clamped between his lips pointed at me.

"Hey Mac, move that jeep outta here! Emergency vehicles only!"

"That's Lieutenant Mac to you, Sarge, and this is a goddamn emergency."

I jumped out of the jeep and ran around to Kaz's side. The sergeant came close enough to check my rank and look at Kaz. It didn't take him long to react. He tossed his butt, hollered some orders, and in a minute had Kaz on a stretcher and inside. He didn't bother apologizing for talking to an officer that way, which actually made me think he was okay.

We went down a long dark hallway into a well-lit room with empty beds along one wall, and a few doctors and nurses standing around.

"Hey Doc, got some business for you," the sergeant called out. The stretcher bearers transferred Kaz to a gurney as the doctor moved in for a look.

"Who brought him in?"

"This guy." The sergeant nodded his head

toward me. He was dark-skinned with jet-black hair and thick eyebrows, and sounded like he was from somewhere deep in Brooklyn. His three stripes sported a rocker, so he was a staff sergeant, and obviously in charge, even though the doctor was also a lieutenant. Second louies were a dime a dozen in this Army, but experienced NCOs were worth their weight in gold and they knew it. This one sure did. The doctor put his hand on Kaz's forehead as he listened to his heartbeat with a stethoscope.

"When was he wounded, and when was the bandage last changed?"

"Just yesterday morning," I said, "and no one's looked at it since the medic fixed him up. It started bothering him earlier this evening. What's wrong, Doc?"

He didn't answer me as he snipped off the bandage and Kaz's sleeve. A nurse came over with a tray full of instruments and bandages. He wrinkled his nose as he pulled up the last layer of gauze.

"Jesus Christ! Wet gangrene."

I would have liked a better bedside manner, and maybe a doctor who looked a bit older. This one had barely a few years on me, which meant he didn't have a whole lot of experience. He had blond hair and was trying for a mustache, probably to make himself appear closer to thirty. He had the good teeth of the well-to-do and looked like he'd just stepped out of Harvard Square.

"Doc, are you sure?" I asked, "I didn't think you could get gangrene that quick —"

His eyes snapped up to look at me and give me the once-over. "And where did you get your medical degree?"

"Sorry, Doc . . ."

"And don't call me Doc. I didn't get a medical degree from Harvard to be called by a nickname. It's Doctor Sidney Dunbar, and your friend will be very sorry that he didn't get proper medical attention after that medic bandaged him up. Tight bandages in hot weather are a breeding ground for infection. They cut off the blood supply, allowing the Clostridium bacteria to thrive, leading to necrosis and the death of tissue."

"So how bad is —"

"Sergeant," the doctor interrupted, "we'll need the penicillin. Now. Nurse, move the patient into a room. You, get out of our way."

The last part was for me. They scurried off as a couple of orderlies appeared to wheel Kaz away. I stuck with him, and wondered what the hell penny cillin was, and why they couldn't at least offer him the dime cillin.

They moved Kaz into a hospital room.

113

The concrete walls were whitewashed and you could see where the fresh paint had dribbled down to the bare wood floor. There was a damp, antiseptic smell in the room: cleansers, paint and dust all mixed together. It was furnished with three beds, nightstands, and a table with a white porcelain tray filled with instruments I didn't want to look at. They laid Kaz on the middle bed and left. His face was drained of color now. I sat on an empty bed, watching Kaz breathe and praying that each breath would be followed by another. Finally the sergeant came into the room, holding a small cardboard container.

"Don't mind Doctor Dunbar, Lieutenant," he said. "He's a little on edge."

"I'm glad he's so involved with his patients. I'm Lieutenant Billy Boyle, by the way." I stuck out my hand and he shook it.

"Joe Casselli. Don't think that Dunbar is a humanitarian. He's pissed off that we have to use some of this precious stuff."

He held up the container. In U.S. Army regulation stencil, it said PENICILLIN. FOR INTERNAL USE ONLY.

"What is that stuff?"

"It's what is going to save your friend's life," said Dunbar, striding into the room. "No thanks to you or whatever lame-brained unit you're with. Don't you know anything about first aid and hygiene?"

"We're attached to Headquarters," I said vaguely.

"Which Headquarters?" Dunbar asked as he signed a form Casselli held out for him.

"Uh, Allied Forces Headquarters. I'm Boyle, this is Lieutenant Kazimierz."

There was a silence as Dunbar and Casselli both looked at me, then each other. Casselli gave a little shrug.

"I don't have time to play games, Lieutenant. We'll find out later if you don't want to tell us. Then I'll file a report with your CO letting him know that someone's incompetence has obligated us to waste a valuable resource." With that, Dunbar took the penicillin from Casselli. He drew it off with a syringe and injected Kaz, who gave no sign of feeling the needle.

"You called it penicillin?" I asked, keeping my eyes glued to Kaz. "Never heard of it."

"We're the first hospital in a combat zone to have it," said Dunbar. "It's a real wonder drug. It kills a wide range of bacteria, all of them deadly. Including Clostridium, which is what's causing your friend's gangrene to progress so rapidly."

"It'll stop that?"

"It should." For the first time, Dunbar

didn't sound so cocky.

"Should?"

"Listen, Boyle, this is brand new stuff. We know it knocks out bacteria like nothing we've ever seen. I just don't know if it will kill the bacteria fast enough. If it's already spread throughout his system, it may be too late. We wouldn't need to worry if you had brought him in sooner."

"It's worked every time so far, right Doctor Dunbar?" said Casselli.

"Yes. Everyone we saw yesterday is stabilized."

It took me a second to get what he was saying. "You mean you used this for the first time *yesterday?*"

"I said it was brand new, didn't I?" Dunbar sat on Kaz's bed and began cleaning his wound. He poured alcohol over it but Kaz didn't open his eyes or even flinch.

"This wound has to be debrided," Dunbar said. "Sergeant, would you find a nurse and ask her to bring the instruments? Boyle, you wait outside."

"Debrided?" I asked as I moved toward the door.

"We have to cut away the dead tissue. Nothing to worry about, just not pleasant to watch."

He didn't have to tell me twice. I went

116

into the hall and sat on a bench. In a minute Casselli returned, followed by a nurse carrying a tray of shiny sharp instruments. By the looks of them I was glad Dunbar had kicked me out.

"You look like you could use a cup of joe," Casselli said when he appeared. "Don't worry about your buddy. Dunbar may be a jerk, but he's a good doctor."

"Is he always in such a bad mood?"

"Well," Casselli considered, "I can't say he's ever in a good mood, but this is worse than usual. He lost real bad in a big poker game last night. Not for the first time, either."

"Officers gambling? Isn't that against regulations?" I asked with mock innocence.

"Yeah, right. Our CO is a regular along with Dunbar and a few other guys. They've been playing for pretty big stakes lately. Getting close to the shooting war can have that effect."

"How big?"

"Sawbuck ante."

"Wow. Must make for some really big pots."

"Yep. Dunbar used to do pretty good for himself. Since we left England though, his luck's run out. He's in fairly deep to the CO and a surgeon."

"He looks like he's from money. May not be a big deal."

"Maybe. Maybe not. You want some joe or not? I'm buying."

"Coffee sounds great. Lead on."

The mess hall was a beehive of activity. Tables were being set up for breakfast and the smell of fresh coffee floated out to us. Cases of food and supplies were being unloaded from trucks and carried through the mess hall into the kitchen by GIs in olive drab T-shirts. Double doors leading out into the courtyard stood wide open and the trucks were backed up to them, endless stacks of food and who knows what else being handed down and carried in.

"Pretty amazing, isn't it?" said Casselli as we helped ourselves to coffee from an industrial-sized urn.

"What is?" I asked. We headed for a table and sat.

"Just think about it," said Casselli. "We've only been here three days and already have a whole supply system set up, this General Hospital in operation, field hospitals up the line, all while we're keeping the guys at the front supplied. Tons of supplies are moving down that coast road every hour."

"I took all that stuff for granted. It's

always just . . . there," I said, shrugging my acceptance of enough beans and bullets to get the job done.

"I guess I'll take that as a compliment to supply sergeants everywhere in the ETO," Casselli said. "Nobody thinks about us until they run out of gas. Or coffee. Or if the phones don't work. The lines were all dead when we got here, and Walton blew a fuse. We ran almost a thousand feet of wire to get him his telephone. All in a day's work."

I raised my cup to him. "Here's to the unsung heroes," I said. "Supply sergeants and miracle drugs."

"That penicillin stuff is really something," Casselli said excitedly, leaning forward. "We're the first general hospital to get it. They're just starting to mass-produce it in the States. Scientists have know about it since 1929, but they were never able to produce more than a teaspoonful, until some outfit called Pfizer figured it out last year."

"Showing off again, Joe?" A honey soft voice came from behind us. Casselli jumped a bit, and his face went a little red. He stood up like a small child caught at something by a teacher.

"Lieutenant Boyle, this is Captain Morgan, head of Nursing for the 21st," said

Casselli.

"Why Joe, we're never so formal here, are we? The name is Gloria Morgan, Lieutenant Boyle."

"Billy Boyle, ma'am," I said as I stood up.

"Well, Billy, your Polish friend is indeed lucky. Without this new miracle drug Joe was telling you all about, he'd most likely be dead in twenty-four hours."

Gloria Morgan had my attention, in more ways than one. She was the kind of woman who took over a room with her presence. She had a pile of wavy brown hair tied back and deep brown eyes up front. Her face was wide, more striking than pretty, high cheekbones and a strong chin gave her face a determined look, even when she was just standing there. She looked at me with a bit of a smile on her lips that made anything she said seem like good news, delivered with just a trace of a soft southern accent. She was probably in her mid-thirties, maybe even forty, but it was apparent that she was in great shape, even in the Army fatigues she wore. I struggled to say something, to stop staring at her.

"Well, ma'am . . . uh, Captain, Joe was just filling me in on this penicillin thing . . ."

"Call me Gloria, Billy," she said, "this isn't a parade ground."

"All right, Gloria," I managed to get out. I realized she was the oldest woman I had ever called by her first name. She stood there, smiling at me pleasantly, until I remembered my manners.

"Please, join us," I said as gallantly as I could, holding a chair out for her.

"Why thank you, Billy. I will. Just for a few minutes, before I get back to my shift." She sat down with her cup of coffee and so did we. There was a quiet around the table, as if we were eagerly waiting to hear what she had to say next. I sure was. Then I remembered Kaz.

"How is Kaz? Lieutenant Kazimierz, I mean. My Polish friend." I got my mouth to stop flapping and grinned, probably looking like an idiot.

"You can stop worrying, Billy. His wound has been dressed and we gave him something to make sure he sleeps. He should be out for the rest of the day. Rest and penicillin are all he needs now. You brought him in just in time. He'll be fine."

"Thank you. I can't tell you how relieved that makes me."

"Is Lieutenant Kazimierz on the Headquarters staff too?" asked Casselli. Gloria glanced at him and then focused on me.

"Which HQ are we talking about?" she

asked, as she held her coffee cup up to her mouth and blew on it. A tiny wisp of steam rose from its surface.

"Allied Forces Headquarters," I said, trying not to sound too pompous. "We're both on General Eisenhower's staff."

"What distinguished visitors, Joe!" said Gloria, smiling at me as if I were the guest of honor at a fancy dinner party. "And that reminds me, Joe, we have another visitor on his way. Lieutenant Phillipe Mathenet, from the Gardes Mobiles." She glanced at me. "That's the local French police, Billy."

"I've heard of them."

"Well anyway, Joe, Lieutenant Mathenet is on his way to talk to the locals in Ward C. I'd like you to meet him at the front entrance and escort him."

"Locals?" I asked.

"Yes, mostly young French boys. They got mixed up in this coup attempt and were wounded in a fight with the French troops and police. We have about twenty or so in a separate ward. Lieutenant Mathenet is here to find out if any are well enough to be released into his custody." She took a pack of cigarettes from her pocket and shook one out. Casselli and I each slapped our pockets looking for a pack of matches, like two beaus competing for her favors. I won. I still had that blue matchbook in my pocket.

"I'd like to see them myself," I said, striking a match and holding it for her.

"How come, Lieutenant?" asked Casselli.

Gloria broke in before I could answer. "Joe, be a dear and go wait for Lieutenant Mathenet. He's late and I don't want him wandering around getting in the way."

"Whatever you say, Captain." He nodded at me, and left. Gloria watched him go.

"Joe is a great guy," she said, and from her tone I knew there was a "but" coming. "But he thinks he runs the place and has to know everything. Forgive him if he asked too many questions. He means well."

"I've noticed sergeants usually run most things in the Army."

"You may be right. So what do you do at Allied Forces HQ, Billy?" she asked in a semi-serious tone. It was almost as if she didn't believe me. I get a lot of that.

"Whatever Major Harding wants," I answered, staying vague.

"That wouldn't be Sam Harding, would it?"

"His first name is Samuel," I admitted although, if I had ever thought about it before, I would have said his first name was "Major." "West Point, regular Army kind of guy."

"Yes, that's Sam!" she said. "You might be surprised to learn I'm regular Army too, Billy, although things are a lot more informal in a medical unit than you'd find in a headquarters staff. Especially one with Sam Harding on it."

"Wouldn't be hard," I said. "So you served with him before the war?"

"We were on the same base back in the States for a while," she said. She turned away from me. Something had changed; we weren't going to discuss her relationship with Major Harding. "Sam." Then she smiled again, and it was like the sun coming out from behind a dark cloud.

"When did you come ashore?" I asked, trying to get the conversation going. "I didn't realize there'd be nurses here this soon."

"My nurses and I came ashore with the first wave, Billy, climbing down the cargo nets just like the infantry. We came ashore at Beer White and set up an aid station. As soon as the beach was clear, we headed here. This place had been selected as our main hospital facility because it's near the main road and the rail line. The local hospitals aren't worthy of the name, so we've started one here, from scratch."

"I'm impressed," I said, and I was. I didn't

know army nurses had come along on the invasion.

"I wish the army was a little more impressed by us," she said. "We don't have any uniforms of our own, did you know that? We have to find the smallest men's fatigues we can and roll up the sleeves and pants." She stuck out her leg and I saw that the cuffs of the coverall she was wearing were rolled up tight. "And don't even ask about shoes. I have to wear three pairs of socks just to keep these from falling off my feet."

"But what about back in the States? Didn't you have uniforms there?"

"Sure, standard whites, complete with white stockings and white shoes. Not the most appropriate wear for climbing down cargo nets, cleaning floors, and doing laundry."

"Laundry, floors?"

"A woman's work is never done, Billy," she said as she sipped her coffee. "When we got here, the first thing we had to do was clean out and scrub down the rooms. After duty hours, we have to launder all the linens so our patients won't have to lie on dirty sheets."

"But you're all officers, aren't you? I never heard of officers scrubbing anything."

"I'm regular Army, Medical Corps. But all the other nurses are Army Nurse Corps. They're lieutenants, but the army came up with something called relative rank."

"What's that?"

"With relative rank you get half the pay of a man, and no salutes. It wouldn't do for an enlisted man to salute an officer while she's scrubbing the floor or emptying a bedpan, so no salutes for nurses."

"You must be pretty sore at the army."

"I love the army, Billy. It gives me a chance to serve at the front, and every woman here is proud to do what she can. But I'd like some clothes that fit." She smiled that warm smile again, and all the complaints just vanished.

"Tell me, Billy, why do you want to talk to our French patients? They don't need any unnecessary stress while they're recuperating."

"Don't you think the Gardes Mobiles and their SOL pals are a pretty stressful bunch? Do you have any idea what they do to kids like these?"

"What's the SOL?" she asked.

"Service d'Order Legionnaire, fascist militia . . . and you're avoiding the question."

"You're right. And so are you."

How could I answer her question? Tell her I want to talk to the French rebels because one of them might know Diana and have an idea where she is? Oh, and by the way, she's a spy and I'm Uncle Ike's secret agent when I'm not working for your old boyfriend Sam. Then I remembered. Georgie said he had a kid brother in with the rebels.

"I met a French officer the day we came ashore. He told me his brother was a university student and involved in the coup attempt. I'd like to find out if he's among the wounded."

"All right, Billy. I'll take you to Ward C. Why don't you contact this officer and bring him over here?"

"I can't. The Gardes Mobiles killed him. He was murdered by a Captain Luc Villard."

Gloria looked stunned. She opened her mouth to say something but I couldn't hear it over a high-pitched wail that started out slow and then became a shrill sound that felt like an icepick in the ear.

"Air raid!" someone shouted and then everybody jumped up and made for the door.

CHAPTER NINE

We dove into a slit trench behind the main building and stared up into the blue sky, swiveling our heads, straining to see any sign of enemy aircraft. The sirens were wailing, the shrill sound mixing with the voices of nurses, doctors, and GIs as they tumbled out of the building and made for the newly dug trenches that littered the area. They were yelling to or at each other in high-pitched nervous voices, excited and scared at the same time, trying to sound like they were in charge, still in control of things. Several more people jammed themselves into our trench, one nurse laughing as if this was school recess, another trying not to cry, her hand held to her mouth.

"They wouldn't bomb a hospital, would they?" she asked, the quivering of her lower lip just visible.

Gloria reached over at patted her arm. "Don't you worry, honey. They're probably ours and it's a false alarm."

The sirens wound down and stopped, and another strange sound took its place. The air filled with a low, dull, throb that seemed to come from all around us. The yelling stopped as this new sound enveloped us, growing stronger each second. It took on a nasty, buzzing quality that reminded me of hornets or yellow jackets. People started popping up from the trenches, twisting their necks, looking for the source of the droning, ever-increasing noise. I knew that it might be too late once they saw it.

"Get down!" I yelled. "Get your heads down!" I threw my arm around Gloria, yanking her down, nearly burying our heads in gravelly dirt at the bottom of the trench. As the smell of damp, chalky soil hit my nostrils, I had to force myself to keep my face in it. The sound grew. I didn't know if anyone had heard or listened to me, but I didn't really care right then. They had fair warning. Only a fool goes sightseeing in an air raid.

There was a whistling noise, then a sharp sound like lightning breaking, followed by a blast of air I felt sweep over the ground above our heads. Dirt blew in on us, then more blasts came. The earth shook, rattling every bone in my body and sending shock waves of air and debris flying overhead. Even below ground level, I was hurled against the side of the trench with each bomb blast. The bombs struck closer and closer, more of them now, until the blasts became a single noise of explosions and airplane engines, forcing everything else into silent submission. I looked over at the laughing nurse. Her hands were clapped to her ears, her mouth wide open in an inaudible scream, her eyes squeezed shut, and her head shaking back and forth.

I twisted around to look up and saw dark forms in the sky as they sped by, one after another, their wide curved wings sporting black crosses. *Heinkel 111,* a small voice somewhere in the back of my head said, as I recalled a silhouette from Aircraft Recognition Class in OCS. This was a surprise. I never used to be able to remember anything from my classes when I was at school in Boston. But no one was trying to blow me up then. As I thought about that, I realized it had become quiet. The laughing nurse wasn't screaming anymore, she was crying and I could hear her. Someone else was yelling in the distance, but the bombs had stopped and the aircraft sounds were receding.

Gloria was looking around too, a dazed

expression dulling her face. I took her hand. It was shaking. So was the rest of her. I could feel her muscles tense as she fought for control.

"Are you okay?" I said, a little too loudly in the sudden silence. Her eyes were wide and I thought she might start to cry or panic. She took a breath and I could see her pull herself together. Eyes closed, she shook her head up and down, then opened them. Her hand was still.

"I'm fine. I think I have work to do." She winked at me as she got up to look around, dusting the dirt off her clothes as she stood up. "Come on, girls," she said to the two nurses, "they're going to need our help. We'll do our crying later, honey."

She touched the shoulder of the tearful nurse and bounded out of the trench. The nurses rose, held onto each other, and followed her out. They wiped dust, dirt, and tears away, and went to work, streaks of grime showing on their cheeks where their hands had brushed their faces. I had to admire them. Me, I just wanted to stay in this trench until the end of the war. I began to wonder why Major Harding hadn't hung onto Gloria. She was right up his alley. Or, maybe she hadn't hung onto him. I could think of a lot of reasons for that.

I stuck my head up and took in the view. Smoke was billowing up in front of the building where the vehicles and supplies were stored, and flames licked at a pile of wooden crates. Everyone was running in that direction. I ran towards Kaz's room. I knew I should probably help out but I had to know if Kaz was still in one piece. It was bad enough that I'd gotten him into this fix, without getting him killed in an air raid. Off in the distance I started to hear the sounds of more bombs exploding, far away. *Crump . . . crump . . . crump.* It sounded like the harbor in Algiers was being plastered. We had been hit by a handful of bombers while the rest went on to the harbor. The stacks of supplies outside the hospital must have been a secondary target. Maybe they hadn't marked the building with a red cross yet. In one corridor the wall was blown out and smoke from the fires outside was pouring in. The acrid smell of burning rubber filled the hall and I held my hand over my mouth and nose as I checked the rooms. They were all empty so I kept on toward Kaz, hoping this was the only hit the hospital had taken.

When I got to his corridor, I saw Doctor Dunbar treating a couple of stretcher cases for cuts from flying glass. Nurses and orderlies were running around like ants from a stirred up nest. There was a feeling of controlled hysteria in the air as they did their jobs with eyes still wide from fear and shock. For their first time under fire, they weren't doing too badly. It wasn't my first and yet I was glad I hadn't bawled like a baby when the bombs kept coming and coming.

I opened Kaz's door. His eyes were closed and he was so still I thought for a second he was dead. When I finally saw his chest rise and fall, I let out my breath. I was relieved, but at the same time amazed anyone could be doped up enough to sleep through an air raid. I left Kaz to his dreams and asked a nurse for directions to Ward C.

I headed out of the building, across the courtyard, and into a separate brick structure that jutted out from a tin-roofed white washed stucco building. A sign announced it was a MEDICAL CORPS SUPPLY DEPOT. The modern brick wing had bars on the windows and a small sign that said WARD C. It must have been an Algerian jailhouse until Uncle Sam showed up. There was a guard at the door who saluted.

I entered the reception area. A corridor led off it with doors on either side. The fresh Army-green paint job's smell mingled with the odor of strong disinfectant. A nurse sat at a desk working on charts. I asked if there was a French patient named Dupree in the joint. There was: Jerome Dupree, Georgie's kid brother. I walked down the hall to his room and took a deep breath before I knocked. I'd brought news like this to families a few times before. I didn't like it much.

I rapped twice and opened the door. A young kid, maybe eighteen or nineteen at most, with a mop of thick, dark hair nearly jumped out of his bed. Or would have if he hadn't been chained to it. He had manacles on his ankles attached by a chain that looped through the steel bed frame. The windows were barred and if he was going anywhere, the whole bed was going with him. His arm was in a sling, his head was bandaged, and his eyes were wide with fear. But I wasn't the person he expected and the look of fear disappeared.

"Who are you?" he asked. He spoke slowly, as if figuring out the right order for the words as he went along.

"Billy Boyle is my name. You're Georges's brother, right?"

At the sound of his brother's name he brightened up and started jabbering. "Yes, did he send you? How did you know I was here? Have you been looking for me? I have been waiting for you three days!" His accent was pretty thick and I wondered if I had misunderstood him.

"What do you mean, waiting for me?"

"I did not know it would be you, Monsieur Boyle, but Georges told me he was meeting with some American officers and would put them in touch with me."

"We were on our way to you and the other rebels, but —"

"No, no, not about the coup. About the notebook! Did not Georges tell you everything? There is not much time!"

I was confused. What notebook? I just wanted to get delivering the bad news over with. I tried to remember what my Dad used to say. Tell them it's bad news first thing. Then tell them to sit down. Then tell them. I had watched and listened to him deliver the bad news dozens of times before I had to do it myself, alone. I'm not sure his advice helped, but at least it gave me a plan, and maybe that's all he meant it to do.

"Jerome, back up a second. I have some bad news for you." There. He was already sitting down, so time to deliver.

"What . . . ?" His mouth stayed open, a confused and scared look on his face. His eyes darted around the room, as if he were waiting for someone else to come in.

"Georges is dead. He was shot the morning of the invasion."

"No." His head sank back into the pillow. "No, no. He was supposed to meet the Americans, not fight them. You must be mistaken."

"I'm not mistaken, Jerome. He did meet us. He was taking us to General Juin's residence when we were stopped." I could see in his eyes that he knew what was coming next.

"Stopped by the Gardes Mobiles?"

"Yes. A German officer and a French captain . . ."

"Villard?"

"Yes. He killed your brother. You know Villard?"

Jerome squeezed his eyes shut. Tears leaked out as his lips quivered. He put his good hand up to his face and sobbed. I waited, wanting to be somewhere else. Wondering where Diana was and how I could get out of here to look for her.

"I know him," Jerome said finally, spitting out the words with hatred. "He is a criminal and a traitor. And he will kill me next."

"Why you? You're not in the army."

"It has nothing to do with that, Monsieur Boyle. It has to do with the notebook. That damned notebook!" He slammed his fist on the mattress. "It will get us all killed."

"What notebook? What does it have to do with the invasion?"

"Georges did not mention this at all to you?"

"No, he just said you were one of the leaders of the students and that we'd meet you later that morning."

"They are looking for it, and an officer from the Gardes Mobiles is coming today to escort me to Villard. He must believe I still have it. You must help me."

"I don't understand."

"Someone in the Gardes Mobiles stole the notebook from Villard and gave it to me. I couldn't read it since it was in code. I was going to give it to you, but we were taken. I was shot and passed out. When I woke up here the notebook was gone. We were allowed visitors at first, and I received word that our contact in the Gardes Mobiles had been discovered. He probably talked and told them I had the notebook. I believe that is why they are coming today."

As if on cue, we heard doors slam and the sound of people walking down the hallway.

"What is in this notebook, Jerome?"

"Do not speak of it, and please do not let them take me!" he said in a hushed voice, his eyes watching the door. It opened.

"Oh, excuse me," Gloria said. "I didn't know you were in here, Billy. Is this the young man you were telling me about?"

"Yes. I just was telling him about his brother's death."

Gloria set down a jug of water and a couple of glasses on the bedside table. A nurse followed her in with a tray holding several bottles of pills. Gloria bent over the bed and took Jerome's good hand in hers.

"I am so sorry for your loss. Is there anything I can do for you?"

"You are very kind," Jerome said, struggling to put on a brave face. "No, thank you. I can't think of anything."

"Any chance we could release Jerome into the custody of his parents?" I asked.

"I'm sorry Billy, but this is a restricted ward. I can't release any of these patients. Orders. From Headquarters."

I knew that last bit was aimed right at me, and I deserved it for putting her on the spot. Had to give it a try though.

"Are the French going to take custody of some of these boys today? Can Jerome have some time to get over his shock before you hand him over?"

"That's very considerate of you, Billy, but there's no need to worry. Lieutenant Mathenet is having his shrapnel wounds attended to. Nothing life-threatening, but he won't be questioning anybody today."

"Good . . . How's Joe? Wasn't he with Mathenet?"

"Yes, I haven't seen him since the raid. He's probably busy clearing the bomb damage. Now, get out and let Jerome rest. I have medications to give him and the doctor is making his rounds."

"I'll just sit with him, if that's all right."

"It is not, Lieutenant. You can come back later in the day, but right now, out! That's a medical and a military order." She tapped the captain's bars on her blouse.

"Okay, Captain," I said, raising my arms in mock surrender. "Jerome, I'll see you later and we'll talk some more. Your brother was a very brave officer."

"Thank you for bringing me the news yourself. I appreciate hearing it from someone who knew Georges."

I nodded and looked into his eyes, trying to signal I'd be back as soon as I could. I went out the door and almost collided with Doctor Dunbar, Boy Wonder.

"You still hanging around here, Boyle? Isn't there a war on or something?"

He wasn't looking for a response and I didn't give him one. I sure knew there was a war going on, but I was trying to figure out what the *or something* was. And what this notebook business was all about. My head swam as I half-stumbled, half-shuffled out of the ward.

I was dead on my feet. No sleep the night before, a young soldier shot right in front of me, a secret murder witnessed, an emergency run to the hospital with a dying friend, an air raid with explosions that nearly knocked my teeth out, telling a kid his brother was dead, and hearing about a mysterious notebook, all before lunch. It was too much. I yawned. That only made me more tired.

I tried to focus on Jerome's notebook, but all I could think about was Diana. Why was I still hanging around here when I should be out looking for her? Maybe it was time to blow this joint.

To hell with the notebook. Probably some French political thing, so why should I care? Still, it nagged at me. I needed to see Jerome alone again and find out just a little more. Then I had to figure out a way to get to Bône. That contact at the supply depot was still the only clue that might lead to Diana. I yawned again, and my feet dragged as I headed to the mess hall to get some coffee. My eyelids were getting heavy and I wanted to take a little nap. Maybe some shut-eye would be better than coffee, I thought. No harm in that.

I was so intent on talking myself into taking time to sleep that I never noticed the truck. I kind of heard tires crunching on gravel but I didn't pay any attention until the driver laid on the horn. Only then I realized I was walking down the middle of a road, a long driveway that led from the Supply Depot and around the hospital to the main entrance. I jumped to the right just in time to avoid a deuce and a half truck barreling along as if it was on a racetrack. I turned to yell at the driver and give him the single digit salute, but I never got a word out. I was too stunned. Luc Villard was riding in the passenger's seat, wearing a U.S. Army olive drab shirt and khaki overseas cap, tilted at a jaunty angle. I could swear he smiled at me.

I yelled "Hey Stop!" and swallowed a mouthful of dust and grit kicked up by the truck's tires. I didn't stand a chance but I ran after it anyway, making it around the corner of the main building in time to see it hit the main road and turn right. Away from Algiers. Toward Bône.

I watched the truck disappear, lost in the flow of military traffic. People began to run

141

by me, toward the medical supply depot. One orderly nearly knocked me over in his rush, and I turned to follow him, glad to have someone else take the lead.

CHAPTER TEN

It took only a few minutes for a crowd to gather. There were plenty of doctors and nurses looking on, but that wouldn't do Staff Sergeant Joseph Casselli any good at all. Unless this penicillin stuff could fix a slit throat and put all the blood on the floor back in his veins.

We were crammed into a small storeroom in the Medical Corps Supply Depot. Doctor Dunbar was kneeling over the body, checking the wound. Must've been only professional curiosity, since Casselli was beyond all help. Gloria Morgan stood back, her hand clutching a handkerchief, dabbing her moist eyes. I checked the shelves lining the walls all around us. Cases of medical supplies were stacked up everywhere, but the shelves weren't full. I looked at a clipboard hung on a nail. It was a complete inventory of the stock in the room. There were medical instruments on the list, silk thread, all sorts of bandages and other routine supplies. I flipped to the section marked "Drugs." Morphine, sulfa, penicillin, and a whole bunch more I never heard of.

"Where's the morphine?" I didn't know if this was a drug heist but it was the most logical place to start.

"Who the hell wants to know?" growled a stocky officer, pushing enlisted men out of the way as he squeezed into the storeroom.

"I do, sir. It looks like stuff is missing —"

"And who the hell on God's green earth are you? Goddamn it, someone tell me what's going on here!" His forehead was raging red and I could see a vein pulsing on his temple. Maybe Dunbar was about to have another patient. He was a short colonel — otherwise known as a lieutenant colonel — and sported a big unlit cigar clenched between his teeth. He was thick around the waist and gray at the temples. He looked at home in his U.S. Army khakis and had probably been fighting desk wars since before I was born. I decided to play it straight with this guy.

"Lieutenant Billy Boyle, sir! Doctor Dunbar requested that I assist him here after he discovered Sergeant Casselli's body."

"Joe? Dead? Jesus H. Christ on a crutch!

Dunbar, what happened here?"

Dunbar rose up and automatically dusted his hands off, as if ridding himself of a slight inconvenience. I knew doctors were fanatics about clean hands, but that was about touching patients all day. Live ones. Plus, Casselli hadn't been dead long enough to get the creepy crawlies scurrying over him, so no need to worry there. My dad had always reminded me to watch for the telltale signs that suspects give. Some people can't look you straight in the eye when they lie to you. They'll shift their eyes around and glom onto anything except you. But other people can lie like a rug and never take their peepers off yours. Now, maybe the good doctor wasn't really a suspect, but that gesture made me wonder. Maybe he should be. A doctor would know just where best to slit a throat. It sounds easy — just slide your knife across the other guy's gullet — but it can be bungled. Ask Carmine Lupagia, down at the Boston docks. Only don't expect an answer. Some rookie hit man got his voice box but missed his jugular. The scar isn't pretty but then Carmine never was much to look at anyway.

"I don't know, sir," Dunbar said to the colonel, looking him straight in the eye, which of course told me nothing. "I was going to ask Joe to get some more penicillin for a patient, a friend of the Lieutenant's here. I saw the storeroom door open and when I went to shut it, I saw Joe lying there."

"And the reason you asked Lieutenant Boyle to help you?"

"He brought the patient in this morning, claiming to be from headquarters. Allied Forces HQ. I thought I should check up on him, so I radioed for confirmation. Turns out he is. He's on Eisenhower's staff. Some sort of investigator, so I figured —"

"So you figured that you'd call in a headquarters snoop before you informed your commanding officer of a death on his post? You may be a skilled medical man, Dunbar, but otherwise you've got shit for brains!"

I hadn't really liked Dunbar from the moment I met him, but listening to this short colonel bawl him out was getting even more irritating than he was. I never much cared for the kind of guy who threw his weight around and cursed someone who couldn't give it back as good as he got it. I didn't like it when Brother Aloysius, the vice principal, did it back in high school, didn't like it when Sergeant Halloran did it my first year as a rookie cop, and didn't like it much more when those down-South drill instructors did it at OCS.

"Where's the morphine?" I repeated.

"What the hell are you going on about, and why the hell are you still here?"

"Well, sir, Colonel . . . ?"

"Colonel Maxwell Walton, sonny boy, and you better answer me or I'll kick your ass back to HQ so fast. . . ." He apparently couldn't think of exactly how fast so he just let it hang there. I took the opportunity to get a word in while he thought about it.

"Okay, Colonel Walton. What I'm going on about is the distinct possibility that Sergeant Casselli was murdered by a drug ring, and that you've got morphine missing and who knows what else. Maybe they even took that new penicillin stuff." I watched his eyes dart around the room, focusing on the ransacked shelves, on Gloria, and finally on Dunbar. He was just realizing that he might be in a pickle. Just to twist the knife a little, I kept going.

"I understand you'd like me out from under, sir, so I'll just get back to HQ now and give them a security report on the 21st General Hospital, Colonel Maxwell Walton, commanding." I started to walk away, struggling to keep the smirk I felt coming off of my face.

"Now hold on here, boy," Colonel Walton said. "Maybe for once Headquarters staff could be of some use around here. What kind of investigator are you, anyway?" I knew my youthful good looks — my youth, anyway — did not impress.

"I used to be a cop. Sir. The rest is a long story and my boss would probably shoot me if I told you." Walton eyed me for a minute, trying to decide how much of this was bullshit. He looked at Dunbar. His stare turned from quizzical to hostile. There was no love lost there. Gambling debts didn't make for good relations between COs and junior officers.

"Okay, Doctor," Walton said, nearly spitting out the word. "You take Boyle and conduct an official investigation. I expect a preliminary report before the end of the day, including a tally of all missing items. Got it?"

"Yes, sir," was all Dunbar could say. I began to wonder about the wisdom of leaving a guy with heavy gambling debts in charge of investigating a potential theft of drugs worth a fortune on the black market. But then I remembered I didn't give a hoot for any of this. Too bad Joe had ended up this way; I had other business.

"Sorry I can't help out, Colonel, but I'm due at HQ. I just brought in my buddy for treatment this morning and I've got to get

148

back —"

"You," Walton said, pointing a stubby finger at me, "stay here. I'll call headquarters and straighten this out. Who's your commanding officer?" Before I could say anything, Gloria walked over and laid her hand on Walton's arm.

"It's Major Sam Harding, Max. I know him from back in the States. If I give him a call, I'm sure I can persuade him to let us borrow Billy for a while." She smiled at Walton and he turned into a pussycat. She had a magic touch. I couldn't wait to see Harding under her spell.

Gloria left with Walton and I got rid of everyone else except Dunbar and one GI who I put to work checking the inventory.

"Thanks, Boyle," Dunbar said as soon as the crowd thinned.

"Don't mention it. I've never been a fan of pompous blowhards, especially when they're wearing brass. You're not his favorite MD, are you?"

"Hardly." He looked around uneasily, and jerked his head down toward poor Joe on the floor. "What do we do now?"

"First thing is, you tell me why Walton stuck you with this job."

"That's easy enough. He gets to keep his distance in case this thing goes south. If we find anything, he claims the credit."

"Yeah, that's SOP," I said. "What I want to know is why *you*. Why are you the patsy?"

He shrugged. "I'm here?" His edge was gone now. He wasn't the sarcastic upper-class kid anymore. Alone in a room with only a corpse and me, he seemed like just another guy under the thumb of a lousy boss. A guy in debt. Maybe a guy who'd kill to solve his problems? A little murder to cover a drug theft?

"How deep are you into him?"

"What do you mean?"

I didn't say anything. Sometimes silence is the most effective interrogation technique. I knelt down beside Joe's body and felt his hand. It was still warm and flexible, but a little rubbery. The fingertips had started to turn blue.

"Couple of hours at the most, probably less." I said.

"What do you mean?" Dunbar said, his voice tinged with anger.

"You're the doctor, you ought to know about rigor and all that stuff."

"You know what I'm talking about. Who told you?"

Now that's what I mean about silence. If I had badgered him, he might have clammed up. Instead, he'd already confirmed it was

150

true. I raised Joe's arm up straight.

"This guy. His throat is cut as neat as a cadaver. Any idea who could do such a thing?"

"Fuck you, Boyle." Ah, no more mister nice guy. He turned and walked out.

I laid down Joe's arm and looked at the body's position. His legs pointed to a row of shelves on the back wall. There was a crimson spray across the boxes stacked there; he was probably standing facing them when he was cut. Doing what? Was he ordered to stand there while his killer took the drugs, or was he about to take something himself?

I looked at his throat. The cut went ear to ear, severing all the major veins and arteries. Professional. I checked his pockets. Nothing except a pack of matches. I rolled him over and checked for a wallet. It was in the back pocket of his khakis, sodden with the blood he was laying in. I went through it carefully, laying out the slips of paper and bills on his chest. The usual stuff, nothing that told me anything.

I squatted next to the body, just looking. And thinking. Something bothered me about this killing. It made three deaths that I'd seen so far in North Africa, none of which were courtesy of our official enemies.

151

Georgie at the roadblock and then Pierre at the hotel, both killed by Vichy officers, Villard and Bessette. Now Joe at the hospital, assailant unknown. German commandos raiding medical supplies? Not likely. Was this linked to Pierre's complaints about smuggling and drugs? Maybe. Especially with Villard having shown up. Part of me wanted to bolt and start looking for Diana. The other part of me was trying to put the pieces together, betting they'd add up to something that might help me find her. Although Villard driving around wearing an American uniform and one dead supply sergeant could add up to something I wanted no part of. Smugglers and black marketeers were not what I was interested in. I wanted to find Diana, and Luc Villard had stashed her somewhere in Bône, which is the direction he was headed just a little while ago. I didn't want my search for her complicated by an irrelevant crime, but maybe I could use this murder to get some official muscle working for me. Find one bird and kill another with the same stone, something like that. Or maybe I should just get the hell out of here and have a drink at the Bar Bleu. Only problem with that was, last I heard, the French were still shooting at us out there.

Another problem was right at my feet. I had only met Joe a few hours ago, but he'd seemed like an okay guy. Somebody else didn't think so and that bothered me. Plenty of guys were going to die in this war; there was no cause to murder one more.

I tried to put Diana out of my mind and focus on Joe's body. I had seen my Dad do this at crime scenes more times than I could remember. He always made sure I was called in for crowd control so I could watch and learn the ropes. Too bad I never thought to ask him what exactly he was looking for as he hunched down next to a body, his eyes scanning from head to toe. So I did the same thing, and waited for something to jump out at me. There was a lot of blood. It covered the floor around Joe and soaked into his shirt. I looked again at the arm I had picked up a minute ago, his right arm. The shirt sleeve was soaked in blood but there was something else I hadn't noticed right away. The sleeve was cut, right at the cuff, and underneath there was a deep slash on his forearm. A defensive wound? Had he tried to block the knife and taken the first cut on his arm? I looked at the wound on this throat again. One clean cut. No evidence of a false start. I turned his head to get a better look at his face. There was a small scratch on his right cheek, starting just below the eye and ending just on the edge of his mouth. How did that get there?

"Excuse me, Lieutenant?" It was the GI who was checking the stock. He was a young kid, just a PFC. He was skinny and wore glasses that he kept pushing up as they slid down his nose. He looked pretty pale but I couldn't tell if that was his natural color or if he was going to lose it all over me. I got up and backed up a couple of steps. He kept glancing down at Joe.

"It's better if you look at me, Private. What's your name?"

"Willoughby, sir. I'm Sergeant Casselli's . . . I mean I was the sergeant's supply clerk." He was holding a clipboard with both hands. They were trembling.

"Okay, Willoughby. Let's step outside for a minute."

The idea didn't bother him a bit. It was a little cooler in the hallway and he slouched against the stone wall and let out a deep breath.

"Not a pretty sight," I said. "Is that your first dead body?"

"Well, sir, we had some casualties yesterday that I helped move out for Graves Registration, but they were different. I didn't know them."

"Yeah, it makes a difference. Had you known Joe long?"

"Since England. I got transferred to the 21st when the unit was based at Blackpool. We knew we were gearing up for something big when we got selected to try out this penicillin. Sergeant Casselli was pretty excited about it. He said it was our chance to really make a difference and save lives."

"Was he a good noncom?"

"Well, he wasn't full of himself, like some. He let me do my job. He wanted to transfer to the infantry and get into combat. I admired him."

"I'm sure guys would've been lined up to switch with him," I said. "Why didn't he get the transfer?"

"Colonel Walton wouldn't approve it, is all I know."

"Makes sense," I said, "Joe seemed to be on top of things around here. Walton probably didn't want to lose him."

"It wasn't all Sergeant Casselli," Willoughby said, straightening up from his slouch. "No disrespect intended, but I do a lot of the real work around here. I could run this place. I think something else was going on."

"Like what?"

"If a guy owed you money, would you let

him transfer out? Sir?"

"Poker with Colonel Walton?" I asked.

"That's what they say."

"They? Did Joe ever mention it?"

"No, and I never asked directly. It's an open secret though. The colonel has a group of poker buddies and rumor has it Casselli started joining them just before we shipped out of England. Sounds like he didn't do so well."

"Like Doctor Dunbar?"

"Well, yeah. So the rumors say."

"Regulations say gambling's illegal, as well as fraternization between officers and enlisted men. What other rules do they break around here?"

"I wouldn't know, Lieutenant. I don't really keep up on regulations too much. I guess that's what officers are for."

"Yeah, it does give us something to do. Now what did you want to talk about?"

"Uh, when is the body . . . Sergeant Casselli . . . going to be moved out? I need to finish the inventory and he's in the way. Plus all that blood . . . ?"

"Okay. We'll get it cleaned up and then you can get to work. Do you have a morgue here?"

"Not really. There's a basement where it's kinda cool that Graves Registration works out of. That's it."

"Go tell them to pick up the body but not to dispose of it until they hear from me. Then get a detail to clean up in here. I just need a few minutes more. Why don't you take five and then organize all that?"

"Will do, Lieutenant," he said as he pulled a small pack of Chesterfields from his fatigues. "Got a light by any chance?"

"Sure," I said. I was still holding the pack of matches I'd found on Casselli. I opened it up and struck a match. Willoughby lit up and strolled down the hall. I watched him go and wondered if there was less to Private Willoughby than met the eye. Those small packs of Chesterfields were usually found only in K-Rations, and K-Rations were found only at the front. Or in a supply depot, like the one right next to the hospital. Did he get them in a trade or was he the kind of kid who pilfered supplies, knowing that some dogface in a foxhole who thought the cigarettes were the only decent part of K-Rations was going to go without? Now, I know a thing or two about how stuff in warehouses can take a walk. A busted crate here and there and everyone's happy. The smart ones pass it around to the cop on the beat, and he keeps an eye out for them. At least that's how I did my Christmas shopping. But stealing from GIs would be like stealing from the blind. I shook my head wearily at the evil men do as I was about to fold the matchbook in my hand. Then I noticed something white behind the front row of matches. It was a slip of paper. I pulled it out and stepped back inside the storeroom, where I was sure no one could see. It had one hole punched on the side, like it had come from a notebook. I knew before I unfolded it that this piece of paper was from the notebook Jerome had told me about, and that it would be in code.

DBSSFGPVS, and under that, *MF CBS CMFV.*

Damn.

CHAPTER ELEVEN

I was muttering out loud as I strode from the depot toward Ward C. I could see jeeps and trucks pulling out of the vehicle park onto the main road, heading away from this damn place. Which was exactly what I should be doing. Why the hell did Joe Casselli have to go and get himself killed? How had he obtained that notebook, or at least a page from it? Okay, I told myself, I'll go ask Jerome about this notebook and see if he knows the code, or even what's supposed to be concealed in it. Then I'm out of here, Colonel Walton or no.

It was the colonel himself who greeted me at the entrance to Ward C. He was standing with a Gardes Mobiles officer who had his left arm in a sling.

"Boyle!" Walton barked, crooking a finger at me. "This is Lieutenant Phillipe Mathenet from the local French police. He's here to collect prisoners." Mathenet made a

159

little bow in my direction. With one arm in a sling and the other holding his blue uniform jacket, a handshake wasn't going to work and I wasn't going to salute another lieutenant, especially a Vichy cop. I wasn't big on bowing either, so I just nodded back at him. He was older than I expected a police lieutenant to be, with thinning sandy hair and bags under his eyes. A narrow mouth and long chin made it look like his face had started a long downward slide.

"Lieutenant," I said, "I hope your wound is not too serious."

"No, Lieutenant Boyle," he said, mustering a smile. "It is nothing. A bit of stray shrapnel. I am afraid there is more damage to my uniform than to my arm. My tailor will have to sew me a new sleeve."

He smiled again as he held up his jacket with his good arm. The sleeve was torn and bloody, but the rest of the jacket was fine. It seemed like a custom-made job. His pants and shoes were expensive, and his watch looked like a week's pay. Maybe he'd spent all of his lieutenant's salary on this fancy uniform. Or maybe the tailor was on his beat. Or he'd been lucky at cards. Or he was a crooked throat-slitting son of a bitch.

"Yeah," I said, "War is hell. You taking all of these kids out of here?"

His smile faded, fast. "That is no business of yours, or of the American Army," Mathenet answered. "These rebels tried to overthrow the legitimate government of this province. We do not take such actions lightly."

"Boyle," said Walton, "I ordered you to look into the death of Sergeant Casselli, not to antagonize the representative of the local authorities. Now get to it!"

I couldn't think of a reason to go in to see Jerome that would hold water with Walton, but I needed to talk to him before Mathenet rounded him up. Chained to his bed, I couldn't pretend he'd been a witness to anything, so Walton probably would blow a gasket if I paid him a visit instead of playing Dick Tracy. Before I could think of a pretext, a truck drove by, stopped, and backed up toward the entrance. Another Gardes Mobiles cop got out, saluted Mathenet, and handed him a clipboard. As they all consulted it, I stepped away and quietly went inside.

I opened Jerome's door expecting to find him alone and terrified. Instead, he and Gloria Morgan were both seated by the window, raising glasses in a toast. He was smiling and the manacles and chain had been removed from his leg.

161

"Having a party?" I asked, confused.

"We're celebrating and commiserating, Billy," said Gloria.

"I am to be freed," said Jerome, "and we are saluting your Sergeant Casselli."

"I just came off duty and needed a drink, after everything that happened today." Gloria explained. "I saw a letter from General Juin's headquarters, ordering Jerome to be released as soon as he was healthy enough. Isn't that marvelous? I was so happy to hear some good news that I came by to celebrate. So, bottoms up!" She and Jerome drained their glasses.

"What is that you're drinking?" I asked as I saw them slosh down something green.

"Crème de menthe," answered Gloria. "It's a liqueur, very French. It's an acquired taste, which Jerome and I share. Sorry I can't offer you any, Billy. That was the last of it."

"Don't worry, I like my liquor amber and Irish. That's great news, Jerome. How'd you pull it off?"

"I knew my family was trying to get General Juin to intercede. They are not without influence here, and finally it worked. Just in time," he sighed heavily. He looked tired. Suddenly we heard a commotion in the hallway, shouts and cries in French.

"They're clearing out the ward," said Gloria. "All except a few serious cases. There's nothing we can do. I'm so sorry about your friends, Jerome."

Jerome nodded, sadly, his eyes cast down, his hands cradling his empty glass.

"Well, that's enough excitement for one day. Let's get you back in bed and I'll come and check in later," Gloria said. She helped Jerome up and got him settled, tucking him in and smoothing his hair back from his forehead. He smiled at her and yawned. Gloria smiled back and then picked up the glasses and a small bottle, putting them on a tray and covering it with a hand towel.

"Billy, let's leave Jerome to sleep. You can visit him later. And don't say anything about this," she said, holding up the tray. "It's against regulations, but under the circumstances. . . ."

"Sure," I said. "My lips are sealed. Can I just sit in here with him for a while?"

"No, you may not. Doctor Dunbar gave him something to calm him down earlier. He was very upset about his brother's death, and his friends being taken away. It would be better if he slept now. Later, after it's over, come and visit." Her voice had dropped to a whisper, and she nodded her head toward the door.

"Okay." I looked at Jerome. His eyelids were heavy and he looked like he was about to drop off. It could wait, I decided. Let the poor guy sleep. I followed Gloria out and closed the door. By now, there were about twenty patients, or prisoners, lined up to board the truck. Some were on crutches and all were bandaged. A few tried to appear unconcerned, but most had that same look of terror on their faces I had seen on Jerome's this morning. Now he was sleeping like a lamb, as his friends were being led to the slaughter, courtesy of the ever helpful Colonel Walton, who was slapping Mathenet on the back like an old buddy.

I couldn't watch anymore and decided it was a good time to check on Kaz again. I walked to the main hospital building, passing by the Supply Depot where work crews were busy cleaning up damage from the morning's bombing raid. This war wasn't making a lot of sense so far. The Vichy French fight us, the Germans bomb us, and we turn over the kids who are on our side to the Vichy police. I hoped Uncle Ike knew what he was doing. Inside the hospital, I found Dunbar at the desk near the nurse's station doing paperwork. I filled him in on my conversation with Willoughby, leaving out the matchbook, and told him about moving the body to Graves Registration.

"Thanks, Boyle. Sorry I blew up before. I don't like being interrogated like a suspect."

"Everyone's a suspect. Nothing personal. Sometimes you just have to ask a lot of dumb questions to get one good answer."

"Kind of like making a diagnosis, maybe?" He tossed down his pen. I wondered how long before he blew up again. This guy was under some kind of pressure.

"Yeah, probably. How's Kaz doing?"

"Very well. I just saw him and there's a marked improvement. His fever's down, and the swelling and inflammation are almost gone. He responded very well to the treatment. Go see for yourself."

"I will. And thanks, Doctor. You saved his life."

"Actually, you did, Boyle. If you hadn't brought him in he'd have lasted only a few hours."

I mumbled something and took off down the hall. I didn't want to confess that Kaz was in this fix because of me in the first place. I was glad to hear the good news, but I was still worried. Kaz was a little guy in lousy health, and that was before he took a slug and then got gangrene waiting for yours truly.

I needn't have worried. I found Kaz sitting up in bed, a huge white bandage wrapped around his arm, with a pretty redheaded nurse feeding him soup.

"Really?" she was saying as I walked in, "a real baron? I never met royalty before." She stuck a spoonful of soup into Kaz's mouth as he noticed me in the doorway. He smiled weakly as he swallowed and gave a little apologetic shrug.

"There," the nurse said, dabbing the corner of Kaz's mouth with a napkin, "I'll leave you to your visitor, Baron, and come back to check on you later."

"Thank you, Rita," Kaz said. "But I am fine."

"It's no problem at all," she said, keeping her eyes on Kaz. She walked by me like I was a piece of furniture. Kaz looked away from me, and raised his good hand to wipe away a tear, then covered up by making a show of adjusting his glasses.

"It's okay if a pretty girl makes a fuss over you, Kaz," I said in a low voice as I took the chair Rita had just vacated. "You don't have to give her the cold shoulder."

"Why would my shoulder be cold? We are practically in the desert here."

"Don't change the subject," I said. Kaz loved American slang and he and Daphne used to go to gangster movies just to pick up new phrases. I thought he might know this one already but wanted to divert my attention.

Kaz turned away to stare at nothing.

"Sorry," I said. "I just hate seeing you all torn up."

"She is very pretty, and kind," Kaz said in a tired, low voice. "But all she can do is to remind me of what Daphne and I once had. I would rather she was plain and heartless. I have no room for kindness."

I couldn't think of anything to say, or do. Someone dropped something out in the hallway and the clatter and cursing echoed off the tiles. I was glad of the distraction.

"You look better, Kaz. Last night was pretty bad."

"Thank you for taking care of me, Billy. They say I would have died if you hadn't brought me here."

"Yeah, well, you wouldn't have gotten shot if you hadn't rescued me, and your arm wouldn't have gotten so bad if you hadn't waited for me last night, so we're even. Forget about it. How are you feeling?"

"Much better. I woke up a while ago and was actually surprised to feel so well, even though my arm hurts. They had to clean out the wound and re-stitch it. Rita told me about the penicillin they gave me. It's a miracle drug. Do you know about it?"

"More than I want to. I've got a lot to tell you —"

"Tell both of us, Boyle." The deep voice of Major Sam Harding boomed out from the doorway where he stood; the expression on his face said he was not pleased. Gloria Morgan stood right in back of him. Her face told a different story. She looked very happy to be in the major's company. She gave me a little raise of her eyebrow and a coy smile, then vanished as Harding shut the door behind him, but not before he'd given her a smile and a nod. I had a feeling they'd be doing some catching up later.

"How are you, Lieutenant Kazimierz?" Harding asked as he took off his helmet and sat next to Kaz's bed on the chair I had occupied before his arrival.

"Fine, sir. My arm hurts a bit, but they said that would pass. I am very lucky Billy got me here in time."

"Good. Now tell me what the hell is going on," Harding said, his eyes drilling me. "This morning I got your message that you'd brought Lieutenant Kazimierz here, but I assumed it was just to check his wound. Then I get a phone call from Gloria . . . Captain Morgan . . . informing me that it was gangrene and that oh, by the way, the CO here wants you to investigate a murder!"

"Bet it was a real surprise hearing from her, Major," I said.

His look said the topic was off limits. The room went totally silent.

Kaz glanced between us. "Do you know Captain Morgan, Major?" he asked, tentatively. A couple of seconds passed very slowly as Harding turned his gaze toward Kaz, who obviously was unaware of their history. Some of the grimness left Harding's face, mostly because he wasn't looking at me anymore. It made me wonder about what had happened between him and Gloria. And what might happen next.

"Yes. We served together for a while back in the States. She's career Army Medical Corps."

More silence. That was going to be it. I looked at Kaz. He looked at Harding. Harding looked at me. Right back where we started.

"Start at the beginning, Boyle," Harding said as he shook a cigarette out of a pack of Lucky Strikes and lit up with his Zippo.

That reminded me of Willoughby's Chester-fields.

"Just one quick question, first," I said, "sir." Always helps to remember to call 'em sir when they're in a bad mood. "Those little four-packs of Chesterfields, do they only come in K-Rations?"

"Yes," answered Harding. "Why?"

"And K-Rations are only issued to guys in the front-lines, right?"

"Who else would want to eat them? Now what's this all about?"

I thought about Willoughby and how he was probably just a little rat who pilfered supplies when he had the chance. That was a court-martial offense, but turning him in wouldn't get me anywhere. Better to leave a little leverage in case I needed it later.

"Probably nothing. Not worth going into. So where do we start, Kaz?"

We were each thinking fast, trying to come up with some explanation as to how we'd gotten the information from Bessette's of-fice. An explanation that didn't involve rooftops and late night burglary.

"Late last night we made contact with Agency Africa," Kaz blurted out first, as if he didn't trust me to concoct a good story. I had forgotten that his job was to find out if any part of the pre-war Polish spy network still existed and make contact after we were established in Algiers. "We asked if they knew anything about the political prisoners," Kaz continued, "and gave them the names of the French officers involved, Villard and Bessette." Then he looked up at me. Not a bad cover story. I picked it up, using Agency Africa as the source of the information I'd discovered.

"They said Bessette is as crooked as they come, that he's involved in drug smuggling. He recently had a French Army officer killed after he threatened to expose him."

"Do they have proof?" Harding asked.

"An eyewitness, but no other hard evidence. They did tell us two things about the supply depot at Bône where Villard was headed with the prisoners. First is the password: Le Carrefour."

"Crossroads," Kaz translated for us.

"Go on," said Harding. I took a deep breath. It was just a hunch, and I had been wrong before, but there was something about that matchbook, and all those bills in Bessette's desk drawer.

"A contact for the smuggling operation can be made in a bar, Le Bar Bleu, in Bône, near the supply depot. There's a link between Villard, the prisoners, and the smuggling operation."

I didn't know that there was such a link. Maybe Bessette just collected matchbooks. But I had to keep this thing going in the same direction that Diana was headed, or I'd never see her again.

"Interesting," said Harding, giving me a once-over that said he believed me about as much as he believed we'd be home by Christmas. "What was the name of this contact?"

I looked at Kaz, who simply shrugged. "We were not given a name, Major."

"Man or woman?" he asked. We both hesitated for a heartbeat, but it was long enough for Harding.

"Never mind," Harding said, "I don't want to undermine the enthusiasm of my junior officers, even if they use unorthodox and illegal means."

"You know!" I exclaimed.

"All I know is that you have about fifty feet of rope stowed under your cot, and there was a dark rust-colored stain on the floor in Bessette's office when I met him there this morning. Some Arabs delivered a new rug and rolled it out while I was there. Even a regular army guy can figure stuff out sometimes, Boyle."

"Did he tell you anything?"

"Regular appointments are nice but this

one didn't yield as much information as your unannounced visit. I told him we were concerned about the fate of civilian prisoners taken after the attempted coup. He told me it was none of his business since it was a police matter, and none of mine since it was a French police matter."

"Major, I saw him bash in the head of a French Army captain who was yelling at him about drugs, smuggling, Americans — I couldn't understand most of it. Bessette grabbed a candlestick and killed him with it. His guards reacted like it was business as usual."

"Americans? What do you think he meant by that?"

"I don't know, sir. I couldn't make it out. It sounded like the captain — Pierre was the only name I heard — was threatening Bessette. Bessette pretended to give in, then picked up the candlestick and beaned Pierre. It was all over in a second."

"Then what happened?"

"They left with the body wrapped in the rug he fell on. I went through Bessette's desk and files as best I could. I found the password written on a copy of the same travel orders we found at police headquarters. I figure this place may have something to do with it." I handed Harding the blue

173

matchbook for Le Bar Bleu.

"And when do we get to the murder you're investigating?"

"Oh, yeah. Noncom named Joe Casselli got his throat slit this afternoon. He was the supply sergeant, in charge of this penicillin as well as all the other medical drugs. Do you know about this stuff, sir?"

"I do, but you shouldn't. These medical people should learn to keep their mouths shut. This is a top-secret test. If everything works like the eggheads say it should, penicillin is going to save thousands of lives. And only we have it."

"Do the Germans know that?" Kaz asked.

"They know all about penicillin. The trick isn't making it, it's producing enough of it to be useful. This hospital's supply is the first batch from a new production process. That's why we want to keep it a secret."

"So this stuff is valuable?" I asked.

"Billy," Kaz said, "I would be dead without it. I think it's very valuable."

"Exactly," said Harding. "There's no telling what it would be worth on the black market. Is any of it missing?"

"They're doing an inventory now. We can go check over at the depot. As far as the murder goes, I'm pretty sure who did it."

"Who?" Kaz and Harding asked at the

same time.

"Villard. I saw him driving out of here in a truck, wearing an American uniform, just before they found Casselli's body. I'll bet that truck was full of medical supplies, including penicillin."

"Goddamn," Harding said. Kaz said something in Polish that was probably along the same lines.

"I do have some good news, though. Remember Georgie — Lieutenant Dupree? He had a younger brother, Jerome, who was with the rebels? Well, he's here, in the hospital. He was all worked up about a notebook that the rebels had managed to lift from Bessette at some point. He had it when they brought him in, but now it's gone. I found this sheet of paper, from a notebook, inside a matchbook on Casselli's body." I handed the slip of paper with the code on it to Harding.

"Pretty good work so far, Boyle. Let's go check on the inventory and interview Jerome. Lieutenant Kazimierz, if you're up to it, will you work on this?"

"I am, Major," Kaz said as he took the paper. "I quite enjoy deciphering codes." Puzzling out that jumble of letters, Kaz looked happy as we left. I wasn't. I needed sleep, I had a headache, and my eyes felt like they were full of grit. I started out last night climbing rooftops and since then Kaz had almost died, I had been bombed by the Germans, and then I'd been shanghaied for a murder investigation. I was used to long hours, but the army didn't pay overtime.

CHAPTER TWELVE

There's nothing like a corpse to put things into perspective. I was tired, but Jerome was dead. I could tell by the hospital sheet over his head. We had come into the room to find Dr. Dunbar standing next to the bed, making notes on Jerome's chart.

"I just found him a minute ago," Dunbar said after he gave Harding a salute as an afterthought. "He must've died very recently."

"I was in here with him about an hour ago," I said. "He was tired and going to sleep."

"Could have been a complication from his head injury. He had a severe concussion when he came in. Happens sometimes." He hung the chart back up and walked out. I went up to the bed and pulled back the sheet. A lock of his long dark brown hair hung down over Jerome's forehead. He looked relaxed, and I would have thought he was asleep except for his eyes. They were still open. I tried to avoid looking at them, but couldn't. They seemed to seek me out, as if Jerome had a last message to pass on. All I got was a shiver up my spine as I reached down and closed them. They were hazel green, just like Georgie's, the contracted pupils showing off their full color as if they had blossomed in death. Two brothers dead for what they believed in when they both could have sat it out and played it safe. Like I'd expected I'd be doing back in D.C., where I should have been, in a cushy staff job. Yet I was glad I had gotten into the war, because otherwise I wouldn't have met Diana. But in this hospital room, with a young kid lying dead under a coarse, dingy sheet, I couldn't feel glad about anything.

"Let's go, Boyle," Harding said, his hand on my shoulder. "He can't talk to us now."

If only the dead could speak. I had looked into those eyes, and couldn't escape the feeling they were trying to tell me something, something important but just out of my reach. I followed Harding out of the room, then led the way to the Supply Depot. We found Willoughby leaning up against the brickwork wall outside the supply room where Casselli had been killed. He was adding up columns on the inventory sheet on his clipboard. He came to attention and saluted like a soldier when he saw Harding. There were brand new corporal's stripes sewn onto his sleeves. I returned the salute and pointed at the stripes.

"That was fast. From Private First Class to Corporal already," I said.

"Colonel Walton put me in charge, Lieutenant. I told you I did most of the real work around here anyway. The colonel said I deserved it," he added as an afterthought.

"Didn't say you don't, Willoughby," I said, watching his eyes. They darted between Harding and me.

"Tell us what you've got, Corporal," Harding said.

"Yes sir. I did the best I could, Lieutenant," he said. He gave a nervous glance back at the major. "Graves Registration hasn't shown up yet, so I had to work around Joe. I mean, Joe's body." He shuffled his feet, rubbing his face with one hand. He worked in a hospital in the middle of a war, but this might have been the first dead body he'd ever seen. I gave him an encouraging nod to continue.

"They got the penicillin, two full cases. All that's left in the hospital is less than a case. Plus they got about half our supply of morphine, including all the spare syrettes for the medics. Five cases of sulfa, a box of ten 1cc vials of nalorphine, and two bottles of chloral hydrate."

"What's chloral hydrate, Corporal?" Harding asked. Willoughby shrugged.

"Sleeping pills. Your basic ingredient for a Mickey Finn," I answered.

"How do you know that?" Harding asked.

"You can buy knockout drops, or chloral hydrate, back in Boston for the right price if you know the right gangster. Drop 'em in a drink and you have a Mickey Finn. Guaranteed to put anyone out, temporary or permanent, depending on how many drops."

"Now you can buy them in Algiers," Harding said, "courtesy of the U.S. Army." He went into the supply room, shaking his head in disgust.

"If you're all done here, Corporal, go see what's taking Graves Registration so long. It's too hot to keep a dead body lying around," I told him.

"Yes, sir." He handed me the inventory report and took off. People are always glad to leave when there are dead bodies around. I went inside. Casselli was starting to smell. He didn't look peaceful, like Jerome. He looked like a corpse with a slit throat decomposing in the heat of North Africa.

"Professional job," Harding said. "The

killer could have been trained by the Commandos. Or me."

"I was thinking more along the lines of the Mob," I said.

"Sicilians?"

"There's lots of organized crime out of Marseilles. Maybe there's some connection between them and smuggling here. Or maybe it was an Arab, using one of those curved knives."

"It was a sharp knife, I can tell you that much," Harding said.

"Major," I asked. "How would you train somebody to slit a throat?"

"Hopefully you won't need to, Boyle."

"No, really, show me how you'd do it, sir."

Harding pulled me away from Casselli's body and stood behind me. With his left hand he grabbed my chin. "First, you pull up the chin so you can get at the throat." He pulled his right hand across my bare neck. This must have been the last thing Casselli felt. I thrust my right hand up, protecting my neck.

"Would that work?" I asked. Harding drew his hand across my wrist. We both looked at Casselli's right arm. He had a slice across the cuff, at exactly the same spot.

"It only delayed the inevitable," Harding said. "If someone had him from behind, and

181

knew what they were doing, his arm wouldn't protect him for long."

"Try it again," I said, giving Harding a pencil. "Use that as the knife."

He grabbed my chin and brought his right arm around with the pencil. I grabbed it with my right hand and pushed it away and then to the left, dragging the pencil across his left hand as it held my chin. He broke my grip and went at my neck again. I protected it with my right hand. Harding let go.

"Do you know someone with slash marks on his left arm?" he asked.

"Lieutenant Phillipe Mathenet. A Vichy cop who said he got hit by shrapnel in the left arm. His sleeve was in shreds."

"You said earlier that you knew Villard had killed Casselli."

"That was before we worked this out. Mathenet's sleeve bothered me. It seemed too coincidental. But Villard was here at the same time he was, and he had to be in on it."

"Why?"

"Who else held Casselli's right arm so Mathenet could make a clean cut? One on one, Casselli was holding him off."

Harding thought for a minute, then lit a cigarette, the blue smoke helping to cover up the coppery smell of dried blood and the fouler odors of the shit and piss Casselli had let go when his lights went out. I looked down at Casselli, the supply sergeant, and wondered at the struggle he had put up. The dead eyes looked up at me, pupils wide in amazement, as if the thought of death had never occurred to him before. Probably hadn't.

We walked outside, leaving the smell of decay and dried blood behind. Harding stood in the sun and drew on his cigarette. My head was spinning. It was way past chow time and I needed some. And some coffee, or sleep. Food and sleep. That sounded great. Then I'd worry about these dead bodies, and getting out of here to find Diana, and . . . I couldn't even think about what else. I rubbed my eyes. My eyes. Something about my eyes nibbled at the back of my mind. What? My eyes or someone else's? I had no clue. Literally.

"I need some chow and a cup of joe, Major, before I fall asleep in my tracks."

"Let's check on Lieutenant Kazimierz first. I'd like to know when they're going to release him."

I trudged after Harding, wondering who was going to release me, and what was it about eyes? Damn his eyes? The ayes have it? The eye of the beholder? I want to go home? I gave up and shuffled along to Kaz's room.

Kaz held up a slip of paper as we walked in with "Carrefour" and "Le Bar Bleu" written on it.

"I already told you the password and about the bar," I said. I wasn't thinking quickly.

"You cracked the code," Harding said.

"It's hardly a code at all," said Kaz, sounding disappointed. "It's more like an improvised shorthand. In a proper code, one doesn't leave spaces between the words. This is nothing more than a single letter displacement. B for A, C for B, and so on. DBSSFGPVS is Carrefour if you shift each letter one place."

"Simple," I said, now that I understood.

"Simple enough to be able to write and read it quickly if you know the secret, but still enough to keep prying eyes from understanding it right away," said Harding.

Prying eyes. Eyes again. I almost had it . . . then Rita the nurse walked in, a ray of cheery sunshine, visiting her prince.

"Baron, time for your medicine! Excuse me, gentleman." She set down her tray and gave Kaz four pills as she poured a glass of water. She did have very pretty green eyes.

Green eyes like Jerome. Kaz beamed at the attention and scooped up the pills. His eyes were blue. Different eyes. That was it!

"What are all those for?" I asked.

"That's for his blood pressure, it's a little high," she said chattily, pointing out different pills, "and this is something to help him sleep." The elevated blood pressure was probably due to his heart condition but I didn't want to say anything about that. Kaz was having an adventure, and would hate being sent back to a real hospital in England. I had to humor him.

"Chloral hydrate?"

"Why, yes, Lieutenant. You certainly know something about drugs. Were you a medical student before the war?"

"No, a student of human nature. How much longer is he going to be taking that penicillin?"

"I'll have to ask Doctor Dunbar."

"Please do that. Now."

"I have to finish —"

"Now!" Sometimes I surprise myself. I can actually sound like a tight-ass officer when I need to. Nothing to be proud of, but it got her out of the room.

"Jerome didn't die of complications. He was murdered, and we've got to get Kaz out of here."

Harding and Kaz just looked at me like I was a blithering idiot.

"Now!" Why not try it on them?

"Explain yourself, Boyle!" Harding yelled without raising his voice.

"It's the eyes! I'm not a hundred percent certain, but one thing I do know is that a morphine overdose makes your pupils shrink down to a pinpoint. I've seen the look on the faces of addicts who checked out plenty of times. Jerome's eyes were just like that."

"But Boyle, maybe it was just the light in the room," said Harding patiently.

"No, it couldn't be. Listen, sir, I know you've seen plenty of dead men in the Great War. Probably a lot more than me, but my job is to study them when we find them murdered. One thing my Dad told me when he took me to my first crime scene was about the Dead Man's Stare."

"The dead do look as if they're seeing something beyond us," Kaz said quietly.

I took a breath before going on. I knew he was thinking about Daphne now and I hated to get clinical, but I had to.

"Yeah, and a lot of rookies get spooked by that. But he taught me that the pupils in your eyes widen right after death. It's the muscles relaxing or something like that. He said knowing why made it easier to look at them. It did."

"Didn't Jerome's eyes look like that?" Harding asked, sitting down on one of the empty beds and folding his arms.

"They probably will soon. But the effects of the morphine trumped the natural process."

"So he overdosed on morphine?" asked Kaz.

"No. Somebody gave him an overdose. Bit of a difference. That makes two people murdered in this hospital, both of whom knew about this missing notebook. And anyone can walk in here and give Kaz whatever kind of pills or injections they want, night or day!" I tried to slow down. I knew I sounded hysterical, but things were beginning to fall into place.

I tried to be calm and rational. "The notebook that Jerome and his pals lifted from Bessette must contain information about the smuggling operation. It points to the same place in Bône — Le Bar Bleu — as the matches and receipts I found in Bessette's office. And the same password shows up on Villard's travel orders to the supply depot at Bône. Don't you get it? Le Carrefour, the crossroads!"

"Bône is the crossroads of the smuggling

operation," Kaz said, "and the contact is at this bar."

"Could be," said Harding. "But how is Villard involved?"

"Remember, right after Villard shot Georgie, Jerome's brother? That German officer, Remke, was telling us that Villard had connections to the local underworld here. He's probably the connection between them and Bessette. That's why Bessette killed that French Army captain last night. He must have been protesting the smuggling of drugs taken from the Americans."

"Hold on a minute," Harding said, as he rubbed his chin, and paced up and down the little room. "You're saying that this whole operation to raid American drug supplies, including our top secret drug, penicillin, was organized within two or three days of the invasion? The Vichy French didn't know we were coming. Even if they did, how did they learn about our medical supplies? Or that we'd store them here? It doesn't make sense."

I realized he had a point. How could they have known about any of this?

"There's always a black market when supplies are short. Maybe they guessed a lot of military supplies, German or Allied, were going to land here someday. In the meantime, they ran what they could through Bône. I'm sure supplies came in from Marseille all the time. Maybe they took a cut at the docks and sent heroin to France in return. Villard or Bessette had to have some angle."

"It's a stretch, Boyle," Harding said.

"It is a lot to assume, Billy," added Kaz. I wasn't getting any support for my theory.

"If Dunbar is willing to release Kaz, can we at least get him out of here?" I asked Harding.

"Colonel Walton wants you to investigate Caselli's murder," he answered. "You'd do more good here."

"But if the killing is linked to the smuggling operation, I ought to go to Bône."

"Boyle, the fact that Villard has probably taken Diana Seaton to Bône wouldn't be influencing your judgment, would it?"

"I gotta be honest, sir. It has absolutely nothing to do with it. I think Kaz is in danger here and that Villard is behind the killings and theft. I say Bône is our best bet."

I must've really been tired. I gave away the lie by saying I was going to be honest. But Harding hadn't sat through as many police interrogations as I had, and he didn't know that was usually the big tip-off. If you're honest, there's no need to announce the fact.

CHAPTER THIRTEEN

Harding bought it, because half an hour later we had Kaz bundled into the jeep, with a supply of penicillin for the next five days, strict instructions for him to see a medic every day for his shot and to get his dressing changed, and a story ready for Colonel Walton about following up promising leads. Dunbar had checked Kaz out and pronounced him fit to travel. Rita had kissed Kaz goodbye and told him to come back and see her in four days to have the stitches removed. I'd seen Harding and Gloria Morgan whispering about something, maybe catching up on changes to the Army field manual since they last parted company. We were headed back to the St. George Hotel and now all I had to do was find a way to get to Bône from there. I reminded myself that Bône was still beyond our front lines, and might be defended by Vichy troops or even Germans, if they had already reached the town. Or both. I thought it might be time to inquire as to the progress of the war.

"Are we still shooting at the Vichies, Major?" I asked as I drove as carefully as I could to keep Kaz from bumping his arm. The road outside the hospital was rough hard packed gravel and sand that sent jolts through the jeep even at twenty miles an hour. A hot breeze blew dust at our backs and the sand hitting the back of my neck felt like sandpaper on soft pine.

"Not around here," Harding said, turning up his collar. "Darlan surrendered all French forces in the Algiers area; the French troops are in their barracks under orders not to resist. It's a mixed bag outside of Algiers. First, Darlan ordered all French forces in North Africa not to resist us. Then Petain overruled him, but before Darlan could countermand his orders we arrested him. Right now everything's quiet in and around Algiers. There's some fighting in Oran and we don't know what to expect when we move east toward Tunisia. Reports are in that the Germans are landing there and the French are not opposing them."

"They fired on us when we came to liberate them from the Germans, but they let the Germans in to fight us?"

Harding nodded. "It's a crazy war so far.

A lot of civilian rebels were freed when the fighting in Algiers stopped, but others still haven't been released. I heard that Colonel Baril has been arrested," Harding said, his jaw clenching.

"I'm sorry, Major. He seemed like a good guy."

"The best. We need to get this mess straightened out, fast. There's no time to play politics here while the Germans are forming up against us."

"I'm afraid you may find politics are not that easy to get away from," said Kaz from the back seat. "There are the Vichy politicians, the French army, the Arabs, all wanting something. General Eisenhower will have to accommodate them if he wishes to move against the Germans rapidly." He grimaced as we hit a pothole.

"Why?" I asked, downshifting to take a corner as slowly as I could.

"He can either garrison this country with his army . . ." Kaz stopped and hung on as we rounded the bend.

". . . or keep the Vichy structure in place to govern it for him so the army can fight," he finished.

"What about de Gaulle and the Free French? Why don't we let them take over?"

"You saw how most French officers here

feel about following orders," Harding explained. "To them de Gaulle is an opportunist who disobeyed the lawful orders of his government when he kept on fighting. Darlan hates him, Giraud thinks de Gaulle should report to him. . . . There'd be a civil war if we brought the Free French in."

"And then there are the Arabs," Kaz added, with a sharp gasp as I hit another bump.

"Sorry, Kaz. What about them?"

"You may have noticed that there are quite a few of them here," Kaz said.

"You're a funny guy. So, what, are the natives restless?"

"Some want independence, but most want stability. They are conservative, and for the most part go along with the right-wing Vichy policies. Like repression of the Jews. The Vichy government has stripped Jews in North Africa of their French citizenship. That made many friends for them among the Arabs."

"Isn't that the kind of thing we're supposed to be fighting against?" I asked, knowing that I sounded like a naïve schoolkid as soon as I spoke.

"We're supposed to be fighting, and defeating, the Axis powers. That's Germany and Italy in Europe," Harding said. "If we stop along the way to make everything right in North Africa we might never get to Berlin. We may need to leave the Vichy structure in place so we can move through Algeria quickly and take Tunisia before Rommel gets there."

"Wait a minute! The Vichies are the bad guys, remember? The collaborators, the ones shooting at us. Are we going to leave a bunch of junior-league fascists like them in power?" I was almost yelling, and had to relax my grip on the steering wheel as the road curved slightly and we entered a residential area, palm trees and green bushes casting welcome lines of shade in front of us.

"It may come to that, or face a civil war in our rear areas. Or an Arab revolt, which the Germans would be only too glad to foment," Kaz said. "Welcome to the world of European politics, Billy."

"Major, he can't be right, can he?" I asked. Harding didn't say a word. I wanted to be reassured that we were the good guys, not pawns in some power play that let killers and thieves stay on top while guys like Colonel Baril rotted in jail and Georgie and Jerome did the same in the ground. I drove as slowly as I could toward the setting sun as we passed a column of trucks heading out of Algiers. Dust choked the road as the deuce and a halfs, crammed with GIs, headed for the front. I hoped none of them had someone along explaining the intricacies of French politics. It would confuse things when the bullets started flying.

The last truck rolled by and we drove out of the dust, into the city. A cool breeze came off the water as I turned down a side street toward the hotel. I slowed at a curve and glanced back at Kaz to be sure he was all right. The windscreen cracked in front of me as I heard a sharp noise and felt something tug at my sleeve. Harding was pulling out his automatic and saying something I couldn't understand. I tried to take in what was happening. I heard the noise again, a shot. I swerved hard to the right, driving down an alley between two buildings. At the end of a driveway I saw a wooden gate between two houses and I floored it. I had no plans to be caught in a dead-end ambush. Hot steam was gushing from the engine and pouring over the shattered windshield as we headed for the gate.

"Hang on!" I yelled as we hit the gate with a thud and it toppled off its hinges. The jeep went over it with a jolt that made Kaz yell, so I knew he was still alive. I drove like a maniac until we reached the next street with two solid rows of houses between the shooter and us. Steam and water hissed out of the engine and there were shards of glass all over the floorboards.

"Kaz, are you all right?" I asked.

"Yes, Billy," he said, grasping his bad arm and gritting his teeth. He looked around as Harding jumped out, holstered his automatic, and pulled a Thompson from under the seat. I was still gripping the steering wheel. I felt the blood drain from my face. The evening was cool but I started to sweat. I looked at the windscreen. A bullet had struck the metal frame where it joined the window, leaving a half-moon hole in the frame and shattered glass inside the jeep. I got up slowly, making sure I wouldn't fall flat on my face. My hands were shaking and my legs felt like jelly.

"Billy," Kaz said, "look at your right shoulder."

There was a neat hole in my Parsons jacket, beneath my lieutenant's bar. Two neat holes, actually, one in and one out, right where the fabric was bunched up at the seam. I stuck my finger in one and wiggled it out the other.

"Damn close," Harding said. "The second shot hit the engine, so he could pick us off when the jeep stopped. Good thinking, Boyle, to take that turn."

A nod was about all I could manage. Someone had tried to kill *me*. Me, not just any dogface, but me in particular. Me.

"Let's go," Harding said. "We can hoof it to the hotel. We're not hanging around here." He grabbed his gear and I took the keys. I helped Kaz out of the back seat and we followed Harding down the road. I looked back to see a bunch of Arab kids appear from behind houses and doors and gather around the jeep, which was still leaking steam and water. I should've taken the jack. Those tires would be history as soon as we turned the corner. It was kind of comforting, sort of like being back home, in the wrong neighborhood.

As we took a left and came to the next intersection, Harding held up his hand. We stopped. Across the street, the same street we had been driving down, there was a low stone wall encircling a small park. Inside was a water fountain, palm trees, and a bunch of green, shady plants, with nice chalk-white benches to sit on. Very peaceful. At the corner, the wall made a right angle and then there was an entrance from the street. We followed Harding at a trot as he made for it. In the distance I could hear someone laying on the jeep's horn. Kids will be kids. Kaz and I caught up as Harding pointed the Thompson over the wall, glancing in each direction. "No one home," he said. "This was where he hid. Look at this." He pointed to some branches that had recently been snapped. I looked down on the other side of the wall and could see where the ground had been scuffed up.

"Yep," I said. "He had a clear line of fire once he got those branches out of the way. He had us in his sights as soon as we turned the corner. He should have waited a few seconds longer for a better shot."

"Billy," Kaz said, "please do not offer these hints to anyone. I have no wish to give this renegade Vichy a second chance."

"This was no fascist renegade, Kaz," I said as I ran my hand over the ground.

"How do you know that?" he asked. "There are still many Vichy French who do not wish to fight for the Allies."

"We did expect some trouble when we agreed to the cease-fire," Harding said. "The French troops still have weapons. One of them with a grudge could have slipped out, taken a potshot, and then gone back to his barracks."

"How many times has that happened?"

"None that I know of," admitted Harding. "But with thousands of French soldiers in this city who were shooting at us a day ago, anything's possible."

"Well," I said, "how many soldiers in this war take away their shell casings after a firefight?" I could see Kaz's eyes widen. Harding looked at the bare ground where the shooter had been, still puzzled.

"It's a professional habit. Not of soldiers but of hired killers," I said. "Hit men don't leave anything behind to link them to the murder."

"Murder? In the middle of a war?" Harding asked.

"Best time for it," I said. "Now let's get some food."

CHAPTER FOURTEEN

We ate in a mess tent outside the hotel as the sun set and breezes coming off the Mediterranean cooled the evening air. I wolfed down beef stew and rye bread until I had caught up with my two missed meals. Looking up at the palm fronds swaying in the slight wind I remembered how they had looked from the roof of the hotel. Was that only last night? Last night Joe Casselli and Jerome Dupree had both been alive. Had either of them realized it would be their final night on earth? Had they felt the cool breezes before they died?

Most murders are unfair and unequal struggles. A few you can make sense of, but usually it's greed or brutality that causes someone to kill another human being, whether out of sudden rage or studied calculation. There was something much more than unfair about Joe and Jerome's murders. Something was very wrong, upside down, as if the rules had suddenly changed and no one had bothered to tell them. In a war, there's enough chance for a guy to get killed, even a supply sergeant or a college kid caught up in the thrill of plots and revolts. But to be murdered for what? A notebook? Drugs? In a hospital, where they had the right to feel safe and secure? It wasn't right. If they had been killed in the air raid, it would have part of the deal, part of the war. But they had lived through that, only to become victims of some two-bit drug racketeers.

A gust of wind kicked up and the palm trees swished loudly for a few seconds before the fronds dropped silently back in place. I started to wonder how I would know if this were my last night alive, and what I would do differently if I did. Lots of thoughts passed through my mind, but they all seemed petty and childish. Not to say lewd. Maybe it's better not to know, and to go on doing whatever seems important.

That was all the deep thinking I had time for. Harding had organized a room for the three of us, on account of Kaz's wound and the fact that we'd be sitting ducks sleeping in a hallway, even inside the headquarters hotel. Kaz got the bed, Harding took the couch, and I fell asleep in my boots on top of a sleeping bag on the floor, in front of the door. Like a good guard dog.

I woke up with a groan, and twisted around to get more comfortable. The floor was as unforgiving as a nun with a ruler. Kaz was sitting up in bed, sunlight streaming in through the open bay windows. Harding was gone. He would've had to step over me and open the door right in my face. I guess this sleeping dog had been best left to lie.

"Where's Harding?" I asked. I yawned and grimaced at the same time I tried to straighten up.

"He left near dawn. He ordered me to rest, and I decided it was an order worth following. He said he'd be back by nine o'clock with something for you to do."

"Great. Let me get washed up and I'll get some breakfast for us from the mess tent."

"No need, Billy," Kaz said with a smile as he gestured toward the old-fashioned ornate telephone on the bedstand. "The hotel is still operating and room service is quite dependable. I ordered breakfast which should be here any moment."

"Room service?"

"Billy, just because one is wounded on the African continent in the midst of a war, there is no justification for eating powdered eggs when there are more civilized alternatives. I did have to promise a substantial tip, nearly a bribe, really, but it should be worth it."

"Room service," I mumbled to myself as I unlaced my boots and shuffled off to the bathroom. "What a war."

When I returned, a room service cart had been rolled up to the edge of Kaz's bed. Shiny silverware and real china was laid out for us and we ate eggs benedict, hot rolls, figs, and grapes washed down with sweet black coffee. Or I should say I did. Kaz picked at his food, and worked at keeping up chatter about everything and nothing. He was going through the motions of being himself without putting his heart into it. That didn't stop me from gobbling up everything on my plate, including the figs, which I had never seen before. I was just starting to feel human again when Harding walked in.

"Why am I not surprised?" he said, looking at the room service cart as he helped himself to coffee.

"You said I should rest, Major," Kaz said with a faint smile.

"I'm glad to see my subordinates are following orders," Harding said, gulping his coffee from a china cup. "Now, Lieutenant

Kazimierz, a British doctor will come this morning to check your wound and give you your shot. If he says you're up to it, tomorrow I want you to see what you can find out about organized crime here in Algiers. Find out if Villard and Bessette are involved. Ask who's working the black market. Don't strain yourself, just talk to people, especially your Agency Africa contacts."

"Shouldn't I take that assignment, Major?" I said. "The Vichy cops are more likely to talk to another cop, even if he's an American. Kaz could come along to translate for me."

"I've got another job for you, Boyle. First, we go back to the 21st General Hospital and you question everyone who might be involved in the murders and the drug heist. Lean on them, see if you can shake things up. They won't expect that after we beat feet out of there, so maybe someone will become nervous and run to the smugglers."

"What do we do second?"

"Second, you take a boat trip. To Bône."

"When?" I nearly shouted, quickly remembering to add "sir" in a normal voice.

"You'll leave late tonight, from a Motor Torpedo Boat base about twenty kilometers east of here. British MTBs are going into the harbor at Bône with two destroyers to land the 6th Commando. A battalion of paratroopers will be dropped over the airfield later in the day to capture it. We don't think there are any Vichy combat units in the area, but we can't be sure and don't know if they'll fight if they're there. You go in on one of the MTBs, with a two-man shore escort — a translator and someone to protect you."

"Do we know where the Vichy supply depot is?"

Harding pulled out a map of the Algerian coast around Bône, and spread it out on the bed, covering Kaz's legs. It had a city street map in one corner and just off the dock area was a gray square marked "Le Dépôt de Provision."

"Looks like less than a kilometer from where you'll land," said Harding, pointing to a spot just above Kaz's knee.

"Major, I need the Commandos to seal off that area. If Villard's still there —"

"Whoa, hold your horses, Lieutenant," Harding cut in. He poured some more coffee and walked to the open bay window, looking out over the rooftops. "Do you have any idea what it took to get permission for you to go along on this mission? It's a British show, not ours. I had to call in a few chips just to get you on that boat, so forget about anything else. The Commandos are tasked to take the harbor and ensure none of the facilities are destroyed. The paratroops are taking the airfield for an advanced fighter base, which we need very badly."

"Yessir. Understood." What I understood was that I was going into Vichy territory with two other guys to find a renegade smuggler who had enough troops to hold Diana and twenty-four others hostage. Great.

"Good. Do you have the address of that bar? We can mark it on the map."

I picked up my Parsons jacket, feeling the scorched holes near the collar, and rummaged through the pockets until I found the matchbook. I flipped it over, opened it up, but no address. Just the name and phone number. I shook my head. I held it in my hand and looked at the matches. I thought back to the last time I'd used one, to light Gloria's cigarette. Casselli and I had been racing to give her a light. Then I felt those holes again.

"Give it to me," said Kaz from the bed. I handed it to him and tried to let the thought that was forming in my mind take shape. Kaz picked up the phone and I heard him ask for the hotel operator, then read out the telephone number from the matchbook. I tried not to pay attention as the thought took shape. He had a brief conversation in French, asked a question, said "Merci!" and hung up.

"Sometimes it pays to think like a man who wants a drink instead of like a policeman, Billy. Le Bar Bleu is in business at 410 Rue de Napoleon, which is off the Boulevard Fesch, the main road along the quay at the harbor." He flipped the matchbook back to me and smiled. A happy, debonair smile from the old Kaz. I smiled, too, because something had just made sense to me. I pulled my jacket on and stuffed the matchbook in my pocket.

"Thanks, Kaz," I said as I traced my finger over the map and found the two streets. "That just made things a lot easier."

"Get going, Boyle," Harding snapped as he moved toward the door. "I'm going to visit the central police office and try and find Mathenet. Your orders are being prepared now. You'll need them to get on the MTB base. I'll pick them up and meet you at the hospital at 1600 hours. That ought to give you enough time to question the staff there."

"Will you be interviewing Captain Morgan while you're there, sir?"

"None of your damn business, Boyle. Now

get moving!" With that, Harding slammed the door behind him.

"Billy," Kaz said as he folded up the map on his lap, "there was no reason to anger the Major . . ."

"Yes there was," I said, holding up the matchbook. "I was having coffee yesterday morning with Joe Casselli and Gloria Morgan. I lit her cigarette with one of these matches. And within hours two people were dead."

"She and Casselli both saw the matchbook? And the name of the bar?"

"They could have, if they looked. Maybe it doesn't mean anything. Or maybe one of them did see it and made a connection that started the chain of events that led to two deaths."

"Perhaps Sergeant Casselli saw it. If he was involved with the smugglers, when Villard came for the supplies, he could have told him that an American officer knew about Le Bar Bleu, and Villard decided to eliminate anyone who could link him to the thefts."

"Or," I said, "Gloria saw it and put two and two together."

"In which case," Kaz said, "Major Harding may be in danger."

"No. If she were involved she'd pump him

for information. Which means that if he tells her about this side trip to Bône, I'm the one in danger. All she — or anyone — would have to do is drop a nickel on me."

"A nickel?"

"Make a phone call, tip off their pals. Then when I go in, I get a lead cocktail, compliments of the management."

"A lead cocktail, I like that," laughed Kaz, ever the eager student of American gangster slang. "Very good, Billy."

"Yeah, great. I'm so glad my time in the Army gives you the opportunity to learn new terms for death and mayhem."

"Billy, isn't that what war is all about?"

I nodded. "That's what I don't like about it, in case you haven't noticed."

"You know, I think it is what I am beginning to like about it."

I'd thought he was kidding, but that got my attention. Kaz looked deadly serious.

"What do you mean?"

"You have a home and family to go back to, Billy. The Nazis killed my family and enslaved my country. I've lost the only woman I ever loved, or expect to love. So death? What do I have to fear from death? I have greater cause to fear what else life may offer me."

"You're not going to . . . do anything

stupid, are you?"

Kaz laughed. "Stupid? No, not while I have you to look out for, Billy. You do provide a distraction which keeps me amused."

"Distraction? You've been shot, nearly died, then shot at again. Some distraction!"

"Exactly, I can't wait to see what happens tomorrow."

"Me either. It will help if I'm around when tomorrow comes."

We didn't say much else. Kaz looked out the window. I thought about home. That summed it up, both of us together, in our separate worlds.

Finally, I picked up my gear. "Gotta go, Kaz. You need anything?"

"No, Billy, I'll be fine until the doctor arrives."

"Okay. Do me a favor? If the doc lets you up, check with the Army base back in England at Blackpool and see if there was any funny business there with supplies. Call the Provost Marshal's office for that military district and see if they've uncovered any black market activity."

"Or murder?"

"Yeah. Or murder."

CHAPTER FIFTEEN

Colonel Walton's office looked more like a whorehouse parlor than an army hospital administrator's digs. Thick deep purple drapes hung over the windows, blocking out the sun and heat. Oriental rugs were spread over the floor, and a velvet couch sat next to the antique walnut table that served as his desk. A big, ornate telephone and a glass ashtray stood on either side; otherwise the table was bare. There was a matching table at the other end of the room with six chairs around it. Probably for poker games, although there was a map open on it now. It was a National Geographic map of the Mediterranean, dated 1935. Hardly a top-secret document. On the wall opposite the window, a bookshelf was half-filled with army manuals and a few scattered medical books.

I was seated in front of Walton's desk, waiting for him to finish the delicate business of lighting a cigar. He clipped the end, fired up his Zippo, and pulled on the stogie until it glowed red like a taillight at a stop sign. He finally blew out a substantial puff of smoke and appeared to be satisfied. He looked at the cigar like it was the only thing in his world and smiled. He took his eyes off of it and laid them on me, and the smile faded to a frown. Next topic on the agenda.

"Well, Lieutenant Boyle? What have you found out so far?"

"If I were a gambling man, Colonel, I'd bet it was an inside job."

He went back to puffing on his cigar, and gazed at me through a cloud of blue smoke.

"I am a gambling man, junior, but then you probably know that already." He blew smoke in my direction and looked at the stogie again, rolling it between his thumb and thick fingers. The tobacco leaf crinkled faintly under the pressure.

"Yessir, I do. I know that officers under your command owe you money, and that makes me wonder what they'd do to pay you back."

"Dunbar doesn't have the balls to kill a soul. The rest of them don't owe enough to worry about."

"Colonel, doesn't it bother you that gambling is against regulations? You're the commanding officer —"

"Regulations, hell, sonny boy. This is a war, and we aren't stateside, in case you haven't noticed. I've got a major hospital to run here, as well as being responsible for half a dozen field hospitals just behind the front. This isn't your spit and polish regular Army unit, it's a medical unit, and I make sure it runs as smooth as a baby's bottom. A little recreational game of chance now and then lets everyone blow off some steam. No one's forced to play, and if the brass doesn't like it they can get someone else to be CO. Send me back to England! Who the hell wants to be in North Africa anyway?"

I couldn't find a lot to disagree about. I liked his attitude. Unfortunately, I had just a few hours to prod these folks with a stick and see who jumped the highest.

"How much money did Sergeant Casselli owe you?"

"Listen, Lieutenant Boyle, if you want to run some chicken shit investigation into card games at this hospital, you go right ahead, after you figure out who killed Casselli and stole my drugs. Otherwise, I'm liable to think you're a lazy sonofabitch who couldn't figure out how to pour piss out of a boot if the directions were written on the heel. Now is there anything of substance

214

you have for me?"

"Well, yes, there's something I've been wondering about. How do medics in the field administer morphine? Do they have needles?"

"No, they have self-contained doses in sealed syrettes. That's usually enough to take care of the pain until the soldier gets to an aid station."

"So how do the doctors know how much a wounded GI has had already?"

Walton stopped puffing on his cigar for a second, and looked at me as if he were deciding whether to answer me or throw me out. I waited for him to ask me why I wanted to know all this, but instead his eyes narrowed and he gave me a little lecture.

"Medics are supposed to pin each used syrette to the wounded man's collar so he won't be accidentally overdosed at the aid station. Sometimes, in real cold weather, the effects of morphine may be delayed until the body warms up. When it's a cold night, you can usually count on some nervous medic giving too many doses for the GI's own good. Soon as we warm him up, we have double trouble, the wound and a morphine overdose."

"So what do you do?"

"Give him a morphine antidote, nalorphine. It's a new drug, and works pretty well, unless you wait too long to administer it. Then we treat the wound, and make sure the patient survives both problems."

"Nalorphine, penicillin. Lots of new drugs around here."

"War is the great accelerator of medical progress, Lieutenant Boyle. I sometimes wonder if after all the deaths in battle are added up, we save more lives in the long term with the medical advances we make."

It wasn't what I expected from Colonel Maxwell Walton. It sounded thoughtful, and he wasn't yelling. I didn't like his theory of medical progress, but maybe he was right. I didn't care to do the accounting. I had all I needed. I got up, thanked him for his time, and turned to leave.

"Two C notes," he said.

"What?"

"You asked what Casselli owed me. He's dead, I'm out one good supply sergeant, and short two hundred bucks. Does that make me a murderer in your book?"

"Not much there in the motive department."

The telephone on his desk rang.

"I agree. Now go find someone who's got one." He picked up the phone and barked his name into it.

I left, crossing Walton off my list of suspects for now. He hadn't looked at all surprised to see me, which meant either he was a good actor or he wasn't the one who'd called up a French hit man. He was right about motive, too. There was nothing in it for him, as far as I could see. He could be getting a cut of the take, but all this killing on his home turf seemed too messy. He wouldn't want to draw so much attention to his own command. And how could he be connected to the French underworld in Algeria? Actually, that last question applied to everyone involved in this case. There had to have been some advance work done. I could see Villard and his pals setting up their own smuggling operation to take advantage of whichever way the war went. But how could anyone on the inside of the U.S. Army hook up with them so quickly? I gave up trying to figure that one out and went to look for Corporal Willoughby. Something told me he knew more than he let on about what went on around here.

I left the main building and started to cross the courtyard, heading toward the supply depot, when I caught sight of Willoughby. I started to yell to him, but caught myself. He was headed for a row of supply trucks parked on the side of the road that ran between the hospital and the depot. I could see a work crew loading the last two trucks with crates and cases of who knows what. Willoughby made for the first truck, swiveling his head around to be sure no one spotted him. He was paying attention to the work crew, not me, so I stayed behind him and watched as he climbed in. I trotted over to the side of the canvas-covered deuce and a half where I could hear Willoughby clattering around inside. Maybe he was checking to be sure everything was tied down tight. Or maybe he was pilfering Chesterfields. I decided to wait a minute and let him get deep into whichever it was. Then I walked to the back of the truck and lifted the flap.

"I thought the point was to send that stuff to the front," I said. Willoughby turned, one hand holding the top of a wooden carton, the other in the pocket of his fatigue pants. I was pretty sure he wasn't making a personal donation. I hoisted myself up into the truck bed and made my way down a narrow aisle between stacks of cartons, all marked "U.S. Army Medical Supplies."

"Graduated from Chesterfields, have we, Corporal?"

"It's sergeant, now, sir," Willoughby said, with a certain pride that didn't really match the circumstances. "Colonel Walton decided I should have the same rank as Casselli."

"You won't for long," I said as I grabbed his left arm and pulled his hand out of his pocket. A bunch of little cardboard containers, about as long as your finger, fell to the floor. One was still in his hand and I took it.

"Solution of Morphine, 1/2 Grain, Syrette. Warning: May Be Habit Forming," I read. These were the morphine syrettes Walton mentioned.

"So, Willoughby, are you volunteering for duty as a front-line medic?"

"Sir, this isn't what it looks like," he said, with a wide-eyed nervousness as the thought of going to the front or to prison began to dawn on him. I didn't know which would be worse and I could tell he didn't want to find out.

"Did you not heed the warning, or is this a business deal?"

"I'm not a addict, if that's what you mean," he said, in a disgusted tone of voice, as he leaned down and picked up the syrette boxes on the floor. He put them back in the shipping carton, stacking them neatly, as if he could undo everything by putting them back.

"Addict or thief, it really doesn't matter

now, boy-o, your little racket is done for," I intoned, going for the intimidating sound of a Boston cop making a collar. I wanted Willoughby to look at me and see his entire future in my hands. This might be just the link I needed. If Willoughby had a connection on the black market to dispose of this stuff, he might be able to tell me who else was involved and how the whole thing was set up. If it was for personal use, then tough luck for him. Morphine withdrawal in a cell wasn't anything I wanted to see.

"I don't have a racket, sir."

"Roll up your sleeves and shut up."

He did both and I checked his veins. No telltale tracks.

"Or a habit," he said quietly.

"That's too bad. They might have gone easy on you if you did. Diminished capacity, the lawyers call it."

"Lieutenant, you gotta believe me, I've never done anything like this before. It was supposed to be a one-time thing, just to get a little extra cash!"

"Never? What about those packs of Chesterfields?"

"Aww, come on, sir, with all this stuff lying around, everyone takes something. Couple of cartons get dropped, break open, you know how it is."

I did, but I wasn't going to admit it. It was a tradition in my family among those of us who were cops, which included every male over twenty, that when we recovered stolen goods, there was a right to "spillage." Just the thing Willoughby was talking about. If we caught a guy who boosted a truckload of booze, everyone would go home with a case. I figured that the owners owed us, since we recovered their stolen property. Who's to say that the thieves hadn't disposed of a percentage before we got to them? The crooks wouldn't tell if they wanted to keep the bluecoats from pulling out their billy clubs. I gave up thinking about the good old days and zeroed in on Willoughby.

"You're not playing in the minor leagues here, Willoughby. This is the big time, a felony, not to mention a goddamn low thing to do. Did you ever think about some GI out there, wounded and in pain, and a medic shows up fresh out of syrettes?"

"A felony?"

I could see Willoughby had more sense of self-preservation than feelings of guilt.

"Larceny with intent to sell, and probably some charges related to falsification of records, since I'm sure you signed out a certain amount of supplies to be delivered to the front. You waited until they were out of your jurisdiction and then lifted them, so if anyone discovered it at the other end, the finger would point at the driver or some other poor slob."

"He told me to —" Willoughby caught himself, trapped between the desire to explain away his actions and the fear of implicating someone else.

"Who?"

"Why should I tell you anything? You're going to turn me in, take my stripes, and have me court-martialed."

"That all depends on what I saw in here. I'm pretty sure I saw you stealing morphine from the U.S. Army. But maybe you were checking the shipment and that carton fell and broke open?"

Willoughby thought for a minute, flogging his brain cells to come up with a course of action. I decided to hurry it along a bit.

"Just so you know, we're talking about ten years at hard labor. Or not." That was pretty easy math, even for him.

"Okay. I tell you who and we forget the whole thing?"

"If I believe you, and if it checks out."

"You're not going to tell him I squealed?"

"Ten years. Splitting rocks every day."

"Okay, okay. I get it. It was Doctor Dunbar. He's been after me ever since Joe got killed. He owes Colonel Walton and some other officers. He's been on a big losing streak and he wanted to get even. He told me to take the syrettes after I logged them out of the supply depot. We were supposed to split the take."

"Who is the buyer?"

"I don't know. He said he'd find someone at the Kasbah in Algiers. Officers have been cleared to go into town when they're off duty. I haven't been anywhere since I got here."

He sounded frantic. He knew everything depended on my believing him. Dunbar had managed to keep his hands clean. He could deny everything and Willoughby would be hung out to dry. Willoughby was sweating, little beads of moisture forming on his forehead and cascading over his face. It was hot in back of the truck, under the canvas, standing in the narrow passageway between stacked cartons of supplies. I decided to turn the heat up some more.

"When were you supposed to hand the stuff over to him?"

"Right now. He pulled two shifts in a row and he's off duty for the rest of the day. He was going to head into Algiers and nose around the Kasbah. Let me give him some of these syrettes and then you'll see it was his idea! He wouldn't take them otherwise, would he?"

I had seen honor among thieves, so I knew it existed. But not today, not here, not with this guy. I told Willoughby to give Dunbar half a dozen syrettes and tell him he'd get a lot more tomorrow. Dunbar could take the six samples with him and find a buyer. I was betting that he already had the buyer and was working Willoughby, hooking him with the idea of a one-time heist with no intention of stopping at that. If I was right, I had the connection I needed. If not, then I had a couple of small-time punks.

It sounded like a plan. Just what I liked, a plan, a suspect, clues, the works. The only problem was that I wasn't any closer to finding Diana. I had to be sure to get back here and meet Harding at four o'clock to get to the MTB base in time for my little jaunt. If this lead didn't pan out by mid-afternoon, I'd leave Dunbar with his six syrettes and take off. Willoughby, I had other plans for.

CHAPTER SIXTEEN

A phone call and a jeep ride later I was standing in a narrow, dusty passageway near the entrance to the Kasbah, the Arab marketplace in the center of Algiers. As we neared the market, French shops had begun to give way to Arab shops and the streets narrowed, with an ancient feel to them, as if the centuries were looking down on us. Kaz stood beside me, looking chipper in a khaki sling that matched his tropical British battledress. I looked like a rumpled colonial country cousin in comparison. Arabs swirled around us, their robes and turbans dazzling in all sorts of bright colors. They looked exotic and colorful, until they got close. A glance and a whiff revealed the robes to be filthy and smelly. Flies buzzed around my head and then I figured out what the turbans were for.

A civilian in a dark suit approached us.

"This could be him," Kaz whispered to

me. He had set up a meeting with one of the Agency Africa agents that the Polish government-in-exile operated. Kaz, with his sling, was easy to spot and his contact had given him a recognition code to exchange. The guy in the suit stopped in front of us. He had a black mustache, a couple of day's growth of beard, and blue eyes that darted everywhere, checking doorways and exits. He and Kaz exchanged some French I didn't catch, then shook hands and spoke quietly in Polish for a few seconds.

"Billy," Kaz said, "this is Vincent. He's lived in Algiers ten years, and knows where certain commodities are bought and sold in the Kasbah."

"Pleased to meet you, Lieutenant. I am glad to be of service."

His English was good, very precise but spoken slowly, as if he was thinking about how to say the next few words.

"Vincent, thanks for coming. The guy we're watching for is another American lieutenant, a doctor. He has a small amount of morphine to sell, with the promise of more to follow. He may or may not have a buyer lined up. Any idea where he'd start?"

"There are a few obvious places. He is in great danger though, if he asks openly about buying or selling drugs. One must be introduced by the right people."

"Who are the right people?"

"There are several. The Sicilians are represented in the Algiers underworld. There are two major French crime families, as well. The Grimauds have connections with the nomadic Arabs and deal in smuggling and caravans from the interior. The Bessettes run the docks and —"

"Bessettes? As in Captain Henri Bessette?" I asked.

"Yes, he is part of that family. He used to be a colonel in France, they say, but was demoted and sent back here in disgrace after killing a man. It could not be proved, but the army was not pleased. It is rumored he bribed his way to a staff position here."

"Well, it seems he may be working on his retirement plan. He hasn't stopped killing people either. I saw him bash a French officer's head in a couple of nights ago."

"Bessette's family owns a carpet business. It is his trademark. We know about Captain Pierre Labaule's death. He made the mistake of being an honest man, and reporting the corruption he found. Follow me."

Vincent took us to a seedy little bar on a side street just off the main marketplace. There were a few tables outside, shaded by a covering arcade. It was cool, and we had a good view of the square. Vincent spoke to the Arab waiter and in a few minutes three glasses of hot mint tea appeared.

"The Arabs believe hot sweet tea will cool you on a hot day," Vincent explained. "I've come to agree with them. Try it; it is very refreshing."

"Look, Vincent, I'm sure the tea's great, but shouldn't we be looking for Dunbar?"

"We are," he answered, keeping his eyes on the square as he sipped his tea. "Watch that stall, the one with the red awning at the end of the row. They sell Arab knives and metalwork, but their main business is distributing drugs."

"Do you think Dunbar will show up there?"

"It is very possible. This is a small-time operation, run by Arabs, the Tabriz brothers. They do business with all the organized crime gangs, including the Bessettes. If your doctor asks around in the Kasbah, this is where he would be sent."

"Why?"

"Because if he is with the military police, then no one will care if the Tabriz brothers are arrested. It won't make trouble for the Sicilians or for the French mob. Also, one of them speaks English. It is my best guess. In any event, if Doctor Dunbar has a meeting set up with any of the main crime families, then we would not be able to follow him. Not if we are concerned with staying alive."

"It's a big concern of mine, Vincent, but I don't have a lot of time."

"You are speaking to a man who has lived the last ten years of his life in Algiers, Lieutenant Boyle. I have learned here that we all have the same amount of time." He smiled thinly and sipped his tea, eyes darting across the square. I decided not to debate the nature of time with Vincent and drank my tea. It was pretty good, but it didn't cool me off. I guess it took a few years here to achieve that effect. I wondered how long the war was going to last and if I'd still be in North Africa in a couple of years, an old hand with strange acquired habits, still very far from home.

I tried to not keep looking at my watch, but I couldn't help it. After about the twentieth time, I looked up to see a U.S. Army officer walking among the stalls. He had blond hair like Dunbar's under his fore and aft cap, but I couldn't make out his face or rank. He was wearing a khaki uniform jacket with big pockets, just right for carrying half a dozen small cardboard boxes.

"That could be him," Kaz said before I could.

"If he comes this way, Vincent, we'll duck into the bar and you keep an eye on him," I said as I strained to see between the stalls and awnings in the marketplace. He turned toward us and I could see his face clearly. It was Dunbar, and he was looking over his shoulder, like a guy carrying stolen drugs in a bad part of town.

"It's him," I said as Kaz threw some francs down on the table and we got up to follow at a distance.

"Wait," Vincent said, holding up his hand to keep us back. "He is being followed, see there?" Two bull-necked guys in dark, dusty suits were trailing Dunbar, stopping to look at a stall full of dates or nuts or grapes every time Dunbar looked around. I couldn't tell if they were French or Arab, but one thing was for certain, they weren't there for the fruit.

An Arab kid ran up to Dunbar and said something, pointing to an alleyway at the end of the square. He nodded and dropped some coins into the kid's palm. He went off toward the alley with the two goons in his wake. It's amazing how a guy smart enough to be a doctor can be dumb enough to get in a fix like this.

"He's being hustled," I said, "let's go."

"I must leave you now," Vincent said. "I cannot be involved any further. Your friend Doctor Dunbar is not a very clever drug dealer."

"He's neither. Thanks, Vincent." I heard Kaz say goodbye — or who knows what — in Polish as I trotted across the square, trying not to be noticed by the two big guys whose backs were just disappearing into the dark alleyway.

The sound of a big meaty fist smashing into a ribcage is really unpleasant, but I knew I'd rather hear it than feel it. It came from inside a doorway in the alley, and was followed by a loud thud, a groan, and a yell. I made it to the alley in time for someone to throw Dunbar onto the ground. I could hear the door slam as he fell against me, knocking me down, too. I had my hand on my .45, but there was no one else around except Kaz, a few paces behind me. He pulled Dunbar off me and leaned him up against the wall. The doctor's eye was puffing up and he held his ribs, wincing every time he drew a breath.

"Boyle . . . what are you . . ." That was all he could manage. I gave him the once-over. No broken bones. He had gotten a nice professional beating. No blood on the bad guy's hands, lots of close-in work to the torso. He'd have cracked ribs at the least. No syrettes in his pockets, and no wallet. No shoes, either. That made me laugh.

"Doc, you are one goddamn dumb Barney."

Dunbar moaned.

"Barney?" Kaz asked. "Is that American slang for a doctor?"

"No, it's strictly a Boston term. We call the Harvard boys Barneys, because of the trolley barns that used to be near the university. And this chowderhead is the dumbest Barney I've ever come across."

"The Arab boy . . . he was supposed to. . . ." Dunbar stopped to wince again.

"He was supposed to take you to meet someone who would buy your drugs," I said, trying to finish the sentence for him.

"Oh God," Dunbar wailed, "what have I done?" He started crying.

"For starters, stolen U.S. Army property and conspired to sell it for personal profit."

His face went white. Tears were still streaming out of the corners of his eyes, but he seemed too stunned to take notice. Before I could say anything else, he doubled over and vomited.

"Good thing you don't have those nice leather dress shoes to worry about anymore," I said as I jumped back to dodge the splatter. I grabbed an arm and dragged him back across the marketplace, where the Arabs who didn't ignore us looked at each other and laughed. The whole place seemed to know what had happened. We walked under the arched entrance to the Kasbah and back to the jeep. Dunbar was still out of breath, rubbing his nose with his sleeve, and trying not to blubber.

"It was . . . just supposed to be . . . a one-time thing," Dunbar said, gasping for air as I helped him into the jeep, barefoot, dribbled stains on his tie and shirt, his cover gone. He was definitely out of uniform, which was the least of his problems right now.

"Sure, sure. Now just sit there and lean out the side if you feel sick again." I turned to Kaz, who was surveying the situation with that slightly amused look that usually seemed to be on his face. Around me, anyway.

"Big waste of time, huh?" I said.

"Well, Billy, I think you can eliminate the good doctor from suspicion of being the brains of a smuggling ring."

"Maybe that's what he wants us to think?"

"If so, then I am very impressed by his ability to vomit on command just to con-

233

vince us he is a frightened incompetent."

We both managed a laugh. I heard Dunbar moan a bit as he tried to find a comfortable position and that made me feel better too. I plopped myself down behind the wheel as Kaz pulled himself into the passenger's seat.

"Okay, let's get back on track, Kaz. How's your arm feeling?"

"It hurts, but I'm fine. The doctor said I could have the stitches out the day after tomorrow."

"If you're up to it, can you work on the Blackpool connection?"

"Yes, I was just about to start when you called. Vincent is inquiring quietly about smuggling connections into Tunisia, assuming that Villard and Bessette are selling to the Germans. He also knows dockworkers who may have information about a smuggling route, through neutral vessels in the harbor. He said he's heard of refugees being smuggled into Portugal in the holds of merchant ships flying neutral flags."

"That fits with the Bessette family's control of the docks."

"Yes, but they will have to find an alternate route for the Germans or Italians now that Algiers is in Allied hands. We will search the vessels more thoroughly than the Vichy did, when they weren't bribed to look the other way."

Something in the conversation clicked in my mind. I had no idea what, but something Kaz said started the wheels turning. What was it? Bribes, Portugal, dockworkers . . . ? I had the feeling that somehow he had given me the answer to a big question, but all I could think of was a million little ones.

"Billy, are you listening to me?"

"Yeah, Kaz, yeah, I am. Sorry. What were you saying?"

"I will use the radio link at Headquarters to contact the base at Blackpool and the Provost Marshal's office. Call the hotel and ask for me anytime. The staff will know how to find me."

"I'll bet. In the bar or the dining room, if I know you."

"Are you going to turn me in?" whined Dunbar from the back of the jeep.

"Shut up," I said over my shoulder. "Kaz, I have to get back, unload this bozo, and meet Harding. I'll drop you at the hotel and be in touch as soon as I can."

I started the jeep and gunned the engine as I drove down the narrow street. I was rewarded with a grunt and a groan from Dunbar as he was thrown back against his hard seat. Kaz was laughing as I pulled in front of the hotel and hit the brakes just enough to throw Dunbar around some more.

"Good luck, Billy," Kaz said as the smile disappeared from his face. "Stay alive and find Diana."

He put his good hand out and we shook. There was a lump in my throat. I watched the emotion sweep over his face as he wished for me what he could never again have for himself. I nodded my head, and watched him walk up the steps to the hotel, whistling a tune.

"Can we get the hell out of here now?" Dunbar said. "I need medical care in case you haven't noticed."

How do people turn out so differently? Kaz had lost his family, his country, his true love, was scarred for life, almost killed, and could still wish me luck and whistle as he went up the steps. Dunbar lost his shoes and took a few lumps, had blubbered like a baby, and now was acting like one. Time he grew up.

CHAPTER SEVENTEEN

"It's not just Walton," Dunbar said in between bumps and potholes in the road as we drove to the hospital. "I'm in hock to a couple of other guys too. About a thousand, all told. I had a string of bad luck. Kept making stupid bets to try to win it back."

"And then you hit on this really good idea to break even? Selling morphine meant for the front?"

"Boyle, you should see all the stuff that comes through the supply depot. There's enough for an army!"

I was about to explain to Dunbar how that was exactly the point, but if he didn't understand now he never would. He was one of those guys who put their own problems, no matter how small, in front of everyone else's, no matter how large. That meant I had to make it a big problem in order to get his attention. I downshifted to take a corner, and looked around for a place to pull over. We were on the outskirts of the city where palm trees lined the road and peddlers pulling donkeys plodded along on the shady side of the street.

"Do you want me to shoot you right now, Dunbar, or would you rather wait for the firing squad?" I had to turn my head and yell at Dunbar, to be heard over the sound of the engine and tires in the open jeep.

"That's not funny, Boyle," Dunbar said. He spoke in gasps, as if talking emptied his lungs of air. Broken rib, maybe a couple.

"I think it's hilarious. Nice Harvard boy gets mixed up with gambling and drugs, ruins promising career, disgraces his family. Just the story to amuse an Irish kid from Southie."

"You can't prove a thing, anyway."

"You don't actually trust that rat Willoughby, do you? How do you think I got to you so fast?"

"Jesus," he said, again in that whining, airless voice. "I thought. . . . What am I supposed to do?"

"I couldn't care less. Why should I help you figure that out? What can you do for me anyway, give me free poker lessons?"

"Will you help me if I help you?"

That's what I wanted to hear. But I shrugged. As if I were indifferent.

"Maybe you wandered into the wrong part of town and I happened by at the right time. Or not. It all depends on what you can tell me."

"What about Willoughby?"

"Leave him to me."

"Aw, Christ. What do you want to know?"

"Anything about drug thefts, Vichy officers coming by the hospital, anything suspicious, or even just odd."

"This was the first time I took anything, honest . . ."

"I'm talking about penicillin, the wonder drug, remember? Not your pathetic little pilfering. A real heist. Did you see anybody casing the joint before Casselli got killed? Any other drugs gone missing?"

"Oh. No. I was pretty busy getting things organized. I picked the location for the medical supplies when we first got here, then left it to Casselli."

"So you walked the grounds and chose that spot by yourself?"

"Why do you ask?"

That did it. I pulled the jeep over to the side of the road. We had cleared the city and they hadn't bothered to plant nice rows of shady palms out here. Just sand and a gravelly gully leading to more sand, rocks, and boulders. No Frenchies, donkeys or

Arabs. I took my .45 out of the holster and ran a round into the chamber. That sound always had a nice, threatening ring to it, a metallic *snick click* that meant business. I held it in my left hand, pointing at Dunbar.

"Now listen up, you worthless piece of dog meat. This isn't a social conversation. I ask, you answer. If you answer right, maybe I'll save your bacon. Piss me off again and I'll shoot you and leave you for the Arabs to strip."

"You wouldn't . . ."

I clicked the hammer back. Another *snick*.

"Okay, okay, okay!" He put his hands up in a cross in front of his face, palms toward me. I had found a small-time drug dealer once, with holes in both palms and another where his left eye had been. He was flat on his back, arms outstretched, a Jesus on the pavement. Funny the things you think about at the oddest times. I waited for Dunbar to drop his hands and lowered the .45, but kept it pointed in his general direction and waved it as an invitation for him to keep talking.

"Casselli was with me when we walked the grounds. The place used to be a military base but was closed down. There was plenty of room, we just needed to decide what went where."

"Why did you put the Medical Supply Depot in a separate building?"

"Casselli thought it would be better for the patients, so the loading and unloading wouldn't disturb them."

"So it was Casselli's idea, not yours?"

"Well, yeah, I guess so, now that you mention it."

Any sergeant worth his salt knew how to "suggest" things so an officer thought it was his idea. Casselli was no different. It was no more Dunbar's idea than it was Ike's.

"How long did you know Casselli?"

"He joined up with us about three months ago, in England, after our first supply sergeant deserted."

"What? Deserted? In England? Where the hell did he go?"

"No one knows. Captain Morgan saw him leave in a jeep one night, after lights out, and he never came back. He must've had someplace to hide out."

"Where were you based again?"

"Outside of Blackpool, on the coast. It had a port and we got a lot of our supplies right from the Liberty Ships that docked there. Pretty big operation."

It's amazing how chatty a loaded .45 automatic can make a guy, especially one who's just been rolled in an Arab bazaar. I eased the hammer down and holstered the piece. So Casselli was the second supply sergeant to lose the job, one way or the other. I wondered where the first guy was. I wondered where they'd found his jeep. I wondered what Gloria Morgan was doing out after lights out, and who she was doing it with.

"Okay, let's get you taken care of."

"Are you going to report me?"

"No."

"Thanks, Boyle, I really owe you."

I pulled back onto the road and didn't say you're welcome. I only promised not to report him. If he wanted to feel thankful about that, he didn't have much of an imagination. I did.

Ten minutes later Gloria Morgan herself was comforting poor Doctor Dunbar as Rita taped his chest.

"What were you doing alone in the Kasbah, Doctor? You know we were told not to go there alone," Gloria said. She was patting his hand and her soft southern voice had a singsong lilt to it, as if she was reminding a small child to look both ways before crossing. Dunbar was eating it up.

"I was lucky Boyle showed up when he did. Those two hoodlums took my wallet, my shoes, my hat. . . . Who knows what else they would have done to me!"

He was so amazed at his own luck that he forgot to thank me. He looked to Gloria for some more warm sympathy as Rita caught my eye and pulled the tape tightly across his bruised ribs. He gasped.

"Ow! What are you doing, trying to kill me?" Dunbar demanded.

"Don't worry, Doctor," Rita said, "Billy is here to protect you."

Gloria turned her head, too much the senior officer and Southern belle to laugh at a doctor's discomfort. Rita didn't even crack a smile. I did, for all of us.

"I've had enough of your snotty comments!" Dunbar yelled, jumping up and grimacing as his ribs failed to cooperate. Still, he took a step toward Rita and she instinctively pulled back. This guy could turn mean in a heartbeat, and I wasn't surprised that he took it out on the weakest one in the room. I half turned to get between them.

"You sure you don't need some morphine, Doc?" I asked "You must be in a lot of pain." He looked panic-stricken, stepped back, and regained the little self-control he had left.

"We don't prescribe morphine for minor injuries, and don't call me doc."

He grabbed his jacket and walked out of the examining room. A little stiffly, but with all the grace of a Harvard man. A shoeless, thieving, broken-ribbed Harvard man.

"Poor fellow," Gloria said.

"Yeah, I guess he's just too trusting to be let out on his own."

"If I didn't know better, I'd say you didn't like our young Doctor Dunbar, Billy," Gloria said, drilling me with those killer eyes.

"Oh, he's swell. I'm just a Townie, that's all. We never get along with the Harvard guys."

"But you seem to be the kind of fellow who gets along with everyone, Billy. People around here could learn something from you."

"Thank you, Captain. I'm sure I could learn from them, too." *About theft, smuggling, corruption, and murder.*

Gloria walked out, throwing a look over her shoulder that said she'd be thinking of nobody but me until we met again. She was good. She was so good that she seemed to draw all attention to herself, and it was only when she was gone that I noticed Rita was still here, cleaning up bandages, tape, and gauze left over from patching Dunbar.

"She's meeting your Major Harding, you

know," Rita said.

"I'm not surprised. Apparently they used to be an item back in the States. Does Gloria . . . the captain, I mean, have anyone special here?"

"First, don't worry about the military courtesies here. We're a pretty loose outfit. First names are fine, unless it's Dunbar or Colonel Walton."

"And second?"

"Secondly, Gloria likes to get her way with men. She can twist them around her little finger, in case you haven't noticed. But she hasn't gotten tied down with anyone since I've known her."

"How long has that been?"

"Since we formed up in the States. I was in the first group of nurses assigned to the 21st."

"So you were at the base outside of Blackpool?"

"Sure. We had it easy there. No casualties, occasionally a few patients, leave now and then. It was great."

"Did you know the original supply sergeant, the one before Casselli?"

"Freddie? He was a nice guy. No one could understand why he took off like that."

"What was his full name?"

"Frederick Hotchkiss. Why?"

"Do you think there's anything suspicious about two supply sergeants being taken out of the picture?"

"But Freddie deserted!" She frowned as she tossed the waste into a trashcan.

"How do you know that?"

"Gloria saw him drive out the main gate. He never came back. His personal gear was missing, so it seemed clear that he was gone for good."

"Maybe Gloria was mistaken. Did anybody else see him leave?"

"No. It was late, after lights out."

"No sentry at the gate?"

"No, we're a hospital, not a top secret military unit. People come and go all the time." She tucked a loose strand of hair behind her ear and touched her sleeve to her forehead, leaving little damp sweat spots on the soft green material. She looked tired.

"What was Gloria doing out that night?"

"I don't know, I don't keep tabs on her. You're a suspicious fellow, aren't you?"

"Goes with the job. How about you? Did you kill both sergeants?"

"No, I take care of patients. Doctors kill them." She picked up a tray of instruments, turned, and walked out, giving me an imitation over-the-shoulder look like Gloria's, fluttering her eyelashes.

"Tell that cute friend of yours to come back so I can change his bandages. He's not married or anything, is he?"

"Kaz? No, not married. Or anything."

She gave a little happy laugh as she left. I wondered if people understood how lucky they were when they could just be with someone they cared about. It sounded so easy. I started to think about Diana and suddenly realized that I was alone in the examining room for no good reason. Alone. It scared me. Stuck in a room alone, never able to move on and find the woman I love. It felt like a dream, a real bad dream. Like Kaz, waking up every day to the memory of loss, and the impossibility of ever having anything like the life he had once had. Or Vincent, sitting alone at a bar, sipping mint tea in an Arab bazaar, his homeland more memory than anything else, the dust of Algiers more familiar now than the streets of Warsaw. I looked at the four walls and shuddered a bit. I walked out without looking back over my shoulder.

Chapter Eighteen

I was right on time, Johnny-on-the-spot, with a jeep to take Harding and me east, up the coast to the British Motor Torpedo Boat base. He'd drive back by himself. I thought about that return trip, with Harding alone at the wheel, and I felt as empty as the passenger seat beside him. Feelings of loneliness and fear still had me by the throat. I tried to shake off the willies and looked at my watch and the front entrance to the hospital, again. No Harding. I killed the engine and the sudden silence sprang out at me. I jumped a bit, sat back, then took a deep breath, trying to imagine what lay ahead, on the other side of Harding's solo return trip.

Villard's destination was known to the commander of the Vichy French supply depot at Bône. I'd be there tomorrow, and I had to hope he was the kind of CO who would stay at his post and not retire when the British Commandos on a couple of destroyers crashed the docks. I also hoped he was the kind of guy who would spill the beans about Villard's next stop. Of course, the best bet for a snitch wouldn't be a guy who'd stay at his post when things got hot and heavy. I'd have to get to the depot quickly, ahead of the Commandos, and do some fast talking, courtesy of the French-speaking British officer they were sending in with me.

I looked at my watch again. Harding was late, which wasn't like him. Was he sneaking in some time with his old girlfriend? Come to think of it, that wasn't like him either. That was like me. I was becoming irritated. There wasn't much to count on in this war, but Harding had been a consistent hard-ass West Pointer since I'd first met him in England. Now he was showing signs of being a normal guy, a Buy-you-a-drink-buddy? kinda guy. I didn't like it. I preferred my bosses predictable, so I could rely on them, one way or the other. It only meant trouble for me if he started acting like he had half a heart.

A corkscrew wind blew up and dust gusted around the jeep. I closed my eyes and felt the fine sand pepper my face and force itself into every fold and crevice of my clothes. It

249

was late afternoon and the sun was low in the western sky, pointing long fingerlike shadows toward the eastern hills. Toward Bône, Villard, Diana, and the Germans. It was getting cold, and I pulled up the collar of my field jacket. My body shivered from bottom to top as I jammed my hands in my pockets, and waited some more.

Harding came trotting out of the main entrance of the hospital and jumped into the passenger's seat of the jeep. There was a smile on his face and I thought it was almost funny: It was as if we had somehow traded places and he was the happy-go-lucky Yank in love and I was the grim one, sandblasted and focused on my mission, no time for diversions or stories of lost and found love. All of a sudden I had the urge to punch that smile off his face. I started the jeep instead.

"Sorry I'm late, Boyle," he said as he threw his web belt and gear into the back seat and put his helmet on. I thought about commenting on the fact that I'd never seen him sorry or late before, not to mention both at once, plus smiling. It would have been funny. My kind of trademark smart-ass comment. I didn't bother.

"No problem, Major," I said instead, looking straight ahead, easing up on the clutch and heading down the gravel drive to the main road. There was a convoy passing by, deuce and a half trucks and flatbeds with M-3 Stuart light tanks chained down. We waited as the men and armor rolled along, just like a parade. A jeep with a mounted .30 caliber machine gun brought up the rear, the GIs riding in it wearing goggles and covered in dust.

"Hold up for a few minutes, or we'll be eating dirt like those tail-end Charlies," Harding said. We sat and watched the convoy move down the road, trucks and tanks disappearing into a dust storm that blew down on us like cinders in city soot. More waiting. I felt helpless, frustrated, about to go crazy. I had to say something, anything.

"Did you get to spend time with Captain Morgan, sir?" That's it, get Harding to talk about his lady friend.

"A bit. She told me you pulled Doctor Dunbar's fat out of the fire."

"Yeah. Lucky I came along."

"She also told me you were obviously covering up for him."

"That's one smart lady. Sir."

"Tell me about it."

I didn't know if he was referring to her or if he wanted to hear more about Dunbar. I went with Dunbar. Going over this again might help me figure something out.

"The good news is we can eliminate Dunbar and the supply clerk as suspects in this smuggling operation. They're both small-time operators without enough sense to come in out of the rain. Dunbar got rolled trying to freelance half a dozen morphine syrettes Willoughby lifted for him." I told him about Willoughby and the supply truck and Dunbar at the Kasbah and his gambling debts. It felt good to talk, to take my mind off . . . what? What was bothering me? I couldn't pin it down, but I knew that Vincent had spooked me.

"They don't sound like the throat-slitting types," Harding agreed. "But that doesn't mean they shouldn't be court-martialed."

"I kind of had to promise a few things to get information out of them." I kept my eyes on the tail of the convoy and waited for Harding to blow up. Not that a lieutenant's promise meant much to a major.

"What information?"

"I got Willoughby to admit it was Dunbar put him up to stealing the morphine, and Dunbar told me that their first supply sergeant went missing when the 21st was back in England. He took off one night after lights out. Captain Morgan was the last one to see him."

I let that sink in. For the next minute Harding didn't say a thing.

"What promise?" It took me a minute to get what he was asking.

"I promised not to turn them in."

"Boyle, according to the Articles of War —"

"Major," I interrupted, "I know. They shouldn't get away with it. But why should they sit out the war in a stockade?" He took a second, shifting in his seat, as if he was trying to get used to a new idea.

"What exactly do you mean?"

"Transfers. Willoughby to an infantry outfit at the front, and Dunbar to a Battalion Aid Station, as close to the front as any MD will ever get."

"Aid stations can be dangerous places," Harding said, nodding. "They're usually within enemy artillery range. Should cure the good doctor of his gambling problem. I think I have some paperwork to do when I get back to HQ."

With that, Harding nodded toward the road and I turned right onto the two-lane highway. We picked up speed, the wind whipping around us and biting through my field jacket. It seemed to blow some of the sand away, and the cold wind made my face feel cleaner. I didn't want to punch Harding

253

any more, at least, but that uneasy feeling stayed in the pit of my stomach.

I was glad I had switched to a wool shirt, courtesy of Willoughby's supply stores. He'd also given me lined leather gloves, a scarf, and a wool cap. Kind of a thank you for not having him court-martialed, but I didn't think I'd be getting any more gifts from him. He'd be too busy trying to stay alive, and hoping no rear-area slob lifted the smokes from *his* rations. It felt good for a minute to think about that, but I couldn't keep my thoughts together. Everything was a jumble. Kaz, Diana, Harding — everyone was finding or losing somebody. I didn't like how things were adding up, and I didn't want to be the one to break it to Harding. I downshifted as the road rose up and snaked over a ridge. The wind from the south blew harder, scattering dust across our path. And, I had to admit, I didn't want his reaction to screw up my search for Diana.

"It'll be colder inland," Harding said, pulling out his own gloves. "If you end up in the hills, get ready for some really cold nights. It's almost tropical along the coast here, but don't count on it lasting."

"You can't really count on many things lasting, can you, sir?"

"Guess not, Boyle." Harding looked at me

sideways, trying to figure out what I was getting at. I wasn't much at subtlety, so I didn't say anything else.

"The one thing I can't figure out is the link between the smuggling ring and whoever killed Casselli and Jerome," I said. I switched on my headlights. They were taped over, just a little slit open to let a bit of light out. A precaution against snipers, night fighters and who knows what other dangers up at the front. They illuminated enough of the road to show me what I was just about to run into, but not enough to warn me in time to avoid it. About as logical as the army got. It would protect me against the Luftwaffe spotting me from two thousand feet up, but not against a donkey in the road. I slowed down.

"It might not be the same killer," offered Harding. "And those two deaths might not be connected."

"Maybe not," I said. I thought about Casselli's slit throat, and how that was probably the work of a man. But Jerome's overdose, or poisoning, could easily be a woman's work. It was too soon to suggest that to Harding, and anyway the phantom man and woman could have been working together.

"Jerome was involved in a revolt against the government here. There could be a

255

number of people who'd want him dead," Harding said. "Are you sure there has to be a link?"

"If they were only after morphine, anybody could figure out that a military hospital and medical supply depot would have a lot of morphine on hand. But how many people in French Northwest Africa knew about penicillin before we landed?"

"A few doctors would know about it in theory, but that we can produce large quantities? Nobody."

"Then how come, a few days after we land, a crooked Vichy officer shows up and steals our entire supply? How did he know about it? How could he have hooked up with anyone fast enough to set it up? How did he obtain an American uniform? It was obvious from the crime scene that Casselli knew and trusted whoever killed him. How could he have become acquainted with an outsider well enough to trust him after just a couple of days?"

"Find Villard and ask him," Harding said, as if all I had to do was look him up in the phone book.

"I'll do that," I said, thinking that as long as Villard was the key to finding Diana, I'd damn well find him, and soon. "Meanwhile, can you get to Bessette again and really question him?"

"Not right now. Negotiations with Darlan are still very delicate. We can't grab one of his aides without seeming to implicate Darlan himself. Orders are to keep hands off."

"Orders from who?" I asked, even though I knew the answer.

"Somebody's Uncle."

CHAPTER NINETEEN

The rest of the ride was silent, except for the sound of wind-driven sand pelting the side of the jeep whenever a big gust kicked up. It peppered my helmet as I squinted to make out the bit of illuminated road in front of me. We stopped once at a crossroads to check the map. Harding clicked on his flashlight, cupping his hands over it to keep the light from leaking out into the darkness surrounding us. He hand-signaled left and killed the light. I spun the wheel and headed down toward the coast to the MTB base. The wind was at our back now, beginning to lessen as the landscape sloped down, away from the rolling brown hills and rock outcroppings inland. It was late evening, the only light coming from a half-moon drifting up from the horizon. The stars were splashed across the sky like diamonds on a jeweler's black velvet cloth in a Washington

Street shop. It was beautiful, and I didn't care.

My head was filled with a jumble of thoughts that wouldn't quit, my heart was pumping like a six-inch hose at a four-alarmer, and my gut ached like I had swallowed a bone. There was just too much going on, too many things changing when I needed them to stay the same. I knew myself well enough to know that I worked best on familiar ground. When I knew where I was, and the people around me. I liked things nice and steady, even though I didn't always let on. I always gave officers, whether they were cops or U.S. Army, a hard time when I could get away with it. Someone with more brains than me might ask why I'd gone into law enforcement in the first place. Sure, it was sort of expected in my family, but I could've done something else. Pumped gas, worked down at the docks, any job that didn't have a guy wearing brass telling me what to do. Truth was, I didn't mind it that much. I liked to smart-mouth back once in a while; it really suited me. Everybody, including me, knew what was expected of them. It was like that in the army, too. Except now. Kaz was close to cracking up, I couldn't trust Harding with my latest suspicion, Diana was who-knows-where, and now Uncle Ike was getting in the way of this investigation, which was my only ticket to finding Diana. Plus, I had no idea how the whole thing hung together. I couldn't make it add up. And I liked things to add up at the end of the day. Maybe that's really why I liked being on the cops. It gave me a chance to set things right. Right, the way they ought to be, but never really were. I looked up at the stars and wondered, not for the first time, why did God in heaven leave things so screwed up down here? My Mom would've whacked me good if she ever heard me say it, but God disappointed me more often than He should.

I stopped thinking and started watching the road, which was just as difficult. It had narrowed down to one good lane and I could catch a whiff of salt air. Soon I could make out a white gate in the distance, and a small light glowing in a guard shack. I slowed down as Harding pulled a set of folded orders out of his field jacket, shaking the sand loose as he opened them.

A British Marine, flashlight in one hand, the other resting on the grip of his holstered revolver, stood in front of the gate. Two others stood casually by on either side, holding Lee-Enfield rifles instead of flashlights.

Harding showed the Marine the orders, and he read them like it was his great-aunt's last will and testament. He seemed sorry everything was in order and reluctantly had the gate pulled up. Must've been a slow night. I drove down a gravel driveway, tires crunching on the loose stone, as the smell from the sea grew stronger. Salt and diesel fuel were in the air, mixing with woodsmoke and the faint odor of cabbage. The scent of war.

"Pull in here," Harding said as we came upon a long, narrow two-story building that seemed to be the only intact structure around. The stucco was worn off and the exposed brickwork was crumbling. Weather-beaten wooden doors and shutters hung loose on their hinges. Light leaked out from the rooms around blackout curtains as figures went in and out of the main doorway. There were tents everywhere else, arranged around other buildings that had long since collapsed or lost their roofs. I could make out the docks and pier about fifty feet away, clear enough in the faintly reflected moonlight which danced on waves as they lapped the shore. Low, still, dark forms blotted out the light, six of them, high speed Motor Torpedo Boats. Even at rest, they looked like sleek, impatient killers. They bobbed slightly as the waves rolled under them, as if they were uneasy, straining to be let loose. I already knew something about MTBs, more than I wanted to know, or remember.

I pulled the jeep up in front of the building, killed the engine, set the brake, and let out a long sigh. It just never ended. Things that I thought I would never have to think about came around again and again. They were never gone. It was warmer here right on the coast, but I still shivered. I couldn't shake the cold, just like the last time, out in the North Sea.

"Let's go, Boyle," said Harding. He got out and jumped up and down a bit, trying to shake the sand out of his clothes and gear. He seemed to be about to order me to get a move on, when he came around to my side of the jeep and put a hand on my shoulder.

"Don't worry. It won't be like before. This is just a short hop down the coast," he said. He patted my shoulder like a coach after a pep talk and bounded up the steps to the door. Jesus H. Christ.

I did my own sand dance and followed him in.

We found the exec and gave him my orders. He told me where to find a tent with a spare bunk in which to stash my gear and that we had thirty minutes to grab some chow before the briefing. Of course he was English so it all sounded a lot nicer than that. Unfortunately, the food was also English, so after a plate of boiled beef, stewed tomatoes, cabbage, and Brussels sprouts, we happily left the field kitchen behind for the briefing tent.

The sentry standing guard at the tent lifted the canvas flap for us. The red band around his cap marking him as a Royal Marine made me think about redcoats and that made me think about how my Uncle Dan would curse me out for consorting with the British. Colors were important to Uncle Dan. Green, of course, was good; orange was bad. I remember Uncle Dan, when I was maybe seven or eight years old, explaining why I must never wear orange. That was the color of the Orangemen, he said, and they were even worse than the English, since they were Irish-born. It wasn't until later that I understood they were Protestant Irish. In my child's heart orange was still the color of the devil. My world was divided up into many colors: black and white, green and orange, khaki and blood red, police blue and every other hue. Uncle Dan was a good Irishman, a great cop, and a loyal American, roughly in that order. I had always looked up to him, but in a different way than I looked up to my father. It wasn't merely because he was my uncle, it was because of who he was: a fighter, a rebel, a man who stood his ground. Now he seemed almost quaint, like an old man telling stories of fairies and the little people. This war made everything else fade into the past, losing value as the hard, grinding realities of combat, death, and destruction sunk in.

A gale blew up and the sides of the tent flapped, pulling at the rope lines, straining to rise up and blow away. Pieces of paper flew into the air and half a dozen khaki arms rose up to catch them as they floated around inside the tent. About twenty folding chairs were set up with a narrow aisle in the middle. Up front was a bulletin board with a long map of the coastline tacked on it. We grabbed two seats in the back row and watched the last few stragglers come in. They were a seedy bunch, dressed in a variety of wrinkled and faded khaki or corduroy pants with sweaters and field jackets in various combinations. They wore crumpled white naval caps, various styles of beards, and looked more like pirates than officers in His Majesty's Navy. Of course, these were MTB guys, like our PT boat crews in the Pacific. Which according to the newsreels were all part buccaneer, by way of Ivy

League schools and yachting clubs. Rich kids who knew how to sail and handle small boats, and who were used to giving orders. Probably no different in England.

The oldest guy in the room, almost forty, walked over to the map. He pulled out a pipe and lit up, watching the group as he did so. The chatter subsided and he nodded approvingly. "All right, chaps, listen up. For the benefit of our American visitors, I am Captain Charles Mannering, Royal Navy Reserve. Welcome to Motor Torpedo Squadron 18. Glad to have you along for this little show!"

Mannering smiled and lifted an eyebrow at his audience. "You Yanks will have to excuse appearances here. I'm sure we look like ragamuffins, but the supply ship with our cold weather gear didn't make it. Rather disappointing. So here we are, still kitted out for a nice cruise to Crete or the sunny Aegean. Not that we mind a change of scenery, right boys?"

This was greeted by a chorus of boos, jeers, and laughter. Mannering joined in with the rest of them. He had an easy way with his men, and I could tell they liked him. He pointed at one guy in the audience, raised both eyebrows, and the room rippled with laughter again. A private joke, no words needed, the shared bond of silent understanding. Then he casually raised his hand, a smile still playing on his face. The room fell silent. All eyes were on him. He stood quietly, looking at his men. Something seemed to pass between them, something out of my grasp, perhaps born out of long days under the sun, longer cold nights riding out rough water, and the occasional sudden explosion of water, flame, and steel. Pride and sadness, perhaps, I don't know. Maybe this is what it's like after fighting a war for three years, for those left alive, anyway.

Another little smile and a nod, as if they had all been praying, and the spell was broken.

"We've been over this before, but one more time, if you please," said Mannering.

He picked up a pointer and whacked the map. "Bône. This is the objective. Two destroyers will land 6 Commando at the docks and they will deploy to the town. Bône has intact docking facilities and a key railhead which must be taken. It is our job to cover the landing and insure that no vessel — German, Italian, or French — interferes with 6 Commando getting ashore."

He then went over details of rendezvous points, patrol areas, departure times for each boat, and a lot of other stuff that I didn't pay much attention to. I must've rested my eyes a bit because the next thing I knew Harding nudged me with his elbow.

". . . and that brings us to our American friend," Mannering was saying. "76 Boat will make for the piers at the west end of town, near the warehouses and the French Army supply depot. Lieutenant Dickinson and one crewman will escort him ashore and return to the boat as soon as practical. I'm sure it's all very hush-hush, but good luck to you Yanks. Dismissed."

With the mention of the name Dickinson I scanned the room. Could it be? Last time I'd seen Harry it was off the coast of Norway. Could he be in North Africa? Harding looked at me, his eyebrows knitted in a question that didn't need asking.

"Yeah," I said. "That was his name. Harry Dickinson. But it can't be the same guy."

Everybody was getting up and it was hard to see faces. There were greetings, and a few "Good luck, chaps!" as we stood there. Captain Mannering made his way toward us as the crowd thinned. It was just Mannering, Harding and me, standing amid the folding chairs. The map on the bulletin board was loose in one corner, and flapped furiously in the wind like an ace of spades in the spokes on a kid's bike. The three of us — and Lieutenant Harry Dickinson, Royal Navy Reserve, who stood there, arm extended and shaking, his finger pointed at me like a knife, his rage mounting.

"You!"

"Lieutenant Dickinson!" Mannering said, gaping in disbelief. He grabbed Harry's arm.

"Harry . . ." I began.

"Shut up!" Harry yelled, and then turned to Mannering. "Captain, I don't know what this man is doing here, but a few months ago in England he presented forged orders for my boat to take him to Norway. Two good men died getting him there, and when we finally made it back I found out about the phony orders. He could be a German spy!"

"Harry, you know I'm not a German or a spy."

"Then why did you forge those orders? I looked for you and I know you were taken into custody when you got back. You should be in prison, if not hanged!"

Harry was trembling in anger. His face was red and his hands were balled into fists and shaking. I could tell he wasn't in a mood to have things explained to him. Not that I had much of an explanation.

"Is any of this true?" Mannering said, looking at Harding, not me.

Harding held up both of his hands in a calming gesture. "It is true that the orders Lieutenant Boyle presented at the Royal Navy base in Scotland were not officially authorized. It is also true that his mission there was of great assistance to the Allied cause, and that General Eisenhower himself met with Lieutenant Boyle upon his return. I can't tell you any more than that."

"Have you checked their orders out with Headquarters, sir?" Harry asked Mannering. So much for Harding's diplomatic explanation. While not exactly truthful, it would be hard to say it was a lie.

"I shall, and immediately. Major Harding, would you accompany me to the signals tent?"

"Sure," said Harding. "Lead the way."

They left, and Harry followed them out of the tent. I went after him. I don't know what I wanted to say, but I had to let him know . . . what? That it still haunted me? That I felt guilty? Or maybe that if I hadn't come along he would've gone out on a different mission and his whole crew could've bought it? I had gone over all those excuses a million times. What I knew I couldn't say was that I had gotten him involved because of my own personal desire for revenge, my need to catch Daphne's killer at all costs.

"Harry," I said, grabbing him by the shoulder.

He stopped. He looked back at me, then ahead to Mannering and Harding as they walked away toward a large tent with antennas and wires all around it. He turned and all I saw was knuckles coming straight at me. Next thing I knew I was on the ground tasting warm blood, seeing stars and looking up at Harry.

"Touch me again and I'll kill you," he said.

He kicked up little spits of sand that shot toward me as he walked off into the darkness, nursing his righteous anger, shaking his right hand as if he'd hurt it when I hit it with my jaw. Alone on the ground, spitting blood and feeling the ghosts of dead men at the back of my neck, I couldn't figure out why I should bother to get up. We had been at war less than a year and I had been in the Army less than that, and already I was at the end of my rope. Beat and beaten up. Dead tired and almost dead half a dozen times. I couldn't imagine what it would be like next week, and then next month, if I survived. Why couldn't it be like it was for those MTB guys, all one big family, all in this together and all that crap? Instead, I get knocked on my ass by a guy who was once my friend and now hated me. My other good friend was as likely to blow his brains out as sneeze if he got bored, and it looked like my boss was head over heels with my prime suspect.

I started to laugh. I laughed and laughed, wanting to tell someone how funny it was. I looked around, but there was no one to tell, and that was pretty funny, too, so I laughed some more, pounding the sand with my fist until the laughter was nothing more than a long sigh. I was still alone, the wind blowing sand in my face, listening to the soft, rhythmic sound of waves breaking on the shore. I cupped sand in my hand and let it run out through my fingers, like a kid at the beach. I wanted desperately to see Diana, I longed for her to come and rescue *me*. I wanted to cry. Maybe I did.

CHAPTER TWENTY

"Orders are orders, and yours are as good as they get, straight from Allied Forces HQ," said Harry. "So I'll take you into Bône and wherever you need to go. Don't expect anything else."

Harry wouldn't even look at me while he spoke. Instead, he glanced over his shoulder at the stern as the crew cast off from the dock and he eased his boat out, advancing the throttle slightly, bringing a deep, throaty rumble from the four diesel engines below-deck. As he turned the wheel I saw he had a bandage wrapped around the knuckles of his right hand. I felt the bruise on my jaw and figured maybe we'd come out even, except for the part where I ended up flat on the ground.

It was a beautiful morning. The sea was calm and we were heading east, into the sunrise. I tried to cheer up and convince myself that Diana would still be in Bône and that soon I'd find her. I wondered what the day would bring, and fingered the Thompson slung over my shoulder. I was geared up with extra clips, my .45, a couple of pineapples that hung from suspenders, and an M3 combat knife, in case things got personal. My field pack was stuffed with first aid supplies, cigarettes, socks, and K-Rations. Dressed in warm olive-drab wool, with my Parsons jacket tucked in the back of my web belt, and all that gear, plus the helmet on my head, I figured a life preserver wouldn't do me much good if I went in the drink.

I let the light winds whip around me as the boat gained speed and the shoreline faded into the distance off the starboard side. The air was clean and pure, with the promise of a new day. Salt spray kicked up around us as we sped over the low swells and Harry opened up at full throttle. I breathed in the fresh smell of salt air, and for the first time in a while I felt good, as if things might really turn out okay.

The rest of the squadron was out in front of us, their wakes splitting the sea like arrows pointing the way. I wondered what that would look like from the air. I gazed up, into the deep blue sky, wishing for some cloudy weather to ruin this crystal clear day.

Just enough to keep the Luftwaffe from spotting us. Everyone else looked up too, every chance they had. We were running hard now, the only sound besides the engines was a rhythmic *thump . . . thump* as we sped over the low rolling swells. Behind the bridge were two turrets with twin mounted .50 caliber machine guns. They added a soft mechanical whine as the sailors manning them traversed the skies, watching for a glint of sunlight off metal to buy a few second's warning.

"Tea's brewed up, Captain," came a voice from below deck.

"Bring up two cups, Stubbins."

"Aye, sir."

I took that as an opening.

"Thanks, Harry."

"No reason to be uncivil, is there?"

"Then what do you call last night?"

"Here you go, sirs," said Stubbins, coming up behind us and interrupting my attempt at a heart to heart. "I hope you like it dark and sweet the way Captain does, 'cause that's what you got. No coffee here, sorry to say."

Harry ignored me and stared at the sky. Stubbins held out two chipped porcelain mugs with one hand while he climbed the steps to the bridge. He was bald, scrawny, wore a stained apron over his khakis and looked like he'd been born with his sea legs. He didn't spill a drop.

"Thanks," I said.

"Aye, sir. Anything else, Captain?"

"Yes, ask Petty Officer Banville to join us."

"Aye, sir."

Stubbins stepped down from the bridge and we both sipped the hot, strong tea. I didn't know what to say, but I was glad Harry at least tolerated me on the bridge. I watched him, and he looked like the same Harry I had met just a few months ago, but worn, tired, and thinner. He was about my age, with shiny blond hair that the breeze was blowing in every direction and whipping against his face. He was tanned, lines showing at the corner of his eyes from squinting into the sun, like he was doing right now. He had bags under the bags under his eyes.

"Pretty big boat," I said, trying to make conversation.

"She's a Fairmile D, newest model," Harry said, not taking his eyes off the horizon. "Bigger than the boat I took you out on last. Over 115 feet long with a crew of twelve. She can do twenty-eight knots without even trying. And this time we have torpedoes, four tubes."

"How long have you been with this squadron?"

"Less than a month."

"Why'd you leave your boat in Scotland?"

"I didn't. Keep a lookout, will you?" That was that. We stared at the sky and drank tea.

"Captain?"

We both jumped a bit at the voice, like a couple of nervous Nellies.

"Yes, ah, take the wheel, will you, Banville?"

Harry stepped aside and cupped his hands around the tea mug, planting his legs wide as the boat skimmed the waves. "Petty Officer Banville, this is Lieutenant Billy Boyle."

"Welcome aboard, Lieutenant," said Banville, taking his place at the wheel and looking straight ahead. "I'm going ashore with you and the captain, since I parlez fairly well. I learnt my French working trawlers between Boulogne and Brest, hauling everything from potatoes to scrap metal. Between the docks and the whorehouses, I managed to pick up a good bit of the lingo. I'll do my best to get the point across when the time comes."

"Banville's a good man ashore as well as at sea," Harry said. "I hear he can handle himself in a brawl."

"That's what comes of a misspent youth at sea," said Banville with a wink. There was a scar at the corner of his eye and his nose had been broken at least once. He was a wiry, dark-haired guy with a scrubby beard, a knife on his belt, and a crumpled once-white naval cap on his head. He looked like someone you wanted on your side if you were walking down a dark alley, which we well could be before long.

Banville gave me the once over. "By the looks of that hardware I'd say we should expect trouble," he said.

"I hope not," I said. "We're only looking for a couple of people but I like to be prepared."

He looked at my jaw and swollen lip, then at Harry's bandaged hand. "Good advice," he said, as he turned back to stare over the bow.

"I'm going below for a radio check," Harry said. "We're supposed to contact your Major Harding back at base as soon as we land." He left the bridge and Banville and I remained, swiveling our necks.

"So you knew the captain back in England?" Banville asked.

"We did a job together," I said. "But he doesn't seem too happy to see me again."

"So I noticed. But he's not been that

happy about anything since he got here. Not that any of us are thrilled to be here, but we try to make the best of it. Nothing wrong with a good time ashore now and then, right?"

"Not a thing. What about Harry?"

"Keeps to himself, he does. He's a good captain, no doubt, but he holds his cards close to the chest. Doesn't pal around a lot with the other officers, either."

That didn't sound much like the Harry I'd known, however briefly, back in England. He had been cheerful and even wild, ready to take on the German Navy and the North Sea weather. He had been close with his crew, friendly, and down-to-earth. He seemed distant now: not quite aloof, but detached.

"Something must've happened," I said. "A man doesn't change that much for no reason."

"Aye. Not in peacetime, anyway."

"He said he didn't leave his boat. Any idea what he meant by that?"

Banville frowned and shook his head. "He told us about his runs between Scotland and Norway, and what that was like. Not a mention of his crew, though. I asked him about his boat, and he told me plenty about how it was kitted out, but that was all. Near as I can figure it, something happened that he doesn't want to talk about. Or think much about. Some of the boys are worried he's bad luck, but there's been no sign of it yet."

"He was good luck for me last time we were out," I said.

"Well then, maybe you'll be good luck for him," Banville said.

I knew sailors could be superstitious, so I didn't let on that I hadn't been good luck for some of his last crew. Better to let him think I was a walking rabbit's foot.

We cruised along the coast for another hour, the seas growing rougher as the wind freshened. I watched the squadron ahead of us peel off, taking up positions farther forward to cover the approach of the two destroyers. We kept on due east and then began to angle in toward the shore. The sun was high in the sky, beating down on the rolling water and creating sparkles of light everywhere as waves heaved around us. I had to hang on as the waves grew larger and we began hitting each one hard as we changed course. Harry came up and trained his binoculars on the shore.

"There's Bône, dead ahead," he said. "I

hope the chaps you're looking for are home."

"Me too," I said. "Me too."

CHAPTER
TWENTY-ONE

We watched the two destroyers cut across our wake, making for the central wharf. I could see the dome of a big church beyond the docks dead center, but other than that Bône didn't seem much different than Algiers. Smaller, sure, but with that same mix of regular buildings you'd see in any small city back home, with Arab mud brick houses around the edges. Minarets poked up around the city like fingers pointing to heaven. The destroyers slowed as they approached the docks, guns trained on the shore, seeking out any opposition hidden in the city. No one knew if the Vichy forces were going to put up a fight, or if they'd already fled.

"No sign of the enemy, French or otherwise," said Harry, lowering his binoculars. "Lots of locals standing around and watching, rather like they're waiting for a parade."

"Good," I said. "They'll pay less attention to us."

Harry scanned the shore ahead of us. We were close to a group of dilapidated warehouse buildings, one of which had half-collapsed into the water where the pier it was built on had rotted away.

"Take her in there," said Harry, pointing to a relatively intact dock between two wooden buildings. Banville guided the boat in slowly, as two crewmen stood on the port side holding lines to tie up at the dock, and two others stood at the bow, Sten guns at the ready.

The wooden dock was weathered gray, with broken planks leaving gaping holes over the dark water beneath them. The warehouse seemed to be empty, a rough wooden door hanging open crookedly, swaying on a single hinge. Its rusty corrugated tin roof looked as if the next good wind would carry it into the Sahara, but there wasn't any wind, just the stillness of heat rising from dry wood. With the sun high in the sky, the heat was unforgiving. I tossed my jacket to the deck and took off my extra wool shirt, quick. I rolled up my sleeves and while Harry and Banville fiddled with lines and barked nautical orders to the crew, I hoisted myself up onto the dock and looked around.

As I edged along the warehouse wall to the doorway, I found that the wood was soft and swollen, damp on the outside and rotten inside. The door was hanging from the top hinge, so I knelt down to get a better view, poked the barrel of my Thompson inside, and saw a dozen small forms scattering from a pile of broken crates. Rats. Rats and garbage. The smell hit me just before the flies did, and I backed off, swatting them from my eyes. I stopped myself just before I reached the edge of the dock, waving my free arm like a pinwheel while hanging onto the Thompson with the other as I tried to fan the flies away.

I tried to ignore the laughter from the crew and make believe that my face wasn't turning seven shades of red. Harry climbed up on the dock and only stopped laughing when an insect darted into his mouth.

"Damn flies," he spat.

"Algiers isn't too bad," Banville said, "but most of these smaller towns are breeding grounds for insects and filth." He kept his hand moving in a lazy motion in front of his face. Both he and Harry had leather straps hung around their necks from which Sten guns were suspended. They had replaced their white naval caps with those soup bowl helmets the English wear. Sweat ran in little streams down their temples and necks. I was hot under my helmet, too. It felt like the heat rising from the ground was cooking my head, like cabbage in a pot.

"Let's go," I said.

We walked along the waterfront. A concrete embankment ran along the shore, with wharfs and pilings jutting out into the water, none of which looked like they could survive a normal day's work down at the docks in Boston. A small two-masted boat had sunk at its mooring, rotting strands of rope still tying it to the dock. Palm trees lining the walkway along the embankment had dropped the brown and brittle fronds crunching under our boots. A dog darted out from a shack on the pier, and turned to bark at us once before slinking off into the shade of the palms.

"Where are we headed, exactly?" asked Harry.

"To Le Bar Bleu, 410 Rue de Napoleon, off the Boulevard Fesch."

"A bar?" Banville said hopefully.

"Is this another of your stupid tricks?" Harry asked, stopping in his tracks. The flies caught up with us. I kept walking.

"Le Bar Bleu may be a rendezvous for a

smuggling ring. I need to find out if anything there points to where stolen medical supplies have been hidden."

"All this for a few stolen supplies?" Harry asked, as he trotted up to us.

"It's a new wonder drug that's supposed to cure infections better than anything else, and two people, maybe three, have been murdered over it."

"Frenchies or Arabs?" Banville asked.

"French, pretty well-connected too. The Army and the Gardes Mobiles are involved."

My answers seemed to satisfy Harry. We kept walking along the embankment until it curved left and came to a road. We went on, grateful for the shade of a row of three-story buildings facing the water. They were built of stone, with fancy ironwork grills over the bottom-floor windows which were shuttered tightly, like summer homes in Gloucester when the rich folks went wherever they go after Labor Day. Now we could see the main city pier where the British destroyers were docked. The Commandos were ashore, and things must have been going well. It was quiet.

The road we were following curved away from the water as the buildings grew smaller, packed in more tightly. Stone turned to cinderblock and smooth pavement turned to flat stones, narrowing down to an alleyway marked in the middle with a damp brown stain. The flies found us again. For the first time we saw people, Arabs in white robes with strips of colored cloth wound about them. A group of them came toward us, talking to each other in Arabic or whatever they speak in Algeria. They looked at us as if we were ghosts: interesting, but not of their world. A swirl of robes parted as we passed and closed up again, as if we had disappeared.

We came to a large square, filled with Arabs walking among market stalls and vendors selling leather bags, dates, nuts, melons, and lots more food I didn't recognize. Strange smells filled the air, the stink of unwashed bodies and garbage out too long in the hot sun mixing with spices from the cooking pots in the stalls. Clouds of flies rose from heaps of rotting fruit piled up against the walls. Now I knew why Arabs wore those long cloths they could wind around their faces. Barefoot kids in rags darted around us, in and out of the stalls.

Down one side street I saw two columns of Commandos doing double time, Sten guns held high on their chests, boots clomping to the rhythm of ready violence. We were headed in the opposite direction, moving quietly, our guns, heavy with the heat, pointed down, the grips slippery with sweat that streaked down our arms and pooled in the palms of our hands. I felt dull, hot, and thick as the air. Kids ran around us again, yelling to each other as if they were playing a game.

"Boulevard Fesch," said Banville, pointing to a blue enamel sign with white lettering fixed to the side of a building. We followed him toward the boulevard, and stopped at the beginning of the wide road. It faced the water, another row of solid stone buildings and fancy ironwork denoting the French section. I knew the Rue de Napoleon was one of the first few streets running off to the left. A couple of kids ran by us again. One looked at me and laughed. He smelled to high heaven and had open sores on his leg, but he seemed to be enjoying himself. I watched as he took off to the end of the block and stopped there.

"We're being followed," I said. "By experts."

"Who?" asked Harry, swiveling his head around. Banville turned around and raised his gun. A gaggle of raggedy kids behind us scattered.

"Them," I said. "All those kids. They run ahead and wait to see which street we take.

They've been sending runners off to report to someone. I should have seen it sooner." But I hadn't. Just a bunch of dirty Arab beggar kids, nothing to worry about. Yeah, right. They must have had us from the boat.

"Let's go," I said, and broke into a trot. I knew we couldn't outrun these kids, but at least we could cut down on the warning time they gave. I saw the sign marking the first street and it wasn't ours. I ran faster and caught sight of the next street. Rue de Napoleon.

We hooked left on the run and I started watching the signs hanging in front of the shops and stores that lined the street. This was a French neighborhood, but it was closed up tight, no French ladies shopping for dresses or stopping for lunch while English Commandos roamed the streets. The kid with the sores on his legs darted into an alley on the right. That told me the bar was on that side; he was probably headed for a back entrance.

"Banville, stay here," I said. "Don't let anybody pass, especially any vehicles. Shoot out their tires if you have to." Banville looked to Harry, who shrugged and nodded.

"Aye, sir," he answered, and faded into a doorway, giving himself some cover and shade. I went after the kid, following the alley to the first left turn, and took it, figuring it ran along the rear of the shops facing the street. It was wide enough for one car, if it could make its way around the piles of garbage and empty boxes stacked up against the buildings. The flat paving stones were greasy with the remains of whatever people tossed out of their backdoors, and the smell of heated, rotting garbage rose up and slammed into my nostrils. The insects were back. As we ran by each pile of refuse, fat flies rose up, confused about whether to continue feasting on the slop or to begin to play in our eyes and ears. I tried to ignore them.

I saw a packing crate that looked like it could hold my weight and I jumped up, trying to get a better view down the alley. Ahead, just before the buildings curved to the right, I could see a truck parked, facing away from us. Behind it was a black sedan. I got down.

"That could be it up there," I whispered to Harry. "They must know we're coming, but if that kid didn't spot us, they're probably watching the front."

"And what exactly do you plan to do?"

That was just the kind of question I hated. My only plans were to not to get killed and to find out whatever I could from a contact at Le Bar Bleu. The problem was that there seemed to be more activity there than I had counted on. I knew Harry wasn't keen on this whole side trip, and while he'd follow orders, he'd be the first to point out that bursting into a nest of armed smugglers wasn't included in those orders.

"Let's see what's in the truck," I answered. I took off, staying low and taking cover as best I could as I tried to shut down my nostrils and blink away the flies swarming the sweat dripping down over my eyes. Harry followed, apparently deciding his orders covered a peek under a truck tarp.

We were one store away from the truck and the car. I could see LE BAR BLEU painted above the rear door of the building up ahead. The foul, yeasty smell of spilled wine and the sharp smell of urine mingled with the other odors in the alleyway and I had to work at not gagging. Broken bottles littered the ground and wooden barrels were stacked up against the wall in front of us. I could hear the muffled sound of voices and of doors slamming from inside the bar. Then one shot was fired. Harry and I both looked around, unsure of where the sound came from. Two shots followed, then a burst of machine gun fire, coming from out front.

We looked at each other, wondering if Banville was in trouble. But what we heard wasn't the stuttering metallic hammering of a Sten gun. It was the throaty, rapid sound of a large caliber machine gun, and it was getting closer. I could hear the ricochet of bullets off stone, and the sound of pistol and rifle fire from inside the bar. From the uneven sound of the firing, I knew what was going to happen next. I rose and aimed my Thompson at the rear door.

Five seconds passed before the door flew open, and three civilians wearing black armbands spilled out, trying to get out of each other's way as they rushed toward the truck. They each carried wooden crates with "U.S. Army" stenciled on them in big black letters. That got my attention almost as much as the "SOL" on the civilians' armbands. I took a couple of steps forward, holding the Tommy gun pointed at the guy in the center.

"Halt!" I hoped it meant the same thing in French. The lead guy was almost to the truck, and he skidded to a stop as he looked over his shoulder and saw me. His two pals were a second slower and jammed up against him, knocking him off balance. He righted himself and faced me. Now the three of them were in a row looking at each other, and me.

Holding a gun on a guy with his arms full wasn't the easiest way to make an arrest. It has the value of letting you know where the guy's hands are, and that he's not holding a gun, but it does give him options, like throwing the stuff he's holding at you, which had happened to me once. This was familiar territory, except I didn't know how to say "hands up" in French, which was probably a good thing, since their hands already were up. I asked Harry if he spoke French.

"I can order a meal and a good bottle of wine," he offered.

"No thanks, not hungry."

With the barrel of my gun, I gestured to the ground so they would set the crates down. The first guy said something in French, and they began to bend. Another flurry of shots came from the front and the next thing I knew the three of them dove in front of the car and popped up, revolvers in hand and firing. Bullets hit the wall to my side and I felt one whiz by my head. Then I let go with the Thompson and at the same time Harry opened up with his Sten gun. That drove the SOL guys to ground in between the sedan and the truck. Our bullets riddled the sedan. Glass shattered and flew in every direction. We emptied our clips, then hugged the wall while we jammed new ones in. I signaled Harry to go up the right side while I went up the left. We took off and there were more shots. At least two of the SOL guys were still alive and firing through the broken front windshield. We let go again, stitching holes in metal from one end of the sedan to the other. Now I was mad. Shots from the front of the bar mingled with the noise from our guns. All I could hear was firing and the pounding in my head. Then there was a sudden silence when I ran out of ammo. Smoke drifted up from the car and the smell of gas filled my nostrils. As it did, I heard a thin splashing sound, followed by a much smaller sound, a tiny *whump* and I knew we were in for it. I dove to my right, knocking Harry down as the gas tank exploded, sending a ball of flame over us as the car rose a foot or so off the ground. The sedan settled on burning tires, choking the alleyway with thick black rubbery smoke.

I looked down and there were wisps of smoke curling up from half a dozen spots on my fatigues. I swatted at them and checked Harry. His face was black from soot but he seemed okay. Dazed, but okay. He looked at me and tried to focus.

"I think we got them," he said.

"Yeah, and the flies are gone too," I said, coughing out the last word as the smoke surrounding us grew thicker. I stood, dropped the empty clip and shoved in a new one, working a round into the chamber as I tried to see what was happening near the door. Harry yelled as he tried to get up, and held his leg, blood seeping through his fingers as he pressed his hand to his thigh.

"I've been shot," he said, his mouth opening in amazement as if he had never considered such a thing happening to him.

The door opened and three or four more figures came out firing shots in my direction. I saw a flash of long blonde hair through the smoke and flame. More shots. I had no idea where they were coming from. One guy turned and fired back into the bar, then collapsed as shots from inside found him.

"No," I yelled, "no!"

I dropped the Thompson and ran through the flames blossoming from the wrecked sedan, my right arm over my eyes as I held my breath. Red heat tore at my skin and the fire sucked the air from around me as it lashed at my bare hands. It seemed to take forever to run the length of the car. Finally, I stumbled out of the flames and dropped my arm. I saw a man in a blue uniform, the familiar Gardes Mobiles blue, right in front of me. He was holding a woman, half-dragging and half-carrying her to the truck, his left arm wrapped around her waist. With his right hand he raised his revolver and fired into the bar. As he turned to fire I recognized him. Mathenet. I saw the bit of white bandage on his arm, sticking out from his nicely tailored uniform sleeve. All I could see of the woman was her blonde hair. She was dressed in a khaki coverall, and seemed to be unconscious.

Mathenet saw me then. With a startled glance of recognition, he leveled his revolver straight at my chest and pulled the trigger. Click. Click again. I launched myself at him as he raised the revolver, then felt it smash down on my head. I fell to my knees, intense vivid pain spreading through my skull. I grabbed at his right leg, feeling myself fading away. I held onto it and he had to turn to kick at me with his left. Then I saw her face. It was Diana. She looked down at me, but her eyes were empty. A smile partially lifted her lips. She looked as though she was surprised to see me but couldn't quite place my face, or didn't really care. Then Mathenet's heel connected with the side of my head and it was lights out.

CHAPTER
TWENTY-TWO

I felt something damp and cool on my forehead and almost woke up.

"What a lump . . ."

"Careful, he's burned . . ."

". . . more soot than burn . . ."

". . . damn fool."

I wondered who they were talking about. Then I wondered who they were and tried to wake up to find out. I felt water on my face and hands and managed to get both eyes open. My head hurt. Twice in one week. It wasn't a record for me, but it was enough.

I was in a bar. I looked around and noticed I was actually *on* the bar. A couple of commandos had my medical kit spread out between my legs and were washing my face and hands with a bar rag.

"Thought you was burned right good, sir," one of them said. "But it's mostly soot from the fire, especially them tires. You're a bit red in the face and hands, but it ain't half as bad as it looks. Course, that knot on your head is as bad as it looks, if not worse."

"How's Harry?"

"You mean that RN bloke what got 'imself shot?" the other Commando said. "Just fine. An in and out it was, no bones nicked and no 'eavy bleedin'. If 'e was in the Commandos we'd be asking 'im what the bother was. Seeing as 'ow 'e's Royal Navy, well 'e's entitled to a bit of complaining. Them boys ain't used to using their legs, not like us, right Rodney?"

"Right as rain you are, Corporal."

I thought I understood most of what he said. Harry was okay, but wounded.

"Thanks, guys," I said as I sat up. I fought to stay up as someone pounded my head with a sledgehammer. Rodney grabbed me by the shoulders.

"Hold on, sir, you're going to be a bit woozy for a while. You might have a concussion."

"Are you guys doctors in your spare time?"

"Spare time, that's a good one, sir. We're all trained as medics in the Royal Commandos."

With Rodney's help, I stayed up this time. He was just a skinny kid, but he had a good grip and the kind of confidence that comes from knowing how to maim people twenty different ways, and then bind up their wounds. I looked at the other commando, an older guy, mid-thirties maybe, stocky, with a broken nose and hams for hands.

"Corporal . . . ?"

"Corporal Peter Duxbury, at your service, sir. And this is Lance Corporal Rodney Longsmith."

"Well, Corporal Duxbury, help me down and tell me what happened."

I got down from the bar. When my feet hit the floor the shock went through my body and rattled my head. I took a couple of deep breaths and looked at myself. My hands were black, rubbed clean in a few places where they had checked for burns, but otherwise caked with soot. My uniform had scorch marks on it and my web belt was charred in a couple of places. I realized I didn't know how much time had passed since I'd blacked out.

"How long has it been?"

"Since what, sir?"

"Since I got knocked out!"

"Oh, you've been out about 'alf an 'our, sir."

"Jesus Christ! Where are Banville and Harry?"

"The Chief is in there with his Captain, finishing up the bandaging. We figured you was worse off than he was, so we left 'im to start on you."

Rodney pointed to a side room off the bar. I started walking, staggered, and had to hold onto the wall to stay upright. It was cool to the touch, rough stucco with little framed pictures at eye level. The first one was Petain, then some other old guys I didn't recognize: this may have been the French Fascist Hall of Fame. A small archway, complete with those hanging strands of beads you always see in the movies, framed the entrance to a café restaurant. Inside, Banville was sitting at a table with Harry, who had his leg propped up on a chair. Banville was ripping the end of the bandage down the middle and bringing one end around to tie it off. There was a bottle of brandy, a revolver, and a couple of empty glasses on the table. A cigarette dangled from Harry's lips. They looked like gangsters in a B movie set in the Kasbah.

"Give me a hand, I've got to search this place," I said, and tried to turn around. It didn't go well. Rodney, who had followed me in, caught me before I fell.

"Have a seat, Billy. Have a drink for that matter," said Harry. "I certainly needed one.

Never having been shot before, I wasn't quite prepared for it. Not to mention watching you walk through fire." He looked at me with a question in his eyes, as if he were considering my sanity and coming up a few marbles short.

I ended up in the seat next to Harry, with Rodney pushing, or guiding, me down. I didn't have time to deal with a concussion, but standing up seemed a bit of an ordeal, so I decided sitting was enough of an improvement over being unconscious, for now. Trying to think through everything that happened and get moving at the same time, was too much. My head was pounding and thinking was like slogging uphill through molasses. Seeing Diana like that was way too much. I didn't understand it. What was wrong with her? It was as if she didn't care that I was right in front of her.

I became dimly aware that I didn't know everything that had happened. Where had that machine gun fire come from? What were these two commandos doing here? I looked around at Rodney and into the bar at Corporal Duxbury packing up my medical gear. I turned to Banville and tried to form a question.

"The cavalry," said Banville before I could ask. "I was watching the corner when they came by. Said they were doing some recon, but it seemed to me they were just out looking for a fight."

"Well, the landing was unopposed, sir," said Rodney, rather apologetically.

"They drove up in a jeep with a mounted .30 caliber machine gun," continued Banville, "and we saw those chaps with the black armbands . . ."

"Service d'Order Legionnaire," I said, trying to make it sound French. "SOL."

". . . ah, the French Fascists," said Harry, nodding as if now being shot made sense.

"As soon as we got close," Banville said as he gave Harry's bandage a tug, "they started firing at us. You must've been near the rear entrance. I thought you could use a diversion, so the corporal opened up with the .30 caliber. That sent them scrambling. All right, Captain, try that leg now." Banville patted Harry on the shoulder. He grimaced as he swung his leg off the chair.

"Did anyone look around here yet?" I asked, trying to stand. I made it but I had to grip the edge of the chair. My legs were wobbly, the room spun a bit, but I stayed vertical.

"I've been too busy bleeding," said Harry, who was putting weight on his wounded leg, taking little gingerly half steps across the floor.

"We checked out the rooms upstairs, sir," chimed in Rodney. "No one up there, but we didn't have time to search 'em proper."

"Okay, let's start down here," I said. "Look for any paperwork and any mention of U.S. Army supplies. Harry, take a seat in the bar where you can watch the front and rear entrances. We don't want any surprises."

With Harry in the main barroom, seated at a table with a view front and back, we split up and went through the ground floor. Banville took the restaurant, searching a chest of drawers and a couple of packing crates. Nothing but cutlery and wine bottles. Duxbury and Longsmith eagerly pulled out bottles and the drinking debris that tends to gather on bar shelves. Tankards, playing cards, stacks of matchbooks just like the one I had, a billy club, and a set of brass knuckles were all tossed onto the top of the bar. I checked out a door to the right of the bar, just before a stairway that went up to the second floor. It was the most disgusting bathroom I'd ever seen. There was a hole in the floor and a place for your feet. They could've hidden a fortune in diamonds down there and I'd have passed it up. I held my breath and looked around for a couple of seconds to be sure I didn't miss anything. Nothing but dead flies on the floor. Even they couldn't live in this stench. I shut the door and stumbled backward into the barroom, almost colliding with Duxbury as I let out my breath.

"That place almost made me 'omesick for the old East End, it did," laughed Duxbury, enjoying my discomfort. "Four families sharing one loo, and that backed up often as she flushed. One of the reasons I love the Army. The loo is always scrubbed down nice!"

"Clean toilets, three squares, and new threads. I guess it could be worse," I admitted.

"Square what, sir, if you don't mind me asking?" said Duxbury.

"Meals. Square meals, and threads are clothes." I was glad he had as hard a time understanding me as I did him.

I checked the cash register behind the bar. Lots of francs and notes that looked like IOUs. I lifted up the cash drawer.

"Well, I'll be damned," I muttered. "Wonder who's been drinking their schnapps here?" I held up two fifty Reichsmark notes.

"Blimey," said Duxbury. "Bleedin' Jerries get drinks and we get shot at!"

"Don't seem right, do it?" asked Rodney, shaking his head slowly at the injustice of it all, eyeing the array of bottles stacked up on the wall behind the bar.

"Gentlemen," I said, "it hurts me to say this, but we have to stay sober. We're going to need you to drive us somewhere after we finish here."

"Yes, back to the boat," Harry said, his eyes on the open front door, where a dead SOL guy was doing double duty as a door-stop.

"No, to the French Army supply depot," I corrected.

"Billy, I've taken a bullet in the leg on this little expedition of yours, and now it's time to get back. I need to have this taken care of."

"Well, sir," Rodney said carefully, "it was an in and out. Keep the flies off of it, change that bandage tonight, and you'll be just fine."

Harry didn't look pleased. He frowned and turned to check the rear door. I reached into the cash drawer and counted out the francs into three equal piles. I gave one each to the Commandos and the third to Banville as he came in from checking the kitchen.

"No use in letting collaborators and smugglers keep their profits, boys. Sorry, Harry, but officers aren't supposed to loot."

"No one is supposed to loot," Harry answered, but he didn't say anything when Banville rolled his francs into a wad and stuffed it into his pocket. The Reichsmarks went into my pocket, but not as loot, since I didn't plan on being anywhere where they'd be valid currency in the near future. Just souvenirs.

"Let's go upstairs," I suggested, and took the narrow stairway from a little nook to the right of the bar, my paid assistants following me while Harry stayed below on guard, a sour look on his face. There was something bothering him, and it wasn't having been shot. I wondered about what had happened to him, and his boat, back in England. I didn't know why he was here, but I knew he wasn't in the Mediterranean for his health. Something had brought him — or chased him — here. But that was a problem for another day.

The landing on the second floor was a big room, a loft with bare wooden beams at angles on either side, forming part of the roofline. There were open windows under the beams, letting a breeze flow through and displaying a view of the rooftops of the mostly single-story buildings below. Orange tiles, rounded white stucco, and tarpaper mingled together in a combination of European, North African, and shantytown architecture.

Against the far wall was a door, and I could tell there was a small room tucked away behind an interior wall. We spread out, walking through the large room, shuffling aside crumpled newspapers with our feet. Other than scattered papers and a few empty cardboard boxes, the space was empty. It had the feel of a place that had been cleared out. The papers and boxes weren't stacked and covered in dust. They looked as if recently they had been tossed aside by someone in a hurry. There were ground-out cigarette butts on the hardwood floor, the paper still white, the ash smudged across the floorboards. My guess was, this is where they had kept the drugs and other stolen supplies. When they heard about the commandos landing at the dock they'd started clearing out, and we'd hurried them along when we showed up.

But what had Diana been doing here? This whole place was a big waste of time so far as I was concerned if there was nothing to tell us why Diana had been here. As I approached the door to the small room I was itching to blow this joint. I turned the doorknob and kicked it open, standing back in case someone was hiding inside. It was empty. The door slammed against the wall and bounced back, almost shut, startling me as I started to enter the room. Peeling paint the color of pea soup cracked and flaked off on my palm as I held the door open. It was a narrow, long room, created by throwing up a wall across the end of the loft as cheaply as possible. The interior wall wasn't finished off, and sharp points of nails showed where they had broken through the thin wood slats. Through an open double window the warm breeze blew the dirty, stained curtains up from the floor, where they fluttered lazily for a second before falling flat, waiting for the next little gust to start. Always moving, going nowhere.

There was a table to the right, and a mattress on the floor to the left. I went to the table first, and pushed aside a plate of stale bread, black olives dripping in green oil, and a piece of hard, yellowed cheese. This disturbed a couple of fat, slow moving flies at their feast and they halfheartedly lifted off to buzz my face. An open bottle of brandy stood on the desk and a couple of empties had rolled into a corner of the floor. I pushed around a stack of newspapers, yellowed sheets that looked like invoices for liquor shipments, and old magazines. Nothing. An ashtray overflowing with cigarette butts and burned out matches sat on top of a small metal box. I moved it and coughed as I waved away the cloud of ashes that drifted for a moment in the stagnant air when I set it down. The room felt close and airless, even with the windows open. The air had nowhere to go and all the old smells of food, dust and cigarettes had settled, coating every surface with their odors. Something else, too. Sweat?

Banville was somewhere behind me and I could hear Rodney and Duxbury chatting outside the room, in accents so thick that it seemed like a foreign language, different enough that unless I concentrated, they could've been speaking Chinese for all the sense it made to me. I opened the box.

"Jesus," said Banville in a half whisper, as I looked inside.

"Lieutenant, you should see this," Banville said, standing over the mattress.

"In a second," I told him.

The box held writing paper, envelopes, stamps, and a couple of pens. I dumped the contents out. All blank, except for one page. It was the start of a letter, addressed to a Monsieur Baudouin in Algiers. It went on but the address was all I could make out. I turned to give it to Banville.

"Can you translate . . . ?" I stopped. He had pulled back the rough brown blanket that covered the mattress. I glimpsed a bit of blue fabric caught up in the folds of the blanket. There was no sheet. The mattress was stained rust red with dried blood, not a lot, just enough to show that someone had been beaten and left there. On the floor next to the mattress were a couple of small tubes. They looked familiar. I felt sick. My face went white-hot and my hands started trembling. It seemed I was watching myself, looking down on this other guy who was starting to fall apart.

"Solution of Morphine, one half Grain, Syrette. Warning: May Be Habit Forming," I said, from memory. I didn't need to read the label on the used-up tube.

Banville nodded and motioned with his thumb toward a big tin can, like those big tins of peas they use in the mess hall. It was empty, the label long gone, doing service as a trash can. Inside were a half-dozen empty syrettes. And a couple of used condoms.

I wanted to turn and run and keep going until I hit the boat, take off, and leave this goddamned country behind. Instead, I closed my eyes and took a deep breath. I opened them, turned around, and knelt down by the mattress. Now I knew what that other smell was. Not just sweat, but the musky smell of sex and fear. I shook the blanket until the piece of light blue fabric fell out. Sky blue, to match her eyes. A four-inch ragged strip with lace along the collar, delicate and feminine, but the dark splotches of dried blood were horrible and masculine, as were the ripped buttons and torn stitching. I laid it down gently on the floor, and tried to remember for certain if that was the blouse I had seen Diana wearing a few days ago. Nothing came to me, no image of her. Just him.

"Here," I said, handing the unfinished letter to Banville. "Tell me what this says later. Now get out of here."

"What do you mean? I can translate it now if you want."

I went over to the table, gathered up the blank papers, and old newspapers and magazines, and threw them on top of the mattress. I grabbed the bottle of brandy and shook it out over the paper-strewn mattress.

"What the hell are you doing, sir?" asked Banville, his voice rising with every word. I could sense Rodney and Duxbury in the doorway, attracted by his tone of voice. I dropped the empty bottle, knelt down, and picked up the torn blouse. I brought it up to my nose to try to recapture her scent, to feel a connection with Diana. The ruined cloth gave back nothing but the dull metallic smell of dried blood and the thin feathery feel of torn stitching.

I reached into my pocket and pulled out the matchbook. Le Bar Bleu.

"I told you to get out," I repeated.

This time Banville did as he was told, pushing back the two commandos as well. I fumbled with the matchbook, finally pulling out a match. My hands weren't shaking anymore, but everything felt slow and difficult. I wasn't angry. I just knew what I had to do. Burn this fucking place to the ground.

I struck the match and threw it on the brandy-soaked papers. There was a small *whoosh* and crinkling of paper as the blue flames danced along the curled edges of newsprint, bills, and blank sheets of stationery. The blanket caught fire and I kicked it with my boot over to the window. The flames climbed up the curtains as the breeze fanned the fire and it began to eat at the peeling paint on the wall.

"Lieutenant!" Banville yelled, his hand on my shoulder pulling me back. I shrugged him off, holding the pale blue fabric in my hand for a second longer, before I dropped it in the flames.

CHAPTER TWENTY-THREE

I walked out of the room with flames at my back. Smoke roiled along the ceiling and chased us to the stairs. Duxbury and Rodney clomped down the steps, their boots and combat gear adding noise and weight to their confused retreat. Banville was alongside me, his arm behind my back as if to prevent me from returning to that little room. He glanced down the stairs at Rodney who was looking up at us, eyes wide with fear and incomprehension.

"After you, sir," Banville said, as if he were holding a door open at a fancy hotel, or maybe a sanatorium. The smoke was turning the air gray and the flames were starting to run along the dry wood beams of the ceiling. It was time to go.

"Sure." I took the stairs slowly, trying to regain a sense of connection with the people and things around me. But all I cared about, all I could think about, was Diana. Diana in that room, and Villard. And how he was going to suffer. For what he'd done to her, and for how he was making me suffer now. For making me want to kill him even more than I wanted to be with Diana.

The air began to clear but I knew it wouldn't last, that as soon as the fire burned along the roofline, it would spread down the walls, dropping embers that would eat at the floorboards, opening gaping, black charred holes that would suck up the fresh air and turn it into bright flames, devouring everything that just moments before had been solid, permanent, dependable. And leave a smoking ruined mass of rubble, one or two beams left, holding up nothing but air.

I reached the bottom and waited for Banville who was a couple of steps behind me. He walked by me, the air current created by his passage drawing a little puff of smoke behind him.

"Captain," he bellowed as he turned the corner into the bar where we had left Harry. "We've got to leave, now."

He seemed to be taking over, with one officer wounded and the other loony. Rodney and Duxbury trotted after him, knowing the voice of authority when they heard it. I trailed them into the bar. Banville was helping Harry up and Rodney was already at the door, scanning the street to see if it was more dangerous than remaining in a burning building.

"What's going on? I smell smoke." Harry looked to me, then Banville, who had hoisted Harry's arm over his shoulder and was helping him hop towards the doorway.

"There's a fire," Banville answered, in a noncommittal tone. Harry shot a look over his shoulder at me. He locked onto my eyes and didn't let up. I had to turn away.

"Why did you start it?" Harry asked.

I picked up my helmet and put it on. It felt solid, heavy, blessedly real. I felt like I was waking up from a nightmare although I hadn't been asleep.

"It's a long story."

"Bloody hell."

I could tell he wasn't satisfied with my answer, but that was nothing new. We left the bar and walked into the street, the heat jumping off the white paving stones, a hot bright haze floating up to our eyeballs. The fire behind us was crackling and popping now, the smoke and sound attracting a crowd. Arabs chattered to each other, and a few Frenchmen pointed to the burning building, their arms waving wildly as they signaled to a vehicle coming down the street. It was an ancient fire truck, a hand-pump job that would've been an antique at the turn of the century.

"Let's get out of here," I said. No one disagreed, and as Banville helped Harry into the passenger seat of our jeep Rodney swiveled the .30 caliber machine gun toward the crowd. The barrel was tilted up toward the sky, but the message was clear. The crowd backed off. Duxbury pulled out as the fire truck rattled up behind us. They were starting to work the hand pump as we turned the corner, a dirty gray column of smoke marking the sky behind us.

"Which way to your boat, Captain?" Duxbury asked Harry.

"We're not going back to the boat," I said, before Harry could respond. "We're going to the French Supply Depot." I unfolded a map and pointed to a spot about three kilometers from where we were. "Here."

"What's so important about that depot?" Harry asked, wincing a bit as he held one hand over his bandaged leg. "Or that bar? Why did you set it on fire?"

"The depot is part of this investigation. It may be a rendezvous for smugglers."

"I thought the bar was the rendezvous?"

"I was wrong." I couldn't say anything more. I looked at the buildings ahead of us, more whitewashed Arab houses, and palm trees lining the road, which had changed to hard-packed dirt after we left the French section of town. I moved around in my seat to get comfortable, and to avoid Harry's eyes. Rodney, Banville, and I were crammed in the rear of the jeep, and Rodney took up a lot of room with the .30 caliber on its swivel. I didn't want to explain; I just wanted to get my hands on Villard.

"Who was that girl?" Harry asked. He wouldn't let up.

"Which girl?"

"The one you raced through fire to reach, when you thought she might get hit. Remember her?"

"Yeah. She's connected with this."

"You know her."

"Yeah."

We came to an intersection, and Duxbury stopped for an Arab leading a couple of donkeys weighed down with packs. He crossed in front of us slowly, the donkeys clip-clopping along and the flap of the Arab's sandals keeping time. Slow time. He didn't even look at us, as if jeeps, machine guns, and soldiers were merely part of the scenery. One of the donkeys lifted his tail and dropped a load as he passed. Kind of a salute.

Harry raised his hand before Duxbury could take off.

"Wait," he said, waving his hand to ward off the gathering flies. The donkey shit was putting out an all-points bulletin, and a few curious incomers buzzed us before diving into the feast.

"I'm senior officer here," Harry said, "and —"

"At sea," I said. "You're senior at sea, but now we're on land and this is a U.S. Army operation. You know the orders."

"I've been thinking about those orders. They looked as good as the phony ones you gave me in Scotland."

"But you checked with Headquarters, right? And they verified them?"

"Yes," Harry admitted, "they did, but these chaps don't know what you're capable of. I don't trust you, Billy. There's something decidedly odd about that girl and you."

"Let's find us some shade," said Duxbury, and gunned the jeep through the intersection, down a narrow lane that ran alongside railroad tracks. Houses and buildings thinned out here, and Duxbury pulled over into a grove of palm trees and green shrubbery. He faced me and kind of squinted as if to see me more clearly.

"Keep a sharp eye, Rodney," he said. "Now sirs, why don't you explain, real simple like, so's I can understand, what this is all about? Rodney and me, we'll take you where you need to go, if it's all on the up and up. If not, then maybe we'll just take you back to our CO and let 'im sort things out."

I climbed out of the cramped back seat, took my helmet off and poured water from my canteen over my head. It was hot. My head was hot and it still ached. I didn't want to face a bunch of questions from some tight-assed English officer and end up cooling my heels while Villard took Diana to some other place, some other room. I tried to calm down, feeling the water soak into my shirt, mingling with the sweat that dripped down my neck, spreading a warm dampness across my chest. I took a breath.

"Captain Dickinson and I met in England, Scotland, actually. I used forged orders to hitch a ride on his MTB to Norway. But these orders are legit," I said, pulling the folded papers from inside my shirt. They were limp with my sweat.

"Two men died on that trip," Harry said. His statement hung in the air. Rodney and Duxbury were exchanging looks that seemed to say, There's two of us, too.

"Forging official orders ain't an easy thing. 'ow'd you do it?" asked Duxbury.

"I didn't have to forge the whole thing. I had a set of orders from British headquarters giving me authority to investigate a murder. They ran for several pages, instructing all units to render aid as required. I just pulled one page and substituted another in its place."

"So what you handed me was real, except for one page?" asked Harry.

"Yeah. It was another guy's idea. He said that if the front and back looked real, no one would question the contents."

"And the Captain 'ere checked out your orders for this mission, you said?" Duxbury asked me. I didn't reply. Something was eating at me. Something I had just said reminded me of something I had seen. Orders. False orders hidden within real ones. Front and back. What was it?

"Lieutenant?" Duxbury said.

"Yeah, yeah. He checked them out. Right, Harry?"

"Yes, but there's something strange going on," Harry said to Duxbury, pointing his finger at me. "How did he know the girl at the bar, the one that French policeman was dragging out the back door?"

"She's English," I said.

"That right? The Vichy copper got 'imself an English girl?" Duxbury's face took on a questioning, threatening look.

"There's more to it than one English girl," said Banville, leaning in from the back seat. "That letter you found in the upstairs room, addressed to Monsieur Baudouin. It was a ransom note."

My mind was struggling to keep up with all the ideas flying around. Ransom letter. Okay, Villard is holding the kids hostage, trying to make some francs on the side by getting their families to pay up. But which one of them had no family to pay up? Diana, since her false identity probably didn't include actual parents in Algeria. There was nowhere to send a ransom letter for her.

"The letters!" I blurted out.

"What bloody letters?" Harry said.

"The letters I saw in Bessette's office. There was a letter to Jules Bessette, Blackpool, England on his desk. It was addressed and sealed, but not stamped."

"Has the heat gotten to you? Or are you still concussed?" Harry asked.

"No, no, listen, listen! Bessette is a captain at French Army HQ. I broke into his office a few nights ago, don't ask how. He had letters on his desk. One was addressed to a Mademoiselle Bessette in Marseilles, another to Jules Bessette in England."

"So, he keeps in touch with his family," Harry said.

Everything came together in my head and I tried to assemble my thoughts. But they were all jumbled up.

"It was talking about orders that made everything click. About hiding something within something else. I remember that the letter to Jules Bessette wasn't stamped. That's because the Bessette family has another way of getting letters to England. Bypassing the censors. Bessette is corrupt, and so is the entire family. They run the docks and operate a smuggling operation from here to Portugal: people, drugs, whatever has value. I couldn't figure out how they geared up so fast to grab the morphine and penicillin, but they were told about the arrival of the drugs by letters smuggled to them on neutral steamers, just like they smuggled in anything else."

"Slow down a bit, Lieutenant," Banville said. "What does this have to do with the ransom letter you found upstairs?"

"Nothing and everything," I said. They all seemed slow and stupid. "When you mentioned the letter it all fell into place. Villard and Bessette are in this together, aided by someone who knew about the penicillin coming to Algiers, someone on our side. Bessette supplied the information, which reached him via his smuggling operation from his contacts in England. His brother Jules lives in Blackpool, which is where the U.S. Army hospital now in Algiers was based. Jules got the lowdown from someone there, then passed it on via their smuggling route. That's why there was no stamp on the envelope. Some sailor just walks off the ship when it docks in England, licks a stamp, and mails it there. No censors to worry about. On the return route, they use the same method." I took a breath and looked at the four of them. Furrowed brows, sideways glances, but I could see they were trying to think it through.

"Then 'ow does this English girl fit in?" Duxbury asked.

I supposed there was no reason why they couldn't know about Diana. They were Royal Commandos.

"She's SOE, sent down here to help organize the revolt against the Vichy regime. They failed and she was taken prisoner with those French kids. Villard is working all the angles, so he's extorting the families for a payoff to release their sons and daughters. Only she . . . Diana . . . doesn't have any family here."

"So he found another use for her," Banville said. No one else had seen the room. "He used morphine on her and raped her."

The words were cold and hard. I wasn't ready to hear them said out loud. I shied away from the jeep and the eyes looking at me. My guts twisted and I felt dizzy, like I was about to faint. I grabbed the trunk of a palm tree and steadied myself.

"Do you mean to tell me that this damn Frog is stealing drugs from our 'ospitals and using them on a brave English girl and then 'avin' 'is bleedin' way with 'er?" Duxbury's voice rose with each word, as if he could hardly believe what he had heard.

I nodded. I couldn't speak.

"Then what the bloody hell are we waiting for?" Rodney asked, his hands clenched tightly on the machine gun.

"Get in, Billy," Harry said, in a sad voice. "We're still on land, this is your show."

I doused my head with water again, washing away the tears I prayed they hadn't seen. I got in, put on my helmet, and checked the clip in my Thompson as Duxbury gunned the jeep out of the palm grove and into the fading heat of the day.

CHAPTER
TWENTY-FOUR

The railroad tracks led directly to the supply depot. Duxbury parked the jeep behind a low building that was crumbling into the ground; it was hard to tell where the back wall ended and the pile of rocks began. Banville and I crept along behind it until we could get a good look at the entrance to the depot. We were on a small rise and could look down into it, over the tops of scrub brush that hung onto rocky soil sloping up from the tracks by the front gate. A barbed wire fence encircled the place, or so it seemed. I couldn't see the back, but the fence I could view in front and along the sides was over six feet high. The main gate was open, and three trucks and a couple of cars were parked inside randomly.

"Looks like the headquarters building to the right of the entrance," said Banville, shielding his eyes from the sun. "And a barracks beyond that. That's a garage on the left."

"Yeah, lots of activity, too." The HQ, barracks, and garage formed a U-shape, facing the gate, leaving a wide-open area in front. In back of the barracks were rows of warehouses. Men were running to and from the buildings, and others were bringing up boxes and crates from the warehouses, loading them into the trucks parked in the main courtyard.

"Is that the only entrance?" I asked.

"Far as I can see," said Banville. "Which means it's the only exit."

"Looks like they're getting ready to pull out."

"That's odd," said Banville.

"What is?"

"Those are all SOL blokes down there. Those fellows with the black armbands. Where are the French soldiers? This is an army depot, right?"

"You're right." I scanned the perimeter and didn't see any guards, no one standing sentry duty, no officers watching in the shade. Just guys in civvies with SOL armbands.

"Let's get back to the jeep," I said.

"You guys got any wirecutters?" I asked

Duxbury and Rodney when we reached them.

"I'd be caught dead without 'em," said Duxbury. "Caught dead, get it?" He reached into his pack and pulled out the wirecutters, the handles wrapped in black electrical tape. "Heh, heh, good one, eh?"

"You're a regular Bob Hope," I said as I took the cutters.

"Do you have a plan?" asked Harry, who, reasonably, didn't want to get shot a second time.

"Sure. Give me five minutes and then drive around to the front of the depot. You guys keep them occupied up front while I go around the back. Banville will explain the setup. Don't get too close, but make sure they see the machine gun. Don't let anyone out. I'll cut through the wire and see if I can find Diana."

"We'll get their attention with a burst from the .30 caliber," Rodney said, "that'll let you know we're in position."

"That's a plan? Cut the wire and fire a burst from a machine gun?" said Harry.

"Got a better idea?"

"Go get more commandos?"

"No time. They're getting ready to pull out now. You guys have got to get their attention and keep them from leaving. If you have to shoot at the trucks, shoot the tires out. They may have prisoners in some of them."

"He's right," said Banville, nodding agreement. "There's not much time."

I took a long drink from my canteen and then left as much of my gear as I could with them. I took one grenade and three clips for the Thompson. I had my knife on my belt and the wirecutters stuffed in my pocket. I tossed the canteen to Harry.

"Good luck," he said.

I ran down the street and crossed the railroad tracks, crouching low. The rail bed was raised up a few feet, with a drainage ditch running along each side. Keeping the tracks between me and the depot, I scuttled along, peeking up now and then to get my bearings.

I made it beyond the entrance area, past the garage, opposite the backs of the warehouse buildings. There were guard towers along the fence, but nobody was standing guard. I heard the .30 caliber let loose, one long burst, our knock on the front door. I heard a lot of yelling in French and a few return shots fired, and saw half a dozen SOL men from the rear buildings run toward the entrance.

Grabbing the wirecutters from my pocket,

I ran over the tracks, stooping, head down, and went straight to the fence. My boots kicked up dry dust and I prayed nobody was paying attention as I started on a bottom wire. The first snip sounded like a cymbal clanging. The taut wire gave out a twang that I was sure they'd hear all along the fence. I kept snipping, using both hands on the cutters to get good pressure. Snip. Twang. How could they not hear this? I was glad Rodney had taped the handles. My palms were sweating so much the bare metal would've slipped or flown out of my hands. I cut about three feet up and then worked down the other side, taking about a square yard out of the fence. If I had to pull Diana through here I'd need enough room to do it fast. I went through the hole easy. Now came the hard part.

I ran to the back of a storehouse and flattened myself against it. I could make out voices in the courtyard but couldn't tell what was going on. Ten yards farther along the fence stood one of the guard towers. The platform, about ten feet up, had a corrugated tin roof for shade with a railing around the side. They may have used the towers to watch the wire for anyone breaking in to steal supplies, but if I reached the platform it would give me a good view of what was going on inside too. There was a fair chance no one would bother to look up, so I ran for it.

Up the ladder I went in no time, crouching low, trying to squeeze myself behind the corner post. I peered around the side and could see over the tops of the storehouses and into the courtyard. The trucks and cars were lined up now, reaching almost to the gate. There were maybe ten SOL guys milling around. The door of the headquarters building opened and two uniforms came out. Gardes Mobiles. One big guy and one dapper Dan. Villard and Mathenet. It was too far for a burst from the Thompson, but I was tempted. Villard stopped and pushed Mathenet, pointing to the gate. Mathenet didn't seem too eager. There was a lot of hand waving and pointing toward the jeep. Finally, Villard rested his hand on his holster as two of his thugs came over and bracketed him. That settled it.

Mathenet walked towards the gate. I could see the snout of the machine gun over the top of a low stone wall, about fifty yards from the entrance. Duxbury had chosen a good spot. He had cover for the jeep and men, with room for the .30 caliber to have a clear field of fire. Rodney shot a short burst toward the entrance, three rounds kicking up columns of dust exactly in the middle of the road, between the doors of the open gate. Mathenet was less than ten feet away. He got the message. He stopped and cupped his hands to his mouth, yelling something in French, then in English, but I couldn't make the words out. Someone yelled back, Banville, I think, about surrendering. Mathenet looked toward Villard, who signaled some of his men to follow him. They went toward the garage. I eased myself down the ladder, hoping everyone would stay focused on that front gate.

I worked my way toward the barracks building which was set back from the entrance, between the garage and the headquarters, and lifted my head to peer into the first window. It was at the end of a long room lined with bunk beds, footlockers against the far wall. It looked just like every barracks I had seen so far in the army: neat and tidy, a drill sergeant's dream.

Staying low, I ran along the wall, down to the first window facing into the next room. Same setup, except the place was a mess. Unmade beds, footlockers open with the contents strewn around the room, and two SOL men sitting at a table, smoking. What were they doing in there with all the action going on outside? I ducked and ran the length of that room.

Two more windows at the end of the building. I raised my head again, and peeked in, grabbing onto the windowsill, the gritty, peeling paint crumbling beneath my fingers.

I saw Diana. She was lying on a bed, hands tied in front of her. There was another bed in the room, a desk, and a table. Officer's quarters? One SOL guard stood at the door. Diana didn't move. The guard left, maybe to check on things outside. Diana's head turned toward the doorway as she raised her bound hands to her face to pull at the knots with her teeth. I felt my heart race. She was awake, aware, and active! Should I tap on the window to signal her? I couldn't take the chance. If the guard heard, it would be all over.

I considered my chances. Three guards that I knew of inside. Maybe one more at the main door, which was within plain sight of the courtyard. But if no one was at that door, there was a chance I could get inside. If I could take care of the man guarding Diana, quickly and quietly, we'd be out the window and home free. Sure. If my luck held, and if I could do it, fast and silent. I pulled my combat knife from its sheath, held it in my right hand, and steadied the Thompson hanging from my neck with my left. Quick. And quiet. Don't think, just do what they taught you in Basic Training. I'd seen the results dozens of times on the beat — only back then it was a crime. Now it was me with the knife in my hand, heading for some slob who didn't know he was enjoying the last minute of his life. If I succeeded.

I heard the sound of an engine racing. If I acted now, the noise would be a distraction. I stood, took off my helmet, and strolled around the corner of the building. Someone might notice a slouched, running figure out of the corner of his eye. But walking casually, as if I owned the place, I might not draw a second look. I held the Thompson slung down at my side, the knife held blade up in my palm. I could see guys getting into their trucks and others running around, yelling and pointing. I made it to the front of the barracks and turned right. No one looked at me. Three more paces to the door. I mounted the wooden steps and turned the handle. It was dark inside. It took a second for my eyes to adjust. I was in a corridor that ran the length of the building. I shut the door behind me, kicking it closed with my foot to keep both hands free.

It was too loud. A voice, in French, came from the room Diana was in, off to my right.

"Albert?"

"Hmmn," I grunted, and flattened my back against the wall, as I heard the shuffling of heavy feet, and in a second the large form of a man filled the doorway to the room. He was holding his rifle by the barrel, dragging it along the floor as if he couldn't be bothered to pick it up. I pivoted on my left foot and brought my right hand around in an upward arc, driving the knife between his ribs and into his heart. He looked surprised, his mouth hung open for a second, and then I felt a weight pressing down on my hand as his legs trembled a bit and gave out from under him, so that all that was holding him up was the knife blade in his ribs. The rifle dropped from his hand. I stopped it with my foot so it wouldn't make a racket. I eased him down, grabbing his shirt with my left hand so he wouldn't hit the floor like a sack of potatoes. His eyes sought me out and a small sound escaped his mouth, a gasp, or a last word, I don't know. By the time he was flat on the floor he was dead, even though his eyes were still locked on mine. I went around him and pulled his body into the room, so it couldn't be seen. When I drew out the knife, thick blood dripped from the blade, drops splattering on the dead man's face. I focused on the knife, not wanting to look at him. Everything seemed like it was happening in slow motion, and now I couldn't get back up to speed. The air itself felt thick, slow and deathly.

"Billy. Billy!"

Her voice snapped me out of it. Diana was sitting on the bed, holding up her hands, which were still tied with a thick, knotted rope, although she had chewed part of the rope almost through.

"Hang on," I said as gently as I could.

I started to wipe the blood from the knife on my pants, then thought better of that and wiped the blade on the shirt of the guy on the floor. I had expected to feel something more, but it had happened too fast, there was too much to manage, the weight of him, the rifle, the need for silence. Then the stunned aftermath. And now Diana.

I went to her, knelt down and whispered, "Be very quiet. We're getting out of here, now."

She stared at me, as if my words were hard to understand. Then she nodded, slowly. She held up her bound hands. I brought up the knife to cut the rope. There was still sticky blood between my fingers.

The front door to the room began to open. I backed away from Diana and stood against the adjacent wall, next to the corpse. She lay down again in the position I had seen her in through the window.

Mathenet strode in. He went right to the desk, to the left of the door. He hadn't seen me or the body. He opened a drawer with a key and took something out, put it in his jacket pocket and picked up a briefcase from under the desk.

"Jean?" he called out as he straightened up. I had the Thompson leveled at his gut. He opened his mouth again but no sound came out.

"If you don't want that nice uniform all messed up, then do what I tell you."

His face went white. He nodded.

"Shut the door," I said.

He did. Diana sat again, holding her hands out to me. I cut through the rope, and I saw Mathenet's eyes dart to the guard's body and back to the knife.

"What do you want?" he said.

I was about to say, to get the hell out of here in one piece, when I heard yelling and footsteps outside. Loud engine noises reverberated in the courtyard again, and then the door flew open, in the midst of a torrent of French from Villard. He stopped in mid-sentence when he saw me, one hand on the doorknob, the other at his holster.

"No," I said.

Moving the Thompson to cover him, I debated killing him right then and there, but we needed to make a getaway and pissing off a dozen or so SOL thugs by gunning down their boss would not help us. Diana walked over to pick up the dead guard's rifle.

"No," I said again, for her benefit.

"Lieutenant Boyle, once again I must protest your interference with purely French internal affairs. Formulation of charges will have to wait though, as we must be on our way. Lieutenant Mathenet, give me the briefcase," said Villard as he held out his hand.

"Not so fast," I said.

"What are you going to do? Shoot us? Then what? You will be dead within the minute."

"It's not a very good plan, I'll admit, but it does have something going for it," I said.

"What is that?" Villard said with a sneer.

"You'll die first."

He laughed. "You are too gallant to sacrifice the life of this young lady in order to kill me," Villard said. "Come, Mathenet, now!"

Mathenet was still thinking. He didn't have Villard's bravado and his indecision showed. Villard took a step toward Mathenet and grabbed him by the collar. I tried to keep my aim on Villard but he ducked behind Mathenet and then propelled him toward us, as he snatched the briefcase from his hand. The door slammed behind him as Mathenet bumped into us. Diana went down, her rifle firing into the ceiling. I staggered, trying to keep my balance as Mathenet struggled to untangle himself from her, but I steadied myself a split second before he broke free and gave him a rap on the head with the butt of the Thompson. He fell to the floor just as the door opened and two SOL goons spilled into the room. I pulled the trigger and sprayed them with the Tommy gun. They went down with arms and legs flailing. Smoking cartridges littered the floor and now there were three dead Frenchmen in the room plus one who was unconscious. It was getting crowded.

I lifted Diana. She still looked dazed, not quite sure where she was.

"Are you hurt?" I asked, my eyes on the door.

"You came for me," she said. "I was dreaming about you. . . . You were on fire."

"I'll explain later. We've got to blow this joint in a hurry. Come on."

"Wait." She knelt and unbuckled Mathenet's holster. She pulled out his revolver, cocked the trigger and held it to his head.

"No!" I said. "I need him. I need his evidence."

"He injected me, kept me drugged. I won't let him escape." The barrel was still pointed at his temple.

"No, he won't. We've got the exit covered, but you and I need to get out now!" I grabbed her arm and pulled her along. She held on to the revolver but she followed me. We stepped over the twisted bodies of the two guards in the doorway. I had expected the SOL to send reinforcements, but no one else was in the building. The other barracks room was empty, the only sign of life two cigarettes in an ashtray burning down, the gray smoke curling up from them, left by the two dead guards.

I heard a faint, muffled yelling coming from somewhere. Then, from outside, a loud noise of engines again, and machine gun fire. It sounded like a full-fledged battle. Maybe the rest of the commandos had arrived. I ran to the doorway, signaling Diana to stay low, leaned around the door-frame and saw a bright muzzle flash as bullets hit the wall just above my head, wood splintering, concrete from the walls spraying me with gray dust.

I lay in the hallway, my head buried under my arms. What the hell was that, I asked myself.

"Armored car," said Diana.

"Whose?" I said.

"They have an armored car in the garage. An old model, from the First War."

"Damn!"

I sneaked another look. The armored car was there all right, moving up to the front of the line with its machine gun chattering, firing away at the jeep from behind the safety of steel plate.

Villard must've given us a parting shot with that burst. Now he was focused on the exit, and forcing his way through. I ran toward the gate, wondering if I could get close enough to lob a grenade under his vehicle. Then the tarp on the back of the last truck in line flew up; more rifles than I could count were pointed at me. I dove and rolled to the side of the headquarters building as bullets sang past my ears. Lying flat on the ground as more shots dug up dust and dirt, and slammed into the wood at the corner of the building, I caught a glimpse of Diana, still standing in the doorway. She had her revolver up, the grip cupped in the palm of her left hand, squeezing off carefully aimed shots at the guys shooting at me. After the fourth shot, they turned their fire on her, and she dropped to the floor.

Slugs from the SOL men peppered the doorway. I stood and fired a burst at them, then ran around the back of the headquarters building, discarding the empty clip and ramming a new one in as I went. The shooting died down. As I peered around the corner, I could see the armored car going through the entrance as Duxbury backed up the jeep, wisely retreating. There was no way four men in an open jeep could take on an armored car. Villard led the procession, the column of SOL trucks and cars following. I could have peppered any of them, but I didn't know which held prisoners, who were now hostages. And without the machine gun firing to cover me, the SOL riflemen would gun me down in a minute. I watched the column disappear down the dirt road, out toward the desert.

Diana! Had she been hit?

She was alone. With Mathenet, and he was the only link I had to Villard now. I ran to her, hoping not to hear a single revolver shot.

CHAPTER
TWENTY-FIVE

Diana was inside the room, unharmed, leaning against the desk, reloading the revolver. She had emptied Mathenet's cartridge pouch and tied his hands, using the same rope on him that she had been bound with. He had a nasty cut on his forehead from where I'd whacked him, but he was awake, murmuring in French and wincing every time he moved his head.

Diana didn't look at me. She chambered the last round and closed the cylinder. I touched her shoulder and she flinched.

"Sorry," I said. "Are you all right?"

"I'm glad you're alive." She reached up and touched my arm, to be sure I was real. Her hand didn't linger. As if she couldn't wait to trade the feel of flesh for steel, it closed around her other hand which held the revolver.

"What now?" she said.

"Watch him for a minute. We have friends

outside."

I went into the courtyard, saw Banville on foot at the entrance, and the others waving from the jeep. I waved back and they drove in, parking in front of the barracks. I heard muffled shouting, but I couldn't tell where it was coming from.

"Is there a basement in this building?" I shouted to Diana.

"Yes, I'll show you, if you find someone else to watch Mathenet."

I told Duxbury to guard our prisoner. I thought he was faking now, waiting for us to leave him alone. Rodney stayed on the .30 caliber, Harry with him in the jeep, complaining about his leg. Banville came with Diana and me.

"Anything we can do to help you, Miss?" he asked Diana, trying to take her arm, as if she were crippled. She jerked it away from him, giving him a startled look, her eyebrows raised in a question.

"Help me get these men out; they've been down in the cellar for two days." She led us into the other room of the barracks, where the SOL men had been posted and pointed to a trapdoor closed by an iron padlock, attached to a ring on the floor. We could hear pounding and yelling more clearly now.

"Who are they?" Banville asked.

"Twelve men from this post," Diana said quickly. "The others were called away on some pretext, then Villard and his men took over. I think he still has the key."

"Stand back," Banville said. He took out his Webley revolver and aimed at the lock. The first round dented it, the second shattered it. He lifted the door.

French soldiers poured up from their underground prison, shielding their eyes from the light. Carefully, they hoisted up their captain. His face was bruised, his uniform tunic stained with blood. They helped him to a chair. He issued orders. I couldn't understand what he said, but I could tell they were commands by his tone of voice and the way his men jumped to. Most scurried off, while one man brought him water. He drank and only then seemed to notice us.

"Americans?" he asked.

"American and British, sir. Can you tell me what happened here?"

"My name is Captain Victor Gauthier, and what happened here is a crime."

"What exactly do you mean, sir?" I asked. One man's crime may be another man's natural exuberance.

"My men and I were ready to welcome the Allies and join the fight against the

Germans. We are not among those who believe in collaborating with our enemy. When that Gardes Mobiles officer came here with his orders, we had to obey, to give him food and supplies, to house his prisoners. Orders from Headquarters," he said, almost spitting out the word.

"Signed by Captain Bessette," I added.

"Yes, how did you know?" He looked up, surprised.

"There's no shortage of crime here, Captain, in your army or mine."

"I refused to obey his orders when I saw his treatment of his prisoners," Gauthier said.

I tensed, wondering what he had seen. I watched Diana. She was seated, her expression blank.

"What treatment?" I asked.

"He is a criminal, a corrupt policeman and — *contrebandier* — smuggler, yes?"

I nodded. He had Villard pegged.

"Villard used some of my men, whom he took prisoner, to move supplies he has stolen to an outpost in the desert. From there, he makes contact with the Germans, or Arab caravans that buy from him and take the goods to Dakar."

"Where is this outpost?"

"That I do not know," said Gauthier,

shaking his head, his eyes fixed on the floor. "Villard thought I did and had me beaten. Then he threw me, with my remaining men, into the basement storeroom. I think they would have killed us — left us to starve or suffocate — if you had not come."

"Thank you, Captain," I said. "Allied forces landed at the harbor in Bône this morning. We'll be glad of your support." I tried to sound like Major Harding. He was good at this diplomatic stuff.

We left Gauthier in the care of his men and walked back to see Mathenet. He was sitting on the bed, holding his head in his hands.

"Take your jacket off," I told him. He looked at me dully, as if he were trying to gather his wits. Maybe that knock on the head had been too hard.

When I raised the butt of my Tommy gun as if I was going to hit him again, he wailed in a high-pitched voice. "Yes, yes, please do not strike me." He had his well-tailored jacket off in a flash. I grabbed his left arm, ripped open his shirt cuff and rolled up his sleeve. A gauze bandage covered his forearm.

"How's the shrapnel wound, Lieutenant?"

"It is healing well, why —"

I ripped off the bandage. It was as I had

expected. "Ever see such nice, neat, straight shrapnel wounds?" I asked. Banville and Duxbury leaned over and stared at Mathenet's arm. Diana didn't take any notice. She sat near the desk, holding the revolver in both hands, as if in prayer. I looked at Mathenet again.

"Can't say as I 'ave, sir," Duxbury said. "Looks like a razor or knife cut to me."

"Aye," said Banville. "Shrapnel makes a nasty, jagged cut, not like these wounds."

"It was shrapnel," said Mathenet, "I was caught in the air raid —"

"You were cleaning up loose ends for Villard," I said. "Just like you were doing here, fetching his briefcase like a trained dog. And what did he do? How does he reward you?"

I let go of his arm and pushed him down onto the bed.

"He uses you for a shield, gives you up, and runs for it. He cared more for that briefcase than he did for you."

"What do you want of me?" Mathenet said, his voice catching.

"I want you to hang for the murder of Sergeant Joseph Casselli."

"You cannot prove that —"

"You're right, not on the basis of those cuts alone. If that were all I had, I'd shoot you right now. Anybody here mind?"

"Never had much use for coppers, never mind Frog coppers," growled Duxbury.

"I'll do it," said Diana, the pistol clasped between her hands.

"Miss," Banville said, "perhaps you should wait outside —"

"Perhaps you should mind your own damn business," she snapped back. She looked up, angry, her lips compressed and her eyes narrowed, staring Banville down, daring him to offer assistance or sympathy again. He didn't.

"As I was saying," I announced, trying to get the interrogation back on course, "all we need to do before bringing charges is to find out who stitched up your wound and thought up the shrapnel story."

"What does your hospital staff know of war wounds?" Mathenet said dismissively. "You Americans know nothing and act as if you know everything. France has been in this war since it began!"

"I don't think a crooked, murdering Vichy cop should speak for France. Not for men like Colonel Baril and the Dupree brothers! Did you kill Jerome Dupree as well?"

"No." He started to protest, then caught himself. "I think I recall a Dupree from the prisoner's list, but he was reprieved at the last minute."

"Who did kill him?"

"I know nothing about that."

"Where is Villard's outpost in the desert?"

"I have not been there."

"I didn't ask you that. I asked you where it was."

"Truly, I do not know. I have never been there," Mathenet said with a desperate edge to his voice. It was hard to tell if he was lying. He sounded sincere, but I couldn't tell for sure.

"Were you Villard's second in command?"

"He was my superior officer, yes."

"No, I mean in his smuggling and ransom operation. I have written proof of this racket." That caught him by surprise and deflated him. His head fell back into his hands.

"He should not have left me."

"It was a lousy thing to do," I agreed.

"I thought coppers stuck together," said Duxbury.

"They do, in the States. A guy would never toss a fellow officer to the wolves."

Mathenet may not have quite understood the part about wolves, but he got the point.

"He left me because he thought he had what he wanted," Mathenet said, with a hint of pride. He raised his chin and looked me straight in the eyes for the first time.

"So, you outsmarted him?"

"He's too pathetic to outsmart anyone," Diana said, in disgust.

There was nothing I wanted more than to take her in my arms and comfort her. I could still hardly believe I had found her. But dealing with Mathenet wouldn't wait. He was off balance now, having been abandoned by Villard after being clonked on the head by me. Now, when he was softened up, was the time to get him to cooperate. The way to accomplish that was to convince him I was his best and only hope. That was going to be hard to do with Diana threatening to blow his brains out with his own gun. It made it hard for him to concentrate.

"Excuse us for a minute," I said to Mathenet. I glanced at Duxbury, then back at Mathenet. Duxbury nodded and moved in front of the door.

I walked over to Diana and put my arm around her shoulder. "Let's go outside," I said.

She shrugged off my arm. Her lips were pressed together yet she was trembling. She was on the verge of breaking down but pride wouldn't let her lose her self-control. She looked at Mathenet and at me. Her mouth opened as if she was going to say something. Nothing came out. She wheeled and walked out of the room. I followed her outside.

She stood in the courtyard, her face lifted to the sky. Her eyes were shut.

"This is the first time I've been outside since you saw me in that courtyard in Algiers," she said. Her voice was calm, her face relaxed. She seemed to have left her tension inside.

I moved close to her and took her hand, still holding the gun, in mine.

"You don't need this anymore," I said. "We'll protect you."

"Nobody protected me from Villard," she said. "Who else was looking for us? What took you so long?"

I didn't expect to be thanked for her rescue, but I wasn't prepared to answer that question. She pulled her hand away.

"Things got complicated. And we didn't want to blow your cover." I stammered to a halt.

"My cover didn't matter. We were all working for the Allies. Those students risked their lives. With thousands of troops coming ashore, why couldn't you just . . . just come and get us?" Her voice broke and she turned away from me.

"I'm sorry, Diana. Harding said you'd be freed as soon as they worked out a deal with Darlan."

"A deal? They're making a deal with that fascist? What was it all for if they're making a deal with these people?" She gestured with the pistol toward the barracks, Mathenet, her memories. "Why did we attempt a coup? People died, you know, Billy."

"Diana, I don't make the rules. I would have come for you sooner, but I had my orders. Once I knew the smuggling operation was connected to Le Bar Bleu and this depot —"

"How did you know I was here?" she asked.

"We found orders at police headquarters in Algiers directing Villard to bring the prisoners here, and then move them to another base in the desert. Do you know where that is?"

"No, but I heard him talk about it. We were supposed to be taken there in a few days. He was waiting for some kind of shipment first. But wait a minute, I don't understand. You knew Villard was bringing the prisoners here. But how did you find out about his smuggling operation?"

"There was a theft of supplies from the army hospital in Algiers, and two murders. I found a notebook page, with the name of Le Bar Blue and a password on it: Le Carrefour, the crossroads. We figured the bar was a hideout for the smugglers, so Harding had me sent, along with the British Commandos, on this mission to capture Bône. We've taken the town. . . . I mean the commandos have."

Diana's squinted and her forehead wrinkled. She was trying to work something out, but it looked like she was having trouble. She'd been drugged and couldn't have been thinking clearly. Which was why I wanted to get that pistol away from her. She paced back and forth, holding her free hand up to shield her eyes from the sun. She scuffed up dust, kicking at the ground as she thought.

"What you're telling me, Billy, is that no one cared enough to come after us right away."

"What do you mean?" I asked, knowing exactly what she meant.

She confronted me. "Villard was stealing drugs from the army, so they sent you after him. I only *happened* to be here."

"You're right." There was nothing else to say. I could explain about how I angled to be sent to Bône, how I would have lied through my teeth to come after her, but it didn't matter. She knew how the war worked.

"So the rest of the prisoners, the ones no

one will ransom, what happens to them? Does anyone care if they live or die?" Her voice rose into an hysterical pitch.

"Diana, you were on a mission. It failed. It wasn't your fault. You're safe now —"

I knew as soon as I spoke the words that I'd made a mistake. It was the same thing that had happened to her before, as a FANY on the destroyer laden with evacuees from Dunkirk. She was caring for the wounded on deck when they were hit, and sunk. She had been on a mission. It failed. They died in the water. It wasn't her fault then either. But here she was, still alive, while the others were dying. It seemed as if it was long ago, in another world, but it was really not quite six months ago, in England, that she had told me about her nightmares. She stood on the deck of a sinking destroyer, and huge waves would wash the wounded overboard. She'd try to save one and just miss him as he went over the side. Then another, and another, until the destroyer sank while she floated, peacefully watching the bobbing heads disappear, one by one.

"I was so confused, Billy," she said, tears streaking her face. "I didn't know if I was dreaming or if what happened to me was real. I'm not even sure if *this* is real."

She began to back away from me. As the

gap between us widened, fear flooded me. I could feel the blood pumping in my head. I took one step closer and she retreated a step.

"Diana . . ." I implored her.

"He kept giving me drugs and everything seemed so pleasant and peaceful and then it didn't. I dreamed awful things. I think I dreamed you were walking through fire. Or did that really happen? It couldn't have, could it? I mean, here you are."

I held out my hand, trying to keep it from shaking.

"Stop, Diana, just stop. We'll find the others, and free them, I promise."

"Yes. Find them, Billy. Save them."

Her hand holding the pistol rose, slowly. I could only watch it, carried upward by that strong and graceful arm, in an arc I knew would end in oblivion. I tried to move, to launch myself across the distance separating us, but I knew there wasn't enough time to reach her. I kept my eyes on hers, willing her to stay with me. But there was nothing to lock onto. Her eyes looked right through me to some other place, somewhere else she wanted to go to.

I didn't see Harry dash toward her until he tackled her and they both fell onto the sand. There was a melee as they struggled for possession of the gun. He pushed it away from her, down onto the ground. Diana was thrashing and kicking and screaming. I ran and picked up the pistol before she could seize it again.

"Get him off me! Get him off!" she screamed.

Harry rolled to the side, holding his wounded leg with both hands.

"Get off!" she screamed again, pushing at the air with her hands. I flung the pistol away and knelt at her side, trying to take one of her flailing hands in mine.

"Get him off me, please," she cried. She drew her knees up to her chest, went limp and covered her face with her hands. I cradled her so her face wouldn't rest on the sand.

"It's okay, it's okay now. I'm really here. And I will find them. It'll be all right, everything will be okay," I said, lying over and over again, in my gentlest voice.

CHAPTER
TWENTY-SIX

Diana was quiet as we got her into the jeep. Rodney knew shock when he saw it and covered her with a thick woolen blanket from the rear of the vehicle.

"There you go, miss," he cooed to her. "You sit tight. We're here now."

He sat with her in the back seat, tucking the blanket in around her and urging her to sip from his canteen. She still had a faraway look in her eyes, but at least she was quiet. I stood at the side of the jeep. When I put my hand on her shoulder she didn't flinch.

"I'll be right back, Diana," I said. "Rodney and Harry will take good care of you. I won't be long." I waited until she met my eyes.

"Billy?"

"I'll be right back," I repeated. "Okay? Rodney's right here, he'll stay with you."

She nodded.

"We'll be all right, Lieutenant," Rodney

said with a cheerful voice that didn't match his expression. "You go on and . . . take care of things."

Harry limped up to the Jeep and leaned against it. The bandage around his leg was soaked with blood.

"Thank you, Harry." It seemed so little to say, but I couldn't think of anything else. I put my hand on his shoulder and squeezed. He placed his hand over mine. I thought he intended to push mine away, but he kept it there.

"I guessed what she intended to do," he said.

"How? I didn't, until too late."

He shrugged, and looked down at the ground. "I realized as soon as she stepped into the daylight. It was the way she held the gun, pacing back and forth, like an animal in a cage, realizing there was no way out."

"Except . . ."

"Yes," Harry said, "except for that. The quick way out." A flush of shame reddened his face. I realized why he'd been able to interpret the signs so easily, but this wasn't the time or place.

"I'll just be a few minutes. You all right?"

"I'll be fine. It's just a through and through, right?"

"Sure, pal."

On my way back to the barracks I picked up Mathenet's revolver from the ground, blew the sand from it, and wiped it on my pants leg as I entered the barracks. It was a relief to have the sun off my back as I hit the shade. I stood in the corridor, catching my breath and letting the sweat drip off my face. It wasn't exactly cool inside, but it was cooler. I looked at the gun in my hand and waited. When I was calm I strolled into the room where I had left Mathenet. He was still sitting on the edge of the bed, fear and hope flickering in his eyes, as he watched me and then Duxbury.

"Corporal Duxbury," I said, "did the Commandos bring along a medical unit and a doctor?"

"Medics, we did, Lieutenant, but no doctor. You Yanks landed a parachute battalion on the airfield east of town this morning, and it was unopposed as well. They told us transports would be coming in to set up a field 'ospital and evacuate the wounded. Does the young lady need a doctor?"

"Yes, it would be good for her to see a doctor, I think."

I faced Mathenet and lifted the revolver just a few inches, pulled back on the hammer, and heard the cylinder click with a nice, well-oiled sound. I pulled the trigger and the sound reverberated in the small room. Mathenet jumped in surprise and then stared at his left foot. There was a round hole dead center right through his shoe, where the laces ended. Blood bubbled up as he lifted his foot to hold it by the ankle. There was a bullet hole in the floor, too.

"I think he's going to need one as well," I said.

"A through and through, just like the captain," said Duxbury, viewing the shot with professional interest. "Lucky chap."

Mathenet was moaning, mumbling in French, and trying to untie his shoe. As he managed to get it off he started screaming as the blood poured out of it.

"Help me, please, I will bleed to death. Why did you shoot me?"

I let that pass. "Here, put your foot up on the pillow," I said as I helped him to lie down on the bed. "Corporal, get something to tie around his foot, please."

Duxbury grabbed a sheet and started ripping it into long pieces. Mathenet looked at me with wide eyes, confused.

"What are you doing . . . ?"

"Shhhh," I said. "Take it easy."

Duxbury wrapped the strips around Mathenet's foot and tied it off tightly. The blood flow eased.

I stood over him. "Just so you know, that was for nothing. Nothing at all. Do you understand?"

He shook his head no, and tried to form the word with his mouth but nothing emerged. "That's all right. You need to understand that if you lie to me, if you even hesitate to tell me the whole truth, the next one will be for something. Something permanent."

I raised the revolver again and let the barrel rest on his kneecap. The hammer wasn't back and my finger wasn't even on the trigger, but he didn't seem comforted.

"Non, non, non. . . ." Now he got the word out.

"Okay, tell me the truth."

"Oui, oui, I will." Now his head bobbed up and down, eagerly.

"Where is Villard going with the prisoners?"

"Oh, no, I do not know, really, please . . ."

I put my finger on the trigger.

"He did not tell me everything, he kept secrets from everyone!"

I pulled the hammer back, and that quiet metallic sound — the click of a bullet arriving at just the right spot for its date with the firing pin — seemed to echo.

"The crossroads," he sobbed. "That is all I know, really. The crossroads."

"Carrefour? Isn't that a password?"

"No, no. It is a place. You found the paper? From the notebook?" There was a touch of hope in his voice. We were having a conversation, which appealed to him more than picking pieces of his kneecap out of a dirty mattress.

"Yeah, I found it. What do you mean, a place?"

"The bar, that was the first place, the first place to meet. Then, if that didn't work, the crossroads. But I swear, he never told me where it was. He said if we needed to go there, then I would know."

I released the hammer and took my finger off the trigger. That same sound again, but reversed, like time going backward.

"Who were you going to meet there?"

"Customers, Arab traders, whoever would pay the most."

This time I just had to move my finger only a quarter of an inch.

"The Germans, he was in touch with the Germans. They wanted all the penicillin he could deliver. They were going to pay in gold, as soon as he got the next shipment." He spoke in a rush, hurrying to get the words out that would move my finger back. But I didn't shift it. Next shipment? No one had said a word about *another* shipment. I had to think it through.

"When and where will the next shipment arrive?"

"In two nights, but I do not know where. I would tell you, I owe that pig nothing!"

Yeah, now we were pals. No one liked Villard.

"Anything else you can tell me?" I asked.

"No, Villard did not trust me with any information. He always told me things right before they were about to happen."

"So that's it?" I asked.

"Yes, truly. Please take me to the doctor now."

I patted down his uniform jacket pocket, the pocket I saw him put something in when he'd taken the briefcase. I felt a notebook inside and reached in for it. A black leather notebook, full of pages just like the sheet I found on Casselli.

"You missed a page when you killed Casselli, by the way. It was folded inside the matchbook," I offered, just being helpful. I flipped through the pages, seeing nothing but a lot of letters that didn't make sense. Code again. "Smart move palming the notebook. A nice insurance package in case your boss turned against you," I said. "But it was not smart to lie to me."

He started to shake again, his whole body trembling, waiting for my hand to raise the gun and make that sound again. I wanted to, I wanted to empty his goddamn pistol into his chest and watch him die. Then I wanted him to come back, so I could do it all over again.

"Ain't worth it, Lieutenant," Duxbury said quietly. "Not even a rotten piece of garbage like that one."

I had to agree. "Let's go," I said. But I knew someone else who was well worth it.

CHAPTER
TWENTY-SEVEN

Captain Gauthier was happy to take Mathenet into custody, and I was happy he didn't ask about the hole in Mathenet's foot. Duxbury had given it a good bandaging, and the last I saw of Mathenet, a grinning French sergeant was opening the trap door to that hole Villard had kept Gauthier and his men in for two days. Mathenet had tried to protest, but I told him he didn't have a leg to stand on. Duxbury thought it was funny, but I guess it lost something in translation since Mathenet didn't laugh.

Duxbury and Rodney dropped us off at Harry's boat. They said it had been fun, and I don't think they were kidding. We traded handshakes and cigarettes, and I pretended to be glad to fork over a couple of packs of Lucky Strikes for English cigarettes, which tended to taste more like straw than tobacco.

Harry's crewmen helped him aboard and

then promptly ignored him while they made Diana comfortable. Banville got on the radio and contacted base. They relayed our situation to HQ in Algiers, and we were told that Harding had issued orders for an RAF Catalina flying boat to pick us up just outside the harbor. Harry, Diana, and I were to be taken to the 21st General Hospital in Algiers. Back to square one. But now I had Diana with me.

Aboard the giant seaplane, watching Banville turn the MTB out to sea for the long ride back, I observed Diana as the Catalina took off. Its two engines revved high and the hull bounced hard each time it sliced through a wave until it finally lifted off, leaving the heavy seas behind. The Catalina was outfitted for Air-Sea rescue; Diana lay on a stretcher, covered in blankets. Her eyes were closed, but I knew she wasn't sleeping because I could see her brace herself every time the Catalina hit one of those waves. I reached over to place my hand on her shoulder, and she stiffened. I took it away and I made believe she was sleeping too.

Harry had his leg propped up on a case of ammo. Just beyond him were the waist gunners, who had great views from the observation blisters that jutted out from the narrow fuselage. Great, except when what you saw were German or Italian fighters diving toward you. The waist gunners ignored us as they swiveled their guns around and scanned the sky, which was fine with me.

"How's the leg?" I asked, settling down on the metal seat next to Harry.

"Hurts like the devil, not that I dare complain about a little through and through, as our Commando friends kept reminding me."

"Shot is shot," I said. "The human body wasn't built to have red hot lead smash through it. You have a right to complain."

He didn't say anything. After a minute or so he pointed with his thumb to Diana.

"How is she?"

"Asleep. I think, or hope. You saved her life, and I owe you for that."

"Trick is, Billy, will she think I did her a favor? And did I? She's obviously suffering, and I've just given her the chance to face more sleepless nights, more anguish, more memories . . ."

"What happened?"

"What do you mean?"

"What happened to your last boat?"

More silence. His eyes stayed glued to the floor.

"You knew what she was going to do before I did," I said. "Maybe even before she did. You knew what she was feeling by the way she moved. Like a caged animal, looking for a way out, you said."

"Only there is no way out," he finished.

"Except —"

"Yes, except that. By your own hand, or someone else's, what does it matter? This is war, people die all the time!" Harry bit off those last words with anger, his face turning red.

"Before I ran into you, back in England, I was questioning a woman about a murder. Her husband had gone down with his bomber and she didn't know if he was alive or dead. Know what she said to me?"

"What?"

"She said, thousands die every day, and they send no one. One old man dies, and they send you."

"The difference being?"

"That old man didn't have to die. Diana didn't either. It wasn't her time. You don't, at least not by your own hand."

Harry laughed at that, more of a grunt, really, with a lazy smile tacked onto the end of it.

"I couldn't, anyway. Too much of a bloody coward. But it did seem like the only way out, when the walls were closing in and nothing made any sense at all."

"So what happened?"

"Deuce of it is, I don't really know. Or remember. We were on patrol, nothing special really. Last thing I remember is coming up on deck. Then, being in the drink. I woke up with blood in my eyes, floating in the water, my boat capsized and burning. I couldn't remember how I got there, or what had happened. I looked around for the others, and there was no one. I saw one body, yards away, badly burned and obviously dead. That was it. Everybody gone, just me with a gash on my head bobbing around in my life jacket, watching my boat burn and go under. Maybe we hit a mine and it happened all in a second, or maybe we were jumped by S-Boats or Messerschmitts. I have no idea. I found a piece of wreckage and floated on it, and one of our own boats finally found me. Just by chance, too. How lucky is that, Billy, to be spared death in an explosion and then to be picked up before I could die of exposure?"

"If you were really lucky, you would've been ordered to stay in port that day."

Harry grunted again, his slight grin offering the hope there might be something to really smile about someday. He looked out the small round window behind his head. The sea was choppy and there were small white plumes riding the crests of a thousand waves below. I thought about Harry floating in a sea like that, all alone, and remembered something. What had been just a story now seemed very real and terrifying.

"My Uncle Dan had something like that happen to him," I said.

"Yes . . . ?"

"He fought in the First World War, in France. His squad had crawled out on a night patrol in No Man's Land to cut wire. That night it was his turn as rear guard, to make sure a German patrol hadn't spotted them, to stay put in a shell hole while the rest of the squad crawled back to their trench."

I could see Uncle Dan out there now in a way I never could before, all alone and listening for any tell-tale sound in the darkness.

"He said the Germans sent up a flare, so he buried his head in the mud and didn't move a muscle. Then he heard the artillery start up. He heard the shells whistling overhead and felt the ground shake as they hit behind him. He couldn't tell how long it lasted, but it seemed to go on forever. When it stopped, he waited and waited, not moving a muscle. Then he started crawling back, heading the same way his squad had. He never found them, not a trace. They could have been blown to pieces, or been buried in the mud; he never knew. They were gone, and he was fine. Just gone."

Harry didn't look at me, or speak. We were quiet for a while.

"So it made sense to you, did it?" Harry said, not taking his gaze off the water below.

"What?"

"Being sent because one old man died."

"It's about the only thing that does."

"Why? The pursuit of justice and all that rot?"

"Justice? What the hell do I know about justice? I'm not a lawyer or politician, thank God. I don't know a damn thing about justice. Injustice, that's easier. You know injustice when you see it. That old man's dead body. Sergeant Casselli with his throat slit. And . . ."

I pointed to Diana.

"Look how easy it is to spot," I said. "Everything looks wrong, like some terrible hand from hell reached up and turned people's lives upside down, broke their hearts, ruined their dreams."

I realized my voice had risen; I was almost yelling. The waist gunners both were looking at me as if I was crazy, and maybe they had a point. I made a gesture with one hand that said, Never mind, I'm okay, just a little worked up. They went back to craning their necks.

"So you're here to set things right," Harry said.

"I know there's damn few dreams left in this war, Harry. The thing is, that's what makes murder so hard to take. War's going to take lives, we know that. So why let some bastard get away with murdering somebody who might otherwise have a chance?"

"It must be the pain, but I think you're actually making sense," Harry said, bracing his bad leg with both hands.

I shrugged. I was done explaining myself. But it bothered me, like when you walk by a picture hung crooked on the wall. It can bug you until you have to turn around and fix it. In my line of work, it just requires a little more effort to get things back in order.

I felt the Catalina start to lose altitude. Through the window across from me I could see the coast with Algiers harbor ahead.

"Almost there," I said to Harry. "How's the leg?"

"Starting to throb like the dickens. I almost wish I'd taken that dose of morphine Rodney offered."

"Why didn't you? It would have made the

ride a lot more comfortable."

"I can't abide needles of any sort. I really am a coward at heart, you know. The thought of being stuck with one of those gives me nightmares. And I don't think much of hospitals, either."

"You'll love this one, then. This is the place the drugs were stolen from, where that supply sergeant was murdered and the kid overdosed on morphine."

"Thank you very much for that information," Harry said. "Now I have to worry about idiot doctors as well as needles. Don't they know how to measure doses?"

"I'm not really sure how that happened. But the good news is they do have some pretty nurses there," I said, trying to make up for worrying him.

"I'm all for pretty nurses, but I prefer to see them off duty and outside of a hospital. As far as I'm concerned, if you can walk into a hospital under your own power, don't. There are more chances of getting sick inside than outside."

"Well, you could probably *hop* into a hospital under your own power. Does that count?"

"Go ahead and have your laugh, Billy. But this is almost like a religion in my family. My grandmother had nothing to do with doctors all her life, after her mother went to hospital for an ache in her side and never set foot out of it. Alive anyway. And Grandmamma lived to be ninety-six, and was in good health until a few weeks before she died. I plan to do the same, if this war doesn't interfere."

"All right, I give up," I said. "I suppose she didn't like needles either."

"Not one bit," Harry said, and then smiled. "Actually, I think she's the one who instilled that fear in me when I was a child, always going on about doctors and their long needles. She was a very nice woman, but just a trifle touchy on the subject of medicine. She finally came down with some kind of cancer just after her ninety-fifth birthday. She allowed a doctor to come to the house, but after he diagnosed her she refused to go to hospital. She carried on just as she always had, until the pain and weakness were too much for her."

"So no needles, even at the end?"

"She wouldn't allow it. The doctor did give her morphine, mixed in with liquor, which helped. We stayed with her, Mother and I, until the end. I have to say it was a lot better than being in a sterile hospital."

"You won't have to worry about that in Algiers. Nothing is sterile there." I smiled and patted his shoulder. "I'm going to check on Diana."

"Billy, I'm sorry I punched you. You didn't deserve it. I . . . I mean I keep thinking, maybe there was something I could have done that would have changed things, that would have kept my crew alive. But I don't know. Sometimes it gets to be too much and then I explode. You were convenient, and I thought I could at least blame you for those deaths in Norway."

"I blame myself, Harry."

"But don't you see, they were all dead men already," he said, gripping my arm. "It was just a fortnight later that it happened, whatever it was. It didn't matter what you did, where you took us. They already had a date with death. We were already headed for that mine, or whatever it was, we just didn't know it. So what does it matter? I might as well blame the chap who wrote the orders for that patrol. Anyway, I'm sorry."

"Yeah, me too. I wish I never got you involved in that mission, but I wasn't thinking straight."

"You had to put things right. That makes some sense, more sense than waking up in the water wondering where all your chaps went. Now, go tend to that young lady before I do. She's quite beautiful, you know.

I may hop over there any second."

He let go of my arm. It was strange that they each had a boat sink from under them. And then I thought that hanging around survivors like them wasn't such a bad idea. Maybe their luck would rub off, although from the shape they were both in, that kind of luck carried a steep price tag.

I knelt beside Diana, started to take her hand, then thought better of it.

"Diana, it's Billy," I whispered. "You're safe, and the plane is about to land in Algiers. Then we're going to a hospital. There will be privacy, clean sheets, and doctors and nurses to take care of you. And I'll be there. Major Harding and Kaz too. We'll be together and you'll be safe."

Her eyes stayed closed but I could see her hands grip the blankets more tightly. She squeezed her eyelids shut, but tears leaked out. Her hands let go of the blankets and searched the air for mine. She grasped my hand in hers and pulled it to her face. She didn't say a thing as she held my hand against her tears.

I felt in that moment how much I loved her, and how even that small gesture meant everything in the world to me: The feel of her palms surrounding my hand, the softness of her moist cheek, brought back the past. After everything she had been through, she still trusted me.

I had only one thought, aside from Diana. I would have to kill Villard, to keep him from haunting us. I felt ashamed that it was his leering face I saw when I closed my eyes.

The plane hit the water and bounced on the waves three of four times before it settled and taxied into the harbor toward a pier where another Catalina was tied up. The jolt had almost knocked me over, and in so doing it knocked Villard's image from my mind, but I knew it would be back.

Diana still had her eyes closed and I wondered what she'd see written on my face when she opened them.

CHAPTER TWENTY-EIGHT

"Boyle, wake up."

"Ummmm."

"Now, Boyle!" Harding's voice drifted into my dream and took it over. I was dreaming that I was lost in a city, unable to find the train station. Then Harry was there, trying to tell me something important, but I couldn't understand him. He turned into Harding. My tough luck.

"Okay, Major. I'm up." I felt the hard wooden slats of the cot digging into my ribs as I forced my eyelids apart.

"Lieutenant Kazimierz is on his way in from Headquarters," Harding said. "We'll meet in the Officer's Mess at 0700."

Harding didn't wait to see if that fit in with my morning plans. I managed to keep one eye open long enough to observe the heels of his combat boots retreating to the door. I had to focus to figure out where I was. Oh yeah. Algiers. Back at the goddamn hospital. I looked around. There were half a dozen cots in the room, a flophouse for doctors and orderlies on duty. Light from the rising sun filtered into the room from the single window above me. The walls were stark white, still smelling of whitewash and lye, the army's standard scheme for redecorating. There were lumps in two other cots and one of them snored.

It had been dark when the ambulance met us at the harbor. When we reached the hospital Harding met us at the entrance with a guard detail, guys from Headquarters Company, not from the General Hospital detachment. He had stationed men out front, by the Medical Supply Depot and the motor pool. After we got Diana to a room, he left a GI by her door too. I liked that. I also liked that my old pal, Doc Dunbar, was on his way to the front with the 1st Armored Division, posted to a Battalion Aid Station. Sergeant Willoughby, too, except now he was a private again. Dunbar's replacement, Doctor Perrini, had shipped in straight from the States, and Diana was his patient. I liked that, too, since Perrini had no connection with anyone else at the hospital. He was from Chicago, and seemed like a regular guy. First thing he did was to have a couple of nurses clean Diana up, check her over, and give her a sedative. Then he examined Harry's wound, changed the bandage, and approved of the job our Commando pals had done to patch him up. I left before he could pull out a needle.

I had told Harding about the second shipment of penicillin coming through, got something to eat, found this cot, and claimed it. I think I remember taking my boots off, but that was it.

I was still dead tired, but I didn't have time for any more shut-eye. I put on a fresh pair of socks from my pack and headed to the washroom. There was only cold water, but I dumped a helmet-full over my head, washed up, and managed to shave without massacring my face. I hoped I looked presentable. And that Diana would want to see me, would want to hold my hand, would let me sooth and reassure her. I wanted her to be the Diana with the sparkling eyes full of fun I had known and loved in England, all passion, temper, and tenderness. Not the Diana who had put a gun to her head. Not the Diana who had been . . . I didn't even want to think about it. But it was all I could think about. I looked at myself in the cracked mirror above the sink. I smiled, and it was the same face that had always smiled back at me. Yet it wasn't. It couldn't be, not with everything that had happened. The smile didn't last, and I looked away from the reflection. Villard's face floated through my mind and he was smiling too, laughing at me. I wondered if I could ever think of Diana without remembering what he'd done to her. How could I hold her without thinking about where his hands had been? It didn't make me proud, but there it was.

I stashed my gear under the cot and put on my web belt with the .45 in its holster. I took its grip in my hand and pressed with all my strength until I could feel the little cross-hatchings against my skin. It was some relief. I felt better. I still had ten minutes and decided to drop in on Diana to see if she was awake. As I walked down the hall, past everyone going on shift or off, I realized the real reason I wanted to see her now instead of later. To get it over with. But I didn't like admitting it, even to myself.

The guard at the door to the ward checked my dogtags and found my name on a list.

"Okay, Lieutenant, knock and check with the nurse."

I went up to the closed door and gave a little rap on the frosted glass. I thought for a second that no one was going to answer. I could just go away. The door was opened by

Rita, the nurse who had taken a liking to Kaz.

"Billy, come in," she whispered as she took me by the arm and pulled me into the room. There were four beds against the wall, empty except for the one by the window. Diana was asleep, her blonde hair framing her face. She looked better, now that she was cleaned up and in a fresh white room.

"She asked for you when she woke up an hour or so ago. Doctor Perrini gave her a sedative. She can't stay awake long. Sit by the bed, I'll let her know you're here."

"Wait," I said in a low voice. "How is she? Did she have any injuries . . . internal injuries, or anything?"

"She was beaten, but not on the face. She's badly bruised. She was a little confused and disoriented from the drugs she'd been injected with, but they're almost all out of her system now."

"Did she tell you what happened?"

Rita gave me a probing look, trying to figure out how much to tell me, and if I could take it. I didn't know the answer to that myself.

"Yes. They gave her chloral hydrate to knock her out when they moved her. That was after she tried to escape."

"Jesus." I wondered when that was. When

I was having breakfast at the St. George Hotel? Or maybe while I was having coffee with Casselli? I went over to the chair by the bed and sat down. I didn't want to hear any more.

"Miss Seaton," Rita said, taking hold of Diana's hand. "You have a visitor. Can you wake up for me?"

Diana shook her head, as if she was dreaming, and mumbled something I couldn't understand. I wondered if she was lost in a strange city, too. Then her eyes opened.

"Billy."

"I'm here, Diana."

"Don't go . . ."

I was about to tell her I had to, when her eyelids drooped and she was asleep again. "I have to go," I said anyway. I reached up and touched her forehead. It was cool, and she smiled, like a child hearing a lullaby as she drifts off to sleep.

"I do have to go," I said to Rita as I got up. "Tell her . . . I was here."

"I'll tell her you'll be back," she said with determination.

"Yeah, I'll be back. Later. I will."

"And bring that nice Polish guy with you," she said, the hardness in her eyes gone, the test passed.

I saw that nice Polish guy a few minutes later sitting with Harding at a corner table in the Officer's Mess. They had a beat up coffee pot, burned black on the bottom, and a plate of doughnuts on the table. The enlisted men's mess and kitchen were just across the hall, and the smell of army powdered eggs, burnt toast, and cigarettes drifting in almost killed what little appetite I had. They hadn't gotten around to white-washing this part of the hospital, but the floor was clean and the red brick walls gave the room a cool, pleasant feel.

"Okay, first things first," said Harding as I poured coffee into a chipped mug. Pieces of eggshell floated on top and I dredged them out with my finger. "How's Miss Seaton?"

"Pretty good, considering," I said, trying to sound confident. "Bruised quite a bit, and still a little woozy."

I didn't tell them what I hadn't told Rita either. That Diana had been pretty lively back in Bône until she almost blew her brains out. Maybe it had been shock, maybe the drugs, or both. I hoped.

"She will be all right?" asked Kaz, leaning in and speaking quietly.

"Yeah, I saw her a few minutes ago. Still groggy, but she'll be fine."

"Good," declared Harding, closing the

subject of personal relationships. I wondered how he and Gloria Morgan were doing. He didn't give me a chance to ask.

"I notified HQ about the new penicillin shipment. It's traveling by ship to Oran and then by train to Algiers. It's coming by rail because the Luftwaffe has been targeting vessels entering Algiers harbor. It's a big shipment, twenty cases, which is about eighty percent of the entire world supply at the moment."

Kaz whistled.

"How much would it be worth?" I asked.

"It's invaluable," answered Harding. "Which means a lot of money."

"And no one at this hospital thought it worth mentioning, after the first supply was stolen?" I asked.

"You find out about that, Boyle, when we're done here. Who knew, and why didn't they speak up?"

"Yes, sir. I assume you've added security for this shipment?"

"Damn right. It's being guarded like the crown jewels."

"And when is it due here?"

"The train from Oran will arrive at 0300 hours tomorrow morning. A truck will bring the shipment of penicillin from the station to the depot here, to be parceled out to field hospitals the next day. I've got a platoon of Rangers on the train with it now. They'll guard the truck until it leaves here."

"I think, sir, that we should keep the existence of our extra security quiet for now."

"Why?" asked Harding.

"Because someone went to a lot of effort to hide this delivery from us, and maybe from the rest of the hospital staff. Villard may be planning to hit the truck en route. He'd have time to get away with a fortune in penicillin before anyone even knew it was gone."

"So we let him have a go at it?" Harding asked, as if I had just gone around the bend.

"We shouldn't tip our hand too soon. We might have a chance to trap him and his accomplices."

"How?" asked Kaz, as he dumped sugar into his coffee.

"We keep quiet about the Rangers guarding the penicillin for now. If we let the information out late tonight, whoever is working with Villard will try to get word to him. We have to watch the phones, to see if anyone tries to get to the radio, or whether someone leaves the hospital for no reason. Then we'll have them."

"And if his inside person doesn't manage to get word out, Villard will still try to hit the truck."

"Yes sir. That's why I want to be in that truck when it makes the pickup."

Harding eyed me, trying to figure out what was going on. I didn't usually volunteer, and with Diana safe here, he probably thought I'd be angling to stay put. He started to say something but stopped as a couple of officers sat down at the table next to us.

"I'll think about it," he said in a low voice. "Meantime, we'll keep it zipped about the escort. Lieutenant Kazimierz, you work on this." He produced the notebook that I had given him last night. Kaz flipped through the pages. He frowned.

"What's the matter?" I asked.

"I am not certain, but this looks much more complicated than the other code you showed me. That was actually a substitution cipher, really not a code at all."

"What's the difference?" I asked.

"Ciphers are different from codes. When you substitute one word for another word or sentence, you have a code. When you mix up or substitute letters, you have a cipher. You can also combine codes and ciphers by substituting one word for another and then mixing up the result. There are two types of ciphers also. Substitution ciphers replace letters with other letters or symbols, keeping the order in which the symbols fall the same. Transposition ciphers keep all of the original letters intact, but mix up the order. Of course, you can use both methods, one after the other, to further confuse anyone who intercepts the message."

"I'm confused," I admitted. I had stopped following his explanation before he was half done.

"Look here," said Kaz, warming up to his subject. "These last pages do seem to be the same shorthand cipher we saw before. The words look intact. But here, on these pages, the letters are all in five letter groups. Here, there are just numbers in groups of three, separated by a dash. 45-16-4, 109-22-26, 8-31-38, and so on. No logical order. Whoever set this up used a number of different techniques, and then used the substitution cipher for quick messages."

"When we're done here, find a quiet place and work on it," Harding said.

He didn't like it and neither did I. We had both thought deciphering the contents of the notebook would be a quick fix to a tough problem. It would allow us to bring evidence to Ike of corruption at high levels within the Vichy French regime here, a reason to clean house. But it wasn't going to be that easy.

"All right, Boyle, tell us what you found out in Bône," Harding said, leaning back and sipping his coffee.

I told them about Le Bar Bleu, but not the room upstairs, or the fact that I'd burned the place down. I told them about the depot, finding Diana, and how I got the notebook, but not about shooting Mathenet in the foot. I told them about The Crossroads being the code name for the detention center in the desert, to which Villard now had moved the last of his slave laborers and his hijacked supplies, waiting for the highest bidder. Germans, Arabs, the Mafia, everyone on the wrong side of the war or the law was probably itching to get their hands on the new wonder drug. I didn't tell them about promising Diana I'd get the rest of the prisoners out of his hands, since I had no idea how I could pull that off. By the time I finished figuring out what to leave in and what to leave out, I had only one question left. I refilled my cup with hot coffee and took a doughnut. Reporting is hard work.

"You know the thing that bothered me was how Villard and Bessette got this smuggling operation set up so quickly, as if they had known ahead of time about the hospital being opened here and even about the penicillin and how valuable it would be."

"Right," said Harding. "What did you come up with?"

"I think I have it figured out. Bessette's family is involved in shipping between Algeria, France, and Portugal. I bet they use the ships for smuggling as well. He has a brother, Jules, who lives in Blackpool, England, where the 21st General Hospital was posted before being transported here. It'd be easy for Bessette to send a letter with a sailor going to Portugal with instructions to hand it off there to someone on a neutral vessel headed for England. When that sailor arrives, he simply mails the letter at a local post office."

"Because the British censor international mail, but not internal mail," Kaz said, nodding his head.

"What about getting information back to Algiers?" Harding asked. "That wouldn't be so easy."

"It wouldn't have to be done the same way," said Kaz, quickly. "They could have set up a simple code, word for word. Jules could write back, 'My good friend, John, will be visiting London in three weeks.' That could actually mean someone named John would be in Algiers in six weeks, depending on whatever previous arrangement they made for signifying numbers and places."

"But even so, how could they have found out? Everything about the invasion was top secret," Harding said.

"But Major, what does top secret really mean? Just how secret is it?" I asked.

"Well, a lot of people did have to know," admitted Harding. "Planning staff, logistical staff, civil affairs. As the date got closer, the circle of those in the know grew larger and larger."

"Would the Medical Corps be in that circle?"

Harding let that question hang in the air for a minute as he thought.

"They'd have to be, especially to prepare for the kinds of indigenous diseases they'd have to deal with," he finally said.

"And certainly if they were involved in the testing of a new miracle drug," added Kaz.

Harding took more coffee, poured milk into it and tapped his spoon on the edge of the thick ceramic mug. *Clink clink clink.*

"I don't like what I'm hearing. You're suggesting that a U.S. Army officer would betray secret plans for the invasion of North Africa for personal gain. But I agree it's possible. Does your speculation fit with Lieutenant Kazimierz's information?" Harding nodded at Kaz.

"Scotland Yard is quite familiar with Jules Bessette and his associates in Blackpool," Kaz said, leaning forward and lowering his voice, even though the tables around us were empty. "I first called the Provost Marshal's office, and they referred me to Scotland Yard, and I was told that Jules Bessette is suspected of everything from running the black market to murder, but he is very careful. They have no concrete evidence against him or anyone in his organization. Except . . ." Kaz stopped and took a sip of coffee. He loved the drama of all this.

"Okay, I'm hooked," I said. "Except for what?"

"Except for the case of Sergeant Frederick Hotchkiss, of the 21st General Hospital, who supposedly deserted."

"He was the supply sergeant before Casselli," I said.

"Yes. The man who drove off in a jeep one night never to be seen again. But the jeep was, or the engine, at least. It was found in a local garage."

"Let me guess, a garage owned by Jules Bessette," I said.

"Exactly!"

"So why didn't they arrest Bessette?"

Harding asked.

"He owned the garage but was seldom there. Scotland Yard had their eye on it as a link in a black market operation. Vehicles could come and go from a garage without arousing suspicion. Someone reported that Hotchkiss had been seen at the garage the day he deserted. The Provost Marshal's office and Scotland Yard searched the place and found the jeep's engine lying among other auto parts, but no sign of Hotchkiss or the rest of the jeep. The odd thing was, the manager of the garage was found floating face down in Blackpool harbor a few nights later. The investigation went nowhere."

"Which is exactly what brother Jules wanted," I said, thinking out loud.

"What do you mean?" asked Harding.

"I'd bet dollars to doughnuts that Hotchkiss was killed at the garage, and the manager was supposed to dispose of the body and the vehicle. The jeep, intact, would be too hot to try to sell or salvage. But somebody got greedy and thought they could stash the engine away until all the fuss died down."

"Ah," said Kaz, "so when Jules found out, he had the manager killed, to eliminate the link to him . . ."

"And to set an example. Follow orders or else, like in the army."

"If I threw you in the harbor every time you didn't obey orders, Boyle, you'd still be treading water," said Harding, setting down his coffee mug with a thump on the wooden tabletop. "Anything else?"

"Yes sir," I said, wanting to sound like an authentic officer to keep Harding from getting any ideas. "I got a look at Mathenet's wounds that he supposedly got in the air raid. It wasn't from shrapnel. They were knife wounds."

"Like we figured the assailant got when he tried to slit Casselli's throat?"

"Exactly like that. I'm certain Mathenet won't be going anywhere soon, so we can get our hands on him anytime we want. But I'd like to find out who treated him for those wounds. I don't think anyone with medical knowledge would buy the shrapnel story."

"Go ahead," Harding said, "but I wouldn't be surprised if some of the doctors and nurses here didn't know shrapnel from shinola. This is their first posting in a combat zone. Guy comes in bleeding and said something hit him during the air raid. What are they going to do, give him the third degree?"

"As long as it's okay with you, I'll ask around."

"Knock yourself out. Now, with all this new information, who seems to be our most likely suspect?"

"Well, who would know both that North Africa was our destination and that penicillin would be sent to this hospital?" I asked.

"That would be *both* shipments of penicillin," Kaz added.

"Yeah. And, who had access to the morphine to give Jerome an overdose?"

"Hold on," Harding interrupted, holding up his hand. "That happened after the theft, so it could have been anybody. We don't know if the morphine that killed Jerome came from the stolen lot or the remaining supplies."

"That's right," I said, rapping my fingers on the table. "Some of that stolen stuff could have stayed right here. Which means that it could be anybody —"

"*If* they knew about the unit's destination and about the penicillin," said Kaz.

"Or it could mean two of our people are involved," I said. "Actually I should have said three, because it's obvious Casselli was involved to some degree. Maybe with petty stuff at first, and then he may have gotten nervous about going big-time."

"Like the former supply sergeant, Hotch-kiss?" asked Harding.

"Maybe, or maybe Hotchkiss was too much of a Boy Scout for them. He may even have been going to report some funny business."

Harding pushed back his chair and got up, his mouth set in a frown of frustration.

"We could play the maybe game all day. Let's get some facts. Lieutenant Kazimierz, you work on that notebook. Boyle, you start with Walton and find out if this fish stinks from the head. I've got to get back to HQ. Ike is in town."

"What's happening, sir?"

"The deal with Darlan is about to happen, and all hell is going to break loose."

"Here? Why?"

"Not here. Even though Darlan is a double-crossing fascist, he'll do a deal that will make things easier for us. Darlan will be in charge politically and General Giraud will be in command of the French Armed Forces in North Africa. We won't have to worry about our rear areas. And the French will join us in fighting the Germans."

"But we're still making a deal with a fascist."

"Right. The politicians and the news-papers back home are going to have a field day. Once the news gets out, half the country will want Ike's head. Your uncle may make it home before any of us. In the meantime, I'll meet you two back here at 1500 hours."

Kaz's eyebrows were raised. I shrugged. I hate to admit it, but the first thing I thought about wasn't Uncle Ike losing his job. It was about what would happen to me if he did. I doubted if I'd be lucky enough to be sent home in disgrace.

CHAPTER
TWENTY-NINE

"Billy, I'm so glad you're back with us, safe and sound."

I felt the hand on my shoulder before I heard Gloria Morgan's honeyed Southern voice.

I stopped in the busy hospital hallway and said, "Yes, ma'am. I am, too."

"Now Billy, remember, you don't have to be so formal here."

She hooked her arm through mine and we strolled down the hall together. I could feel the softness of her body as her arm pressed mine to her side. She smelled like real soap and perfume, not whitewash and lye.

"Sure . . . Gloria. . . . It's just that Major Harding has me well-trained when it comes to addressing superior officers."

"I'll bet he does. I don't think of myself as outranking you, Billy. I'm only a nurse. You know I can't even give you an order, even though I am a captain." She stressed those last words, as if she needed to remind me, or herself.

"No, I didn't. So lady officers can only order other lady officers around?"

"That's the way the army likes it, Billy. At least among the Nurse Corps, anyway. I can't even order the dumbest, lowest private to empty a bedpan."

I stopped. I needed to go left, down the hall to Walton's office, and Gloria seemed to be propelling me along for the ride to wherever she was headed.

"Yeah, but I bet you could ask real nice and get him to do what you wanted." I said it with a smile, and she didn't miss a beat.

"I might try that out on you someday, Billy." She peered up at me through long eyelashes, and I could almost see her licking her lips. "Say hello to your lady friend for me. I checked up on her this morning, and she asked me to tell you she was feeling much better."

"You did? She seemed okay?"

"Fine, she's fine. I've got to go, Billy. We've got some new doctors arriving and I need to check on arrangements for them. See you later, sweetheart." She turned, fluttering her fingers in a wave.

"Oh, wait a second, Gloria. I wanted to ask you, do you remember after the aid raid, when you told me that Lieutenant Mathenet was being treated for a shrapnel wound?"

"Yes, I do. I ran into you when you were visiting that poor French boy who died . . ."

"Jerome."

"Yes, Jerome . . . Dupree it was. You asked me if the Lieutenant was going to be taking him into custody."

"You told me he was being treated. Who was caring for him?"

"Why, I'm certain I don't know. The fellow stumbled into the emergency room, with blood running down his arm. I pointed him to the triage area and that was the last I saw of him."

"Did you look at his wound?"

"I could tell it wasn't very serious by the small amount of blood. But no, I didn't look at it closely. Why, is he having a problem with it?" Her eyebrows rose with the question, all professional curiosity.

"No, it's healing up fine. I just wanted to check on who was where and when. Routine cop stuff."

"Sorry I can't help. See you later, Billy." She gave me a little wink and sashayed away.

I nodded and watched her go. It took a hell of a woman to make a career out of the Army and put up with everything she had to contend with. Pompous doctors, low pay, and no respect for her rank. For the first time, I wondered why. What did Gloria Morgan get out of the bargain? I wondered about that as I walked down the hall, knocked on Colonel Walton's door, and entered his office.

"Goddamn it Boyle! I thought I'd seen the last of you! I'll tell you something . . ."

Walton got up from behind his desk and advanced on me, wagging the two fingers holding a cigar, ashes falling on the carpet in front of him.

"Now I've got Headquarters troops standing guard in my own hospital, like goddamn prison guards. That Major Harding of yours is a pain in the ass!"

He went back to his chair. I was thinking about telling him I agreed, when he wheeled around and pointed the cigar at me again.

"And you're not much better! Take a seat."

I did. I waited a minute in silence as he puffed on his cigar, staring me down through the smoke.

"You're not as stupid as you look, Boyle," he finally said. "A lot of guys would try to calm me down by explaining themselves. Shutting up is hard for most people."

"What do you need explained, Colonel?"

"Why Harding is bringing in these men, for starters. And why in hell I got orders from HQ to cooperate with you!"

I held up one hand, fingers outstretched.

"Two murders, one theft, an idiot doctor, a crooked supply clerk. . . . What did I leave out?" I looked at my five fingers.

"Petty pilferage. Goes on all the time. I didn't mind losing those two anyway. Dunbar was a prissy sonofabitch and Willoughby deserves to be at the other end of the supply chain. If you investigated every CO when some supplies go missing, you'd have a lifetime occupation."

"But those supplies are drugs, Colonel."

"Wake up, Boyle. I run a hospital here. Of course drugs are missing. If it were a paratroop outfit it'd be jump boots. If it were the Air Corps it'd be leather jackets. If it was Headquarters it'd be champagne."

"Good point, Colonel, but we're talking about this hospital and what's gone on here. Plus, we don't really have champagne that much. Bushmills, yeah." I tried a smile.

"Bullshit is more like it. Ask your goddamn questions, and be quick about it."

I could tell Walton didn't like being pressured to cooperate, and he wanted me to know he didn't like it. Question was, is this the way the guilty party would react? Answer was, maybe, if he were cool and smart. Walton seemed more the fly-off-the-handle than the cool-calculating type to me. I thought I should start easy so he wouldn't fly off that handle and beat me over he head with it. I looked at the books lining the shelves and thought about the first time I came into his office.

"Colonel, you've got everything here from *Gray's Anatomy* to the *U.S. Army Manual for Courts-Martial.* Are you a doctor yourself? Regular Army?"

"No and no. I was a kid in the First World War, infantry. I went to medical school when I got back, but it wasn't for me. I went to work at a hospital instead and ended up as Chief Hospital Administrator, Detroit General. Then the war came along and the army needed to build up the Medical Corps overnight. That's my job, to organize and make things happen in a hurry. Best way to do that in the Army is to know every damn regulation backward and forward, and bury those desk-jockeys at HQ with paperwork if they give you a hard time."

"And the medical texts?" I gestured with my thumb toward *Gray's Anatomy,* the only book with a title that I could understand.

"I like to keep up. Keeps the MD bullshit factor down if I understand every third word."

"Can anyone come in here and borrow them?"

"No one needs to."

"But if they did?"

"The door's locked when I'm not here. My clerk across the hall has a key if he wants anything. I suppose anyone could ask to borrow a book."

"Is this where you play poker too?"

"Yep. And you're not invited."

"Okay, Colonel. Now a more important question. Do you know who bandaged Lieutenant Mathenet's wounds after the air raid?"

"No fucking idea."

"Do you keep records of that sort of thing?"

"For a little scratch, right after we've been bombed by the Nazis? If we had to hospitalize someone, then yes. Otherwise it's just gauze and tape and get the hell out."

"Is that the only working telephone in the hospital?" I pointed to the ornate French-style telephone on his ornate table.

"Yes. Probably the only one for miles around. The Signal Corps ran a wire out here, straight to this room. That's it."

Time for the harder questions. I figured I'd build up to the big one.

"Why do you think Sergeant Hotchkiss

deserted in England?"

"Now that's a mystery I'd like solved. No idea. Not in his character. He up and disappeared one day, no warning, no explanation. His gear, jeep, everything."

"You certain he deserted?"

"Apparently he did. Captain Morgan saw him leave that night, and he was spotted in town the next day. Then nothing. What else could've happened?"

I didn't feel like going into all the possibilities. Next question.

"When did you first learn the destination of your unit?"

"About six weeks before we shipped out, I was told to prepare for two eventualities. One was that Spain was considering getting into the war on our side, and that we should prepare to move to the Pyrenees on the Spanish-French border. The other was that Vichy France was going to come over to us, and that we should prepare to set up a hospital in Algiers as a preliminary step to moving into France."

"Two cover stories, one just a little off the mark."

"Exactly. Nothing was said about an invasion, just to prepare for transport to either locale. We had to research local diseases, health conditions, and stock up on drugs and medications for each."

"Who is 'we' exactly?"

"I mean the hospital. I did the research and gave orders for the supplies."

"When I was in England I saw GIs issued cold weather gear for Norway, as part of a deception plan. Anything like that go on with your unit?"

"That's a laugh. No, no cloak and dagger stuff. Once I got the word, though, I couldn't leave base."

"Could you send and receive mail?"

"Sure. What, do you think I was going to send a note to Adolf?" He laughed.

"No, just curious about the security. When did you learn about the penicillin?"

"I knew the 21st had been selected for the trial run of the first batch months ago. But I didn't know when and where."

"When did you find that out?"

"Three weeks before we left. Medical Corps brass and some pharmaceutical reps paid me a visit. I had to sign the Official Secrets Act and everything, promising not to reveal that piece of information."

"And you didn't?"

"No!"

"Not to a trusted colleague, or to anyone on your staff? It must have been pretty exciting for the doctors when they heard about it."

"Yeah, they were jumping up and down when I told them. Here. After we landed."

"All right, just a cop's suspicious nature."

"Anything else, officer?" Walton drew out the last word, sarcasm dripping off each syllable.

I looked around the room for a few seconds, just to irritate him. "Nooo," I said, tapping my finger against my lips, as if I were trying to come up with something but couldn't.

"Good. I have more supply requisitions here than there are hours in the day." He picked up a pen and started in on a stack of papers about two inches thick. I leaned back in the chair and got comfortable. Crossed my legs, even.

"You know," I said, wagging my finger in the air, "there is just one more thing."

Then I saw it. Walton had been perfect so far. It's hard for a suspect to hide his relief when he thinks the session is over. Innocent or guilty, everyone is glad to have a cop stop asking a million irritating questions. It's even harder to hide disappointment when he starts up again. It's a flicker of resentment, from deep inside the soul of someone who is trying his damnedest to protect a lie. It takes a lot out of a guy, and I saw some of that wind go out of Walton's sails in that brief moment.

"What?" No goddamn this or that — a weary, resigned question.

"You must have taken that Official Secrets Act pretty seriously."

"Have you signed it, Boyle?"

"As a matter of fact, I have."

"Did you read it?"

"I had it explained to me."

"So you know they can string you up by the balls, throw you in a cell, and toss away the key if they even think you've violated it?"

"Well, I wasn't told those details, but I got the drift of the thing."

"So my answer is, Yes, I take it seriously."

"You must. Why else would you have kept the second shipment a secret?"

"Second shipment of what?"

"How many second shipments of things that you had to sign the Official Secrets Act over are you expecting?"

"Spit it out, Boyle! Are you talking about more penicillin coming in?"

"Yes, Colonel, I am. And I'm wondering why you didn't mention that, after the theft of the first."

"No one told me anything about more penicillin! I figured more would be coming, but I had no idea. . . . When is it due?" He looked up at me as if the full impact of my information was just hitting him. "Who else knows about this?"

"I can't say anything more, Colonel. Are you trying to tell me you're ignorant about the second shipment?"

"Dumb-fucking-founded, boy. Ignorant as a Texas mule. You find out who was supposed to have told me about this and ask him if he did. If he says yes, he's a lying bastard! Check the paperwork! The army doesn't let you shit without filing a form! You find me a supply order with my signature on it, telling me I have another shipment of penicillin due, and I'll kiss your Irish ass!"

Walton got up and stalked around his desk toward me, leaning forward so his red face was just above my nose. He put his hands on either arm of the chair. I could smell the cigar and coffee on his breath.

"But you remember this, you worthless rear-area fuck-up! If you find that form with somebody else's name on it, I'm gonna drag you across that parade ground and you're going to kiss my ass, and smile while you're doing it. Now get out before I get all worked up and do something that will cause you to appreciate the quality medical care provided at the 21st General Hospital."

That last word had a fine spin of spittle on it. Walton pushed away from the chair and went back to his desk, puffing on that cigar like a locomotive building up a head of steam. I waited until I got out in the hall to wipe my face. He was hiding something, I was sure. I was also sure that he was either another Clark Gable or he had no clue at all about the penicillin coming in tonight on the 3:00 AM train from Oran. But somebody did.

I walked out of the rear entrance for some fresh air but didn't get much more than dust and a warm, stale breeze. The breeze part was nice, but the dust and heat didn't have much charm. The area between the hospital and the Medical Supply Depot had been neatened up, Army style. They had whitewashed rocks laid out to mark walkways and the roadway. It made me wish I had stock in a whitewash company. The army must buy that stuff by the truckload. The debris that had been out back had been taken away, and there were a couple of real air raid shelters with reinforced roofs instead of slit trenches. I wanted to breath in the fresh air and feel it fill my lungs, send oxygen to my brain, and help me figure all this out. Instead, a couple of deuce and a half trucks rolled through the yard slowly, tires crunching on gravel, raising a cloud of dust when they braked to a halt. I shielded my eyes against the sun and dust, then gave up. No inspiration, no flash of intuition. I kicked a stone and went back inside.

I walked down to Diana's room; the same guard was there. He waved me through. I knocked on the door and opened it slightly, afraid of interrupting some medical or personal activity. Instead, I found Diana up and dressed, sort of, in U.S. Army fatigues big enough for a couple of her. Kaz was packing hospital-issue pajamas and a robe into a small duffle bag.

"Billy," she said, surprised and a little shy, I thought.

"What's going on?" I said to Kaz, not taking my eyes off Diana. She sank onto the edge of the bed, the effort of standing too much for her.

"Doctor Perrini agreed that Diana need not stay here any longer. He prescribed bed rest and relaxation for her. She can be accommodated much more comfortably at the St. George Hotel. Major Harding agreed that we should give up our room so Diana can occupy it." He smiled and continued packing the few meager army-issue items that Diana could call her own.

I perched on the bed next to her. "How are you?" I asked.

She looked at the floor. "Better," she said, after giving it some thought. She nodded, as if she were agreeing with herself. "Better. I'm starting to think more clearly now. I believe I know what really happened and what was a dream, or a delusion."

She still wouldn't look at me.

I took her hand. "It's okay, everything will be all right," I said.

"Will it?" With that question, she gazed straight into my eyes.

I froze. I realized I shouldn't have told her everything would be okay. Everything wasn't okay. I didn't want to lie to her but I didn't want to think about the truth. I glanced around, trying to avoid her eyes. I didn't know what to do. Kaz rescued me.

"Well, not much in the way of luggage, my dear. Quite unusual for such a beautiful woman." He held the duffle bag over his good shoulder and gestured with his other arm which was still in a sling. "Billy, would you be so good as to take Diana's arm? She may need assistance and I am short a working appendage." Kaz was being clever, cheerful, and solicitous. I was being a dunce.

"Yeah, sure, yes." I helped Diana up and offered my arm to her.

She took it, but our eyes did not meet again as we walked down the hall, back out into the heat of the day.

CHAPTER THIRTY

"The last time we made this drive someone shot at us," I said, inclining my head to the right but keeping my eyes on the road. Diana was in the passenger seat, her head tilted back and eyes closed as she let the sun and wind wash over her face. It felt idiotic as soon as I said it, trying to impress her with my brush with danger, while she had been held prisoner, drugged, beaten, and raped.

"Really," she said, without opening her eyes. "How remarkable."

I looked at Kaz and shrugged. I went back to staring at the road, and the scrub brush on the hills around us. Ahead the landscape was greener, palm trees shading both sides of the road, but the five miles between the hospital and edge of Algiers proper was nothing but a dry, stony wasteland.

"It was, actually," Kaz said, leaning forward from the jeep's back seat. "An assassin was laying in wait for us on our route back to the hotel. The first bullet went right between Major Harding and Billy, and I could hear it pass by me. Billy drove like the devil to avoid the next shots. We know it had been an assassin, not just a random sniper, because he took his shell casings away. The shooter." He said that last word with the positive enthusiasm of someone who's mastered a tricky piece of foreign jargon.

That got Diana's attention. She opened her eyes. "You mean that somebody was trying to kill you, specifically?"

"That's my guess," I said, glad that at least she was talking with me. "We took Kaz out of the hospital soon after the killings there. He had deciphered a code, and we thought the killer might make a move on him."

"How did they know where you were going?"

"Plenty of people in the hospital knew we were leaving. A doctor named Dunbar checked Kaz out. Rita, a nurse — you know her — she knew, and so did Captain Morgan. Each of them could've mentioned it to half a dozen people. There's a working phone in Walton's office; he's the Hospital CO. The place is run pretty loosely. Anybody on that staff could've walked into his office and made a phone call."

"No, that's not what I mean, Billy," Diana said, holding onto her long hair as the wind whipped it against her face. "I mean how did they know your route?"

I started to explain it to her, and as soon as I opened my mouth I knew it didn't make sense. "Well, they knew we were attached to headquarters, which is based at the St. George Hotel . . ."

"But you weren't going to HQ exactly, were you?"

"No," I said slowly, thinking it through. I didn't speak for a minute as a small convoy of trucks pulling big 155mm artillery pieces passed us, headed out of the city. The two-wheeled cannons bounced and pounded on the uneven road surface, kicking up a cloud of sand and grit that swirled around us and stung the skin on my face and hands. Diana covered her eyes and mouth until the convoy passed and we drove out of their dust, the hot air flowing around us feeling comparatively fresh and clean as it blew the gritty sand off of us.

"We told Dunbar we were taking Kaz back to his quarters," I said, picking up where I had left off, "but we never said where that was."

"Yes!" Kaz. "I remember thinking that it

would be too ostentatious to mention where we were staying. Whoever contacted the shooter could not have guessed that. The St. George is only for senior officers."

"You didn't tell Rita, when you were filling her in on all the baron stuff?"

"No, Billy, I did not."

"So how did they know?" Diana asked.

"Maybe Colonel Walton found out when he contacted HQ to check us out," I guessed. "That was after we found Casselli's body and he had me assigned to look into the murder. He talked to somebody at headquarters, maybe he got wise to it then."

I gripped the steering wheel hard, until my knuckles were white. I was steamed at myself. It was such a simple thing to overlook, so obvious that I had never even considered it. Somebody had to have known exactly where Kaz was quartered. There were hundreds of guys attached to HQ, spread out all over Algiers, in tents, garages, small hotels, you name it. It couldn't have been a lucky guess.

I didn't feel like talking. I was glad when we drove into the shade and started seeing houses nestled in among palm trees and green, flowering bushes. The Arab homes came first, rounded white stucco houses, decorated with colorful geometric tiles above the doors and windows. Then came the European homes, more widely spaced and built from stone, with white crushed-rock driveways and iron gates. I thought about all those people inside, Arabs and French, leading their lives, going to work, worrying about the rent or mortgage, arguing, kissing, reading the newspaper, yelling at the kids, just a stone's throw away from our jeep. So near to a place where the only color was khaki and daily life was the same routine, over and over again, until you went out and got killed or lost a leg or part of your soul. I looked over at Diana and wanted to reach out and touch her, to comfort her, to bring her to one of those houses disappearing behind us as we drove further into the city, and surround her with the peaceful rhythms of daily life. I wanted to shelter her from the cruelty and evil brought into our lives by this war. But then what? What would I say when she asked me again if everything was going to be all right? What the hell was I supposed to say?

I turned a corner and downshifted, slowing down for a line of traffic headed for the hotel. Jeeps, staff cars, some civilian vehicles, were all jammed together waiting for a security check. Ike was in town, and with the Darlan deal in the works there was good reason to check things thoroughly. We inched forward, then stopped. I tried to think of something to say, and felt like I was back in Boston, in high school and on my first date, trying to make some remark that wouldn't sound like it came from the jerk I knew I was.

"Sorry for the wait," I said. Brilliant. Yeah, speak like a chauffeur, that's a great idea.

"I have time," Diana said. "I'm coming back from a failed mission. No one will be in a hurry to debrief me, I'm sure of that much." She turned away and rubbed her eyes. Was it fatigue? Or tears? Was she crying for her failure, the agony and humiliation, the wasted lives, and for all I knew for the faith she once had in me? I put my hand out and tried to take hers. She shook it off, then buried her face in her hands. Traffic moved and I gunned the engine.

The MPs gave us the once-over, and double-checked Diana's release papers from the hospital. They sent us down the road from the hotel to park the jeep anywhere we could. The place was packed, and lowly lieutenants did not rate their own parking area. We pulled over and got out, walking past stacks of wooden crates, supplies of all kinds, covered by camouflage tarps and guarded by bored GIs walking back and forth, ignoring us and yelling at the occasional Arab who got too close. More tents had sprung up all around the hotel, and some of the gardens had been taken over, sprouting green canvas in place of palm leaves. I took Diana's arm as we went up the steps to the main entrance and she flinched, then relaxed and leaned on me. I guessed I was going to have to take my chances, to wait and see.

Kaz unlocked the door to the room and opened it. Our stuff was still there, just as we'd left it a few days ago, bedrolls and knapsacks stashed in a corner. The long windows on either side of the bed were open, and a cool breeze drifted in off the water. Diana walked ahead of us, went to the window, and drew aside the curtain. Aquamarine water shimmered in the sunshine, and a few white puffy clouds stood out against a clear blue sky. Deep green palm fronds just outside the window swished as the wind coming in from the Mediterranean blew the tops of the trees back and forth, sending a cooling breeze into the room. The gauzy curtains fluttered around Diana, brushed against her like a caress, and then withdrew as the wind pulled them back against the windowframe. On the table there was a glass pitcher beaded with cold moisture holding orange juice, glasses turned upside down on paper doilies, next to flowers in a vase. She turned from the view and looked at the room, the white sheets on the four-poster bed with mosquito netting draped over the top, the vibrant colors of the orange juice and the pink flowers, the couch upholstered in a deep blue fabric, almost the shade of the ocean. There was an odd expression on her face. Maybe she wanted to cry again, but couldn't.

She looked confused. Then she fainted. Her eyes rolled up and her knees buckled. I made a dive to catch her before she cracked her head on the floor. I held her and put my hand under her head, lifted her and put her in bed.

"Diana!" Kaz said, the urgency in his voice betraying the fear that was just under the surface. "What can I do?"

"She's okay," I said, to convince myself as well as him, to calm my own fears. I listened to her breathing and felt her pulse. Normal. It had all been too much, too elegant, too different. Too clean, too white, too pure. I stroked her cheek, one hand still cradling her head, and she half awoke, her eyes opening part way and meeting mine.

"Billy, what happened?"

"You fainted."

"Damn silly . . ." She shook her head as if to deny her weakness, then rested her cheek in the palm of my hand.

I knelt by the bedside, pressed up against the night table, as she curled her hand around my wrist. It wasn't really a comfortable position, but I liked it. I could hear the rhythmic, even sounds of her breathing as she dropped off to sleep.

I heard Kaz open the door. "I will be right back," he whispered.

By the time Kaz returned, I had managed to free my hand without waking Diana. I sat in the armchair near the window, watching her and looking out at the Mediterranean, trying to make believe we were on our honeymoon, at a seaside resort, and Diana was just taking a nap. The oversized fatigues and unlaced combat boots she was wearing didn't help my imagination. There wasn't much in the way of women's clothing available in U.S. Army warehouses, and I was wondering how to find her something else when Kaz walked in, carrying a couple of parcels and trailed by a very pretty young girl.

"Yvette, this is Lieutenant Boyle, and there is our friend, Miss Seaton."

"I am pleased to make your acquaintance,

Lieutenant," she said in slow but proper English, holding her hands together in front of her. She wore a skirt with all sorts of flowers on it, and a white blouse with ruffled sleeves and blue embroidery around the neckline, a peasant blouse I think the girls back home called it. Her hair was brown, short and wavy, and she had a confident smile. Her eyes cautiously flitted around the room, taking in everything, assessing the situation, to see if whatever Kaz had said that had gotten her to accompany a stranger into a hotel room was on the up and up.

"Yvette works in a little shop down the street . . ." Kaz started to explain.

"What were you shopping for?" I asked in a low voice.

"I thought Diana would like some clothes and feminine articles," said Kaz, "so I went in search of a shop. Yvette was very helpful, and speaks excellent English." He nodded to her, and she returned the favor.

"That's nice," I said. "I don't mean to sound rude but what is she doing here?"

"I have engaged Yvette to stay with Diana for the rest of the day and night. She had just finished work at the shop, and is also free tomorrow. Her mother runs the establishment, and agreed once I explained the situation."

"Thanks, Kaz. I hadn't thought that far ahead."

"Yes, well, that is what friends are for, is it not?" Kaz didn't wait for an answer. He sat on the couch, opening the parcels with his good hand as Yvette held them for him. There was perfume, colorful silk pajamas in greens and blues, a long robe that looked almost like an evening gown, lipstick, and a bunch of make-up stuff that I could only guess at.

"Yes, it is, Kaz. Thank you. I'm glad you're here."

He stopped for a moment, then he looked at Diana, and at Yvette, standing in front of him holding an open box with silks spilling out of it in an eruption of colors. "You know," he said, a hint of amazement creeping into his voice, "I am glad also."

"Glad of what?"

We all turned to see Diana, awake and propped up on her elbows, blinking her eyes and looking at Yvette.

"Glad to see you, and to be among friends," Kaz continued, a smile lighting up his face. "This is Yvette, and she will stay with you tonight. Billy and I have some business to attend to."

Diana pushed herself up and said, "Be careful, both of you."

"We will be, my dear," Kaz answered. "We have all sorts of things here that Yvette picked out. I told her you were without anything a young lady needs and she has supplied you with all the basics." He spread his hands out to indicate the boxes strewn around the couch.

"Perhaps tomorrow, Miss Seaton, I can go out and purchase some dresses for you, if you tell me what you like."

"That sounds nice, Yvette," Diana said. "Very nice. And please call me Diana."

"Oui. Today, we can perhaps wash your hair, Diana," Yvette said. She had a very precise way of speaking, as if she were thinking about each word, which she probably was. Diana said something to her in French, not as slowly, and they both laughed.

"And shoes, also," Yvette said as she moved around the bed to help Diana take off the combat boots. "Yes, definitely shoes."

"I must go now," said Kaz. "I will speak to the kitchen about your meals and they will be brought to you. No army food will be allowed in this room, I promise you. I will meet you at the jeep, Billy." He made a little bow and smiled at Yvette before giving her the room key.

Her face lit up. One thing I could never figure out is the effect Kaz had on women.

He's a short, thin guy with glasses, with a long scar on one side of his face. But there's something about him that drives women wild. Maybe it's that he's the kind of guy who thinks about buying soft frilly things. Or maybe it's the bow. I couldn't see myself pulling that one off.

I sat on the side of Diana's bed. Yvette got busy around the couch, picking up clothes, folding them, and putting them away in the dresser drawers.

"We'll be back in the morning," I said.

"You don't have to come back, you know," Diana said, watching Yvette opening drawers. "You came to Bône to rescue me, I know that. If it wasn't for you, I might be dead right now." Her voice trailed off, and I wondered if she was thinking back to that courtyard at the French supply depot and remembering raising that pistol to her head. Or, was she recalling Villard.

"But I will come back," I assured her.

"I'm not sure I want you to."

"Why? What do you mean?"

"You figure it out, you're the detective." Her eyes were filled with pain and hurt. She spoke again before I could, but she was done talking to me. "Yvette, help me up, please. I'd love to get out of these men's clothes and to bathe." She tried to swivel her legs around, pushing up with her hands. As she rose into a sitting position at the end of the bed, she winced.

"Can I help?" I asked, sounding like a little kid in the kitchen with his mother.

"No, no, no," said Yvette, advancing on me and wagging a finger. "This is work for women only. You must leave."

"Billy, please go, I know you have things to do," said Diana.

"Okay," I said, trying hard not to sound like a chump getting the heave-ho. "I just want to wash up for a minute before I go. I'll knock before I come out to make sure you're decent." I retreated to the bathroom. It was big, with a marble sink, nickel-plated fixtures, and a big freestanding tub on little claw feet with soft towels hung on either side. Nice bathroom for the honeymoon suite, I thought glumly as I looked at myself in the mirror. Everything about me was rumpled. Shirt, hair, even my face. I ran some water and washed, wanting to feel clean and fresh. I wet my hair and ran a comb through it, finding the part and noticing that my hair was already turning lighter and my skin darker as I spent more time under the North African sun. I gave myself the patented Billy Boyle smile, guaranteed to charm every time. I saw pearly whites against tan skin, but not a touch of charm. Then I heard a shriek. Without thinking I quickly opened the door.

Yvette was standing on the other side of the bed, holding her hands over her mouth, her eyes wide. I moved around the bed as she shook off whatever had scared her and kneeled.

"She got up too quickly and fainted, Monsieur. Je suis désolée." I think that meant she was sorry.

Then I saw why Yvette had screamed. Diana lay on her side on the floor. The robe she was wearing had fallen open. She was naked, her body covered in welts and bruises, the kind of marks a real sadist leaves. No blood, no cuts, just ugly black, blue, dark red, and grayish-green colors decorating her like a tattooed nightmare. Yvette grabbed one end of the robe and covered her, but not before I could see the large dark, bruises between her thighs and the red welts on her breasts.

"Je suis désolée," Yvette said again, this time to Diana as she patted her cheeks. "Je suis désolée." I'm sorry. I'm sorry. Diana came to suddenly, grabbed at her robe and pulled it tightly closed.

"I got up too quickly —"

"I know. Let me help you," I said, trying

to make light of her state, as if she had merely been a bit dizzy.

She didn't say anything. Yvette and I each took an elbow and lifted her, seating her on the edge of the bed. Our eyes locked for an instant and a silent message passed between us. Diana didn't need to know that we had both seen.

"I will start the hot water running in the tub," Yvette said, now in command of her English once more. "Do not get up, I will help you into the bathroom in a minute." She went into the bathroom and I was left alone with Diana. I struggled to stay in control, to sound normal, to pretend I hadn't just seen the marks of a torturer's hands all over her. I didn't know what I was feeling. A numbness had settled in over my heart.

"I don't know what's wrong, but I have to stop this fainting," Diana said.

"You've been through a lot. You'll feel better after a few days of bed rest." I tried to sound chipper, like I knew what the hell I was talking about.

"You remember that you said you'd find them," Diana said, not really a question but a statement. I had to struggle to think about what it was she was talking about.

"You mean the other prisoners?"

"Yes. You promised."

"I'll start tomorrow," I said, "first we have to take care of something tonight. I'll come see you in the morning and then —"

"No," Diana said, clipping off the word with a firmness I didn't think she still had. "Go find them now. I don't need to see you. You must find them before he starts on someone else. Go."

She sat with her robe bunched up in two clenched fists, shielding her wounds from the world. And from me.

"Okay, I will," I told her.

CHAPTER
THIRTY-ONE

I took the stairs two at a time, my hand sliding along the brass banister as my heels smacked the marble stairs leading into the main lobby. I wanted to leave the hotel, to flee the vision of Diana's bruised body, to disappear into the desert and let the sun scorch my eyes and burn away what I'd seen and what I still imagined.

"Billy," Kaz said, coming toward me from the lobby. I halted at the landing, only a few steps left before the main floor and the open doors, escape beckoning to me with ocean breezes.

"What?" I said, with more irritation than I meant to. I couldn't look at Kaz, I couldn't trust my face to hide the effects of what I had seen and how it was tearing at me inside. Wiping sweat from my forehead with my sleeve, I leaned against the railing, my sight fixed on the sliver of blue sea visible through the double doors.

"General Eisenhower is here, and he wants to see you." Kaz leaned on the railing, and I felt his eyes on me.

"We've got things to do," I said.

"I know," said Kaz, "after we see the general." He put his hand on my arm, like a cop leading a suspect or a mother taking her kid to school. I wanted to shake off his grip and run, but it was Kaz, and I knew he meant well. I also knew I couldn't skip out on Uncle Ike, even as crazed as I was feeling. We walked through the lobby, into a wing of the hotel filled with busy clerks and WACs and admirals, lots of hustle and even more bustle as they organized the new home of Allied Forces Headquarters.

Kaz was about to knock on a door when it flew open and General Mark Clark strode out, all six feet plus of him brushing past us as two aides hurried to keep up. The door remained open, held by a woman in a khaki skirt and blouse that she somehow made look faintly glamorous.

"Hello, Kay," I said. "I heard the general wants to see us."

"Yes, Billy, he's been asking about you. And about Miss Seaton. He's very concerned."

Headquarters staff was like a big family. Everyone knew everyone else's business.

And Kay Summersby was no exception. Kay was Uncle Ike's driver, occasional secretary, and constant companion. Kay had known Daphne, and was good friends with Kaz. So of course she'd heard about Diana, which meant so had Uncle Ike. I braced myself for their pity as Kay led us into the next room.

"William," Unkle Ike said, advancing on me with his right hand extended. His left clasped me on the shoulder. "How are you?"

"Fine, sir," was all I could manage.

"Lieutenant Kazimierz told me about your rescue of Miss Seaton. That was very brave, William."

"It was nothing compared to what she went through, sir." I regretted how that sounded as soon as it came out. I didn't want to make Uncle Ike feel guilty or add to his burden. I only wanted to get out of here and set things right.

"I know, I know, William. She took a tremendous risk, but it was necessary. We had to take every measure to ensure safe landings for our troops and to rally the French to our side."

"I didn't mean —"

"Don't worry, William, I'm growing a thick skin these days. Did you know Edward R. Murrow asked if we were fighting the

433

Nazis in North Africa or sleeping with them? Jesus Christ on the mountain! The press is after me as if I were the devil himself." He reached for a cigarette but the crumpled pack was empty. He threw it away, his mouth twisted in frustration. Before he could say a word, Kay was opening a fresh pack and handing it to him.

"Thanks, Kay," he said. She smiled at him and went back to her seat. She had a way about her, with that faint Irish lilt in her voice and her dark, lively eyes. I could see she calmed the general down by her presence, handing him cigarettes, sitting with him, being someone who made no demands of him.

Uncle Ike drew deep on his cigarette, blowing out blue smoke that rode on a sigh into the air. "I was sick when I heard what Miss Seaton endured, William, I want you to know that. That went beyond all bounds of civilized conduct. She will recover, won't she?"

"Yes — yes, I think so. The man who —"

"Yes, yes, William. You want him held accountable."

Uncle Ike's eyes held mine, and I wondered why he wanted to see me, what could be so important in the midst of everything else he was responsible for. I saw his eyes drift toward Kay, seated in a soft leather chair, her long legs crossed, the heel of her shoe dangling off her foot. Then he closed them, as if he couldn't bear the vision in his mind either. Maybe I was reading too much into it, maybe I was thinking about myself, but I sensed loss and regret and longing in those averted eyes.

"Yes, sir, I do."

"You have to leave that aside, for now, William. Not everything we want in this life comes to pass. These are delicate times. One mistake, and everything we've worked for can be destroyed. You have to leave things as they are. Do you understand, William?"

I didn't understand a damn thing, except that Uncle Ike felt he had to explain himself to me, and that he felt guilty enough to take the time to tell me it was important to lay off Villard. Maybe he knew all those reporters had a point. Maybe he wished he could do what he wanted, not simply what was best for the war effort. For all I knew, Darlan himself was cooling his heels in the hallway while we had this little talk, and Uncle Ike needed to steel himself to shake hands with a snake. No, I didn't understand anything, as I began to comprehend how the world really worked.

"Sure, Uncle Ike," I said in a whisper, allowing myself the familiarity we sometimes shared in private. "Sure."

Kaz and I didn't go straight back to the hospital, although we were supposed to rendezvous there with Harding to plan for meeting up with the train carrying the second penicillin shipment. First we took a detour to the Algiers docks, to a warehouse that served as the headquarters for the Quartermaster Corps. These were the guys who controlled the shipment of all supplies through Algiers and up to the front. If anyone had evidence as to who'd signed off on the receipt for the order detailing the second shipment of penicillin, it would be the Quartermaster Corps.

We drove through the city center, which was filled with shops and cafés. This was France, not Algeria. All the signs were in French, and the only Arabs in sight were sweeping the sidewalks. Men in suits walked hurriedly down the streets between the four- and five-story buildings, all richly decorated with ironwork grills and tall windows. People sat under awnings at sidewalk cafés, sipping tiny cups of thick coffee as they watched the world go by. I was the world going by. I had places to go, people to kill, no time for lolling around a café. As we

436

drove closer to the water, the road skirted the shore. The buildings to our left, each house painted the same light sea-green color that made them look cool even as they baked in the harsh brightness, had their shutters closed tight against the blazing sun. While I admired the architecture, Kaz had been studying the notebook with the codes in it. Or ciphers, if that's what they were. He tapped his finger on an open page, nodding to himself.

"This has to be a book cipher. It has to be."

"What do you mean?"

"Book cipher, or dictionary code in its simplest form —"

"Well, which is it, a code or a cipher?"

"Both, in a way. Did you know the English word *code* comes from the Latin *codex,* which means book? So, actually . . ."

"Okay, okay, I'm sorry I asked. Just tell me what it means. Is it good news or bad?"

"Oh, very bad indeed, for us. Unless we know which book, then it is very good news."

"Kaz, could you start making sense anytime now? That would be fine."

"Very well. Remember when I told you about the sets of three numbers? For instance, like this set, 236-16-5."

"Yeah."

"I think this is a variation on a dictionary code. With that, two people have the same edition of a dictionary. There are two number sets used, such as 90-25. That means go to page ninety and then the twenty-fifth entry. Therefore, 90-25 stands for that word."

"Okay, but we have three numbers."

"Yes, that is why this is so clever. I am guessing that there is a book, but it is not necessarily a dictionary. It could be anything. And, the third number refers to a letter. Page number, line number, then count to the number indicated and you get one letter."

"Is that safer?"

"Quite. One way to break a code is to look for patterns. The most common letters in the English language are E, T, O, A, and R, in that order. You can look for patterns in codes to see how often certain substitutions are used."

"But with this book code, I could use a different three-number combination for every E in my message!"

"Excellent, Billy! Yes, there need never be a repeat. No pattern, nothing to go on. The only way to break this code, if it is what I think it is, would be to discover what book is being used."

"But only the people using the code know that, and it would be incredibly easy to hide."

"Oh, yes, it could be anything. Even a magazine, if it had enough pages. Or a manual, or a novel, or. . . ." He gave up and shrugged.

"Great. So the codebook is useless."

"Yes. I went through the substitution code, the simple one, and that is all place names. I will check a map later but I doubt anything important was consigned to that code. It's only a shorthand, as I said."

"Well, good work anyway, Kaz. Sure would be nice if we could catch a break for a goddamn change." I hit the horn as an Arab leading a couple of donkeys took more than his share of the road. Just one little break, that's all, one damn break.

The shore ahead curved to the right, and so did the road, bringing us into the harbor district. The buildings were of worn, cracked stucco with peeling paint, displaying their age. Piers jutted out into the water, which had turned from a brilliant blue to a dark, oil-stained pool where dead fish, seaweed, and garbage marked the high tide line. This was the working Algiers, not a single café in sight. Small craft, from sailing boats to tenders, crowded the first piers we passed, and the docks were crammed with even larger ships, unloading tons of supplies every hour. Most of it would make it to the front or wherever it was supposed to go. It was the rest of it that I was interested in.

Farther out, a line of destroyers sat at anchor, guarding the harbor entrance. I could see anti-aircraft emplacements on the heights above the harbor, and as I looked around at the stacks of ammo, fuel, beans, boots, and black oil, I hoped they wouldn't be needed for the next few minutes. Gulls were everywhere, squawking at each other, looking for choice morsels from the broken cases and open boxes that littered the wooden docks in either direction. We stopped at a fork in the road. It went inland to the left, or onto a concrete roadway leading down to the main dockyard on the right. I read the freshly painted signs that were nailed up on a telephone pole, their arrows pointing every which way. Harbormaster, to the right. Local Labor, dead ahead. Quartermaster, hard left. New York City, straight out to sea. Every GI's a joker.

A Quonset hut had already been erected in front of the warehouse, at the far edge of the harbor, not much beyond the breakwater the locals called the Jetée du Nord. A line of Arab workers passed, each guy carrying a sack of flour over his shoulder that looked like it weighed more than he did. A single GI with a carbine walked behind them, telling them to hurry up, but their pace didn't change much one way or the other. The place smelled like saltwater brine, rotting fish, and sweat. I tried not to breath too deeply as we got out of the jeep.

Inside the Quonset hut, an overworked corporal was sitting on two cases of Scotch, typing a form on a typewriter that sat on another two cases of Scotch. It was nice to see the QM Corps making do with what they had. A stack of forms was piled up on either side of the typewriter, and an ashcan filled with cigarette butts sat in front of him. His shirt, showing off his two stripes, was hung over a crate behind him. He was in a sweat-soaked T-shirt, peering intently at the form he was working on, lining up the carriage to fill in those little boxes neatly. He ignored us until he got it right, then looked up at me as he started typing. I told him what I wanted, and he didn't stop clacking the keys, one by one, for even a second. He just nodded toward the end of the hut, gesturing with the cigarette clenched between his lips.

"Knock yerself out, Lieutenant. The files

are all back there. Pardon the mess."

Not exactly the height of military courtesy, but it's amazing how agreeable officers can be to supply clerks with so much Scotch they use it for furniture. I threaded my way between the liquor, radios, cartons of Lucky Strikes, condoms, and all the other highly convertible currency of war. At the end of the aisle there were three large filing cabinets lined up against the wall. The only problem was that they hadn't had time to file any paperwork yet. Two cardboard boxes overflowing with carbon paper and crumpled forms stood in front of the filing cabinets. Really large boxes. I looked at Kaz and shrugged. One for each of us.

It was hot, very hot, not too surprising since the sun was baking the sheet metal skin of the Quonset hut at about 102 degrees this time of day. We each pulled up a wooden crate; Kaz's was marked SPAM and mine was SOCKS, WOOLEN, GREEN. We sat and read U.S. Army requisition forms in the stifling heat, at the back end of this tin hut stuck out on the worst smelling dock outside of Boston harbor in August. And it was all my idea; I couldn't even blame anyone else. I tried to think of something short of bodily injury that could be worse, and came up empty.

About an hour later I had learned that you could requisition a pool table if the order was signed off by a major or higher. I filed that information away for use later, but didn't have more to show than that, other than a small dent in the paperwork in my box. I was going through a stack of requisitions for blister cream when Kaz pulled out a large, worn manila envelope from underneath his pile of papers.

"Billy, this is marked Receipts, Orders!" The envelope was about three inches thick and bulging at the seams. Kaz emptied the contents onto the floor with his good arm and started pawing through them. I came over and lent a hand. There were receipts for movement orders, receipts for orders detailing the distribution of tents, receipts for orders of cooking supplies to Company kitchens, all sorts of acknowledgments of orders to send or receive supplies, none in any discernable order. There was even a receipt for an order of receipt forms. We were more than halfway through the pile when Kaz yelled out.

"Billy! Here it is! An order to the 21st General Hospital, Colonel M. Walton Commanding. For the receipt of a shipment of penicillin, to be delivered tomorrow! It's dated 9 November." He turned it over, looking for the signature on the back of the form indicating receipt by the proper command. It was a carbon copy, so the signature wasn't exactly clear. But it was still unmistakable.

Sgt. J. Casselli.

"Joe signed this on the 9th and was dead the next day," I said.

"Is it normal procedure for a sergeant to sign such a receipt?" asked Kaz.

"Sure, when he's the supply sergeant, like Joe was. Only thing is, normal procedure is to give it to your CO after signing for it. Walton would have gotten the original. Walton had to know about the shipment."

"So he lied to us?"

I thought about that question. Could Casselli have kept the receipt from Walton? Why would he? I sat there with the sweat running down my face, dripping onto the plywood floor, evaporating in a second. I watched as the little drops hit the floor and then disappeared. Now you see it, now you don't, just like the missing orders. I thought about that phone in Walton's office, and how quickly that shooter had had us in his sights. I thought about gambling, and wondered what other vices Walton dabbled in. I thought about Blackpool, and how he was CO of a hospital in a city where the organized crime boss was related to a crooked French soldier in Algiers. I thought about letters, and codes, and disappearing supply sergeants. Now they're here, now they're gone. Drip, splash. Vanishing orders, evaporating in an instant. First here, then gone, now back again. I looked down at the piece of paper in my hand. Joe Casselli had scribbled his own death warrant, never knowing what that hasty scrawl had meant. I wondered what had happened. Had he taken the order to Walton, only to be told to keep it on the QT? Had he refused? Walton would yell and scream, Casselli would stand his ground. Walton would seem to give in . . . and then contact Mathenet, who would arrange to eliminate Casselli, the guy who wasn't crooked enough for their plans.

"Billy?"

"Yeah, he lied. Let's go."

Chapter
Thirty-Two

"Because everything fits, that's why!" I gunned the jeep up the sloping roadway, away from the stinking docks, forcing Kaz to hang on, and hopefully to shut up.

"But there is no real evidence . . ." Kaz said, as he was slammed back in his seat. He alternated using his good arm to hold onto the brim of his service cap and to clutch the frame of the jeep. As usual, nothing stopped him from talking.

"Whaddya mean, no evidence? Walton had to have known about the second supply shipment. If Casselli never gave him the receipt, why did he end up with his throat slit? They must've argued, and Walton decided he had to be silenced. He had access to the only telephone within miles, and he came here from the same city in England where the Bessette family ran the local rackets. Plus, he gambles. He may have gotten in too deep in Blackpool and this is his payback."

I took the next corner hard, glad I had the steering wheel and gearshift to hang onto. Kaz braced himself with his feet and clung to his hat.

"Circumstantial evidence," Kaz said, shifting upright in his seat as I came out of the turn.

"Nothing wrong with circumstantial evidence if there's a ton of it."

"No, no, I mean the film, *Circumstantial Evidence.* We saw it one evening in London, at Headquarters."

Ike loved movies, and nearly every night there was something showing at HQ.

"What about it?" I asked, slowing down in the crowded streets of the business district.

"An American journalist wishes to demonstrate that circumstantial evidence should not be enough to convict someone. So, he arranges evidence that shows he killed a man, and has the so-called victim go into hiding, to reappear after he is convicted."

"Sounds a little farfetched, even for a reporter."

"It would be a scoop, correct?"

"Yeah, I guess. What happened?"

"The alleged victim does not show up, and the reporter is almost executed. Finally, he arrives and saves him."

"So?"

"Well, if that reporter could be convicted only by circumstantial evidence, and it was all false . . ."

"Kaz, no one made this stuff up. People are really dead." We stopped at an intersection. A French cop, directing traffic, held up a white-gloved hand.

"Yes, they are," he said. "And Diana was very badly hurt. Which may cause you to not think quite clearly."

The cop waved us through. I didn't say anything. It's hard to argue with a movie. We drove up a narrow, winding street that finally opened into a thoroughfare that led to the residential area and then out of the city. A stone wall about five feet high ran along one block, enclosing some Frenchman's mansion. A message was painted on it, the whitewash still wet and dripping from the bottom of the letters.

"Darlan à la guillotine!" Kaz read.

"Darlan to the guillotine?" I asked.

"Exactly. The Admiral does not appear too popular here."

"Not my favorite guy either, or the bums he has working for him."

"Your opinion is shared by many, especially in London and amongst the members of the press. Do you know that he has made

448

the SOL legal again? They were outlawed right after the landings, and Darlan has already canceled that."

"Ike must've loved that."

"Yes, I learned some new curses from him . . . 'Jesus Christ on the mountain'!"

Kaz gave that in a passable imitation of Ike's flat Kansas accent, and we both laughed. Just two pals out for a ride, making fun of the boss. It felt like old times, until I thought about Diana and those marks on her body. I understood why'd she contemplated raising that gun to her head, and why Kaz didn't care much for living now that Daphne was gone. Everything fell into place, the perfect misery of it all, the cycle of brutality, death, and guilt and the ruin it brought to those left behind. I had to find a way to stop that wheel from turning, just for a minute, so we could get off without breaking our necks. I knew nothing would ever be the same again, but I also knew that it didn't have to get any worse, not if I had anything to do about it. Darlan à la guillotine. Villard à la guillotine.

We left the thoroughfare and crossed railroad tracks on our way to the coast road and the hospital. The tracks paralleled the road and up ahead we could see a long train, unmoving. There must've been thirty

449

or so cars, so many that I could barely make out the steam from the locomotive up front. Kaz swiveled his head around, looking for something as he cupped his hand to his ear.

"Do you hear that, Billy?"

I heard it the moment he asked. A steady droning sound, coming from where? I checked the train, thinking it was some sort of machinery working on the tracks. I slowed, craning my neck as the droning became a high-pitched scream. The sky behind us was swarming with aircraft, the six lead planes beginning their steep dive, straight at us.

I downshifted and slammed on the gas, not wanting to hang around and offer the Jerries a stationary target. The road sloped off on either side into two deep ditches. There was nowhere to go but straight ahead. We were alongside the train now, about fifty yards separating the roadbed and the tracks. The train whistle blew and I could see the cars jolting forward as the locomotive driver got the same idea I had, except you can't floor it when you're dragging thirty loaded boxcars.

"Ju88s!" Kaz cried out, and I turned for a second and spotted the bulbous glass nose sprouting machine guns as a twin-engine dive-bomber hurtled straight at our jeep.

No, not toward us, of course not! They were headed for the train. A single vehicle was nothing, not when a fat juicy supply train was sitting there, barely moving, just waiting to be blown to bits. Kaz grabbed for my Thompson in the back seat, but with only one hand he couldn't hold it and pull the bolt back. The screaming whine of the six dive bombers grew louder. They were almost on top of us when the first one let go its bomb load and pulled up, about even with us. I could see the swastika on its tail clear as day. I heard explosions before the bombs hit but it was Kaz, blasting away at the next incoming plane with his revolver. Not that it would do much good, but it was better than just sitting there.

The bombs hit wide of the train, crashing into the culvert, blasting dirt and debris over the train, the road, and us. I covered my head with one hand and drove with the other, wishing I had my helmet on. The train had picked up speed, which meant that it was going to stay alongside us for too damn long.

"Hang on!" I yelled and thrust out my right arm to get Kaz's attention. "Hang on tight!"

I slammed on the brakes and spun the steering wheel, sending us on a sideways skid down the road as I fought to keep control and not roll us over. We were dead even with the locomotive, and, as we skidded, I was facing it head on. I saw the engineer look at me and then up into the sky, his eyes and mouth wide open, fear showing on his face as if it had been painted there. The skid slowed and I pumped the brakes, getting the jeep to halt facing back the way we had come. Peeling out, I gave it all I had, racing against time and bombs and what they would do if that train was loaded with munitions.

The next bombs hit their target, and the next, until there was nothing but one continuous detonation. I looked back and saw the engine lift off the tracks and explode, sending a geyser of steam into the air before the next car hit the burning wreck and burst into a huge fireball of black smoke and angry red flames engulfing the front of the train, the road, and everything within a hundred yards of where we had been.

The next planes struck farther back along the train, their bombs impacting just behind us as they methodically took the boxcars apart. There were huge explosions of gas, multiple secondary explosions of all sorts of ordnance, and the screeching, crashing sound of boxcars sliding off the tracks and breaking up before the fire and bombs devoured them. By the time the last of the six dive bombers had hit the rear of the train, we were back to where we had crossed the tracks, looking down the rails at the burning wreckage, fire and smoke filling the air, obscuring where the planes were headed next.

I stopped the jeep and took my hands off the wheel. They were shaking so hard I put them right back, to steady them.

"Billy . . ." Kaz looked at me with wide eyes, his still smoking revolver in his good hand.

"Yes, Kaz, I will teach you how to do that, when your arm is better."

"Thank you."

"No problem. But I need a minute here."

"Thanks to your driving, we have more minutes than we reasonably should have. We would have been incinerated. . . ." He was excited, the thrill of almost dying lighting up his face. I was just about getting my heart back into my chest, and didn't want to hear about how we were nearly blown up.

"Yeah, I know. You hit anything with that?"

Kaz was reloading, still smiling, his grin split by the scar on his cheek.

"I —"

He was cut off by the chatter of a machine gun and a Ju88 flying low out of the smoke. One of them had come back for us. Jesus Christ on the mountain. The bullets chewed up dirt and gravel around us but didn't really come close. If we stayed here we wouldn't be so lucky next time. I pulled a tight turn and headed back for the train, hoping to hide in the smoke until the plane became bored with searching for such a worthless target. I could hear the engines behind us. Since he was flying in the clear, it would be easy for the nose gunner to line us up this time before the smoke concealed us. Kaz kept firing at the airplane with his revolver. I pressed the gas pedal down and didn't let up.

"Stop shooting that thing, you're just making him mad!"

"You use the Thompson, Billy! I can't work it with one hand."

"Screw that —" I was interrupted by bursts of machine gun fire that hit the road ahead of us. I glanced back and saw the Ju88 off to our left a bit, lining up for a better shot. I swerved, trying to throw his aim off yet stay on the road at the same time. The smoke from the burning train was close, but we weren't going to make it. The nose gunner let go a long burst and I swear

I could feel the bullets as they parted the air just above us. The pilot had to pull up. The shadow of the Ju88 spread slowly over us as we raced at top speed and he tried to fly as slowly as he could to give his machine gunner a chance. The shadow faded and I hoped we were home free. Then I saw the rear-facing twin machine guns underneath the fuselage emit bright flashes, like fire-works, as the gunner fired straight down at us. Bullets slammed into the hood of the jeep and I felt the vibrations in the steering wheel as I tried to keep my hands from fly-ing off it. Everything slowed down, and I noticed that the bottom of the airplane was a light blue, just like the sky. It was almost pretty. Kaz had his arm raised and was fir-ing that damn revolver of his again. I heard the *pow, pow, pow* of Kaz's bullets, but they were up against the hard, ripping sound of the twin machine guns spitting hundred of slugs at us. Another burst of fire came from the machine guns as the plane pulled up and away and I heard one of our front tires blow out at the same time as the hood flew up with a mix of smoke and steam. The jeep swerved wildly and I fought to hold on, but the wheel rim couldn't take it and we spun around, off the road, into the air.

CHAPTER
THIRTY-THREE

I was on the ground. There were bodies all around me. My head hurt. I tried to sit up, which took all the strength I had. It wasn't enough. I heard voices. It might have been an hour after the crash, or two seconds. The last thing I remembered was the jeep going off the road, into the ditch. No one was around, just me and Kaz. Kaz? Was he one of the bodies? Who were they?

I was about to open one eye when somebody did it for me. Two fingers pulled my eyelids apart and a pair of eyes stared down at me. The sun made a halo behind the figure standing over me and I turned away. I heard the voices again and tried as hard as I could to understand, but there was a ringing sound coming from somewhere. Was somebody talking to me? To Kaz?

I opened both eyes and looked around. Everything was blurry. I tried to get up, used my hands to push myself up an inch.

What was that? It wasn't the ground. Cold metal. I heard a door slam and an engine roar to life. Someone was moaning and the ringing sound kept on as I felt the vehicle lurch forward. What the hell was going on? I managed to raise myself onto my elbows, my head pounding. Slats of wood were in my way. Canvas. I was on a stretcher. That made sense, and I lay my head back, wondering about Kaz.

Green and white figures moved around me as I heard the engine stop. They took the stretcher and moved me outside. A big red cross floating on pure white appeared and yells pierced the air. More ambulances. My head throbbed and everything rotated around me in a blur. I wanted nothing more than to lie there, but I had to find Kaz. Rolling onto my side, I tried to lever myself onto one knee. It didn't work out well and I found myself face down on the dry, gritty ground. Where was that ringing coming from?

"Whoa, fella, where do you think you're going?" The voice was close to my ear, but tinny and distant. Who was ringing those damn bells?

I turned my head, squinted, tried to get the face in focus.

"What?" I said, even though I had heard

him. I hadn't understood the question.

"Stay right there, you're going to be fine, Mac." I felt hands under my shoulders lifting me back onto the stretcher. Then they were gone. Okay, I was going to be fine, I had to stay here, but somebody needed to stop ringing that goddamn bell. And I had to find Kaz.

"Where am I?" Nobody answered. They probably couldn't hear me with all that ringing going on. I put my hands over my ears but it got louder as I shut out the other noises. My right hand felt sticky. I pulled it away. Blood. Jesus Christ on that fucking mountain. Bells in my head *and* I'm bleeding. What happened? Where was Kaz?

"Get this one inside, X-Ray."

I knew that voice. Hands lifted the stretcher and I went from the hot sun to a cool hallway. X-Ray. Who was that guy? Was he talking about me? I got it.

"Doctor Perrini. Doc!" I tried to yell but it came out a croak. The hospital. This had to be the hospital. I grabbed at the first green leg that walked by me.

"Leggo, Mac! Wait your turn!"

"Is this the 21st? General Hospital?"

"Yeah," green leg said, impatience battling with pity in his voice. He knelt down. "You don't look too bad, Lieutenant, but you have to have an X-Ray to see if you cracked your skull. You probably have a concussion at least."

"Where's the guy I came in with? British uniform." I tried to keep my eyes focused and to understand what he was telling me. I looked at his sleeve. PFC. Must be an orderly.

"No fucking idea, sir. We got casualties from Medjez el Bab coming in. They ran into *beaucoup* Germans up there. Plus the air raid. Krauts hit some ships in the harbor and a convoy of GIs on the road. They really plastered us. We got casualties coming in from everywhere. I never expected it to be like this!"

My vision cleared for a second. He was just a skinny kid, nineteen tops. His face was white, and his thin bony fingers gripped his pants leg in a desperate attempt to hang onto something solid. He didn't appear to want to keep going. He looked up and down the hallway, stretcher cases running the full length of it. He had probably not seen this much suffering in his entire life.

"What's your name?" I asked him. He looked startled.

"Uh, Johnston, Lieutenant."

"No, I mean your first name."

"John, sir, but everybody calls me Jay

because John Johnston sorta sounds silly."

"Okay, Jay. Now listen, I gotta find the guy I came in with. Help me up."

"You're in line for an X-Ray, Lieutenant, I can't —"

"Sure you can. Just help me up and we'll look around. Then bring me back here for the X-Ray." It sounded like a good plan to me. But I needed a little help, and for those bells to stop.

"You got hit on the head too hard, Lieutenant. You have to stay there!"

Jay scurried off. At least he looked more scared of me than of the other casualties now. My head was beginning to clear a little, and the ringing racket going on between my ears was down a few notches. With no help available, it was time to either lay back and forget about Kaz, or get up by myself. I wondered what an X Ray would find. I touched the side of my head again and felt a crusty patch of matted hair and dried blood. I realized my shirt was gone. I found the blood-soaked pieces on the stretcher beside me. They must have cut it off, looking for other wounds. I did a quick check and couldn't find any other sharp pains anywhere. I knew I could move my legs and arms, even if not real well. Screw the X Ray. I just needed a shirt so I could walk around without being put back on a stretcher.

I looked up and down the hall. No Jay, no doctors. I took a deep breath and rolled off the stretcher, onto my knees and elbows. Oh boy. The bells started ringing louder, my skull was pounding, but I stayed steady on all fours. Good so far. I got up on one knee. Still no one in the hallway. I had to stand upright now, while I had the time. Push, I ordered myself.

I was up. My legs were shaking. I rested my hands on my knees while my stomach decided if it was coming with me or not. The hallway started to spin but it slowed to a stop, like a top on its last few turns. My stomach stayed put and I managed to stand up straight. That lasted two seconds, but long enough for me to get one hand to the wall and that was enough to keep me vertical. I took a couple of deep breaths and let my hand fall to my side. Not bad. Who needs an X-Ray anyway?

I took slow steps until I was sure my legs remembered how to work together. They did and I kept going, aiming for the open door on my right. I passed one guy on his stretcher who had his leg in a splint. He smiled and gave me the V for victory sign. I nodded like I was out for a walk in the park. The next guy was unconscious. His chest was taped up and he had a gauze bandage on his head. His breathing was ragged, bubbles of blood popping out of his mouth when he exhaled. If this was the area for guys who weren't hurt too badly and could wait, I didn't want to see the others.

I made it to a door. I went in. No one was inside. Just what I wanted. A supply closet with a sink, soap, and shelves full of bandages, towels, all sorts of medical supplies. I ran the water and stuck my head underneath the spigot. It felt like an ice pick. I gasped but made myself stay under. I had to look presentable, and that meant no dried blood. I washed my face and toweled off, carefully dabbing around the wound above my ear. I had a big goose egg, and a long cut still oozing blood after I cleaned it out. I went through the bandages, found a gauze pad, and wrapped a bandage around it, ripped the ends and tied them off. There wasn't a mirror and I hoped I looked like a discharged walking wounded, not an escaped madman.

Clothes. I needed a shirt. The shelves were stacked with operating gowns but I didn't think I could pass for a doctor. I looked around and saw khaki shirts and pants hanging on the back of the door. Perfect. I checked the shirts. There was one with lieutenant's bars and one with captain's. I decided against adding impersonating a senior office to whatever regulations I was breaking already and took the second louie's shirt.

My hands rested on the sink for a minute. The cold water had cleared my head some. I was still dizzy and things were a bit blurry, but I was ready. I was even getting used to the ringing in my ears. Time to find Kaz.

I moved down the hallway, and recognized where I was. This was a wing off the main hospital. I walked past a double door with X-Ray painted on it. I couldn't bust in to see if Kaz was there, but I checked the stretchers lining the hall. Mostly GIs with broken bones or cracked skulls. A few sailors, maybe from the air raid on the harbor. I was almost to the end of the corridor when a nurse turned the corner and walked toward me.

"Are you all right, Lieutenant?" she asked, concern and confusion wrinkling her brow.

"Yeah, they checked me out and said I was fine, told me to get out of the way," I said, as cheerfully as I could, hooking a thumb back in the general direction of the X-Ray room.

"Well, this is your lucky day, Lieutenant," she said, and hustled by me to kneel down and check one of the sailors. I wanted to tell her if I was really lucky I wouldn't have had this knock on the head, but thought better of it and turned left, toward the main emergency room.

As I got closer I understood why there were so many stretcher cases lined up outside. The place was packed. Nurses and doctors were running back and forth, threading their way between gurneys as orderlies shifted the wounded from waiting areas into treatment rooms or surgery. Some of the doctors had on their white operating gowns, splashed with blood, while others were working on guys right in the hall, doing God knows what. One GI was screaming bloody murder as two nurses held him down while Perrini worked on his leg. I didn't interrupt.

I remembered Gloria had told me they had new doctors coming in, and I figured they got here just in time. The 21st was a General Hospital, not a Field Hospital. They were supposed to get cases sent up the line from the Field Hospitals, not fresh casualties. No one expected the Luftwaffe to be this active so far in our rear. The staff looked a little overwhelmed, and a lot scared.

As I approached the operating theaters,

the odors got worse. Antiseptic, dried blood, the smell of shit and piss mixed with the smoky burned smells of fabric and flesh, all blending into the gut-wrenching stink of the ass-end of war, a military hospital under siege by the wounded and dying.

"Outta the way, outta the way!" An orderly ran by pushing a gurney with a still form on it, a white sheet over his body, soaking up blood wherever it touched him. His eyes were open and staring at the ceiling as I stumbled back, out of the way, wondering if a dirty brown ceiling in a makeshift Algiers hospital was going to be the last thing that kid ever saw.

I had to back up to lean against the wall or fall down. The smells were getting to me and I needed to catch my breath. I moved on, checking the conscious and unconscious wounded on either side of me. No British uniforms, not that I could tell anyway, as most had been cut away.

I began to be able to tell the difference between the GIs who ran into the Germans at the front, and those in the convoy who'd been bombed and strafed just outside of town. The convoy GIs wore clean uniforms. They were dressed in herringbone twill coveralls, with the American flag patch sewn on the shoulder. Their woolen clothes were probably in their duffle bags, blown to hell on some deserted stretch of Algerian highway, with whatever wasn't burned or looted by Arabs. The GIs from the front were dressed in filthy, dirty wool pants, shirts, and twill coveralls in all sorts of combinations. They looked like they had been wearing everything they owned, dressed for cold nights in the desert. As their clothes were cut away by orderlies searching for secondary wounds, each layer would cover another shirt, or long johns, or whatever they had piled on for warmth. I wondered about the cold-weather gear stacked up in the warehouses down by the harbor. Had the army a clue how damn cold it got in the desert?

I passed a hallway leading to another wing of the building, this one also stacked up with wounded on stretchers or sitting on crates. It looked like another holding area for those who could wait for treatment. I walked the corridor searching for Kaz, hoping to see him sitting there with a big grin on his face.

There was some yelling going on. "You get the fuck out of here," hollered a GI, a huge bandage wrapped around one shoulder. It didn't stop him from jabbing a finger on his good side at the guy across from him.

"Shut up, dogface. Don't they teach you

not to talk to an officer that way?" This from a guy in a leather jacket, an Army Air Corps pilot, a lieutenant with his trousers ripped open and bandages on both legs.

"Don't they teach you not to shoot up your own troops? Yesterday two P-38s killed four of our guys, and it wasn't the first time. I'm getting sick of it!" The GI tried to get up but winced at the effort and sat back down.

"You tell him, Morrie," said another GI. There were murmurs of assent and anger, but not one of them seemed to be as willing as Morrie to take on an officer, even if he was Air Corps.

"Listen, Private, it works both ways. You guys are supposed to know aircraft recognition, right? They ever teach you WEFT procedures? Wings, Engine, Fuselage, Tail?"

"Kinda hard to pick out that WEFT bullshit when half a dozen P-38s are blazing away at you with their .50 calibers," Morrie said.

"You probably fired on them first. You know what WEFT really stands for in the infantry? Wrong Every Fucking Time!"

This time Morrie stood up. "Yeah, well you murdering bastard, we have a saying too. If it flies, it dies!" Morrie raised his one good arm in a fist and advanced on the pilot, who lay immobile on his stretcher. Three guys who could get up did and pulled Morrie back. Words continued to fly, but not fists.

I kept checking for Kaz. As I did, on the stretcher to my right, I saw a Luftwaffe pilot, an amused look on his face. His blue tunic displayed the Luftwaffe eagle, grasping a swastika in its claws. I don't know if he spoke English, but he seemed to understand exactly what was going on. Our eyes met and he smiled. His entire left leg was swathed in bandages, and from what was left of his pants, it looked like he'd been burned. He must have been pretty doped up; I doubted he'd be smiling tomorrow.

I wandered back down the hall, feeling weak in the knees, went through the emergency entrance and checked the casualties stacked up there. No Kaz. I went through the treatment rooms, all filled with patients, doctors, and nurses. Everyone was too busy, or in too much pain to notice me. I began to wonder if this was a dream. I seemed to be invisible when I was close to the worst casualties. Whenever I was outside the main treatment area, some nurse or orderly would stop and check me out. I didn't know if I could convince the next one that I was okay. My head was swimming, and although the ringing was down to a reasonable volume, I was feeling more wobbly and I had to keep reminding myself what, or rather who, I was looking for.

Then I saw him. Kaz, on a gurney, being pushed down the hall. A nurse was doing the pushing. I tried to call to her, but I couldn't get my voice to work. My yell came out as a croak, and my head rebelled against the effort. She turned a corner and disappeared down another hallway. I forced myself down the hall after her, stumbling against an orderly carrying a tray of instruments. He and the tray went down with a crash, the noise in my ears ratcheting up the ringing up even worse.

"Hey, those were sterile! Watch it!"

The floor seemed to tilt. I had to swing my arms to keep my balance. I knew I looked like a drunk but I had to catch up. I couldn't hold onto the wall without stepping on the guys lined up alongside it. I focused on the floor in front of me, placing one foot in front of the other, turning the corner just in time to see the back of a nurse leave a patient's room. She was headed down the hall away from me. Had she seen me? I couldn't tell, but this time I managed to call her name out.

"Stop," I called once, and heads turned. I

couldn't tell how loudly I'd said it with all the noise in my head, but I must've yelled pretty loud. Maybe she didn't hear me because she disappeared, her green fatigues blending into a crowd of nurses, orderlies, and wounded. There were three doors on the right but I couldn't remember which one she had walked out of. I looked in the first room, and it was full, three hospital beds and two gurneys crowded in together. I went into the middle room.

Kaz was there, lying on a gurney pushed next to two others. A young nurse was tending to a patient in one of the beds. She was trying to get him to take a pill and he was shaking his head back and forth, mumbling. The others were all asleep or unconscious, nicely cleaned up and bandaged. The sign on the door said Post-Op.

I went over to Kaz. He hadn't been cleaned up, and it didn't look like he had just been operated on. His breathing was harsh, small gasps followed by gulps for air. There was a fresh bandage on his arm, he had a black eye, a cut on his eyebrow, and a serious welt on his forehead. Other than that he looked okay. But why was he in Post-Op?

"Kaz," I said. "Can you hear me?"

"What are you doing in here?" the nurse

asked, glancing at me before she turned back to her patient. She put a pill in his mouth and held his chin as she lifted a glass of water to his lips.

"Just checking on my friend —"

"Out," she said, pointing to the door. "I'll take good care of him."

"What's wrong with him?" I asked. "Why is he here? In Post-Op I mean."

That question delayed her for a second. She looked at me as she went to check the chart hanging on the end of the gurney.

"What's wrong with you?" she asked. "You look like you should be lying down."

"Can't disagree," I said, trying to smile. "Will you just check his chart and tell me what's wrong with him? His breathing doesn't sound right."

She seemed exasperated, but relented, putting a hand on Kaz's chest. His uniform blouse and shirt were open, but not cut away like the others. She frowned as she read the chart. I checked the front pocket on his blouse where Kaz had kept the notebook. It was unbuttoned, and empty. I checked his other pockets. Nothing. It was gone.

"Probable concussion, X-Rayed, no visible fractures. No subdermal bleeding, redressed existing wound. Patient was conscious upon admission," she said, summarizing the information on the chart.

"In other words, he was fine except for a bump on the head," I said. She didn't say anything. She checked his pulse.

"It's weak," she said.

"He has a bad heart," I said.

"Billy," Kaz said weakly. He half opened his eyes. "How are you?" He sounded almost giddy.

"Kaz," I said, "what happened to you?"

"I feel much better now. . . ." I swear he smiled, then closed his eyes. I opened one with my fingers. His face swam back and forth in front of me. The ringing grew louder and the floor started shifting from under me again. I held onto the gurney with one hand, trying to get his face to hold still.

For just one second it did. I saw it, a tiny, contracted pupil, just like Jerome's, only he had already been dead, and Kaz wasn't. Other images popped up in my mind, Kaz in the jeep waiting to go back to the hotel the first time he was admitted here. Dunbar giving him the okay to leave. Rita kissing him goodbye. Gloria and Harding having a heart-to-heart before he got into the jeep for the drive back to the hotel. Jerome. Harry's grandmother. Click, click. Things fell into place and I had to tell this nurse before the floor came up and whacked me.

"Nalorphine," I said. Both hands were on the gurney now and my legs were shaking. "Nalorphine, now! Hurry!"

I turned to look at her and try to explain, but all I saw were her eyes; wide with a fear of me, a raving lunatic. I tried to step forward and tell her something but I couldn't remember what. And why was I thinking about Harry's grandmother? I couldn't remember what was so important and then the goddamn bells drove everything else out of my head and all I felt was the gritty concrete floor slam into my cheekbone as someone picked up the floor and hit me with it.

CHAPTER
THIRTY-FOUR

It was dark when I awoke. There was a light on a small table next to a window. A dark blackout curtain was drawn over the glass panes, the light from the gooseneck lamp lost in the black fabric. It was quiet. No bells rung. A figure was slumped in a chair next to the light, in shadow. I turned to my right and in the half darkness I could see two other beds with sleeping forms lying on them. I lay there, eyes adjusting to the darkness, trying to remember how I'd gotten here. The train. Bombers. The jeep. Ambulance. Kaz.

"Kaz!" I said out loud, and sat up as memory flooded into my waking mind.

"Billy, it's all right," said the form in the chair, getting up and limping over to me.

"Harry? Is that you?" He came closer and I saw that it was. Dressed in U.S. Army fatigues and sporting a .45 automatic in a holster. "Kaz, is he . . ."

"He is fine, sleeping right over there, thanks to you."

"Where's Major Harding?"

"Right here, Boyle," said Harding as he sat up on the bed facing me and swung around. He had been sleeping with his boots and gun belt on, ready for anything. He spoke in a soft voice. "Lieutenant Kazimierz is fine. He's in the last bed against the wall. I don't know how you knew, but you were right. He'd been overdosed with morphine. They administered the antidote to him just in time. You nearly scared that poor nurse to death, but as soon as you fainted, she checked on him. Doc Perrini figures Kaz had about ten minutes left before it would've been too late."

"Is he going to recover?" I had visions of paralysis, brain damage, all sorts of terrible things to add to the agonies Kaz already had to bear.

"According to the doctor, he has recovered. He'll have a headache from that knock on the head, but that's it. You were X-Rayed, too. You have a very slight fracture of the skull and a moderate concussion. You should be fine if you can avoid getting hit on the head for a while."

"The penicillin shipment?"

"It's safe, under heavy guard at the train

station. No one is going to get within fifty yards of it and live."

"Have you seen Diana?"

"Miss Seaton is fine. The young French girl Lieutenant Kazimierz hired is with her, and there's a guard on their room. No need to worry, everything's fine."

It was too much good news, it just couldn't be all true.

"Are we going to pick up Villard?" I asked.

"We'll talk about that later," Harding said. "Lieutenant Kazimierz was awake for a while, and said you had evidence Colonel Walton was involved in these murders?"

"I thought I did, sir, but now I think I was wrong. I need to talk to you about that."

I didn't know how to tell Harding what I had to say. Or what he would do when I told him. I changed the subject quickly to give myself a few minutes grace.

"What time is it anyway?" I asked.

"Just past five-thirty," said Harry Dickinson, glancing at his watch. It was nice to hear a military type tell time the old fashioned way. He pulled the blackout curtain aside. The sky was lit up by a red dawn. "No need for this," he said as he pulled the curtain aside.

"Harry, what are you doing here?"

"I heard you were causing trouble, and

came to see you. Major Harding asked me to stay and stand guard with him. I was going stark raving mad sitting in a hospital bed, so this seemed a nice alternative."

"How's the leg?"

"This little scratch? Just a through and through, as we say."

I was glad to have Harry as a friend. I was glad they were all here, and I thought about nights back in Boston when Dad and Uncle Dan had something going and the house would fill with cops, all watching out for each other. It felt good to be part of something that brought men like these together. Part of it was suffering; I knew that much from Harry and Kaz, and I think Harding too. It was the possibility of death that made men look each other in the eye, grip shoulders, give a nod that said Yes, I will risk everything for you. Harry had that look in his eyes, and I returned it.

Harding opened the door and asked an orderly to bring in a pot of coffee and four cups. Daylight began to fill the room, so he turned out the lamp. Then he cranked up Kaz's bed so Kaz was sitting up. His face was scratched and bruised, and he looked incredibly thin in the hospital pajamas. I wondered how much strain and abuse his body could take. I wondered the same about mine. Then Kaz opened his eyes.

"Billy! So glad to see you." He looked around for his glasses and Harding picked them up from the nightstand, handing them to Kaz. Almost tenderly.

"Same here, buddy." I sat up too and let my feet hang off the side of the bed. It wasn't too bad. I had on the same hospital pajamas as Kaz, and that reminded me: his clothes.

"Kaz, the notebook is gone," I said.

"Major Harding has already asked some of the orderlies to go through the discarded clothing. They should find my jacket there."

"No, you don't understand. It wasn't in your pocket. I searched for it while you were still wearing your jacket."

There was silence in the room, and Kaz and Harding both looked at me, uncomprehending. The door opened and an orderly entered, a tray with a pot of coffee and cups in his hands.

"Here you go, Major." He set it down on the table and left.

"Okay, Boyle, tell me what you know." Harding handed me a cup of black coffee. I took a sip.

"I'll start with a question. Did you tell Gloria Morgan where our quarters were located, the day we left here with Kaz?"

"Why?" Harding's eyes narrowed and he didn't look happy. I knew he didn't like me poking around his personal life, or even knowing he had one.

"Just before we left, you and she were talking outside the entrance to the hospital. Did you tell her where we were headed?"

"Boyle, she knows we're attached to HQ at the Hotel St. George."

"Yes, but not everyone attached to HQ is quartered there." I saw the effect that had on Harding. It was the same thing that happened to me when Diana had brought it up. How could I have been so stupid?

"Yes, I told her. I said perhaps I could take her to dinner there one night."

"What made you mention where we were quartered?"

He looked away from me.

"She asked."

"Yesterday I saw a nurse wheel Kaz into the Post-Op room. He'd just been given an overdose of morphine. I think that nurse was Gloria Morgan."

"Yes," said Kaz, in open-mouthed amazement. "It was Miss Morgan who took care of me. She gave me a shot for the pain . . ."

"And didn't mark it on your chart. Then stashed you away in a room where no one would notice. In the confusion, your death would've been chalked up to an undiagnosed brain injury. No autopsy, no questions, no notebook."

"But why . . ." Harding asked, letting the question hang there. "Why?"

"Her motive? I have no idea. But it does tell us something."

"What?" asked Kaz.

"She had a reason for stealing the notebook and trying to get rid of you. You said the code was virtually unbreakable without knowing what book they were using."

"Dictionary code?" asked Harding.

"A variation, quite complex," Kaz said, nodding. "Yes, it makes sense. The key book is here, otherwise why would she want the notebook?"

"Excuse me, but what are you two talking about?" Harry asked.

"It's a long story, but coded messages have been sent between Blackpool, England, and Algiers, using neutral merchant ships. The code is based on duplicate copies of a certain book, and if you don't know which book, then the code is totally secure."

"So by stealing the codebook, she tipped you off that the book is here," Harry said.

"Yeah. It was the most dangerous situation she could imagine. Both the book and the codebook, with coded messages, in the same place. That's why she killed Jerome, and tried to kill us. Casselli was murdered because he got cold feet, or was too honest for this business."

"What!" Harding slammed his coffee cup down, sending a splash of hot coffee up and onto his hand. He shook it off. "Explain yourself, Boyle!"

"I thought it was Walton, since he had the means and opportunity. Proximity to the Bessette crime family in Blackpool, direct involvement with medical supplies, access to the only telephone in the area so he could inform the shooter when we left him. But when I saw that Gloria had wheeled Kaz into that room to die, I remembered that you and she were talking that day. She knew what route we would have to take, too, and was in a position to make a call from Walton's office. It would have been completely normal for her to be in there."

"Anybody could've made that call, Boyle," Harding said. "And what about accusing her of killing Jerome? What grounds do you have for that?"

"Harry's grandmother," I said.

"What?" all three of them exclaimed at the same time.

"It came to me when I realized Gloria had given Kaz an overdose. Harry told me how his grandmother hated hospitals and needles. When she was dying, her doctor gave her morphine in a liqueur. Alcohol actually increases the effect of the morphine."

"So?" demanded Harding.

"Just before Jerome died, I came into his room and Gloria and he were drinking Crème de Menthe. The perfect liqueur to mask any taste, and liquid morphine is pretty tasteless to start with."

"But you said they were both drinking it," Harding said.

"Kaz, how do you feel right now?"

"My head hurts, but otherwise fine. A little tired, perhaps."

"There you go, sir. She could give herself an injection of nalorphine as soon as she was alone, and she's all set. She was just off duty, so it would have been normal for her to go to her room and rest."

"Could she simply go to the hospital pharmacy and sign out an injection of nalorphine? They just don't hand out drugs, even to head nurses!"

"Sorry, sir, but nalorphine was on the list of drugs stolen when Sergeant Casselli was killed." That did it. Harding slumped in his chair. "I should have known," he said.

"You couldn't have known, sir," I said.

"There's no way . . ."

"No," he said in a low, strangled voice, "no. I mean I should have known she wasn't really interested in me. She wasn't back in the States, either, not really. But I —"

"You loved her," said Kaz quietly. The room was silent. Harding let out a breath that sounded like it had been held since he hit the beach.

"Yes. All these years. I thought I was the luckiest man in the world to see her again, here, of all places."

"We should go to Colonel Walton as soon as possible, Major, and tell him."

But Harding didn't move. He stared out the window at the rising sun, getting used to the idea of being in love with a murderess. He reached for a cigarette and held it between his fingers, rolling it back and forth. I could hear the white paper crinkle against the tobacco. Nobody said a word.

Two hours later we filed into Walton's office. Since Kaz and I both had bandages on our heads, we looked like a parade of walking wounded after a battle. By contrast, Harding stood ramrod straight, with no expression on his face except the one the army issued him. Inside, I knew he was banged up worse than Kaz and I put together. Harry stood guard outside in the hallway, one hand on a cane and the other resting on his holstered automatic. Walton and Gloria were already in the office, seated at the conference table — or poker table — depending on what your priorities were.

"Good morning, gentlemen. Don't you two look a sight! Baron, you've recovered from your accident?" Either she didn't know why we were here or she was one hell of an actress. She flashed a smile at Harding. He nodded back, curtly. A look of surprise flashed across her face. Now she was on guard.

"Lieutenant Kazimierz," Walton said, stumbling a little over the Polish name, "I want to apologize on behalf of the 21st General Hospital. It was chaos here yesterday, our first major influx of wounded, and we were hit from multiple directions. But that's no excuse for putting a patient in jeopardy."

Harding ignored Walton and looked straight at Gloria. "We know everything," he said. I had to admire his self-control. He could've called HQ and had someone else confront her. He didn't.

"Well, that's great!" Gloria said. "Do tell us all about it." She looked at Harding expectantly.

"We know about your connections to Jules

Bessette in Blackpool. Scotland Yard has questioned him and he's told them everything. We know about the letters, the code, how he set you up with his brother here in Algiers, and about how you tipped them off about the penicillin."

"Me? You're talking about *me?*" Gloria put her hand to her breast as if she couldn't believe what she was hearing. She was the picture of innocence. She was quite convincing. So was Harding as he lied about Scotland Yard. That was good.

"We know about Jerome. We know how you were hunting for the codebook. We know about the Crème de Menthe and the morphine. We know you had Casselli killed when he wouldn't play along with you, and that you took the receipt for the orders concerning the second shipment of penicillin from him."

"Sam, what are you talking about? Is this some kind of joke?" Now she turned on the charm, looking back and forth between Walton and Harding, eyelids fluttering, then looked as if she were about to cry. Walton seemed stunned.

"We know about you and Villard."

Now *I* was stunned. Harding made this accusation with conviction. I guessed there was something in their past that caused him to make that leap. This time Gloria was silent. Harding kept on speaking, never taking his eyes from Gloria, tapping the table with his index finger as he made each point.

"We know you tried to kill Lieutenant Kazimierz in order to get the notebook from him, and to eliminate him in case he knew anything that might endanger you. He will testify that you gave him an injection, and there are witnesses. I have men searching your quarters now. We'll search the entire hospital if we have to, and we'll find the code book. We know that's here too. And the nalorphine, and your private supply of morphine. It's all here. We know everything," he added, that last sentence as a quiet afterthought, the only evidence in anything he said of his pain.

"If somebody has done all these terrible things, they could also have framed me, have you considered that?" Gloria tilted her head.

"We know you used this telephone to call Bessette or Villard and arrange to have us ambushed as we drove back to the hotel."

"If you know everything, what more do you need from me, Sam? Do you enjoy seeing me suffer?"

"I want to know why," Harding said.

She laughed. "You know everything, and

nothing." She folded her arms. Not exactly a confession, but not a protestation of innocence either. It was awkward.

There was nothing for me to say, so I glanced around the room. I looked at Walton's books. All the Army manuals, medical texts . . . and one empty space.

"Where's your *Gray's Anatomy*?" I asked Walton, my eyes on Gloria. She flinched.

"What the hell does that matter?" Walton growled. Then he surveyed his shelves. "Damned if I know. People borrow my books all the time."

I looked at Gloria. What would she need to decode now? What was in the notebook that she didn't already know? Then I knew. *Light dawns on Marblehead,* as my dad used to say, whenever he figured out something that should have been obvious from the start.

"Captain Morgan," I said, as calmly as I could "What was it? Bank accounts?"

Everyone in the room looked at me, quizzically.

"Let me guess. Swiss bank accounts. You weren't just after a split of the take from drug thefts, no matter how valuable the penicillin was. You were after that notebook for yourself. You were going to double-cross the Bessettes. With Villard? Or were you double-dealing him, too?"

She said nothing. No more sweet Southern murmurs, no more innocent fluttering eyelashes.

"Captain Morgan," Harding stated, in his official voice, "you will shortly be arraigned for a General Court-Martial on a number of offenses, including murder, attempted murder, larceny, embezzlement, and a host of lesser charges. You will be lucky not to be executed, as these crimes occurred in wartime."

"Why are you telling me this, Sam?"

"Tell us why. Why did you do it? Cooperate. Please." Begging her to explain cost Harding. It revealed his agony.

"Oh, you poor dear man," Gloria said, laughing. "What, will you promise only to shoot me with one bullet instead of ten? You could learn a lot from Billy, Sam. He's more intelligent than he looks."

I felt sympathy for Harding, and even a little for Gloria, but she was a cold-blooded killer who had confessed her guilt. She had been playing everyone, probably even Villard, and there was no way she was going to beg for mercy now. She had counted on making a big haul, and if she couldn't have that she wasn't going to settle for a little pity from Harding.

The noise in my head returned, a low buzzing sound. I rubbed my eyes, wondering if it would go away, but it got louder and louder. I tried to ignore it, but then I noticed everyone else was looking out the windows. The door flew open and Harry burst in.

"Air raid. Get to the shelters!"

There was a rush to the door. Harding took Gloria's hand. I fell in behind them. I expected her to twist away, to reject him or even to try to escape. She didn't. But she looked scared. Maybe she needed a little tenderness. Maybe Harding wanted something from her other than contempt. I don't know. What I wanted was a well-built air raid shelter over my head.

The slit trenches were still there, but there were improved shelters as well. Sloping walkways had been dug into the ground, with entrances covered by wood beams layered with sandbags. Some of them were pretty large, and nurses were guiding the patients who could walk into them. I knew there were plenty of nurses, doctors, and patients left inside, and I prayed the Luftwaffe wouldn't aim at the hospital. At the same time I wished the army would move the goddamn supply dump next to us a good ten miles down the road.

We made our way down into a smaller shelter. We had to duck going in, and the ceiling was low inside as well. I couldn't stand up straight, so like most everybody else I squatted and listened to the insectlike buzzing get nearer and nearer.

"Where's the bloody RAF?" Harry asked no one in particular.

There was a faraway sound of bombs, explosions that sounded like fireworks. It lasted a full minute, the buzzing coming ever closer. I heard the rhythmic, slow, pumping sound of a 40mm anti-aircraft battery, not too far away. I glanced at Harding. He was crouched by the side of the door, still holding Gloria's hand. A jailer or a lover?

The anti-aircraft batteries around the supply dump opened up, and the noise level increased, until we couldn't hear the planes anymore, which didn't matter since the anti-aircraft fire meant they were coming our way. Gloria took her hand away from Harding and lowered her head, covering her ears tightly. Harding put his right arm around her.

As smooth as silk, she made her move. She lowered her left hand, as if she was going to take his again, but it kept going, down to his leather holster. She unsnapped it, pulled out the big .45 automatic, flipped the safety off and raised it to Harding's head.

"Get back. No one move or I'll kill him!" she screamed loud enough to be heard over the anti-aircraft fire and the thudding of bombs that had started to shake the ground. Clumps of dirt shook loose from the sides of the shelter as if someone was just outside hitting it with a sledgehammer.

"Gloria, don't, there's nowhere you can go," Harding pleaded with her. She backed toward the entrance.

"You're right, Sam. Nowhere. You've got me right where you want me. But I'm not playing by your rules. If I can't have it all I'm not going to rot in a stockade waiting for the firing squad."

"Gloria —" Harding began, moving closer to her. She pulled the hammer back and held the automatic, squarely aimed at his forehead.

"I'd hate to do it," she said, "but I will. Back off."

Harding eased back. She unbuttoned two buttons of her fatigues and reached inside her shirt. Hidden within the bulky men's uniform was the notebook.

"You're a smart young man, Billy. Here's your reward. Five million dollars, maybe more. Waiting in Switzerland." She tossed the notebook to the ground and backed out of the shelter. Another load of bombs hit nearby and I could feel the vibrations shake the ground. Harding followed Gloria to the entrance. She fired once, striking the ground in front of him. Then she was gone.

Harding started after her. I grabbed him by the shoulder, to prevent him from jumping out of the shelter.

"You can't go out there, Major!"

"Let go of me, Boyle!"

He turned and swung at me, hitting me on the jaw hard enough to loosen my grip. He scrambled up the walkway and I followed. The enemy aircraft were almost on top of us. I pulled him down. We both crouched as low as we could as tracers lit up the sky and the chatter of machine guns joined in, small puffs from the 40mm guns exploding above us. Straight into this hell flew five, no, six formations of four bombers each. I could hear other bombs going off farther away, and guessed this was only a part of the main raid. Heinkel 111s again, their spade-shaped wings beginning to become visible.

Gloria ran right toward them, as close to the supply dump as she could get. She was about a hundred yards away, all alone above ground. She turned once, gazed in our direction, and dropped the pistol, then calmly walked forward as she raised her arms, palms outstretched. I kept both my hands on Harding, as we watched, transfixed, from the dugout entrance. The drone of the engines mixed with the anti-aircraft fire until sound enveloped us and felt like it would crush our eardrums. We could see the bomb bay doors open, as if in acknowledgment of Gloria's gesture. The lead plane dropped its load and then the others followed, the bombs wobbling in the air for a hesitant second, then gaining speed and becoming blurs that exploded inside the supply dump, throwing up flames, black smoke and crashing thunder that crept toward Gloria, her honey brown hair blown back by their force. The concussion from the blasts staggered her, thrusting her back a step. A final stick of bombs walked their way toward her, the last of them exploding where she stood, eruptions of fire, smoke, and debris covering everything. She was gone. But on her own terms.

I pulled Harding down so he wouldn't have to look out on that scene once the dust settled, but it didn't matter. His eyes were closed and tears traced rivulets through the dust on his face.

CHAPTER
THIRTY-FIVE

It wasn't until the day after the air raid that Harding got around to telling me. I don't blame him for the delay, as he had just watched the woman he loved, and who had broken his heart twice, get blown to bits. But that didn't mean I liked the message much either.

It was hands-off time with the Frenchies. No interference with local affairs allowed. There was still a lot of delicate diplomacy going on, and Ike wanted things running smoothly. Even if those things were run by the same former Vichy officials who had done the Germans' bidding and would probably sell out to the Germans again if they made a return appearance. It was determined that Major Gloria Morgan was behind the murders and theft of the drugs, and that Luc Villard's other activities, such as smuggling, ransom, and murder, were all local concerns, best left to the local authorities to handle. Or not, since Luc Villard was one of those local authorities.

I was pretty steamed over that, but there wasn't anything I could do, at least nothing I could think of right then. Harding had Doctor Perrini check out Kaz and me, and the doc ordered us to stay at the hospital for observation. Harding liked the idea of keeping me out of circulation for a while, in case I tried anything stupid. So he kept us at the 21st, while I tried to think of something that wasn't stupid, that might have a chance of working. Harry Dickinson was well enough to be discharged, so Harding grabbed him from the Royal Navy for limited detached duty while he recuperated fully. Harding wanted a bodyguard for us while Kaz worked on the code. I rested my head and thought about things, while Harry stood watch and Kaz deciphered the notebook. The search of Gloria's quarters had produced *Gray's Anatomy,* with a pencil and paper next to it. Gloria had almost finished deciphering the contents of the notebook when she was called to Walton's office. They found the morphine and nalorphine under a false compartment in her footlocker. She also had her passport hidden there. The Army didn't require one for travel, so I wondered what had been on her mind when the war started. Had she planned to make a big score all along? Then desert, and cross over to a neutral country? Or was she simply prepared for any opportunity that might come her way?

I had sent a note to Diana at the hotel, telling her I might be stuck here a few days. I didn't hear back. I knew she was waiting for me to do something about freeing the prisoners, the kids who had been involved with the coup attempt. But that was one of the local matters we weren't supposed to interfere with.

I watched Kaz work all day to finish transcribing the contents of the notebook, making letter substitutions. With *Gray's Anatomy* in hand, it was easy. We got the names of two banks, one in Berne and one in Zurich, Switzerland, each followed by a series of numbers. It was my guess that Villard was in this with her, and given each of their natures, only one would've been skiing in Switzerland this winter. That was the key to my plan.

Harding came to collect Kaz's transcriptions and decodings the next day. We met in Walton's office. Walton was told to go elsewhere. Thankful to still have his job, he willingly made himself scarce. Kaz went over everything and handed his report to

Harding. Before he could take the notebook, I grabbed it and flipped through it, idly looking at the pages.

"Major, I would guess that whoever we have in Switzerland is going to receive these numbers pretty fast, and these accounts are going to be cleaned out. For the benefit of the war effort."

Harding was silent for a minute, deciding that what I said was so obvious it wasn't worth denying. He just nodded.

"So, I'd guess that by tomorrow, this notebook will be worthless?"

"Yes, we'll have gotten all the value out of it that we can." He took it from my hand. "What are you after?"

"You know, Major," Kaz said, "Miss Seaton is very worried about the rebels that were her fellow prisoners. They are still being held by Villard."

Another silence. Harding stared out the window, watching a work detail filling in bomb craters. He sighed. Finally he tossed the notebook on the table.

"Tomorrow, after twelve noon, this notebook will be so much worthless paper."

I guessed that meant Harding didn't think my idea was stupid. We got Doc Perrini to discharge us, and Kaz, Harry, and I went in search of Captain Henri Bessette. About a local matter.

Kaz enlisted Vincent, our pal the Polish spy, and by nightfall we found ourselves seated at a swank sidewalk café, with a view of the nice part of the waterfront, on the same road Kaz and I had taken to the harbor. There were bushy green plants along the sidewalk and Cinzano umbrellas for shade. Harry sat at another table, sipping a brandy, smoking a cigarette, and trying to look like a Royal Navy lieutenant on leave. He had arrived a half-hour before us, wearing his Webley revolver and carrying a Sten gun, with the shoulder butt folded back, inside a haversack. Honor among thieves only applies when you're a thief, too. I noticed a couple of beefy guys in dark suits who were probably carrying under their jackets. Good. We understood each other.

"There," Kaz said, nodding. Vincent was standing across the street with Bessette and one other uniformed soldier, probably his official bodyguard. I guessed the dark suits were SOL. Vincent pointed to us and waved. Two Gardes Mobiles officers walked past the café, eyeing us, a visual, and not too subtle, warning to not try anything funny.

Bessette and his guy stood across the street for a minute after Vincent left. Then they crossed, waiting another minute on the sidewalk. The cops came back, greeted Bessette, and then he walked over to our table. He sat and took out a package of Gauloises. Before he could light up one of those foul-smelling French cigarettes, I reached for a pack of Luckies. The two dark suits jumped up, pistols at the ready. I smiled and slowly pulled out the Lucky Strikes.

"American cigarette?"

Bessette took the whole pack, and motioned for his men to sit down.

"Merci," he said, lighting a Lucky and savoring it. "Very good."

"You speak some English, Captain Bessette?" I asked.

"Some, not very good. Parlez français?"

"Je parle français," answered Kaz.

"Très bien," said Bessette. "If we need French, him," he said, pointing roughly at Kaz with his cigarette. "Now, you, American, say what you want."

"To do business, what else?" Bessette glanced at Kaz for confirmation. He rattled off some French, ending with a shrug of the shoulders. What else, indeed?

"Business! But we are allies, not businessmen!" Bessette grinned, showing off nicotine-stained teeth. His fingers were yellow where he held the cigarette. "Or are you from Chicago? Gangsters! Al Capone!" He thought this was hilarious and roared with laughter. A bottle of red wine and glasses appeared at the table. No one spoke as the waiter poured. He scurried away and Bessette took a long swallow.

"Business," he said, staring me in the eye. "What business?"

"I have something you want, and you have two things I want."

"That," he said, shaking his head, "is bad business. Two for one? No."

"The one thing I have is worth nothing to me and a great deal to you."

"And the two things I have?"

"One is worth much less, and the other, nothing."

He refilled his wine glass and took another drink.

"Say what it is you want, and what you have to give."

"The first thing I want is Villard's prisoners from Le Carrefour, delivered to the Hotel St. George, at noon tomorrow." I nodded to Kaz to translate, to make sure Bessette understood.

"That is a police matter," he said, once Kaz was done. He waved his hand. "That has nothing to do with me."

"Yes, but the notebook, that does have

something to do with you."

Kaz started to translate but Bessette cut him off.

"You have the notebook? Here?" His eyes flew to the dark suits.

Now it was my turn to laugh. "That would not be good business," I said, and took a drink myself, smiling at Bessette like he was an old pal. He glowered at me, then nodded.

"Very bad business it would be, yes. Notebook for rebels. Good business."

"Half of the pages for the rebels," Kaz translated.

"What will the other pages cost?" Bessette demanded. His English got better as the negotiations went on.

"All I want for the other half," I said, leaning in close to whisper, "is a rug."

CHAPTER
THIRTY-SIX

I looked in the mirror and adjusted my service cap. My bandages had come off yesterday, but I still didn't relish the brim sitting on that bump, so I had to adjust it to just the right angle. Clean khaki shirt, freshly shaved, lieutenant's bars gleaming, I looked like a real staff flunky. I hooked my web belt on and checked my holster, knife, and spare ammo. Everything in place. Kaz and I were back at the St. George, but stuck in a tent with Harry outside on the grounds. Still, we had access to real bathrooms and the restaurant, the latter due to Kaz's constant praising of the chef and his dishes, and his free way with francs.

I walked to the lobby and found Diana and Yvette. Diana was wearing a long summer dress, and a light coat with long sleeves. She looked fashionable, and if you didn't know her clothes were chosen to hide her bruises, you'd think she looked fine. She said she was healing, but she didn't want to talk about it. She had her arm in Yvette's, who was helping her down the lobby steps. But her hand dug into Yvette's forearm, and I knew every step she took was filled with pain and required courage.

"What's the big surprise you've summoned us for, Billy?" Diana asked. She smiled, but it was a distant smile. All lips and no eyes. A re-creation of an emotion from memory.

"Come outside, find a nice spot in the shade, and wait," I said. I wanted to take her by the hand, but I was nervous. It was like that between me and Diana now. We hadn't had much time together the past few days, and when we did, Yvette was always there, fussing with Diana's hair or chatting with her in French. Diana seemed calm when Yvette was by her side. But if we were alone, or if I tried to hold her hand, she became jittery. And I did, too. She wasn't the same, not the same Diana I'd known back in England, not even the same Diana I had glimpsed in that dusty prison courtyard the first day in Algiers. And me? Yeah, I wasn't the same guy either. Things had happened. Nothing as bad as what had happened to Diana, but I had to live with that, too. I felt lousy, like a low-life bum who cared more about his two-bit problems than the people who depended on him. People he loved. Every time I thought about Villard and what he had done, his hands on her, beating her, caressing her, drugging her, raping her, owning her in that room, on that filthy mattress, I'd feel red rage rising up inside me until I wanted to scream. I knew if I had any chance to make things right with Diana, that image had to disappear. Whatever it took.

I found Diana and Yvette a bench in a part of the gardens that hadn't been taken over by tents and trailers yet. When Diana sat down she let out a sigh, as if the short walk downstairs and outside had exhausted her.

"You okay?" I asked, bending down to talk to her. My hand rested on the back of the bench, close to her shoulder. She nodded, offering me a bit of a smile. Not much, but real, her eyes locking on mine. This we could manage. Not an actual conversation, just a quick exchange now and then that caught us both by surprise, our old selves taking over, reminding us of how things had once been.

"Diana," I said, "I have to leave right now with Kaz and Harry. I'll be back later. I just wanted you to see this, and, and to know, that . . . uh, well, you'll see."

"What are you trying to tell me? See what? What's happening, Billy?"

"I've got something to do. It needs doing, and should have been done . . . I don't know, I can't explain it. I just wanted you to know —"

"Know what, Billy?"

"That I kept my promise."

With that I got up and headed for the drive. The main drive leading into the hotel ended in a circular loop that was already lined with parked vehicles but was still wide enough for a large truck to pass. Kaz and Harry were at the entrance to the hotel to escort the truck in. It was noon, and I could hear church bells ringing the hour in the French district. The sun was shining, reflected in the calm sea. In a minute, they drove in, Harry at the wheel of the jeep, leading an old open truck whose canvas sides flapped in the breeze. The decrepit vehicle looked out of place among the freshly painted olive drab army vehicles parked along the drive, but it was a beautiful sight.

The truck was crammed with young kids, rail-thin and dirty, like scarecrows, their clothes in rags, hanging off them. They were cheering like crazy, hugging each other and crying. When the truck braked to a stop, the driver yelled *"Sortez,"* but no one needed to tell them to get out. They jumped down, whooped and hollered, and I saw Diana run to them, a huge smile on her face, more joy than I had seen in her since I got her away from Villard. She jumped up and down like a schoolgirl, going to each and embracing every one of them in turn, all memory of bruises and pain gone.

My eyes met those of the driver. His frown stayed right where it was. He held out his hand. I pulled a wad of notebook paper out of my pocket and placed it in his palm. He took it and grunted. I got in the jeep and we drove out, following him to our next appointment. I looked at my watch. It was 12:15.

XIX Corps Headquarters had moved out of the hotel, which had been taken over entirely by Allied Forces HQ. Corps staff had moved to a big palace on the heights above Algiers, near other French Army staff headquarters. We drove up the winding roads, past churches and large houses that rose up from the slopes to look out over the Mediterranean. Harry had to keep downshifting the jeep to make it around the sharp bends in the road as it wound its way up. The truck chugged along slowly. We didn't rush, knowing that Bessette would want to check out the first half of his payment before letting us in. We arrived at a low, white stone wall with an ornate iron gate barring the drive leading into the palace grounds. We parked off the road, outside the gate. The truck drove up, and we got out, waiting for Bessette. He came down the front steps and yelled orders to the guards at the gate. They opened for the truck and let it through, one of them holding up his hand, signaling us to stop. The truck entered the courtyard, stopping by Bessette. The driver handed him something, the notebook pages I'd given him. Bessette signaled him to park. After several minutes he waved to the guards. They opened the gate and let us walk in.

"Just you," Bessette said, pointing to me. "The others, no."

"Nous attendrons ici," Kaz said, and I thought, damn right you'll wait here. I don't want to be left here with these bastards all by myself.

"When my colleagues see me come out, they'll go to get the rest of the notebook, bring it back and hand it over. Then we'll leave together."

"Okay," said Bessette, enjoying his bit of American slang. "Okay, yes? You, come get your rug!" He threw back his head and laughed as he clapped my shoulder. Good buddies. Good business.

I started to perspire as I walked beside Bessette. Yet it wasn't hot up here. Cool breezes flowed up the hill, making the sun's heat bearable. Even so, I could feel a trickle of sweat running down my back. We entered the building and I saw French soldiers, doing all the stuff HQ staff does everywhere. Carry papers, look busy, look important, stay out of the way of the brass. We hoofed it up two flights of a grand staircase, the kind you might see Fred Astaire and Ginger Rogers dance down in the movies. At the top we took a left, and a soldier snapped to attention as Bessette passed. This was his territory; these were his guys. I was either going to buy a rug or buy the farm.

"Enter," said Bessette, opening a door and motioning inside.

"After you," I said politely.

"Ah! Good business. Yes, after me." He went in and I followed.

Villard sat in a leather armchair, smoking a cigarette. He didn't look surprised to see me.

"Ah. Lieutenant Boyle, we meet again. I understand you have something for us."

No expression crossed Bessette's face. This was nothing more than a business meeting. I looked away from Villard to Bessette's desk on my left. A pair of candlesticks stood on it, just like back at the hotel. One of them had been nicely cleaned up.

"Sorry if I ruined your ransom racket."

"That was nothing," Villard sneered. "A sideline, yes. But with our source out of the picture, the value of the rebel prisoners lessened. Too bad, really."

"She was a handsome woman, the American captain of nurses," Bessette said, more fully in command of English than before.

"Yes, but not as pretty as some," Villard stared at me, spitting out a piece of stray tobacco. "Nor as young. But variety in love is wonderful, no?"

"In love, yes," said Bessette. "In business, no. You fail to discern the difference, Luc."

Villard threw his cigarette in the ashtray. "Henri . . ."

Bessette left, slamming the door behind him. I stood between Villard and the door, as his expression changed from surprise to comprehension. Anger, and maybe a hint of fear flashed across his face before he reached for his revolver. But I was ready. I had no fair fight scruples, no illusions about bringing him in alive and letting the law take its course. The war was the law now, and that war had decreed that Luc Villard was free to go about his business. But the war had taught me a few things, too, things that hadn't been agreed to by generals. I had my knife out already as I closed the distance between us in a step. I had planned on telling him why I was going to kill him. I had planned every word, so he would know exactly why I was doing it, what was going to happen, that he was living his last minutes on this earth, drawing his last breath of air. With one blow, I was going to justify myself, to make everything better, to erase those handprints in black and blue all over Diana, and he was going to know it. It didn't work out that way.

I stepped into him, the knife entering his ribcage as he was still trying to unsnap his holster. He kept trying to get it open but his hand flapped at his side like a bird's injured wing. I pushed him, slamming him against the wall, watching his eyes for some evidence of comprehension and remorse, or even anger at being betrayed. Even anguish would have satisfied me. Instead, there was only desperation, his hot breath in my face, his eyes wide and unfocused, his mouth gasping for air. I twisted the knife and felt a rib crack as he let out a cry. I grabbed his shoulder with my left hand and swung him around, throwing him down on the rug in front of Bessette's desk. I stepped on his chest and pulled out the knife. Blood gurgled out of his mouth as he worked his jaw trying to say something, or maybe choking on his own blood. His right hand flapped around on the floor, still vainly searching for the holstered gun. Then he was still. I squatted next to him for a minute, watching. No movement, no breath, no more bubbles of blood. No heartbeat. Luc Villard was dead. Just like that.

I cleaned my knife on his pants and wiped my hands on his blue cape that was folded over the arm of the chair where he had been sitting. I walked out of the room and Bessette was standing in the hallway. With two of his guards, ready with a new rug to go in the room.

"I was not entirely sure which of you would leave that room," Bessette said.

"We both will, but he's going feet first."

In the courtyard, Harry and Kaz were waiting in the jeep. Harry cradled a Sten gun in his lap, his eyes riveted on Bessette who nipped at my heels. I nodded to Kaz. He reached inside his sling and withdrew the notebook containing the other half of the pages.

I handed Bessette the notebook. Good business.

■ ■ ■ ■

My clothes had blood on them. I changed in the tent as Kaz took the bloody shirt and pants to throw in the garbage. Harry sat outside the tent, smoking, keeping watch. No one spoke. I headed into the hotel, washed my hands, washed my face, and looked in the bathroom mirror. He wasn't the first guy I had killed, but he was the first I'd killed in cold blood. An execution. Murder, some might say. I half-expected to feel guilty, but all I felt was sad, and tired. I wanted to sleep. Or to go down to the bar and get drunk. I looked at the guy in the mirror. He didn't look any different. Was this the old me or the new me? Would Diana recognize which one I was? Could she still love me? Would the red rage return, or would it fade away with her bruises?

I made myself go to Diana's room and knock on her door. She answered it herself. Diana reached up and kissed me on the cheek. She was still happy because of the release of the rebel prisoners. Yvette wasn't there. I went in, wondering which of us needed the other the most, ashamed that I was still thinking of myself.

We stood there, the closed door behind

us, holding each other tightly, as if it were the most natural thing in the world. I had just murdered a man, and I was afraid that the violence still marked me, and that I'd hurt her, without meaning to. I felt ashamed to be in her presence.

"Billy?"

"Yeah?"

"How did you manage it? To free all of them?"

"I made a deal. Ike made his with Darlan, I made mine with Bessette."

Diana raised her head from my shoulder. "What did it cost you?"

"A notebook. Worthless by the time they got it, but they didn't know that. Bessette thought it was very valuable, worth both the prisoners and his partner in crime. Villard is dead."

She tensed at the mention of his name. Her hands gripped my arms tightly. "Good," she said, finally. "Good."

"I . . ."

"What's that noise?" Diana said. The doors to the balcony were open. It was a far-off droning sound that I was beginning to know too well.

"Goddamn it! Another air raid!" I ran onto the balcony, swiveling my head around to try to spot the source of the increasing sound. Diana was right behind me.

"There they are," she shouted, pointing toward the horizon. I followed her finger and found them, a formation of bombers, flying low this time, heading straight for the harbor. Going after the ships docked side by side, trying to sneak in under the radar. They were dark specks, growing larger with each second. The harbor was to our left, and the formation would pass right in front of us if that was their target.

"We should go down to the bomb shelter," I said.

"No. Let's stay here. I don't want to run and hide."

She hooked her arm through mine and something told me that she was right. Cowering in a basement was the last thing Diana needed to do right now. Unless those bombers were aware this was a headquarters building, that is. We stood at the balcony railing, watching the bombers draw closer, coming toward us at an angle, aiming for the harbor. Air raid sirens started to howl throughout the city, as people below us scattered to shelters and slit trenches. I shaded my eyes with my hand and tried to count them. It looked like twenty-five or so. Heinkel 111s again.

A snarling roar came from behind us, and

I ducked instinctively as four RAF Spitfires flew over the hotel, so low that the palm trees bent forward as the planes blasted past us. Diana shrieked in surprise and then we both laughed, crazily. It was like having a ringside seat at the fights, the excitement of the match boiling up inside you. Now *our* boys were in the ring, and I was damned glad those Heinkels wouldn't have such a smooth run this time.

The Spitfires flew on a collision course with the bombers, aiming to break up their formation before they reached the docks. They climbed briefly, rising slightly above the Heinkels, then leveled out. The bombers grew larger as the fighters closed the distance. Suddenly the four fighters split into two groups, one pair swooping head on into the formation, machine guns blazing. The other pair looped around and came in from the side, both firing their guns at the same bomber. It exploded in a ball of fire. The fighters broke off, climbing up and around for another run, as the bombers broke formation to avoid hitting the stricken plane, which flew forward in a flaming wreck until its wings caved in and it crumpled into the water. The first two fighters hadn't brought anyone down, but their attack run had broken up the tight formation. The bombers kept on course, but now they were all over the sky, and the fighters could pick their targets without running into a hail of fire from the machine guns that bristled from their tops and sides.

"Look!" yelled Diana, pointing with a shaky hand.

Another bomber was down, plowing into the sea as it dove, trying to maneuver away from the Spitfire hammering it. As the lead group got closer to the docks it was met by anti-aircraft fire. The Spitfires were staying away from land, content to harass the rear of the formation, out of the line of fire from the ground.

I stood on tiptoe, trying to see over the palm trees to the docks. I heard the first bombs explode, but couldn't tell if they hit anything. Out of the corner of my eye I caught sight of something headed for us. A Heinkel was hurtling straight toward the hotel, a Spitfire slightly above and behind him, both barely above eye level. Machine guns sparkled on the Spit's wings, and little pieces of the bomber flew off as the pilot strained to get away. His bomb bay doors opened and I wondered if the hotel was his target, before I realized he was dropping weight, getting rid of his bombs in hope of climbing and escaping. The planes were so close I could count the bombs as they tumbled out, exploding in the ocean one after another, in a line heading straight for the shore below us. Five, six, seven hit the water and then the bomber was almost over our heads. Eight and nine exploded on the hillside and then I saw the last, number ten. Its tailfins wobbled as it sailed down toward us and the bomber rose and roared over the hotel, the fighter racing behind, chattering machine guns drowning out all other noises as I stood in front of Diana and waited for that last great crashing noise. I felt her arms around me and we both watched, transfixed by the falling bomb that seemed to take forever to reach the ground. I was sure I could follow its trajectory and see right where it would land, below us in the green, manicured gardens. We embraced and I closed my eyes.

A sharp crunching sound, then silence. We looked at each other, amazed to be alive, but eerily calm. Smoke curled in the air from the direction of the harbor, distant explosions fading as the bombers ran for home. We stepped forward, looking down over the edge of the balcony railing. I gripped it hard; the feeling of cold iron steadied in my trembling hands.

Below us dirt was scattered everywhere.

An unexploded 250-pound bomb scarred the garden, its tail fins pointing skyward, its nose buried in the soft ground. It was close enough to spit on. A dud? Or maybe it was set to explode in five minutes, or an hour, who knew? We were alive. We backed into the room, holding hands, moving carefully, as if a heavy step might set it off.

"Billy," Diana said. Her hands were trembling. She grabbed at my shirt and pressed her face to my chest. "I thought I'd never see you again, I thought I'd die there. I wanted to die, so many times."

She pressed her forehead against my chest, as she cried for the first time since she had raised that gun to her head. I put my arms around her.

"Do you understand?" she asked. "Can you?"

I knew what she wanted to hear, what she had to hear from me. I pressed my cheek to hers, feeling our tears mingle. I wanted to tell her how sorry I was, about everything. About everything we had both lost, about all the death and pain and suffering. About Harding's heartbreak. About Gloria walking into the explosions. Maybe even about killing Villard. But mostly about how my hatred of Villard and what he'd done had come between us. Because I had let it come between us, tainting my every thought of her. I'd gotten rid of the poison, but I couldn't help wondering at the price.

"Do you?" she repeated, her moist eyes searching mine for understanding.

I understood. I nodded, holding her face in my hands as I looked into her eyes and whispered.

"*Je suis désolé, je suis désolé, je suis désolé.*"

AUTHOR'S NOTE

Billy's consternation that the first Allied invasion of the war targeted French forces in Algeria and French Morocco may well have echoed the thoughts of some of his fellow American soldiers and sailors, but most thought they would be welcomed as liberators. It was a vain hope, shared by Eisenhower and other generals who had not yet learned the hard realities of war. In five days of fighting, 526 Americans were killed by French forces before they surrendered and became our new allies. The confusion with which Eisenhower's infamous "deal with Darlan" is greeted in this story is mild compared to the firestorm of bad press and political pressure that was actually brought to bear on him. In granting Jean Darlan civil jurisdiction throughout North Africa, Eisenhower believed he was cementing control of his rear areas and gaining French co-operation. But Darlan's well-earned reputation as an anti-Semite and collaborator did not sit well with the folks back home, especially those who owned newspapers. Many demanded Eisenhower's resignation. He managed to hold onto his job, and the problem went away when Darlan was assassinated two months later.

The introduction of penicillin to battlefield hospitals is advanced by several months for plot purposes in this book. However, penicillin did make its debut in North Africa and was instrumental in treating thousands of wounded soldiers, not to mention curing thousands more of venereal disease throughout the course of the war. Discovered by Sir Alexander Fleming in 1928, it had been impossible to produce in useful quantities. After America's entry into the war, a number of medical labs accelerated their research. It was only through innovative production processes pioneered by one company that the drug became available in large quantities. Gambling that a deep-tank fermentation process used to make citric acid would work for penicillin, Pfizer cut back on the production of other chemicals using that process, and devoted itself to producing penicillin. It succeeded and, ultimately, the government authorized nineteen companies to produce the antibiotic using Pfizer's proven deep-tank fermentation process which the company agreed to share with its competitors: a story in and of itself.

Finally, the incredible service of U.S. Army nurses has to be acknowledged and honored. Gloria Morgan and her actions are purely fictitious. What is real is everything she says about the position of nurses in the army. "Relative rank" meant nurses received 50 percent of the pay of male officers of the same rank. And no salutes. Disregarding these inequities, over 59,000 nurses volunteered for the U.S. Army Nurse Corps, and fully half of those volunteered for, and served in, combat zones. More than 1,600 were decorated for meritorious service and bravery under fire. Two hundred seventeen lost their lives. Some of you reading this book would not be alive today if your grandfather or father had not received life-saving care on the battlefields of Guadalcanal, Anzio, Normandy, or elsewhere on land or sea, where volunteer American nurses served in World War II.